ADVENTURES IN THE
BORDERLAND PROVINCES

Authors: Eytan Bernstein, Scott Fitzgerald Gray, Gwendolyn Kestrel, Rhiannon Louve, Ari Marmell, Anthony Pryor, C.A. Suleiman
Developers: Ari Marmell and Matthew J. Finch
Producers: Bill Webb and Matthew J. Finch

Layout and Graphic Design: Charles A. Wright
Front Cover Art: Colin Chan
Interior Art: Terry Pavlet
Cartography: Robert Altbauer

Necromancer Games is not affiliated with Wizards of the Coast™.
We make no claim to or challenge to any trademarks held by Wizards of the Coast™.

NECROMANCER
GAMES

5th Edition Rules,
1st Edition Feel

Table of Contents

Other Products from Frog God Games

You can find these product lines and more at our website, **froggodgames.com**, and on the shelves of many retail game stores. Superscripts indicate the available game systems: "PF" means the Pathfinder Roleplaying Game, "5e" means Fifth Edition, and "S&W" means *Swords & Wizardry*. If there is no superscript it means that it is not specific to a single rule system.

GENERAL RESOURCES

Swords & Wizardry Complete [S&W]
The Tome of Horrors Complete [PF, S&W]
Tome of Horrors 4 [PF, S&W]
Tome of Adventure Design
Monstrosities [S&W]
Bill Webb's Book of Dirty Tricks
Razor Coast: Fire as She Bears [PF]
Book of Lost Spells [5e]
Fifth Edition Foes [5e]
Book of Alchemy* [5e, PF, S&W]

THE LOST LANDS

Rappan Athuk [PF, S&W]
Rappan Athuk Expansions Vol. I [PF, S&W]
The Slumbering Tsar Saga [PF, S&W]
The Black Monastery [PF, S&W]
Cyclopean Deeps Vol. I [PF, S&W]
Cyclopean Deeps Vol. II [PF, S&W]
Razor Coast [PF, S&W]
Razor Coast: Heart of the Razor [PF, S&W]
Razor Coast: Freebooter's Guide to the Razor Coast [PF, S&W]
LL0: The Lost Lands Campaign Setting*
LL1: Stoneheart Valley [PF, S&W]
LL2: The Lost City of Barakus [PF, S&W]

LL3: Sword of Air [PF, S&W]
LL4: Cults of the Sundered Kingdoms [PF, S&W]
LL5: Borderland Provinces [5e, PF, S&W]
LL6: The Northlands Saga Complete [PF, S&W]
LL7: The Blight* [PF, S&W]
LL8: Bard's Gate Complete* [PF, S&W]
LL9: Adventures in the Borderland Provinces [5e, PF, S&W]

QUESTS OF DOOM

Quests of Doom (Vol. 1) [5e]
Quests of Doom (Vol. 2) [5e]
Quests of Doom (includes the 5e Vol. 1 and 2, but for PF and S&W only) [PF, S&W]
Quests of Doom 2 [5e]
Quests of Doom 3* [5e, S&W]
Quests of Doom 4* [5e, PF, S&W]

PERILOUS VISTAS

Dead Man's Chest (pdf only) [PF]
Dunes of Desolation [PF]
Fields of Blood [PF]
Mountains of Madness* [PF]

* (forthcoming from **Frog God Games**)

Introduction

Welcome to the Borderlands. You'll probably die here.

Okay, that's a bit of an exaggeration. The Borderland region isn't *that* hostile. It's home to a great many thriving cultures, humanity and other races building upon century after century's worth of history. Much of the area is fully civilized.

Much of it isn't. The wilds hold monsters, and worse than monsters, surprises to challenge the courage of even the most stalwart adventurer.

And those civilized areas, the provinces and miniature kingdoms? They hold secrets and schemes of their own, creatures and conspiracies at least as dangerous as anything you'll find in the wilderness.

No, the Borderlands don't necessarily spell death for those who brave these outer reaches, but they *do* spell adventure. Peril. Excitement. And they do so in their own way. There's nowhere else quite like the Borderlands, so there's nothing quite like a Borderlands adventure.

The following eight scenarios are intended to challenge your players, of course, but also to showcase the sorts of story potential the Borderlands region can offer. Some of these adventures are dark, bloody, bordering on horrific (and possibly even disturbing to more sensitive players); some are far lighter, almost silly. One focuses on the perils of the untamed wilderness, another is almost entirely urban. Some are quite light on combat, others extremely action-heavy. Like the Borderlands — and like the game itself, throughout its long publishing history and its many editions — these adventures run the gamut, providing an array of experiences. Their common theme, the thread that binds them together in a single book? The Borderlands themselves.

Please note that we assume you have access to the ***Lost Lands: Borderlands Provinces*** book. You'll need to look there for more detail about these regions, governments, and communities. That said, while it requires making up some details of your own and you might miss certain nuances, it shouldn't prove too difficult to make these adventures work for you even if you *don't* have the companion work at hand.

You'll also note that many of the encounters in these adventures don't offer treasure. Because treasure in general, and magic items in particular, differ so greatly from campaign to campaign in the new edition, we've chosen to leave that largely up to the GM. By all means, provide your PCs as much loot, or as little, as your preferred play style warrants.

Other than that, have at it! The Borderlands await your adventurers. No, they may not die out here, on the edge of civilization — but only if they *earn* their survival!

— **Ari Marmell**

On a Lonely Road

> *Like one who, on a lonely road,*
> *Doth walk in fear and dread,*
> *And, having once turned round, walks on,*
> *And turns no more his head;*
> *Because he knows a frightful fiend*
> *Doth close behind him tread.*
> — Samuel Coleridge, *The Rhyme of the Ancient Mariner*

Adventure Background

On a Lonely Road is a wilderness adventure for a party of 4–6 adventurers averaging 2nd level. Intended as an exercise in suspenseful survival horror, the adventure contains several suggestions for amping up the tension, keeping the players nervous, and even facing the possibility that their characters might not survive.

The Yolbiac Vale is known for its strange secrets, but has largely been ignored by historians from outside the Vale itself — though one scholar, Sarrus Togren of the University of Subtleties in the city of Troye, believes the region was once home to an ancient and learned civilization. Long dismissed as a crackpot by his peers Togren has, with the aid of his loyal assistant Nymea Goswynn, at last obtained funding to lead a research expedition to the Vale, specifically a region known locally as the Quillande Ferosc. He now has everything he needs save guards for the hazardous trek into a wilderness region of the Yolbiac. That's where our heroes come in.

The Real Story

Professor Togren's interest in the region is very real, and he has no intention of betraying or leading the party astray. Nymea Goswynn on the other hand, has some very specific goals in mind, for she knows far more about the area than she's letting on.

Togren's hypotheses about the region are entirely correct, though not necessarily in the way he believes. Millennia ago, before the coming of the Hyperboreans, parts of the Yolbiac Vale were inhabited by a race of creatures called the Jaundool (pallid ones, in the original language), now forgotten save in obscure legends and terrified racial memory.

By the time the Hyperboreans walked the lands of Akados, the pallid ones had already faded to a decadent, degenerate shadow of their former selves. Most humans knew to avoid the territory occupied by these corrupt remnants, but some were nowhere near as wise, and in their quest for power some of the old, dark forest tribes actually sought out the surviving Jaundools, offering food, gold and sacrifice in exchange for lost knowledge. As the professor suspects, these activities were centered in the Quillande Ferosc.

The deals that the ancient humans made proved to be mixed blessings at best, for though they gained power, they found themselves infected by the same corruption that had taken the pallid ones. Rituals and magic grew ever darker, and eventually the humans actually interbred with the twisted

creatures, producing chieftains and shamans who bore Jaundool blood.

In time, most of these settlements and bloodlines died out or were hunted down, and the Jaundools were all but forgotten. A few persisted, however, dwindling but not disappearing, in the deep forests, and their bloodline continued to linger in the descendants of the human clans who had mated with the foul creatures.

While reading ancient texts in rotting and unmaintained sections of libraries in Troye, Nymea became convinced that she herself carried the bloodline of the Jaundools, and that her mentor, Professor Togren, bore an even more powerful birthright — he is, she believes, a descendant of a powerful ruler of the Jaundools, a fearsome creature mentioned as the "Pallid King" in one or two fragments of Yolbiac folklore. She believes, with the right inducement and rituals, that Sarrus Togren might be reborn as this fearsome king, and bring about a rebirth of the ancient civilization (with her as his lieutenant, of course).

To this demented end, Nymea began to plant clues for her professor to find and nudged him to act on his desire to lead a full-scale expedition into the Yolbiac Vale. Eventually resorting to blackmailing several governors of the University, Nymea secured permission and funding, and now she seeks to draw her companions into a trap as sport and sacrifice to the things she considers to be "her" people, and to bring about a terrible transformation in Professor Togren, that the pallid ones might live again. Professor Togren mistakenly believes he is pursuing the history of the "Ancient Ones," a prehistoric human civilization of Akados, but the Jaundools are neither human nor related to the Ancient Ones in any way.

Adventure Synopsis

Initially the expedition goes well. The party makes good time to the little-used Quillande Road and the Avauntz Inn — though they learn a few disturbing rumors about disappearances and strange events in the area — and develop relationships, for good or ill, with their fellow expedition members. The party ventures into the wilderness in relatively high spirits.

In the dark forest, the party fights off an attack by bandits, then delves deeper, uncovering signs that seem to verify Togren's hypothesis. The real fear begins when the party locates the bandits, or what is left of them, their bodies ritually mutilated and covered in strange sigils. That night one of the people they are escorting disappears, and soon the expedition is lost in the woods, low on supplies and stalked by an unseen but very real force.

Nymea makes her play at night, unleashing her Jaundool allies on the party in a diversionary attack intended to kidnap Togren and any other sacrificial victims she can acquire. Faced with a terrifying enemy and lost party members, the adventurers must decide on escape or rescue. Either way, with the help of an unexpected ally, they eventually find themselves facing Nymea, with only a single chance to stop her plans from coming to fruition.

Adventure Hooks

While it is entirely acceptable to start the adventure *in medias res* by reading the shaded text below, this adventure is easily placed into a regular ongoing campaign, in which case some of the following hooks may prove useful.

An Offer of Employment

The simplest way to involve the characters is for one of them to spot a flyer asking for brave adventurers to guard an important scholarly expedition, or — if they've already begun to build a reputation (no mean feat at their level!) — to be directly approached by Sarrus and his party. Characters may also overhear a conversation between other adventurers or mercenaries, perhaps at a tavern or in the marketplace. Comments to the effect of, "An expedition to the Yolbiac Vale? I'd rather slit my own throat. You'd have to be insane to go out there," might be sufficient to pique the interests of adventure-hungry characters. Should they follow up, the characters eventually find their way to Sarrus's lodging where he asks them to join his great undertaking.

Members of the Expedition

Characters may already be part of the expedition, as students, assistants or even professors from the University of Subtleties. If some characters start as expedition members, they may contact and persuade their fellow adventurers to join them.

Seekers After Knowledge

This one requires a little preparation, but gives one party member particularly solid motivation. A history expert or other scholarly adventurer may have heard the same rumors as Sarrus, or learned of similar legends and stories, and decided to venture into the Yolbiac independently. In Troye, the character and his or her companions hear rumors about Sarrus' mission and can either seek him out and offer to join forces, or find themselves approached by Sarrus or Nymea with a similar offer. Either way, it should be obvious that cooperation is a better idea than separate, competing expeditions.

Meeting Sarrus

The party first meets Sarrus Togren in the city of Troye, in the common room of the Gilded Mouse Inn, where he and his expedition are staying while they purchase supplies and prepare for departure. The Gilded Mouse is a fairly run-down establishment with cheap rooms and cheaper ale, suggesting that Sarrus is on a tight budget. He does, however, offer to buy the party drinks, after which read or paraphrase the following.

The interior of the Gilded Mouse is anything but gilded, unless gilded is another word for "grimy." A few patrons quietly nurse jacks of foul-smelling brew and a burly innkeeper watches over things with a weary expression.

"I'm pleased to make your acquaintance," says the man you've come to meet. He is a thin fellow of middle years, with a nervous manner and dark, intense eyes. "My name is Sarrus Togren, Tenured Professor of History at the University of Subtleties here in Troye. I have a proposal for you if you'd care to listen. Please, sit. Have a drink, though I can't vouch for its quality."

The table before him Togren piled high with old books, parchments and scrolls. Beside him sits a pretty half-elven woman, who — were she human — would appear to be in her mid-twenties. She introduces herself as Nymea Gosswyn, a Fellow of the College of History who works with the Professor.

Assuming that the characters are interested in talking with Sarrus, which is likely given that he is offering free drinks and possible employment while their belt pouches are light on gold, read or paraphrase the following introduction to the adventure:

Over a round of questionable ale, Sarrus tells his story. You have the uncomfortable feeling that he's giving you a lecture that he's been repeating for years.

He spins a tale of a vast lost civilization that once thrived in the region known as the Yolbiac Vale, probably related to the Ancient Ones, the region's earliest human inhabitants. Its rulers were wise, learned and mastered both arcane and druidic magic. As he speaks, a light flares in his eyes that is both profound and disturbing. His voice is hushed with excitement now, as if he is finally realizing a life-long dream.

"I'm sorry to say that very few in the academic community put much stock in my theories," he reports sadly. "Yet my

---

research has led me to believe that evidence of the Ancient Ones and their magic remain in the area — artifacts, shrines, even dwellings that may contain the secrets of old, deep arcana, undreamed of by even the most wild theorists of today!"

A few heads turn at Sarrus' exclamation, then turn back to their drinks as he falls silent, looking a bit embarrassed at himself.

"In any event," he concludes meekly, "after many years I have finally succeeded in obtaining approval and funding for an expedition, and I am presently making final preparations to venture into the Yolbiac Vale, specifically a small wilderness region known as the Quillande Ferosc."

Nymea glances at her mentor with sympathy as he falls silent and contemplates the depths of his ale mug.

"We know that this part of the province is quite dangerous," she says, picking up where her mentor trailed off. "There are tales of bandits, marauding humanoids, wild animals, even monsters like giants and dragons. Venturing into the wild without protection would be madness. To conserve resources we decided to hire guards here in Troye, and you seem like a capable group. Would you be interested in joining our endeavor?"

As Nymea implied and the characters observed, Sarrus operates on a fairly restricted budget, but at this point they're open to negotiation. The initial offer is 1gp per person per day, and with negotiations this can be increased to 2gp, plus a share of any treasure obtained along the way. As the expedition's leader Sarrus insists that he get first choice of any takings, with special interest in items of archeological significance.

If the party agrees (and hopefully they do, since if they don't the adventure is pretty much over), Sarrus perks up immediately and takes the characters to his rooms where he introduces the other members of the expedition. He is eager to get underway and plans departure for the following morning, giving the characters time to purchase supplies and possibly investigate rumors (see below).

Other Party Members

Sarrus' party consists of a number of fellow expendables... excuse me... scholars, all of whom share his enthusiasm for knowledge and research. The following lists the party members with brief statistics. Also included are optional stats for another professor and two students with character class levels, who can be included if the GM feels it's appropriate.

Professor Sarrus Togren, Human Male Scholar; AC 12; **HP** 12 (5d6–5); **Spd** 30ft; **Melee** staff (+3, 1d6 bludgeoning); **Str** +0, **Dex** +2, **Con** –1, **Int** +4, **Wis** +2, **Cha** +0; **Skills** Arcana +7, History +7, Insight +5, Investigation +7, Medicine +5, Nature +7; **AL** NG; **CR** 1/2; **XP** 100.
> **Equipment:** traveling clothes, backpack, staff.

A dedicated scholar, Sarrus Togren has spent the last 20 years intensely studying the ancient history of the Sinnar Coast region with special attention to the Yolbiac Vale and its most obscure inhabitants. He sincerely believes that the Ancient Ones possessed significant knowledge that could benefit modern civilization, and dismisses tales that they consorted with demons and evil creatures as meaningless folklore or outright lies.

Sarrus is tall and spare, with sparse grey hair, a wispy beard and a studious, thoughtful manner. He rarely is moved to any emotional extreme (except when expounding on his theories and goals), and even when confronted with the horrors of the deep forest he maintains a calm and detached demeanor. While this may be due to his academic professionalism, it might also be an indication of his heritage as a distant descendant of the Jaundool civilization. Nymea believes the latter, and is determined to bring Professor Togren to "his" people, where his deeply buried traits and powers can be brought to fruition.

Nymea Goswynn, Female Half-Elf Sor5 (wild magic): AC 15; **HP** 20 (5d6); **Spd** 30ft; **Melee** +1 dagger (+7, 1d4+4 piercing); **Ranged** +1 dagger (+7, 20ft/60ft, 1d4+4 piercing); **SA** spells (Cha+7, DC 15); **Str** –1, **Dex** +3, **Con** +0 (+3), **Int** +3, **Wis** +3, **Cha** +4 (+7); **Skills** Arcana +6, Religion +6; **Senses** darkvision 60ft; **Traits** font of magic (5 sorcery points), metamagic (empowered spell, subtle spell); **AL** CE; **CR** 4; **XP** 1100.
> **Spells (slots):** 0 (at will)—blade ward, chill touch, dancing lights, mage hand, poison spray; 1st (4)—chromatic orb, mage armor, ray of sickness; 2nd (3)—detect thoughts, shatter; 3rd (2)—fear.
> **Equipment:** traveling clothes, backpack, +1 dagger, 3 potions of healing, 2 potions of greater healing, potion of superior healing, ring of protection, leather armor.

Quiet, intense, intelligent and even beautiful in a reserved, subtle way, Sarrus Togren's academic assistant is careful not to reveal her true intentions or her sorcerous powers. If pressed, she casts spells defensively, saying only that she has studied low-level magic and has a few resources, though her primary interest is the scholarly pursuit of knowledge and the well-being of her mentor, professor Togren.

Physically Nymea is short and slender, but quite dexterous and agile. She dresses and behaves modestly, spending most of her time with books or assisting the professor in his researches. She endeavors to keep him insulated from worries or trouble and anyone who wishes to speak with Togren needs to go through her first.

If the GM feels that the party needs a little extra firepower in combat, the following NPC can be included. Her actions are included in the text below but this is only important if she's actually in the party.

Professor Sigra Ironshoulders, Female Mountain Dwarf Ftr2: AC 16; **HP** 26 (2d10+10); **Spd** 30ft; **Melee** warhammer (+6, 1d8+4 bludgeoning); **Ranged** heavy crossbow (+3, 100ft/400ft; 1d10+1 piercing); **Resist** poison; **Str** +4 (+6), **Dex** +1, **Con** +5 (+7), **Int** +2, **Wis** –1, **Cha** –1; **Skills** Arcana +4, History +4, Insight +1, Investigation +4; **Senses** darkvision 60ft; **Traits** action surge, dwarven resilience (tactical advantage vs. poison), fighting style (defense), second wind, stonecunning; **AL** LN; **CR** 1; **XP** 200.
> **Equipment:** chain shirt, shield, warhammer, heavy crossbow, 20 bolts.

Sigra Ironshoulders is a professor of engineering and geography who is along on the expedition to do some mapping and surveying. She's also an experienced warrior and can serve as a valuable resource during combat. Like many dwarves, her manner is gruff but ultimately comradely. Physically she is solidly built with broad shoulders, strong arms and red braided hair shot with grey. She wears her chain shirt at all times without apparent fatigue, and carries a masterfully-crafted warhammer inscribed with the runic symbols of her clan.

Students

The various students on the expedition are primarily noncombatants with little training in survival. They all share the following stats (unless otherwise noted), but the GM can vary their skills and knowledge depending upon the scenario's needs. They all carry basic equipment such as clothing, backpack, etc.

Student, Human Scholar: AC 11; **HP** 9 (2d6+2); **Spd** 30ft; **Melee** dagger (+3, 1d6+1 piercing); **Str** +0, **Dex** +1, **Con** +1, **Int** +3, **Wis** +0, **Cha** +0; **CR** 1/8; **XP** 25.

Maiesse Tolivant: Maiesse is an athletic, resourceful young woman who has some experience in the wilderness, and has picked up a few ranger skills. She jumped at the chance to go on this expedition, since she dreams of one day being a freelance adventurer.

Optionally, the GM may treat Maiesse as a 1st level ranger and use the following stats:

Maiesse Tolivant: Female Human Rgr1; AC 14; **HP** 12
(1d10+2); **Spd** 30ft; **Melee** shortsword (+5, 1d6+3 piercing);
Ranged longbow (+5, 150ft/600ft, 1d6+3 piercing); **Str**
+1 (+3), **Dex** +3 (+6), **Con** +2, **Int** +0, **Wis** +3, **Cha** +0; **Skills**
Investigation +2, Medicine +5, Nature +2, Perception +5,
Religion +2; **Traits** favored enemy (monstrosities), natural
explorer; **AL** NG; **CR** 1/2; **XP** 100.
    Equipment: leather armor, longbow, 50 arrows,
longsword.

Gedney Foulkes: A gnomish student of arcane history, Gedney hopes to find new information about ancient spellcasting and magical procedures. Like most gnomes he is friendly and almost pathologically optimistic. His enthusiasm will be sorely tested in the coming days.

As with Maiesse, Gedney can be included as a 1st level wizard using the following stats.

Gedney Foulkes, Male Forest Gnome Wiz1: AC 12; **HP** 6
(1d6); **Spd** 25ft; **Melee** dagger (+4, 1d4+3 piercing);
Ranged dagger (+4, 20ft/60ft, 1d4+3 piercing); **SA** spells
(Int+6, DC 14); **Str** –1, **Dex** +2, **Con** +0, **Int** +4 (+6), **Wis**
+1 (+3), **Cha** +2; **Skills** Arcana +6, History +6, Insight +3,
Religion +6; **Senses** darkvision 60ft; **Traits** arcane recovery,
gnome cunning; **AL** CG; **CR** 1/2; **XP** 100.
    Spells (slots): 0 (at will)—*dancing lights, light,
prestidigitation*; 1st (2)—*burning hands, charm person,
comprehend languages, detect magic, mage armor*
    Equipment: traveling clothing, backpack, staff, 2
daggers

Drew Connat: Sincere, bearded and ever so slightly overweight, Drew is an enthusiastic if undistinguished history student, but he is totally unprepared for life on the road, frequently falling off his horse or losing the trail.

Sylva Montrose: Another of Professor Togren's history students, Sylva clearly dislikes Nymea Goswynn and thinks that she's up to something (though right now she only thinks that Nymea is currying favor for better treatment at the university). She has some access to Togren's history books and some knowledge of the area. She can provide the characters with information that Nymea will not divulge and may seek the party out for advice and assistance. She is bright, bookish and friendly, with freckles and strawberry-blonde hair.

Regis Tenebro: No one is really sure why Regis is here. He's dark, sallow and surly, constantly wrapped in a dark hooded cloak, usually complaining about conditions or grunting in monosyllables. He's frequently seen where he shouldn't be — near others' tents, going through their baggage, disappearing at night or wandering off the trail. Regis is a total red herring — though he is a grim and antisocial little creep, he is totally innocent of any involvement in Nymea's plot, and his strange behavior is simply a result of his own lack of interpersonal graces. Feel free to play Regis up as a potential adversary to mislead the party.

Equipment

It's not necessary to maintain detailed records of the expedition's supplies. The party includes two mules carrying tents, blankets, rope, tools and sufficient food for a week in the wilderness. The party also begins riding horses and will provide enough for characters who don't have their own, but these animals will have to be left at the Avauntz Inn once the expedition reaches the Quillande Ferosc area.

Rumors

Characters may want to learn more about Sarrus' proposal and his stories of lost civilizations before departing. If they do some research, make some Investigation checks, with the results as listed below. Information with a more local, and even less savory, orientation can be obtained later in the adventure at the Avauntz Inn, but by then it's probably too late to back out.

DC 12

• The Yolbiac Vale is sparsely populated, and is a common destination for outlaws and fugitives from justice.
• The Quillande Road is the only road leading to the area the professor wants to explore, but it is often in bad repair and is known to be plagued by brigands.
• A place called Timberval was once the largest village in that area, but it is essentially abandoned.

DC 15

• Strange carved stones and images have been found in the forest, but they inevitably bring disaster to their discoverers and so are avoided as cursed.
• A bandit chieftain named Borosha the Black and her followers have taken up residence in the ruins of Timberval. (While true, this rumor is mostly a red herring; it has only limited relevance to the coming adventure, though the characters will encounter some of Borosha's bandits.)
• The few settlements that remain in the western forests have recently been plagued by a rash of disappearances, vandalism and break-ins, mostly blamed on Borosha's bandits.
• There is a lost palace deep in the western forests, full of gold and gems, but guarded by a fierce undead dragon (false).

DC 18

• Some ancient writings and art from the period describes not just humans, but some unfamiliar humanoid creatures, as dwelling in the region.
• Everyone avoids the more deeply-forested regions of the Yolbiac Vale. Except for small villages, the forests contain nothing but secret horrors.
• Among the artifacts of the vanished civilization that are sometimes found in the area are items of more recent manufacture — twig dolls, crudely carved stones and bone knives.
• Ghosts of the ancient human inhabitants of the region still haunt the forests and will grant wisdom and riches to those who help them find rest (false).

DC 20

• Some places in the Yolbiac Vale practiced cannibalism and human sacrifice, and were finally exterminated by the Church of Thyr and the Knights of the Swan. (well, they tried, and continue to try, but this is only very partially true).
• It is said that the Ancient Ones were corrupted by their contacts with unclean spirits and evil demonic beings (partially true, but not the actual Ancient Ones).
• In recent months, hunters and foresters have refused to venture west of the Quillande Road, and few will talk about it other than to say that the woods are now "cursed."

Into the Wild

The day dawns, and with dawn come soaking rains. The morning of your departure is miserable — even with scraps of night-fog still clinging to low ground and tree branches, the rain pours down from the sky like the wrath of an angry god determined to dissuade you from your course of action.

The next several days prove uneventful, for the "road" to Coelum Town (SEE-lum) is not heavily traveled. You are fortunate enough to find inns and shelter along the way, through the mountain pass into the Yolbiac Vale, and after four days of hard travel you eventually reach the spot where the narrow and ill-maintained Quillande Road breaks off from the main road into the forested foothills known as the Quillande Ferosc.

The journey from Troye to the Quillande Road takes four to five days. Make normal encounter checks (see *The Lost Lands: Borderland*

Provinces as a resource), but feel free to replace a dangerous encounter with a mundane one if you think it will delay the adventure unduly.

Characters can take this opportunity to interact with their fellow explorers, but most information exchanged is of relatively minor significance. An occasional hint at the level of Sarrus' obsession and of Nymea's concern for his safety and sanity are all that are required at this point.

Most of the students and professors are polite or even friendly, as they're grateful for the party's presence in this dangerous region. Regis Tenebro is surly and uncommunicative, while Sylva Montrose might be persuaded to share some of her knowledge about the history of the region, possibly preparing her as a source of information later in the adventure. Developing friendships also help give the players a sense of the stakes involved when their companions start disappearing.

Quillande Road

> The relative safety of the Yolbiac Vale's main road vanishes quickly behind you, and soon you find that the Quillande Road runs through a dark, threatening forest. You are deep in gloom, with only wan grey light and fat droplets of icy rainwater filtering down from a grim sky. The trees are old, with black bark and heavy branches sprouting thick needles. The only living things you see are black crows that roost among the boughs and stare coldly down on you, flying off only when Regis wings pinecones at them.
>
> The track ahead of you is narrow and in places overgrown, or blocked by fallen trees, requiring frustrating delays to clear. From time to time you ride past weathered waystones, thick with moss, their inscriptions barely legible, referring to settlements long lost to time — *Timberval 120 leagues*. There are a few newer stones as well — *Avauntz Inn 20 leagues*.

At the party's current pace it takes about two days to reach the Avauntz Inn. Once more, you can roll for normal encounters along the Quillande Road, but the action doesn't really get underway until after they reach the inn.

The party has to camp out at least one night, pitching their tents in the dark and sleeping fitfully under a constant assault of rain. The darkness here is absolute, and fires burn poorly due to the dampness. In addition to the constant drumbeat of falling rain, other sounds echo in the night — the chirp of crickets, the croak of frogs and even the occasional cry of nightjars.

Most of the other party members are oppressed by the weather and miserable conditions, especially Regis, who complains constantly. Even Sarrus is quiet, but he still retains a fair amount of excitement about the adventure as he draws nearer his destination. Nymea continues to see to his comfort, but if she has grown friendly toward a character, she may confide that she is concerned about Sarrus' health and well-being, and possibly subtly suggest that Regis might be up to something unsavory.

The Avauntz Inn

After several days travel into the forbidding forests, the party arrives at the last outpost of civilization for many leagues: the Avauntz Inn. This establishment that caters to a handful of patrons —hunters and trappers, the inhabitants of isolated cottages and hamlets, and the occasional merchant bold enough to brave the forest and its dangers.

> In the depths of the forest, morning and afternoon are scarcely distinguishable, but your body tells you that it is late in the day when the road turns west, revealing a venerable wooden building with a gabled roof and a stable. Smoke rises from its chimney, and a moss-covered sign outside announces that you have arrived at the Avauntz Inn.

The Inn is a welcome change from the deprivation of the previous days. The main building is well-constructed of split logs and at least a century old, with good but basic fare, a common room and ten small rooms, a barn with space for about a half-dozen horses and an outside enclosure with room for more. Party members may need to double up in sleeping rooms, unless some want to spend the night in the barn (it's warmer and more comfortable than one might expect).

The characters may interact with the innkeeper, Barlus Denight (NG male human **commoner**); his daughter Maris (NG female human **commoner**); as well as patrons Thandaela Brightroad (CG female half-elf **commoner**) a merchant passing through on her way south; Donal Farzel (N male human **Ftr3**), a mercenary hoping for employment hunting down bandits; Vertain Solos (CN male human **Drd4**), a priest of the Green Father who has been summoned by villagers to help ward off evils growing in the forest; Armen Toral (NG human **scout**), a hunter who makes his living selling game to the few villages that remain in the region; and Willow Catseye (NG female halfling **commoner**), a halfling villager who is here unwinding after a long week at the farm.

Later that evening as the party dines or relaxes by the fire, Maris approaches them warily, asking what possible reason they might have for venturing into the deep woods. Characters may respond by questioning Maris and other patrons; a combination of roleplaying and Investigation checks reveal some fairly alarming rumors (see next section). Eventually, the party retires for the night. Some may sleep without incident, but others' slumber may be interrupted by disturbing dreams and visions (see below). The next morning, some NPCs, particularly Sylva Montrose, complain of similar bad dreams. (These dreams have no mechanical effect — the characters still gain the full benefits of a long rest, nobody suffers levels of exhaustion, or the like — but play up the description of their restless slumber, so that they feel as if they've only just escaped a more severe penalty.)

Rumors at the Inn

DC 12

• There are a few small homesteads and hamlets in the forest, but these are all found east of the Quillande Road. Few locals venture into the thick woods to the west.

• The ruins of Timberval lie only a league or so off the road to the south, but are generally avoided due to wild animals and bandits.

• In the past few weeks, bandits based in the ruins of Timberval have been raiding homes and hamlets throughout the forest.

DC 15

• Local inhabitants superstitiously avoid the woods west of the Quillande Road, claiming that they are home to demons and ghosts.

• A group of traders left the Avauntz Inn a few weeks ago but never arrived at their destination: the village of Lortz on the southern edge of the forest.

• A hunter venturing into the western wood was unable to find any game and claims that his possessions were stolen and his food spoiled, but has no idea by whom. He has since declared he has no intention of returning to the area.

DC 18

• Present inhabitants of the region believe that the things that inhabit the forest west of the Quillande Road are the ghosts of ancient residents there, or possibly monsters that the old shamans summoned, kept alive by fell magic.

• A single survivor of the group of traders was found, hopelessly mad. He was kept at the inn for a few days, but disappeared in the night and hasn't been heard from since.

• Guests at the inn have complained about scratching or tapping at their windows and doors.

• The handful of locals who live in this part of the forest have been complaining of disappearances and break-ins, but most blame the bandits of Timberval.

DC 20

• Some of the ancient humans still live in the forests, emerging periodically to kill livestock, steal children and even murder lone travelers.

the hidden bandit and the deadfall trap.

Bad Dreams and Omens

Come up with some of your own, or use any of the following suggestions.

• The sleeper dreams of marching through the forest and simply feeling nervous, as if being watched, but when they look into the trees see nothing. Then their point of view shifts, and they now see themselves, as if they are the ones observing the party from a place of concealment.

• The dreamer is alone in the darkness, surrounded by flitting movement and black figures that can be glimpsed only vaguely.

• Flocks of black birds, like the crows that the party has already seen, flap through tree branches, staring and calling out with human voices.

• The dreamer is chained to an altar, menaced by shadowy figures with bone knives and necklaces that resemble human figures crafted from tree twigs.

• Locals have complained of bad dreams and visions of dark forests, invisible pursuers and ancient stone buildings that harbor fearful but unseen creatures.

• A farmer searching for some missing goats found a number of strange artifacts on his property, including bone daggers and small fetishes woven from twigs. The farmer has since disappeared.

Day One

After spending a potentially restless night at the Avauntz Inn, the party wakes bright and early, before the sun has managed to drive off the night fogs, eats a hasty breakfast and pushes westward into the forest under Sarrus' eager guidance. On the first day the party must deal with an attack by Borosha the Black's bandits — a seemingly routine encounter that will have significant consequences later.

Within a few minutes, the safe haven of the Avauntz Inn vanishes among the trees and you begin to feel truly alone. The party moves slowly westward along a narrow, overgrown track that leads straight toward the foothills in the Quillande Ferosc. The rain continues with steady intensity, the land rises slowly, and as you go the trees grow thicker and even more ancient. Sarrus comments that some of the trees have not been felled in centuries, and that the Ancient Ones drew much of their power from their wild spirits.

Bandit Attack

As travel through the region declined, the bandits who have taken up residence in the old city of Timberval have grown hungry and increasingly desperate. Their leader, the woman known as Borosha the Black, has demanded that they work harder, and they have begun to raid homesteads, stealing the locals' meager possessions, the source of some — but not all — of the mysterious disappearances and break-ins. Sarrus' expedition represents a real windfall and when it sets out from the Avauntz, several bandits rush ahead, into the fearsome depths of the forest west of the Quillande Road. They have prepared an ambush and attack the party as it passes.

1. Trail

The western trail grows narrow here, forcing the party to march single-file. Have the players create a marching order, including the NPCs and pack horses. If the players say that the characters are being wary, allow them to make Perception checks before they enter the clearing to detect

2. Deadfall

The bandits have rigged a tree to fall as soon as the party passes, either cutting the group in half or cutting off their escape route. A hidden **bandit** (see below) crouches in the undergrowth, DC 18 Wis (Perception) to spot. If he's spotted he sets off the deadfall immediately so that it falls in the midst of the party. If this happens, anyone in the path of the falling tree takes 2d6 bludgeoning damage. A successful DC 15 Dex save halves this damage. If the party is divided by the deadfall anyone who wishes to get over the tree trunk, either to enter the clearing and help their fellows, or retreat from the bandits' onslaught must use an action to make a successful DC 12 Str (Athletics) check.

3. Clearing

The trail widens slightly here, giving the bandits room to maneuver. They remain hidden in the trees until the archers attack.

4. Forest

The surrounding forest is thick and dense with undergrowth. Perception checks for anyone hiding in the forest are at tactical disadvantage, and the forest itself is difficult terrain.

5. Archers

At each of these locations is a bandit archer. As soon as the deadfall is triggered they open up with shortbows, trying to force the party to go to ground.

Bandit Archer (2): AC 12; HP 11 (2d8+2); Spd 30ft; Melee shortsword (+3, 1d6 piercing); Ranged shortbow (+3, 80ft/320ft, 1d6+1 piercing); Str +0, Dex +1, Con +1, Int +0, Wis +0, Cha +0; AL CE; CR 1/8; XP 25.
  Equipment: leather armor, shortsword, dagger, shortbow, 20 arrows, belt pouch with 1d6sp and 3d6cp.

6. Bandits

Once the archers begin to shoot, a squad of bandits attacks directly from these two locations, trying to take out the most powerful party members. If the bandit who triggered the deadfall survived he joins the others.

Bandit (5): AC 12; HP 11 (2d8+2); Spd 30ft; Melee shortsword (+3, 1d6+1 slashing); Str +0, Dex +1, Con +1, Int +0, Wis +0, Cha +0; AL any non-L; CR 1/8; XP 25.
  Equipment: leather armor, longsword, dagger, belt pouch with 1d6sp and 3d6cp.

7. Fallen Tree

A second tree blocks the exit from the clearing.
The GM has the option of making the encounter more dangerous by including a bandit captain among the party's foes.

Bandit Captain: AC 15; HP 65 (10d8+20); Spd 30ft; Melee scimitar (+5, 1d6+3 slashing), dagger (+5, 1d4+3 piercing); Ranged dagger (+5, 20ft/60ft, 1d4+3 piercing); SA multiattack (scimitar x2, dagger or ranged dagger x2), parry (reaction, +2 AC vs. single melee); Str +2 (+4), Dex +3 (+5), Con +2, Int +2, Wis +0 (+2), Cha +2; Skills Athletics +4, Deception +4; AL any non-L; CR 2; XP 450
  Equipment: leather armor, scimitar, belt pouch with 14sp.

The bandits were hoping to overwhelm the party quickly and make a short struggle of it, but didn't count on the caravan including experienced adventurers. Once three bandits have been slain the remainder retreat and

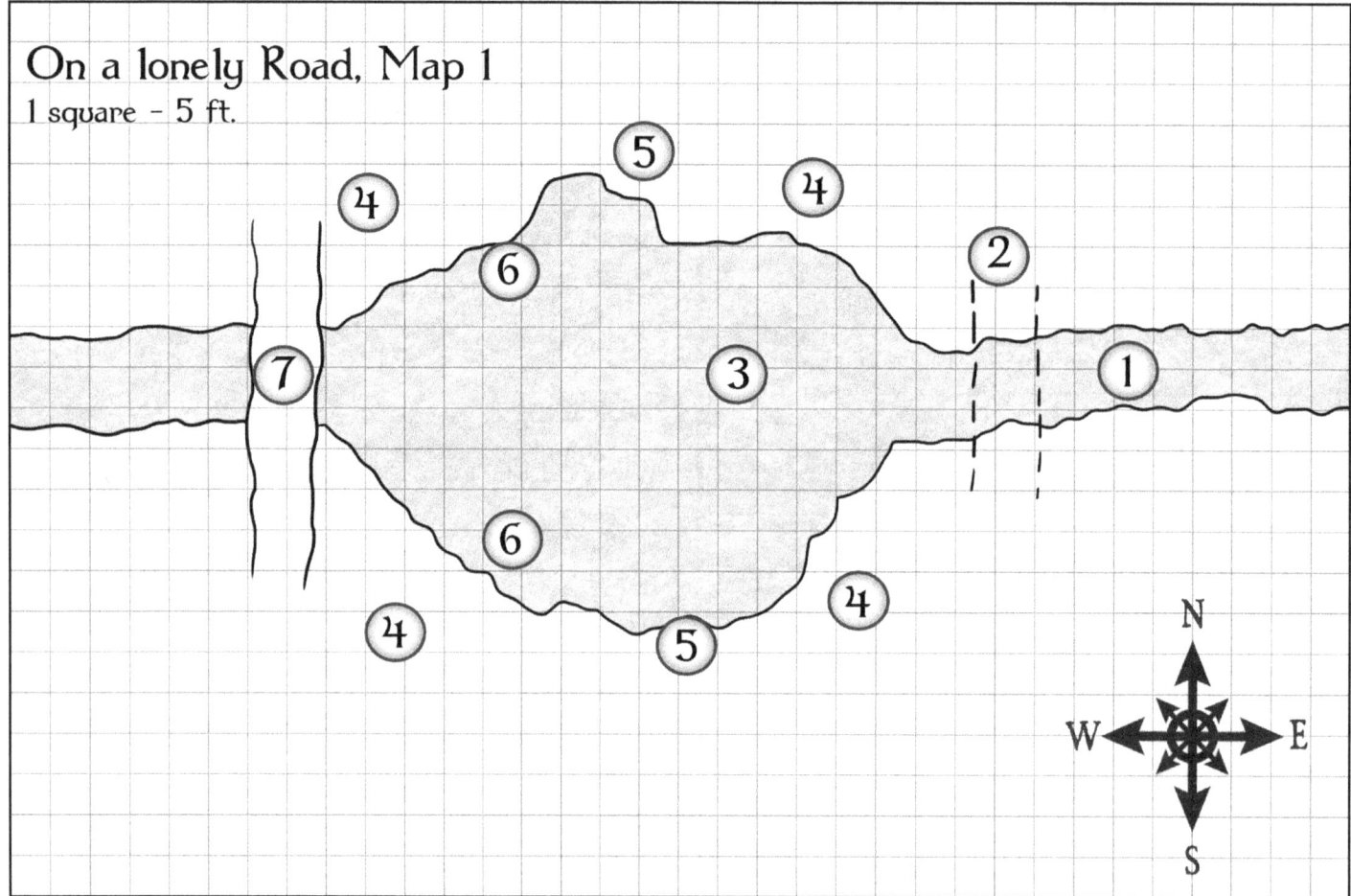

On a lonely Road, Map 1

1 square - 5 ft.

fall back into the woods. The characters can pursue, but the bandits scatter to ensure a least some of them escape. Try to ensure at least one succeeds, as we'll be seeing them again soon.

The party may rest and recover from wounds in the fight's aftermath. Reactions from the various NPCs vary. Sarrus is shaken but seeks refuge in the mission, insisting that it continue despite setbacks, and Nymea quietly supports him. Sigra Ironshoulders is a dwarf through-and-through and shakes off the battle with little reaction, other than to condemn the bandits as a pack of cowards. Maiesse and Gedney were both prepared for mishaps and recover matter-of-factly, while the unfortunate Drew Connat seems frightened, pale and withdrawn at the sight of such violence. Regis Tenebro is quiet but a DC 15 Wis (Insight) check reveals that he is quite fascinated by any blood or dead bodies (another attempt to throw some red herrings at the party).

Night Watch

As the party makes camp, the characters are certain to be on the lookout for more bandits and may set extra watches. The night descends quickly. Regardless of who is on watch, in the early morning hours the near-constant sounds of the forest — crickets, frogs and nocturnal birds — suddenly cease, plunging the camp into absolute silence.

Once this happens it's likely that the characters on watch will rouse the entire camp, anticipating another bandit attack or worse. No such event occurs, but the expedition is stressed out by the false alarm, and sets out the next day tired and in a grim mood.

Day Two

If you wish, have the characters make DC 10 Con saves to determine how well they slept. A failed roll results in one level of exhaustion for the rest of the day due to sleep deprivation and fatigue. Characters who had

disturbing dreams make their Con save at a tactical disadvantage. You can have the characters make these checks each morning that they are in the forest. (Even if you choose to go this route — and you should do so only if the characters are having a particularly easy time of the adventure — do not bestow multiple levels of exhaustion this way. One is quite sufficient.)

The constant assault of rain has finally lessened, but its replacement isn't much of an improvement. A blanket of thick fog enshrouds the forest, rendering anything beyond a few feet all but invisible. Pale grey light shines down from above, and the thick boughs of the ancient trees still drip huge cold drops of water. From time to time you can see winged shapes flapping through the fog and occasionally hear the croak of a crow or raven, but you otherwise feel alone and utterly isolated.

Despite the prior day's mishaps Sarrus remains enthusiastic, if a bit sleep-deprived. He frequently consults his maps and notes, looking eagerly left and right, and directing the party along old trails or through trackless forest. On occasion you must stop and cut your way through brush, circumnavigate ravines or ford small streams. Though you remain on guard, there is no sign of the bandits' return. Perhaps yesterday's drubbing has scared them off for good?

This day will witness a number of strange sights and events, mostly of a baffling or vaguely unsettling nature. Use any or all of the following events spaced throughout the day, and include more descriptions of the oppressive atmosphere, the persistent fogs and the vaguely-seen birds. The birds, it should be noted, are actually under the control of the druidic god the Green Father, whose power in this tainted place is limited, but has sent emissaries to investigate these events. Later in the adventure, their true nature will become clearer, but for now go ahead and use them to make the players worry.

• A character who succeeds on a DC 12 Wis (Perception) check sees a dark form moving in the fog perhaps 30ft distant. If the Wis (Perception) check succeeds by 5 or more, tell the player that the shape appears to be a deer or similarly-sized creature. Repeat this a couple of times, then finally reveal to players who succeeded by 5 or more that the figure looks smallish and vaguely humanoid. If the characters move to investigate they find nothing other than slightly disturbed forest floor detritus that might suggest foot- or hoof-prints.

• After some intensive searching, Sarrus makes a find: a carved stone monolith about 3ft tall. It is black and badly weathered, but clearly bears some curved lines laboriously etched into its surface at some time in the distant past. Sarrus is beside himself with excitement, though he can't immediately identify what the object was or what the carvings depict. A close inspection of the object and a successful DC 15 Wis (Perception) check reveals that the carvings depict humanoid figures gathered around a stone structure of some sort. A check that succeeds by 5 or more reveals one or more of the following:

§ There are two varieties of figures — taller, elf- or human-seeming individuals and smaller, hunched and gnarled humanoids.

§ The structure depicted appears to be an altar of some sort, upon which are laid several bound humanoids.

§ A vague shape looms over the altar, its outlines so badly weathered that it is impossible to determine its exact nature. Viewing this image, though it is not especially clear, nevertheless causes disquiet for reasons the viewer can't quite discern.

• One of the student NPCs turns up missing. A search follows, and you can roll for encounters if you wish. Eventually the missing student is found, slumped against a tree and semiconscious. When questioned the student has no specific memories of getting lost, only vague impressions of drifting off, wandering into the fog, and hearing his or her name being called. At this point the student realizes that a minor possession such as a belt pouch, knife or button is missing, and cannot remember what happened to it.

• A minor object is found. Have the characters make Wis (Perception) checks ranging from 10-15 to see these objects, or have one of the NPCs make the discovery.

§ A steel dagger, covered in blood. This was dropped by one of the bandits as they retreated from battle.

§ A small wooden fetish made of twigs hangs from a branch. It resembles a human figure and appears to be of recent manufacture. Inspecting it closely causes an unaccountable feeling of unease.

§ A white object on the ground nearby proves to be a cunningly-crafted white leaf-blade from a knife or spear. Sarrus is especially excited at this find and exclaims over its exquisite workmanship. A successful DC 10 Int (Nature) check reveals that the blade is carved from bone; if the check succeeds by 5 or more, the observer notes that it appears to be human bone.

§ A pale bone that a DC 10 Wis (Medicine) check confirms comes from a human. If the check succeeds by 5 or more, the observer determines that the bone is at least 1d4 years old.

§ A carved stone with a wizened, toothy face and tiny staring eyes.

§ A miscellaneous carving, obsidian arrowhead, pottery shard or other artifact — feel free to come up with your own ideas here.

• The ground is torn up and a DC 12 Wis (Perception) check reveals dark stains on surrounding trees and bushes, which a further DC 10 Wis (Medicine) check confirms are blood, though it's not certain whether it is human or animal. Some arrows may stand lodged in trees or lying on the ground as well. This is, of course, the site where the unfortunate bandits were ambushed by the Jaundools, though the characters have no way of knowing this as of yet.

Despite the day's difficulties, Sarrus seems quite happy as the party makes camp for the night. Though wary, he believes that the bandits are gone for good and stays up late, making notes, reading and consulting his maps by firelight. He also lays out the party's various discoveries, and Nymea makes small pen-and-ink sketches of them to go with his notes.

Other NPCs are growing less enthusiastic. Drew Connat is withdrawn and scared-looking; he clearly wants to abandon the expedition and go home, but is afraid to say anything. Sigra remains dwarvishly stoic, but is obviously tired. Drew tries to keep busy, while Maiesse continues on with few complaints. Regis — the walking red herring — keeps to himself and may be seen reading a small leather-bound book (if investigated this turns out to be a journal with nothing especially strange or incriminating save some very bad Gothic poetry). On occasion he can be observed staring intently at other party members (there's no reason for this other than his lack of social skills).

Sylva Montrose, however, has been doing her own research, and has also experienced some disturbing dreams. If she feels close to any characters she may sit with them in the evening and share her concerns.

Day Three

At breakfast have the characters make DC 15 Wis (Perception) checks. Those who succeed find that someone or something has rearranged the possessions in their backpacks or saddlebags. Items that were on top are now on the bottom, objects that were secured are lying on the ground, and a few minor knickknacks such as eating utensils, spare clothing or minor spell components, are missing entirely.

A search reveals nothing save foot- and hoofprints left by the party. Accusations against other party members also yield nothing save testy denials. NPCs may bicker over missing items and possibly even engage in scuffles that the characters must break up. Sarrus and Nymea call for calm and insist that there must be a reasonable explanation for the missing or disordered items. Regardless of outcome, the party sets off after breakfast.

Sarrus leads the party deeper into the forest. There are no more tracks, trails or guides now save for your leader's directions. Yesterday's fogs have withdrawn only slightly, lurking 20 to 30 yards distant, keeping you sealed in an isolate bubble, as if this forest is now the entire world and your expedition its only inhabitants.

The leaf mold beneath your feet is thick and seems to have lain undisturbed for years. The trees are even darker and more gnarled here, but are far enough apart to allow you and the party to proceed two-by-two. The birds still linger as well — black crows uttering hollow cries and watching you suspiciously.

Bandits' Fate

The primary encounter today is the discovery of the bandits' remains, but you can throw in a few encounters if you wish, along with more minor artifact discoveries like those of the previous day. Sarrus continues to consult his maps and at one point has the party start excavating a clearing. They may find a few bone arrowheads, but nothing else of any significance.

Just after mid-day the party encounters an especially unpleasant sight. If they are sending out scouts, describe it to them first — either hand them a note or speak to them away from the rest of the group.

The clearing is an abattoir, clearly the site of a recent battle — or, more accurately, a massacre. The ground is soaked in gore, and broad spatters of blood decorate the tree trunks and low-hanging branches. Bodies lie scattered about; you recognize some of the bandits that ambushed you two days ago, but none of them are whole. Some are missing limbs, others headless. Several of those corpses that retain their heads have had their eyes removed. Others are eviscerated, gutted, with entire organs missing. Worse still, the bodies seem purposely arranged in a circle around the perimeter of the clearing, and in the center you see another dark stone monolith — this one is over six feet tall and crusted with dried blood.

The NPCs all react with revulsion, and some — Drew Connat in particular —definitely panic and try to flee. How hard he is to chase down is up to you, but even if forcibly returned to the party, he is an utter nervous wreck, incapable of doing much other than cower in fear.

Once the party has gotten over its initial horror, characters can inspect the scene more closely. The ground is a sodden mess, but a DC 12 Wis (Perception) check shows numerous footprints, some human. Others are those of small humanoids, though it's hard to determine species. The ground is littered with spent arrows and several bandit weapons. A DC 16 Wis (Perception) check reveals several hastily-refilled holes in the ground, 2–3ft in diameter. Excavating these holes yields nothing, as the jaundools have collapsed the tunnels that they dug to cover their tracks.

Characters who succeed on a DC 20 Wis (Perception) check find a bone dagger buried in the muck, and a further DC 15 Int (Investigation) check reveals that it retains remnants of a pasty greenish substance. If a character tries to identify the paste, a DC 20 Int (Nature) check identifies it as something called "verdice," a rare toxin sold only by the most unscrupulous vendors (it's also the favored poison of the jaundools, but no one knows that).

Upon closer inspection, the column is clearly splashed with large quantities of blood. It's composed of a weathered dark grey stone and covered in weathered carvings in the same fashion as those the party previously encountered. In this case, however, it's easier to discern some of the images.

No Wis (Perception) check is needed to see that the carvings depict more human and small humanoid figures. The humans are dressed in loincloths or tunics and elaborate headdresses (these last depict ancient priests), while the smaller figures are 3–4ft tall and appear to be naked, wizened creatures somewhat resembling wrinkled bipedal rats. They bear daggers identical to the one found in the muck. All of the figures are gathered around a ring of stone monoliths and in the center a shape looms up. A DC 15 Wis (Perception) check is required to fully discern the central figure.

The big figure is a towering creature that has some features in common with the wrinkled rat-creatures, as well as what appear to be great membranous wings. The characters cannot determine exactly what this creature is, but anyone watching Sarrus should make a DC 15 Wis (Insight) check to reveal a look of sudden recognition on his face. Sylva Montrose's reaction is even more obvious — she gasps at the sight of the thing, but refuses to explain what disturbed her.

We're Out of Here

At this horrific sight even Sarrus begins to suspect that the party is in over its heads and seriously considers abandoning the expedition and heading back toward safety. At least outwardly, Nymea reluctantly agrees. As the party prepares to make camp for the night — most likely fortifying the site and posting round-the-clock watches — he announces that they will be turning back in the morning and making their way to the Avauntz Inn.

If Sylva has been speaking to any characters, she seeks them out again that night (or possibly speaks quietly to them on the trail as they retreat from the massacre scene). She explains that the situation seems even worse than it had initially seemed.

"I sneaked a look at some of Sarrus' texts," she confides. "They're written in a very archaic dialect of Old Suli, so I couldn't understand a lot of it. I'm not very good with older languages. But I could make out some parts — I think Sarrus hasn't been telling us everything. The people who lived here... They weren't Ancient Ones, not really. They were... exiled? Driven out?... by the true Ancient Ones because they made pacts with evil beings. Demons, devils, the Great Old Ones. They came here to practice their black magic, and found creatures living underground. In tunnels and caves — I wasn't able to find much out about them, but they sound horrible. The bad ones... the exiles... they made friends with them. Allied. Traded knowledge. I think they even..." Sylva

pauses and shudders. "*Bred* with these things... Had *children* with them. The exiles ended up worshipping these creatures' gods along with their own. They performed rituals... Sacrifices... Raided villages for victims... It sounds horrible. And I think..."

She stops again, looking nervously about. "I think that those creatures... They may still be here."

If confronted with this information, Sarrus claims that the stories of subterranean humanoids are exaggerated or entirely mythical, and insist that his expertise in the history of the region can be trusted. He acknowledges that some hostile entity or entities killed the bandits, and agrees that it is best to leave now — possibly returning later in force — but he vehemently denies any evil motives or dire intentions (in this he is being entirely truthful, as he's been manipulated by Nymea the entire time).

If the characters point out that the strange filled-in holes they spotted could indicate tunneling creatures, Sarrus grows quiet but still cannot bring himself to accept (or at least admit) that he may be wrong.

It's also likely that the party has grown of other NPCs such as Regis Tenebro, or Nymea herself. Both deny any involvement in events, but the party may persist and possibly even start a fight. If they do, Regis is innocent but defends himself, while Nymea will not give herself away by fighting — the characters may go so far as to incapacitate and tie up everyone they suspect, but this won't change subsequent events. You can also amp up the tension by having the NPCs bicker with each other, forcing the party to take sides or break up scuffles.

Regardless of the outcome of the discussion and regardless of the truth of Sylva's discoveries, Sarrus insists that it's all moot; he has agreed that the expedition is over and that they must return. Rest for the night is essential, however — many of the party members, especially the students, are exhausted — and the return trip can begin in the morning.

Unfortunately for Sarrus and the party, it's too late for an easy escape. The night promises to be long and filled with both false alarms and bad dreams (as described above). Though no overt attacks take place, the results are terrifying.

Day Four

Upon awakening, it becomes clear that Drew Connat is missing. If the party did headcounts during the night, his absence may be discovered earlier, but in the end there is absolutely no indication of what happened to him or where he went. It is as if this most fragile and disturbed member of the expedition has vanished without a trace. If for some reason the party had Drew restrained or otherwise constantly under guard, you can substitute another NPC.

If anyone thinks to inspect the ground near Drew's tent, a DC 20 Wis (Perception) check reveals more disturbed earth, as if something burrowed up from below. Once more however, the hole has been filled and the tunnel it connected to collapsed.

Inspection of possessions, packs and baggage reveals that they have been rifled through as well, and some food supplies have been stolen or spoiled. Water skins have been slashed, leather straps cut, arrows broken. How this happened isn't clear, as the party certainly maintained a vigilant watch all night.

The party now has to choose between retreating back toward "civilization" and leaving poor Drew to his fate or doing the noble thing and searching for their missing companion. Regardless of which choice the party makes, the outcome is the same. You can check for encounters, but the party has reached the part of the forest where mundane beasts are no longer present, so reroll any such encounters. In addition, the party makes a number of fearful discoveries. Describe some or all of the following to the players at appropriate intervals.

• The small twig fetishes are now found more frequently, hanging from branches along the party's route. They do not detect as magical but still appear to be marking their path, no matter what the party does.

• The expedition approaches a tree covered with the small fetishes — hundreds or thousands, swaying gently from branches high and low.

• Another tree is hung with humanoid skulls — human, dwarvish, elvish, halfling — and a DC 15 Int (Nature) check shows that they range in age from decades to centuries. They have apparently been hanging her for a very long time.

• The party encounters a cluster of three dark stone monoliths, covered in the same carvings as the previous marker. In the center of the trio is a mass of dark blood and possibly the remnants of a corpse. A DC 10 Wis (Medicine) check confirms that the body is not Drew, but is most likely a bandit, still wearing fragments of leather armor.

• Several trees are covered with crows, sitting silently and watching. If a character shoots one or lobs a stone, it easily flaps out of the way and returns to its perch, still staring.

• Random piles of stones also mark the party's route — normal, mundane stones, but clearly stacked intentionally. Some may have small carvings of spirals, circles or hash marks, but it's impossible to tell what these marks signify.

• A torn piece of the missing Drew's clothing or a small possession such as a belt pouch or necklace. If you want to be particularly alarming, perhaps a finger wearing a ring that one of the other students recognizes as Drew's, or other small body part.

The day proves exhausting, frustrating and ultimately futile. Endless hours spent marching or searching simply brings the party back to the scene of the bandit massacre, with the light fading and rain starting to rattle the upper branches of the trees. The party can make camp, try to press on through the night or come up with their own solutions to the dilemma. It's most likely that they'll set up a fortified camp and keep watch through the night, and tonight is when days of stress and fear finally come to their terrifying conclusion. (Should you have characters in the party who normally have abilities that prevent becoming lost, explain to them that memories of vile carvings and half-remembered dreams are interfering. They can tell that this is a supernatural effect, but not how to overcome it.)

Night Assault

Nymea and her allies decide that it is finally time to spring the trap they've been preparing. The night passes with the usual omens, bad dreams and strange events, but in the early morning hours the **jaundools** make their attack. The characters may choose a more defensive layout (with the supplies under guard for example), in which case you can use their layout or modify this one based on their requirements.

Combat takes place in the dark. Attacks made outside the radius of firelight or magic illumination are made at tactical disadvantage unless the attacker has darkvision.

1. Thick Forest

This area around the campsite is considered difficult terrain and provides half cover.

2. Campfire

The fire provides bright illumination to a radius of 20ft, with dim lighting for an additional 20ft.

3. Tents

Each party member has his or her own tent. The surviving members are in the following tents, unless the characters have deliberately arranged them otherwise: (a) Sarrus Togren; (b) Nymea Goswynn; (c) Sigra Ironshoulders; (d) Gedney Foulkes; € Sylva Montrose; (f) Regis Tenebro; (g) player characters (these may be increased/decreased based on the number of party members or moved to suit the players).

4. Animals and Supplies

If the party's pack mules have survived they will be tied up here, along with what's left of the group's supplies.

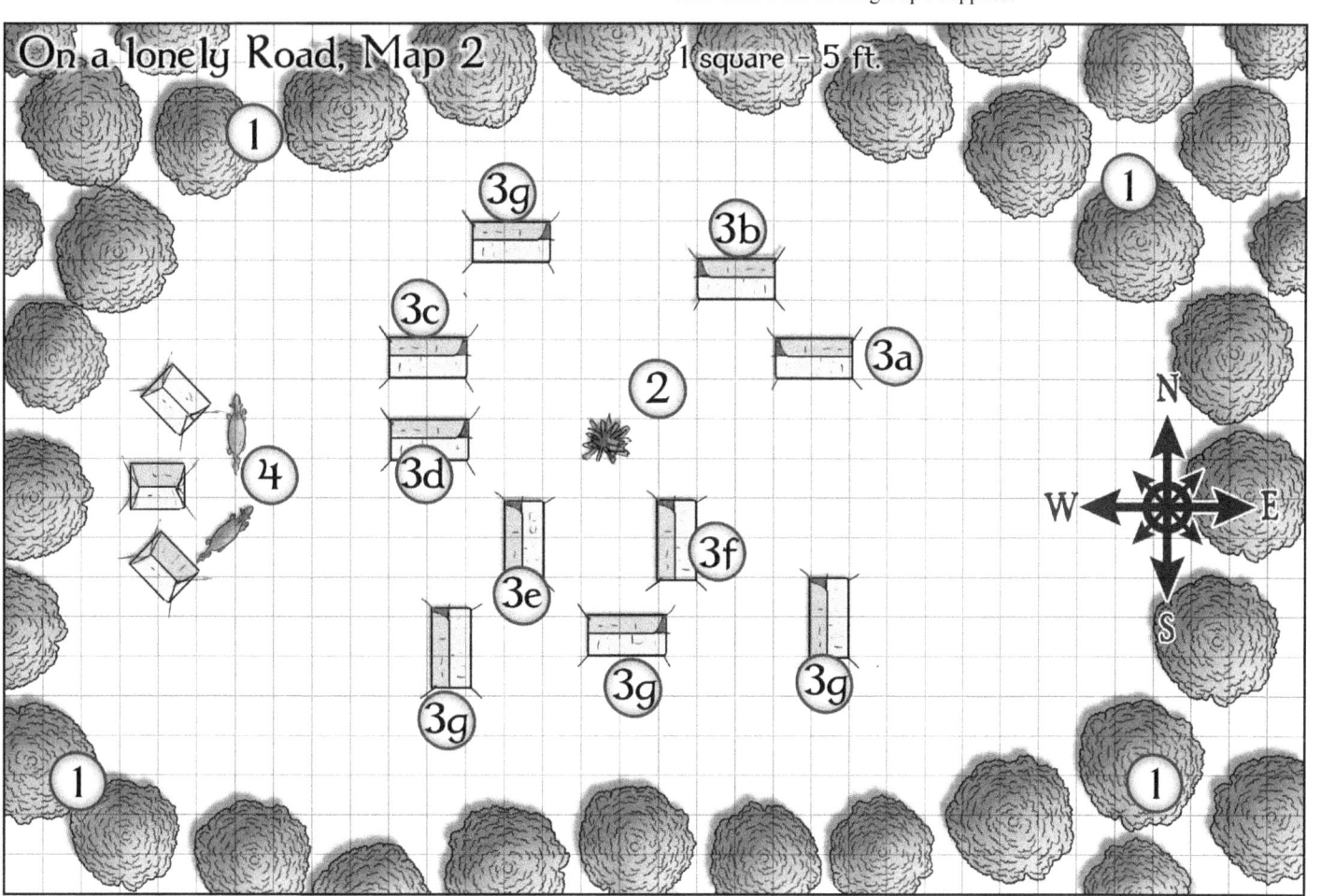

On a lonely Road, Map 2   1 square = 5 ft.

The jaundools possess only a faint remnant of their old wisdom but they are still cunning creatures, and after coordinating with Nymea they have come up with a plan to divert the party's attention while they seize professor Togren and other vulnerable targets.

Initially, the jaundools attack from below, using their burrow attacks on any sentries. After a round or two they then burrow up near the party's supplies, pack animals, or possibly one of the other NPCs in an effort to distract the characters from Professor Togren. If any of the party decide to stay with Togren, Nymea tells them to fight, that she'll keep the professor safe.

No specific number of jaundools make up this encounter. They appear in sufficient numbers to keep the party in combat and away from Togren's tent, and to keep the non-combatant students cowed and terrified, hopefully dragging one of two of them underground as well.

Jaundool (numerous): AC 13; **HP** 27 (6d6+6); **Spd** 20ft, burrow 10ft; **Melee** bite (+5, 1d4+3 piercing), claw (+5, 1d6+3 slashing), bone dagger (+5, 1d4+3 piercing plus poison, DC 11 Con or poisoned for 1d4 hours then DC 11 Con or blinded for 3d6 min; **Ranged** bone dagger (+5, 20ft/60ft, 1d4+3 plus poison); **SA** burrowing attack (DC 13 Dex avoids), multiattack (bite then claw or dagger); **Vulnerable** radiant; **Str** –1, **Dex** +3, **Con** +4, **Int** –1, **Wis** +2, **Cha** –1; **Skills** Perception +4, Stealth +5, Survival +4; **Senses** darkvision 60ft; **Traits** daylight vulnerability, stealthy; **AL** CE; **CR** 1/4; **XP** 50. (**Monster Appendix**)

After the Fight

Once the pallid ones have Togren, they fight on for another round or two, then scurry away or burrow out, collapsing their tunnels behind them. Hopefully the party's attention wandered a few times during the fight and they won't realize until the battle is over that both Togren, Nymea and possibly several other NPCs are gone. It's also possible that some NPCs are slain as well, along with any surviving pack mules. Most of the remaining supplies are stolen or ruined, leaving the party with little food, water or shelter. As dawn pales the sky in the east, it's clear that they are in extremely dire straits.

Day Five

The party has now lost its leader as well as supplies and possibly several NPCs. Whether they can rest long enough to recover spells and lost hit points is up to you, but as the woods grow lighter with morning they are now faced with a stark choice — try to rescue their comrades or simply escape with their lives. As before, it doesn't especially matter what they do, as the outcome in both cases is the same, but don't let them know that, or even hint at it; just keep their decisions in mind when deciding how well to treat them later.

Searching the woods reveals nothing, though a few more artifacts or signs of struggle may turn up. If and when the party begins to march through the forest, either to seek out the missing members or to try to make it back to safety, let them go on for a few hours until they at last face the final realization of Nymea's dark schemes. In the final struggle, however, the party may have an unexpected ally.

The White Raven

The day has passed into cold, bleak afternoon and still you have found no sign of your missing comrades, nor any obvious route of escape. Now, as you approach a lone fir tree, you see that its branches are thick with black crows. Then the mass of birds shifts and you see that among them stands one particular crow, snow white and much larger than its brethren. The white crow springs into the air and alights on the branch of a tree closer to you. It fixes you with a piercing stare and caws once, and now you see that it is not a crow at all but a raven.

Druids and worshippers of the Green Father automatically recognize the white raven as a messenger of the nature god; others may do so with a DC 20 Int (Religion) check. Though his influence in this blighted area is limited, the Green Father has always considered the jaundools to represent a sickness in his domain, and he has finally decided to act through his agents in the forest. The white raven cannot directly communicate with the party, but takes no hostile action and attempts to persuade the party to follow it. A *speak with animals* spell allows the caster to talk to the raven, though its statements are basic ("Follow me," "danger," "your friends," or similar information), while a druid who wild shapes into another raven can get the full story, that the Green Father has sent one of his emissary to aid the party and lead them to the enemy's stronghold.

As previously noted, worshippers of the Green Father may have some inkling about what's going on, but if none of the party members worship this god of nature (or makes the relevant skill check), the intervention of the raven and crows may seem quite mysterious, which is as it should be. GMs may want to include the white raven in future adventures as an omen or messenger.

If the party refuses to follow the raven they eventually arrive at the temple, but only after Togren's transformation is complete, and both he and Nymea are at full power. If they decide to follow, they may arrive in time to stop the ritual and save some of the jaundools' captives.

The Temple

The sun is sinking low as you approach a huge, ancient tree with a vast and gnarled tangle of roots. The white raven is perched above a dark opening amid the roots. Two monoliths flank the opening, as old and eroded as the ones you've already seen, and covered in more indistinct carvings. The raven stares at you for a moment, then glances down at the opening and utters an urgent *caw*.

Most of the surviving jaundools have withdrawn to the ritual chamber deep inside their temple to witness and participate in the summoning of their demon-god under Nymea's guidance. They have left some guardians behind which the party will have to fight through to get to the ritual chamber.

1. Monoliths

Two weathered monoliths flank the entrance. On closer inspection they resemble the monuments previously encountered, with barely-recognizable images of small humanoid creatures engaged in worship and sacrifice of humans and possibly elves.

2. Entrance

A dark entrance yawns between two big roots. Inside the ground is slick and sticky, the walls are a combination of dirt, rocks and intertwined tree roots. The roots extend through and around the tunnels, making footing difficult. Characters who run must make DC 12 Dex saves or fall prone.

3. Idol Chamber

This sizable room represents the jaundools' first line of defense. It contains **5 carved idols** that represent the jaundools' ancient demonic deities and still harbor significant dangerous arcane energy. While there are no jaundools currently here, attackers need to get past the idols and deal with their various magical abilities. (Grant the party 700 XP in total for overcoming this room of idols.)

There are two exits from the room, one to the north and one to the south, but as soon as the first party member enters the room, the roots around the exits contract, sealing off both passages, and the idols all activate. They receive initiative just like characters, and their Initiative bonus is +6. Each idol has an AC of 17 and 18 HP and has a special effect that continues each round until the idol is destroyed. Their Con and Str saves are +6. All other saves are +0, but as they are stationary the idols always fail any Dex saves. The idols' descriptions and powers are as follows:

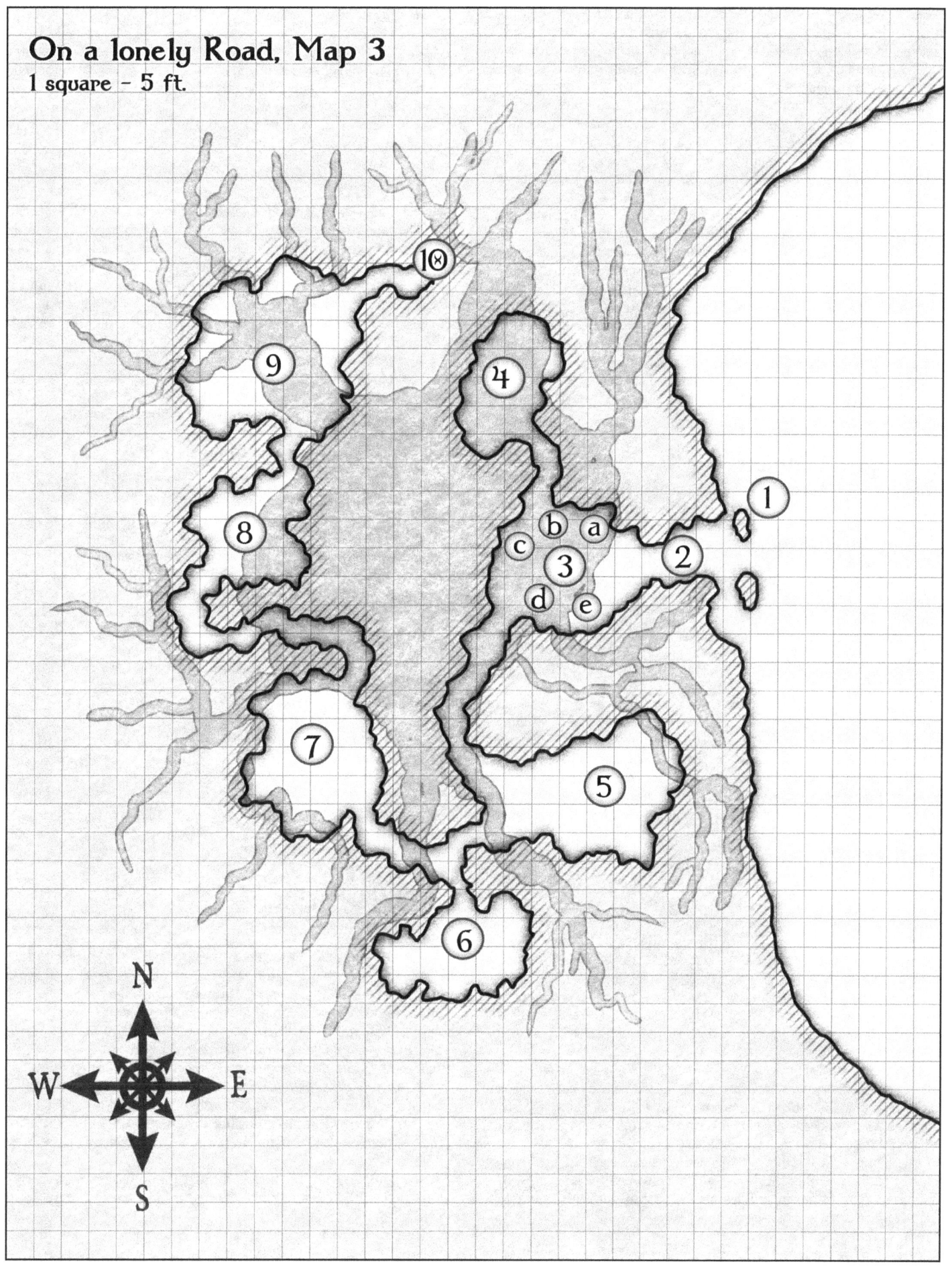

On a lonely Road, Map 3
1 square - 5 ft.

a. Shadow: This idol resembles a dark, hooded figure. Two dark eyes gleam silver in the depths of its hooded face. It represents an ancient and forgotten god of shadows. While the idol is intact, the entire chamber is considered to be in dim light. In addition, each round, the idol can cause one target to make a DC 12 Dex save. Failure results in the target being blinded for one round.

b. Plague Spirit: A rotting, corpse-like creature stares with wide, evil eyes as it reaches out a single emaciated finger. This idol represents another forgotten jaundool god, a demon that visited pestilence and disease on the jaundools' enemies. Each round the idol can cause one creature to make a DC 12 Con save. Failure results in the target receiving the poisoned condition for one round.

c. Tsathogga: A very corroded idol might once have portrayed a fat, toad-like creature. Each round it can cause one creature to make a DC 13 Wis save. Failure results in the target being slowed for one round.

d. Jubilex: This idol portrays an amorphous mass of slime and corruption. Each round it can shoot a stream of corrosive slime 30ft, with a +6 attack. Anyone struck by the slime must make a DC 13 Con save or take 3d6 acid damage. A successful save halves this damage.

e. The Pale King: A stone image of a hulking rat-like creature with great wings, a spiked tail and a demonic visage with glowing red eyes represents the ancient ruler of the jaundools. Each round it can produce one of the following effects (save DC 14): *color spray, magic missile, thunderwave, hold person.*

4. Sleeping Chambers

The jaundools who normally live here have all been called to participate in Nymea's ritual. Normally, they sleep in this filthy burrow, surrounded by various half-eaten creatures and other debris. Among the corpses in this room are the remains of several kidnapped villagers, human and halfling. Several still carry talismans, stone rings, brooches or the remains of recognizable clothing. If the characters gather any of these effects and return them to the druid Vertain at the Avauntz Inn, it will help some grieving families to know their loved ones' fate, however horrible. In this case, the characters gain a bonus 100XP each for the act.

5. Larder

A horrific stench strikes anyone who enters this chamber. The western portion of the room is empty, but the eastern 20–30ft are crammed with corpses — small animals, a few larger creatures and most horrifying of all, human and humanoid bodies, pale and naked, stripped of all valuables. The cave is cold which preserves the bodies to some extent, but the jaundools can eat even the most repellent substances, and don't care if their meals are a little gamey. The corpses all show signs of having been partially butchered, with some internal organs removed, limbs sliced off or sectioned up like sides of beef.

Area 6: Cesspit

Located off the main corridor, this place is even more repugnant than the larder. The jaundools' waste, offal, trash and foodstuffs too rotten even for them is tossed in a pile that has been growing and rotting here for centuries. The chamber is actually a vast pit, at least 60ft deep, but is filled almost to the brim with filth. The stench is all but unbearable, but has no effect on ability checks or attacks. Though there seems to be no reason to remain in this room, a DC 15 Wis (Perception) check reveals both the glint of gold and what appears to be the hilt of a sword extending from the surface of the offal.

Characters who attempt to wade through the waste can move at only 5ft per turn, and must also make a DC 12 Str (Athletics) check each turn or become stuck and be unable to move for that turn. Either the stuck character or an adjacent ally may take an action to free the character with a DC 15 Str (Athletics) check.

In addition to the hazards represented by the garbage itself, the garbage is infested with vermin. Most of these are crawling insects, worms, flies and maggots — disgusting but harmless — but the pit is also home to **6 giant centipedes** who are eager for new prey.

Giant Centipede (6): AC 13; **HP** 4 (1d6+1); **Spd** 30ft, climb 30ft; **Melee** bite (+4, 1d4+2 piercing plus poison; **Str** –3, **Dex**

+2, **Con** +1, **Int** –5, **Wis** –2, **Cha** –4; **Senses** blindsight 30ft; **AL** U; **CR** 1/4; **XP** 50.

After all this, a search of the pit nets 20gp, 31sp and 42cp. The sword is fully functional, though not magical, and clearly very old and of archaic design. The GM can decide to use this sword in a future adventure and may provide it with a longer and more elaborate history, but as it stands the sword is worth 100gp to a historian or collector. Otherwise, it is a very well-made and exotic-looking sword that functions normally.

7. Guardians

The passage widens here into a larger chamber tangled with roots and rocks. The jaundools know routes that allow them to move freely here, but for anyone else the entire room is considered difficult terrain. The jaundools have, over countless generations, trained some of the creatures in this area to ignore them and prey only on outsiders who enter this area. Concealed in burrows throughout the room, DC 18 Wis (Perception) to spot are **6 cave eels.** If not spotted they gain a surprise round, using their viselike jaws ability to seize and gain cover from characters.

Cave Eel (6): AC 12; **HP** 9 (2d8); **Spd** 25ft; **Melee** bite (+4, 1d8+2 piercing plus target grappled and restrained); **Str** +1, **Dex** +2, **Con** +0, **Int** –5, **Wis** +0, **Cha** –4; **Senses** darkvision 60ft; **Traits** concealed burrow, viselike jaws; **AL** U; **CR** 1/4; **XP** 50. (**Fifth Edition Foes** 49)

8. Antechamber

If the characters have gotten this far they're a real threat to the ongoing ritual. Nymea has ordered as many **jaundools** as she can spare to hold the line here, hoping to finish the ritual and see the demon-god reborn in Professor Togren's body. The detailed jaundools will attack mercilessly, utilizing their burrowing attacks and trying to inflict as much damage as possible. This area is relatively free of roots and rocks, and all characters can move normally.

Jaundool (8): AC 13; **HP** 27 (6d6+6); **Spd** 20ft, burrow 10ft; **Melee** bite (+5, 1d4+3 piercing), claw (+5, 1d6+3 slashing), bone dagger (+5, 1d4+3 piercing plus poison, DC 11 Con or poisoned for 1d4 hours then DC 11 Con or blinded for 3d6 min; **Ranged** bone dagger (+5, 20ft/60ft, 1d4+3 plus poison); **SA** burrowing attack (DC 13 Dex avoids), multiattack (bite then claw or dagger); **Vulnerable** radiant; **Str** –1, **Dex** +3, **Con** +4, **Int** –1, **Wis** +2, **Cha** –1; **Skills** Perception +4, Stealth +5, Survival +4; **Senses** darkvision 60ft; **Traits** daylight vulnerability, stealthy; **AL** CE; **CR** 1/4; **XP** 50. (**Monster Appendix**)

9. Ritual Chamber

A pale greenish glow emanates from the fissures and cracks in the tree roots that surround you. In the sickly light you see the skeletal remains of numerous bodies, some very old and still clad in remains of clothing or armor. A crowd of hunched, naked rat-creatures is gathered around a central platform — a gnarled section of ancient root that now serves as an altar stone for the fearsome spectacle unfolding before you. On the altar, covered in dark blood, is the motionless corpse of Drew Connat, and standing beside it, a bone-bladed dagger clutched in one hand, her face distorted and horrific in the green glow, is the missing Professor Togren's assistant, Nymea Goswynn!

She looks up with a fierce, almost diabolical expression, her eyes glinting red. As one, the jaundools turn to stare at you without emotion.

"I don't know whether to be glad or sorry to see you, my friends. I suppose I'm glad, as you can now witness a great event — the rebirth of a god-king!"

A new burst of nauseating light erupts from overhead and to your horror you see the figure of Professor Togren, unconscious and suspended at least 20ft above you, bound by countless tree roots that pierce his skin, pulsating and shining with unclean radiance.

If any of the NPCs or students were taken by the jaundools, they have either already been sacrificed, or held against the wall by tree roots, awaiting their turn. (It's up to the GM how grim circumstances should be, how many can still be saved, but poor Drew Connat has definitely had it). The roots binding each prisoner are AC 15 with 32 HP. Once freed, prisoners can act normally and may be able to help out if the party is in trouble.

There are **20 jaundools** in the chamber, but fortunately for the party, Nymea needs most of them to remain in place if she is to complete her invocation. If the party attacks, jaundools break off from the crowd in groups equal to the number of characters to defend her. The others remain motionless, adding their spiritual energies to the ceremony. Nymea needs five full turns to finish the ritual, which can only be stopped by killing or incapacitating her or by reducing the total number of jaundools participating in the ritual to 5 or fewer.

Pallid ones who are not fighting can be attacked and are particularly vulnerable; a character has tactical advantage on the first attack roll, after which the jaundool will fight, but is no longer considered to be participating in the ritual. Nymea herself cannot move from her spot or engage in physical combat, but she can cast non-concentration spells while performing the ritual.

Jaundool (20): AC 13; **HP** 27 (6d6+6); **Spd** 20ft, burrow 10ft; **Melee** bite (+5, 1d4+3 piercing), claw (+5, 1d6+3 slashing), bone dagger (+5, 1d4+3 piercing plus poison, DC 11 Con or poisoned for 1d4 hours then DC 11 Con or blinded for 3d6 min; **Ranged** bone dagger (+5, 20ft/60ft, 1d4+3 plus poison); **SA** burrowing attack (DC 13 Dex avoids), multiattack (bite then claw or dagger); **Vulnerable** radiant; **Str** −1, **Dex** +3, **Con** +4, **Int** −1, **Wis** +2, **Cha** −1; **Skills** Perception +4, Stealth +5, Survival +4; **Senses** darkvision 60ft; **Traits** daylight vulnerability, stealthy; **AL** CE; **CR** 1/4; **XP** 50. (**Monster Appendix**)

Players needs some cues that the clock is ticking so they'll pull out all the stops. It's obvious that Nymea is performing some kind of ritual, and the green glow that envelops Togren grows brighter on each of Nymea's turns, signaling that something terrible is about to happen.

If 15 jaundools are killed (or otherwise removed from the ritual), or if Nymea is stopped before five turns, the green light fades from Togren's body, and he hangs limp from the roots. If Nymea survives, she may continue to fight or attempt to flee down the tunnel to the lower deeps along with the surviving jaundools, collapsing the passage behind them (see "Concluding the Adventure" below for possible further development).

If Nymea is able to complete five turns performing the ritual with at least five jaundools participating, read or paraphrase the following.

The helpless professor's body is now suffused with the strange green light and begins to transform, growing larger, its head warping into a fearful amalgam of rat and man, its torso hunching, arms growing longer, great wings sprouting from its back. After a moment, the confining roots slip away, leaving a monstrous man-rat-demon hybrid standing above Nymea, gazing at its hands and surroundings curiously. The creatures you've been fighting abruptly stop and turn to stare spellbound at the mighty apparition.

"My master!" Nymea cries, falling on her knees, tears running down her face. "I knew you bore the mark of the pallid ones! That you and I were their final descendants, and

in your veins ran the blood of the ancient demon-god-king! I brought you here, master! I gave you the clues you needed! I led you here! And now I have brought about your glorious rebirth! Make me like you, master! Give me power!"

The winged demon-rat pauses, now gazing at Nymea as she kneels.

There is only the faintest trace of Professor Togren in its ferocious gaze, and after a moment even that is gone when it reaches out and with a clawed hand seizes Nymea by the throat, raising her body up and shaking it like a rag doll, snapping her neck, then casting it aside to lie motionless on the ground.

The gathered pale rat-things exult at this, chittering wildly while genuflecting and cringing on the ground, and with a heavy step the monstrous thing strides toward you.

The Pallid King: AC 15; **HP** 97 (13d10+39); **Spd** 40ft, fly 20ft, burrow 10ft; **Melee** bite (+7, 1d8+4 piercing), claw (+7, x2, 1d6+4 slashing; **Immune** cold; **Resist** normal weapons; **Vulnerable** radiant; **Str** +4 (+7), **Dex** +1, **Con** +3 (+6), **Int** +1, **Wis** +3 (+6), **Cha** +0; **Skills** Perception +6; **Senses** darkvision 120ft; **AL** CE; **CR** 5; **XP** 1800. (**Monster Appendix**)

Once Togren has made his transformation he becomes a serious challenge for the party, especially after what they've gone through to get here. If they choose the better part of valor, rescuing any prisoners they can get and fleeing, Togren pursues for only a few rounds before returning to his worshippers. Fortunately for the characters, any surviving jaundools remain kneeling or prostrate, stunned by the return of their god, and do not participate in the remainder of the encounter.

If the characters flee or are wiped out, the pallid king grows in power and strength, commanding the surviving jaundools and even drawing local inhabitants into its foul cult. Eventually it may become a threat to the entire province, but that would be a matter for further development by the GM — and a chance for the characters to make up for their failure here.

If the characters do by some chance manage to defeat the Pallid King, its surviving worshippers attempt to flee down the tunnel, collapsing it behind them.

Treasure: The jaundools aren't terribly interested in the accumulation of material wealth, but scattered throughout the room — dismembered, partly buried, tangled in roots, etc. — are the remains of centuries' worth of sacrificial victims. Though the jaundools retain little real intelligence, their savage instincts have compelled them to continue abducting victims for food or as offerings to their lost god.

Once all opposition has been killed or fled, the party can search the room. Among the dirt, roots and corpses are the following: 400cp, 6000sp, 1900gp and 120pp; 16 gems (100gp each), a *potion of supreme healing,* a *ring of jumping* and an adamantine chain shirt. Most other equipment and items have long since disintegrated.

10. Exit to Deep Tunnels

Beyond the ritual chamber, this deep, dank tunnel leads still deeper into the earth. More extensive works of the jaundools and even more disturbing things dwell there, and any sensible adventurer should quickly realize that following the tunnel is tantamount to suicide. If the characters seem overly interested in exploring, either oblige them (leading to another adventure beyond the scope of the current work) or have the jaundools collapse the tunnel.

Concluding the Adventure

If the party stops Nymea before the ritual can be completed, any surviving jaundools flee and any imprisoned party members can be freed. Once outside, the party has little trouble getting back to the Avauntz Inn, as the supernatural corruption of the region is swiftly fading, but the white raven will guide them to safety if needed. While a few jaundools

THE LOST LANDS: ADVENTURES IN THE BORDERLAND PROVINCES

survive and continue to stalk the area, they have lost their last connection to ancient greatness and will dwindle, eventually retreating underground to finally vanish forever.

Or do they? The fate of Professor Togren could be used by the GM to create a more ambiguous and disturbing ending. If the party successfully disrupted the ritual and prevented Togren's transformation, you can go for the happy ending (he's unconscious but alive and has learned a valuable lesson about secrets man was not meant to know), tragic (he's dead), or disturbing and uncertain (hopefully). In the final case, wait until an opportune moment when the party's attention is focused elsewhere then inform them that Professor Togren (whether his corpse or his unconscious body) has disappeared from the chamber.

This could also be the case even if the Pallid King is defeated, for the jaundools may be able to escape with the corpse, or perhaps it vanishes mysteriously on its own. Needless to say the characters are left with no alternative but to get out and return to safety. Feel free to throw in occasional false alarms and mysterious incidents on the way back to the Avauntz Inn.

Illusion and Illumination

Adventure Background

Illusion and Illumination is a wilderness adventure for a party of 4-6 player characters averaging 6th level. Light hearted and playful, it lends itself well to a more whimsical style of play unseen in many modern adventures, but readily found within certain older edition scenarios.

Yannick the Candlemaker, a successful merchant in Old Lawson Town, has a fey problem. A pair of sprites from the City of Mirquinoc, 150 miles away, have begun to plague his shop with tricks and mischief in a most unusual fashion. While the sprites of Mirquinoc do have an eccentric reputation, this behavior seems odd even for them. As messengers from Queen Twylinvere of the Mirquin Shee, the sprites have informed Yannick that he has incited her ire, and that he must pay for his crimes, but Yannick has no earthly clue what he's done wrong. Wishing to make amends, he seeks to journey to Mirquinoc to present a gift to the faerie queen in person and beg for her forgiveness before her emissaries destroy his business. Whether as hired guards, coincidental participants, or would-be heroes who have somehow caught wind of abnormal fey activities in the region and seek to put a stop to it, the characters will find themselves swept up in his journey.

The Real Story

While Yannick is as innocent as he seems, Queen Twylinvere is not the villain here either. Rather, she sent two sprite emissaries to perform two different missions near Old Lawson Town, and after an excessive night — involving a band of bored pixies, a crock of Old Lawson's Black Wizard Stout, and an awakened badger — the two sprites' memories of their instructions became completely confused in their minds.

The sprite-emissaries Leaftip and Cattail were sent to pay a visit to Queen Twylinvere's "distant relation," the cruel Oromirlynn, with instructions to, if possible, "bring her to justice". Once finished with Oromirlynn, Leaftip and Cattail were to spend as long as they needed resting up in the nearby settlement of Old Lawson Town, and then to purchase a load of Yannick's magical candles to bring home.

Instead, after the stout beer and the confusion of their instructions, Leaftip reasoned (and became convinced) that since Oromirlynn was a relative of the queen's, however distant, *she* must have been the one whose magical abilities they were sent to hire, while Yannick must be the villain in need of justice. Leaftip is so certain she remembers their instructions correctly, that she has convinced Cattail not to question her. It doesn't help that when the two sprites met Oromirlynn, the evil fey creature was charming and courteous.

However, Cattail has ascertained, using his *heart sight*, that Yannick is a good person. He is convinced that Queen Twylinvere must have intended only some kind of non-violent form of justice for the candlemaker. On the advice of their local pixie friends from the Loamwood Forest (the ones with the bottle of Old Lawson's Black Wizard Stout), Leaftip and Cattail have decided that if they pester Yannick long enough, he'll remember what he did wrong and properly repent. After all, they do vaguely remember having permission to stay in Old Lawson Town for some time.

Meanwhile, the two emissaries have already informed Oromirlynn that the faerie queen of the Mirquin Shee seeks to engage her services to some end or other. Oromirlynn is vain enough to have never questioned this, and when she journeys toward Mirquinoc at the same time as Yannick, she has absolutely no interest in him, his candles, or his armed escort. Thus, despite her delight in others' pain and her tendency to magically enslave random strangers, even Oromirlynn can't fairly be blamed for Yannick's plight.

Adventure Synopsis

At first, the journey from Old Lawson Town goes as expected — dangerous, yes, but that's (at least potentially) why the party was hired. Eventually, however, characters begin to see signs that something dark and terrible may be following them through the forested ravines and rivers. Not only that, but persecution from the fey continues in camp every night and matters begin to escalate.

Depending on the party's choices, the sprites may respond in a number of different ways, but all of them ultimately culminate in both emissaries fleeing back to Queen Twylinvere to inform her of the situation. As for Oromirlynn, regardless of whatever else she learns or doesn't learn about the misunderstanding in play, she eventually decides to take one or more members of the party as her thrall(s), requiring the party to defeat her before they reach Mirquinoc.

Though hints may be dropped before Mirquinoc, ultimately it's Twylinvere herself who fills in the last of the puzzle pieces for Yannick, instructing her sheepish emissaries to apologize for their behavior and making the whole misadventure worth everyone's while.

Adventure Hooks

While this adventure as written begins in the small settlement of Old Lawson Town to the north and east of Mirquinoc in the Gaelon River Valley, nearly any small town with dangerous woods nearby can work. Thus, getting the party into the woods near Yannick's shop should be easy enough. To get the party into contact with Yannick, consider one of the following hooks or, of course, feel free to create your own.

Armed Escort

Once Yannick makes up his mind to hire an armed escort for a trip to Mirquinoc, he does a good job of getting the word out, not just throughout Old Lawson Town but to other nearby riverside settlements. He's willing to pay handsomely for a party of good reputation to accompany him and his goods. Yannick is agreeable and clever, never a foolish negotiator, but leans toward generosity. He seems like he'd make a fine traveling companion, and he has a good reputation. A party who hears about this well-paying, pleasant-sounding job may seek it out themselves.

Further Misunderstanding

Even if the party refuses to work with Yannick, if they meet with Yannick at all, it would not be impossible for Leaftip to get the wrong idea about the characters' relationship with the candlemaker, or for Oromirlynn, watching from the woods, to decide that one of the party members has caught her eye as a potential thrall. Much of this adventure can simply *happen* to the characters regardless of the choices they make; flying, invisible antagonists following them in the background until, for whatever reason, the characters frighten off the sprites, are forced to defeat Oromirlynn in self-defense, and ultimately arrive at Mirquinoc. If the adventure happens without Yannick's participation, be sure to adjust the end with Queen Twylinvere to reflect this.

Problem Pixies

A party who never meets Yannick in Old Lawson Town might find themselves beset by this adventure's pixie mischief for no reason (or rather, for unfathomable pixie reasons), while traveling in the area. As there is only one real road (the Watershed Road) from Old Lawson Town to the King's Road further south, it's only natural to meet other travelers, even though the Watershed Road is little more than a muddy trail with one or two poorly-maintained inns. Yannick is among these fellow travelers, and he proves a friendly traveling companion as well as a generous and excellent cook. By the time the travelers reach the far side of the Loamwood Forest, it will be clear that he too is plagued by the local pixies, and to a much greater degree than the party. After the characters scare away or otherwise defeat the local pixies, Yannick explains that the pixies have frightened off the guards he brought with him from home, and he asks if he can travel with the party up the Watershed Road. If the characters allow Yannick to camp with them along the way, even once or twice, this alone can be enough to draw the attention of the spites and Oromirlynn. Yannick may also attempt to hire the party once he has the funds to do so in Elet.

Notable NPCs

Cattail

Cattail is unusual for a sprite in that he's a bit of a stick in the mud. He loves order and organization, and tends to obsess over details. He is often criticized by fellow sprites for what they see as an imbalanced fixation on minutiae, an inability to step back and examine a broader perspective. Queen Twylinvere chose him to accompany Leaftip in part hoping that the wilder warrior-sprite would help Cattail to relax into a more natural harmony with his path in life, and also because the queen specifically sought Cattail's excessive sense of responsibility to balance out Leaftip's wild side. Instead, Cattail's orders to obey Leaftip as his superior officer have backfired rather dramatically.

First of all, whenever Leaftip has invited him to parties with her pixie friends, Cattail has interpreted the invitation as orders, thus ensuring that he is as confused from pixie cider as she is. Second, Cattail is afraid to disagree with Leaftip's wild ideas about the orders they've lost. He is, however, concerned that she's gotten things wrong, and he's taken a liking to Yannick's candles.

Cattail is generally a bit miserable with the state of affairs on this mission. It may be possible, using reasonable and diplomatic tactics, to convince Cattail to side with Yannick and the party against Leaftip, but not until later in the adventure.

Leaftip

Leaftip is small for a sprite, and unpredictable as well. Her friends tease her that she must be part atomie (a smaller, wilder fey species). She was chosen for this mission because she is among Queen Twylinvere's best winged warriors, and because she already had contacts with local fey in the Old Lawson Town region. Both of these qualifications have backfired on the queen, since the latter have been a terrible influence on the mercurial Leaftip, plying her constantly with Old Lawson's Black Wizard Stout and inciting her toward un-sprite-like mischief, while the former has only enabled Leaftip to cause more trouble.

In general, Leaftip is exceedingly brave, fiercely devoted to Queen Twylinvere, a bit intense and over-passionate even when sober, and hovers on the border between Neutral Good and Chaotic Good, save in regards to her unshakable loyalty to the queen. When she has the town's potent local beer in her system, Leaftip becomes somewhat less compassionate than usual. Lucky for her, what she's best at is guerrilla-style harrying warfare — true of many sprite fighters — so she does know better than to challenge an entire band of strangers in broad daylight, no matter how intoxicated. She'll wait until she knows more about the characters and can take them by surprise.

Because of the garbled version of Queen Twylinvere's orders that she has come to believe, Leaftip is primed to think the worst of Yannick at every turn, and of the party as well for associating with him. No matter how Cattail or the characters attempt to persuade her, she cannot be convinced that Yannick is anything but a villain.

Leaftip has a tendency toward boorish or crass mockery when provoked, though she never takes it far enough to disadvantage herself in combat.

Oromirlynn

Oromirlynn is quietly, happily evil. She is modestly ambitious, hoping to amass a bit of wealth and territory in her lifetime, maybe spawn a local legend or two, but she's hardly a supervillain. She does, however, torture and kill for pleasure — whenever she thinks she can get away with it without upsetting her neighbors. She also keeps around a few magically-enthralled slaves, to fight for her and to keep house. She calls them her "acolytes" and pretends they serve her willingly.

Oromirlynn would not normally be one to travel long distances to serve in anyone's employ, but she's quite flattered that a faerie queen, such as her exceedingly distant cousin Twylinvere, would acknowledge her power and value. Oromirlynn is vain enough that it never occurred to her to question whether this actually made any sense. She knows Twylinvere would object to her murderous habits, but like many evil people, Oromirlynn assumes that most folk enjoy the same "crimes" that she does, and that those who claim otherwise are merely hypocrites, unwilling to acknowledge their true selves.

With such an outlook, it seems perfectly plausible to Oromirlynn that Twylinvere might have a use for someone like her. Nor does Oromirlynn suspect that Twylinvere intended her harm. While she believes anyone's capable of a double-cross, she doesn't think she's done anything noteworthy enough to raise a fey queen's ire.

Queen Twylinvere

Though she doesn't appear until the tail end of the adventure, Queen Twylinvere of the Mirquin Shee is a major driving force of this quest — though not *at all* in any way that she intended.

As a faerie queen, Twylinvere's motivations are understandably obscure, but not quite as obscure in this case as her emissaries have come to imagine. She loves pretty candles and has been impressed with examples of Yannick's work. Her relationship to Oromirlynn is a bit more mysterious, and her reasons for seeking the wildshadow's defeat are unknown even to Oromirlynn, but she does seek genuine justice against a villainous creature.

If asked for her thoughts on the matter, Twylinvere reveals only that Oromirlynn was her responsibility. GMs are free to make as much or as little of this as they wish. Perhaps Twylinvere somehow caused Oromirlynn's descent into cruelty and evil. Perhaps they are closer relations than Oromirlynn is aware. Perhaps Twylinvere has some reason to feel responsible for *all* wildshadows. Perhaps a council of fey leaders in the Borderlands region drew lots for the elimination of fey threats, and Twylinvere happened to draw the "Oromirlynn" straw. Whatever the case, the faerie queen herself does not choose to say, until and unless you choose to build a new adventure out of it.

Yannick the Candlemaker

Agreeable and soft-spoken, Yannick is a particularly handsome halfling, appearing on closer inspection to be partially elven — indeed, almost fully half-elven — in heritage; certainly an unusual mix! He seems just younger than middle-aged, though his mixed blood makes his actual years hard to estimate. He's well-dressed for a backwater town, though not ostentatiously so, and his features have a natural friendliness to them. Right now, however, he looks frazzled and sleepless, with dark circles under his eyes, his hair slipping free of its neat braid, and his clothes rumpled.

In addition to his renown as a master craftsman of candles, Yannick possesses modest skill as a wizard and is also an excellent cook, even over a campfire. If he ends up traveling with the party, he's happy to cook and do dishes for his employees every night, assuring them that their job is simply to keep him safe. He seems to enjoy simple chores and often hums happily while working. He's also startlingly intelligent and happy to learn on any topic any character wants to discuss. He loves stories, too, and will listen to the characters tell of their prior adventures with rapt admiration. It's taken him decades of study and practice to reach his level of wizardry, so adventurers of the party's level seem quite impressive to him (especially other wizards).

Beginning the Adventure

The adventure begins one night out from Old Lawson Town, with the characters traveling north on the Watershed Road from the King's Road.

The Watershed Road leads up from the Gaelon River Valley to the King's Road, a major east-west thoroughfare along the northern border of the Kingdom of Suilley. This remote part of the Gaelon Valley is hilly and cut through with numerous streams and rivulets on their way to join the great river two hundred miles to the north. Most of the area is covered with old-growth forest.

Although the Watershed Road itself is known for its relative safety, as you get closer to Old Lawson Town the great boles of ancient trees give the strange impression that this safety is maintained only at their sufferance, that this little strip of road could be blotted out in moments, if the trees ever so chose — crushed between their trunks to vanish forever, as if the highway and all who travel upon it had never been.

First Hint

Not far outside Old Lawson Town, at the darkest part of the night, all characters with any magical ability sense an odd chill. Anyone awake or sensing the chill may make a DC 18 Wis (Perception) check. Sleeping characters who succeed awaken, feeling as if they are being watched. Characters who were already awake and sleeping characters who beat the DC by 5 or more hear a rustling in the leaves above them, the soft beating of what might be giant moth wings, and a low chuckle of beautiful, feminine laughter. Awake characters who felt the chill but fail the ability check are sure it was their imagination — some trick of the night air perhaps.

This is Oromirlynn, observing the party, as she does live in the area and likes to watch travelers in their sleep. She prefers not to attack people in the Loamwood itself, however — several ancient charms placed upon the road caused her a virulent rash whenever she has attempted this. Unless the characters give pursuit, no further encounter occurs here. If the characters do give chase, keep in mind that Oromirlynn is flying, invisible, and can see in the dark. If they somehow manage to find her, she gives a creepy, musical laugh, uses magic to help her escape, and flees. She is, however, impressed that she was found out and takes note of the party as possible thrall material.

Oromirlynn, Female Wildshadow: AC 15; **HP** 67 (15d6+15); **Spd** 40ft, fly 50ft; **Melee** rapier (+9, 1d8+9 piercing plus *wild thrall*), dagger (+9, 1d4+9 piercing plus *wild thrall*); **Ranged** dart (+9, x2, 20ft/60ft, 1d4+9 piercing plus *wild thrall*); **SA** charm, innate spells (Cha +7, DC 15), multiattack (rapier and dagger or dart x2), superior invisibility; **Str** +1, **Dex** +5 (+8), **Con** +1, **Int** +1, **Wis** +3 (+6), **Cha** +4; **Skills** Deception +5, Perception +6, Stealth +8, Survival +6; **Senses** darkvision 120ft; **Traits** magic resistance, wild enchantment, wild thrall; **AL** NE; **CR** 5; **XP** 1800. **(Monster Appendix)**

   Innate Spells: at will—*dancing lights, mage hand, minor illusion, prestidigitation, vicious mockery*; 3/day—*disguise self, entangle, fog cloud, hypnotic pattern, major image, phantasmal force, silent image, suggestion*; 1/day—*confusion*.

   Equipment: rapier, dagger, 15 darts (all of Oromirlynn's weapons are subject to her *wild enchantment*).

Visiting Old Lawson Town

Old Lawson Town is not a large place, but situated so far out in such odd wilderness, it feels startlingly well-established, shockingly normal. Many ordinary craftspeople do business here, and the taverns (more than one!) serve plenty of beer from the town's excellent brewery. Some sort of magic is deeply embedded in the soil of this particular area, and it has made some of the town's products highly desirable even in distant places. It's only upon engaging the villagers in conversation that one learns just how superstitious is the culture here, undeniably influenced by the local magic aura. Everyone frets that every little thing will bring ill fortune, anger the fair folk, attract witches, and every other manner of worry. Small events are taken as omens, and townsfolk are sometimes known to argue over what each "omen" means.

Despite their superstition, however, the people of Old Lawson Town are friendly enough. They rely on trade with travelers for much of their town's revenue, so they're especially friendly toward visitors with coin and business.

Yannick's "infused" magical candles are locally famous, and the townsfolk are aware that he brings in business from other communities. They are simple tallow candles made from local pig-fat with a bit of alchemy, but due to the local magic infused in the plants eaten by the pigs, the candles have an almost narcotic bacon-like perfume. Yannick himself is well-liked as an upstanding member of the community. Many townsfolk are aware that odd things are happening in his shop lately, and they're worried about him. Some wonder what he's done to anger the faeries, while others shake their heads and blame the local youngsters.

A smaller but significant portion of the townsfolk know that Yannick is seeking to hire an armed escort for a journey. No one knows for sure why he's doing this, though some may have speculations. A DC 8 Wis (Perception) or Cha (Persuasion) check allows characters to overhear or elicit snippets of conversation about Yannick, such as the following (among others):

• He's moving away. He's fed up with high taxes for low results and is taking his business elsewhere. What will we do?

• He's just going on a business trip to trade his candles for other goods and to spread the word of his skills. He's only hiring a large escort to send a message to the mayor about how far the town's law enforcement has fallen.

Old Lawson's Black Wizard Stout

Old Lawson's Black Wizard Stout is affected by the slightly magical effects of the soil around Old Lawson Town. This gives it a certain strength with humans, but a tremendous kick for fey creatures.

The dark, coffee-flavored beer is highly alcoholic, as well as hallucinogenic. A drinker of one full serving (1 ounce per 20 lbs of body weight) must make DC 13 Con saving throw. This saving throw is repeated with every serving, and the DC increases by one (cumulative) for subsequent servings within a 3-hour period. Drinkers who fail a save are subjected to a milder version of the effects listed in the core rules' **short term madness** table (for example, a drinker rolling a 51-60 is merely rude and belligerent, rather than truly violent, while a drinker rolling 76-80 won't eat anything obviously dangerous, etc) for 1d4 hours (with additional servings potentially increasing duration). After the primary effects pass, the drinker continues to be affected as if by 1d3 results from the **long term madness** table, though again, in a much milder version (no mechanical effect — roleplay only) for 1d6 days before the cider fully leaves the drinker's system.

Drinkers who succeed on their saves are affected as if by ordinary dark beer, with a slightly more dreamlike intoxication experience. They have strange dreams when they sleep that night, but no notable lasting effects.

The beer is delicious.

• Oh, he's just taking himself too seriously. A trip out of the valley will remind him how big and mean the world outside can be for merchantfolk. He doesn't really need the kind of protection he's asking for. Should just hire a few local boys to carry spears and look tough.

• Whatever's going on with his shop, he's got to take a journey to lift the curse. I bet he's doing this for the good of the whole town. Wish I could help.

Nearly any villager not otherwise busy would be happy to show the party to Yannick's Candle Shop, though most are currently afraid to go inside, what with the "strange happenings" there.

Yannick's Candle Shop

Yannick's shop is a lovely little storefront, crisply clean and tastefully decorated, if slightly low of ceiling. Not surprisingly, it's full of candles, all neatly sorted and labeled, with prices marked in graceful, readable script. Ordinary candles fill over half the store and come in a remarkable array of colors and shapes. All are of fine quality, crafted with an elegance one would not ordinarily expect in so remote a region. In a major city one might pay five times these prices for candles so lovingly and uniformly made, and ten times as much for the rarer colors. Not to mention that when they burn they smell like a mix of first love and good bacon.

Candle sculptures, some lovely and some adorable, decorate various nooks and ledges. None are lit. In the corners, on sturdy-looking little shelves with remarkably stable-looking candlesticks, burn a small number of cheery little flames, chasing away any shadows that might have lurked within the shop. The place has few windows, perhaps to cut down on cross-breezes, or perhaps to keep the light just a touch low in order to show off the merchandise. Still, the shop boasts a fresh and cheery atmosphere, perfumed undoubtedly by subtly scented candles.

Yannick himself stands in the back of the shop, scrubbing some sort of mess off the wall. Upon closer inspection, it would appear that a lit candle was knocked over, scorching the wall, sending hot wax everywhere, lightly damaging a box of magically-infused merchandise, and utterly destroying what might once have been a pretty little candle sculpture of a flowering tree.

Yannick is busy with his task and doesn't appear to have noticed his shop's tinkling doorbell as you enter. He looks to be a halfling, if a particularly slim one, though he moves with an elvish grace.

When Yannick notices the party, he is flustered and embarrassed to have his shop seen messy, but he manages to remain friendly and ultimately realizes it's for the best that the characters saw the damage done by the overturned candle. He demonstrates how the candle couldn't have fallen by accident, indicating one of those particularly sturdy-looking candlesticks — and a segment of the base that has been clearly chipped. It really does look unlikely that such a candlestick could have spilled a candle, or that the base could have been so readily damaged, in any way other than sabotage.

During this display, Yannick suddenly notices the other lit candles and gasps, hurrying around to snuff them and inspect the other candlesticks for tampering. He explains that the first thing he did after putting out the fire from the spilled candle was to snuff all the others. He's not sure how he managed to miss the others being lit again while he worked, but it is a bright day outside, so even in the shadows of his little shop, any single candle flame isn't readily noticeable.

Unless the party gives Yannick some reason to believe they might be more dangerous to him than what he's already dealing with, he's quite happy to negotiate most generously for their services as an armed escort. He'll buy some equipment for the journey (as needed and reasonable, if it would be obtainable in Old Lawson Town on short notice), has no trouble

Yannick's Candles

Other than the pretty normal candles, Yannick's famous "infused" candles are also on display. Only a few of each are available, and the precise numbers are entirely up to the GM's preference. Some examples include:

Candle: Drifting Light
Length: 30 mins
Price: 10 gp

The person holding the candle can cause its light to drift away at a speed of 5ft/turn, to a distance up to 60ft from the candle. The drifting flame casts dim light in a 10ft radius.

Candle: Friends
Length: 30 mins
Price: 20 gp

Everyone within 15ft of the lit candle has generally positive feelings toward the person who lit it; that person gets tactical advantage on Cha checks (but not attacks) that target humanoids in the candle's radius.

Candle: Light the Path
Length: 30 mins
Price: 5 gp

While holding the lit candle and thinking about a place to which the holder has been, the flame flickers toward the direction of that place. These are popular among folk who must travel at night and are anxious about losing their way back home. One of the local taverns keeps a box of them for revelers who overindulge.

Candle: Mending
Length: 30 secs
Price: 15 gp

If the wax from this rapid-burning candle is dripped onto a broken non-magical object, the object repairs itself exactly as if a *mending* spell had been cast on it. One candle can repair one object.

Candle: Message
Length: 1 min
Price: 30 gp

A message is whispered to the candle while it is lit, then the candle is extinguished. The next time the candle is lit, it repeats the message verbatim. The total burning time of the candle is one minute, so a message that's more than 30 seconds long will be truncated on delivery. The candle works only once, regardless of how short the message is.

Candle: Restfulness
Length: 1 hr
Price: 30 gp

A character who lights this candle at the start of a short rest, and spends an hour basking in its light, recovers from one level of exhaustion. Only the character who lit the candle gets the benefit, and the benefit can be gained only once in a 24-hour period.

Candle: Soothing Sounds
Length: 1 hr
Price: 5 gp

While lit, this candle creates the illusion of a simple, soothing sound. Different candles are labeled and color-coded for different sounds, such as birdsong, frogs and crickets, a burbling stream, wind through leaves, and similar.

The GM should feel free to include other candles as desired, with similar prices. It is easy to see, however, which candles are made by Yannick personally, and which seem to been crafted elsewhere. The *Friends, Mending, Message,* and *Soothing Sounds* candles are all examples of Yannick's own work, and these are much more finely-crafted in appearance than any candles made by other magic-users.

In designing new candles, GMs should take into account the spells described for Yannick's spellbook in the next section. While most of his storefront candles are extremely minor magics, there's nothing to say he can't keep candles for spells up to second level, under lock and key in the back (priced appropriately, of course). Any candle ideas that seem like they might be crafted using spells Yannick would know will reflect Yannick's skill at sculpting in wax. Any that Yannick could not produce himself, such as candles of healing, look like decent-to-nice-quality candles without Yannick's flair for grace or uniformity of form, and certainly without Yannick's impressive array of colors.

---

with covering all expenses while on the road, and makes an initial offer of 100 gp per character each way (that is, 200gp each for a round trip journey). GMs should feel free to adjust this total as appropriate to setting and party. Yannick is willing to haggle, but keep in mind that he is a small-time merchant in an isolated town. As a merchant of magical items, he is likely to be wealthier than his neighbors realize, but too much disposable wealth would still be unrealistic. He can certainly offer to include magical candles in his reward, within reason. All moneys are to be given to the characters upon Yannick's safe return to town.

When the party asks for more details about the journey, such as its destination or purpose, or its connection to his candle issues, Yannick glances around fearfully. He's more than willing to explain his situation, but not in his shop. It's hard to tell if he has a good reason for this or is just as superstitious as the rest of Old Lawson Town.

He closes shop for the day, explaining that most townsfolk won't buy anything from him right now anyway, not since Belena the cobbler had her hair set on fire last week. His only business is from out-of-town traders, and he's starting to worry for their safety. In the long run, it's probably better for business to hurry up and start preparing for his journey. Of course, if characters want to make purchases, he'll let them.

With the shop closed, Yannick leads the party toward the Church of the Forest, a local temple. He explains that this is the only place he can trust he'll be left alone long enough to tell the story and won't endanger others with his presence. He's not sure why, but those dogging him always leave him alone inside the temple.

Before the party can arrive at said temple, however, Yannick is accosted en route. Leaftip appears from invisibility and flutters in the air between Yannick and the entrance to the churchyard. Noticing her before she appears requires a DC 25 Wis (Perception) check, especially since the sound of her wings is covered by the ordinary daytime bustle of the town. Yannick immediately identifies this sprite as one of his candle-shop antagonists.

Leaftip, Female Sprite Ftr7 (champion): AC 19; **HP** 44 (8d4+24); **Spd** 10ft, fly 40ft; **Melee** +2 rapier (+10, x2,1d8+12 piercing); **Ranged** shortbow (+8, x2, 40ft/160ft, 1d6+8 piercing); **SA** heart sight, invisibility, multiattack; **Str** −3 (+0), **Dex** +5, **Con** +3 (+6), **Int** +1, **Wis** −1, **Cha** +0; **Skills** Perception +2, Stealth +11; **Traits** action surge, fighting style (dueling), improved critical, remarkable athlete, second wind; **AL** NG; **CR** 7; **XP** 2,900.

> **Equipment:** studded leather armor, shield, +2 rapier, shortbow, 50 arrows.

A DC 15 Wis (Insight) check shows that this smaller-than-average sprite might be slightly intoxicated; if that check is successful, then a DC 20 Int (Medicine) check suggests the intoxicant is an unusual one. (Don't worry about a third check for this. If anyone makes the Medicine check, allow a local character to make the connection to the brewery's Black Wizard Stout automatically.) Leaftip's state doesn't quite look like ordinary drunkenness either, but it looks more like intoxication from Old Lawson's Black Wizard Stout than regular alcohol or other common substances.

In fact, it's been several days since Leaftip indulged in anything of the kind, but the local brewery makes a drink much stronger than either of the Mirquinoc sprites has yet realized, and it's infused with the magic earth of the area, which has a very strong effect on fey creatures. Leaftip doesn't know that she's still not quite sober from the last time she met with her local pixie friends.

If the characters attack before Leaftip can speak, she makes several terrible, irrationally strong assumptions about them all and flies away, turning invisible. If necessary, Cattail and even a local pixie or two might be nearby to help her escape.

If the encounter begins with conversation, read or paraphrase the following:

"I'm onto you, candlemaker," the little sprite says, sneering down at you all. "You know we're too respectful to attack you in the temple, so you blaspheme upon its grounds with your foul plotting. You have my partner convinced you're not so bad, but I see through you. And who are these ruffians you've gathered? Assassins to threaten our queen?" She shakes her head gravely. "I will stop you, miscreant. I will find a way."

Leaftip is not ready for a pitched battle here in the streets of Old Lawson Town. She flees rather than fight, once any real combat begins. However, she talks for some time if the characters engage her diplomatically. Leaftip refuses to reveal anything about her own purposes, except for her own extreme loyalty to the Queen of the Mirquin Shee. While she may be persuaded to grudgingly like or respect certain party members, she isn't rational right now and can't be convinced that Yannick should be left alone (especially since the characters don't know enough of what's going on to offer any key arguments.)

If the party does not provoke Leaftip to flee, the town's local cleric (**Autzen Jemm**, Neutral (good) male human cleric 6) eventually emerges from the temple and politely requests that Leaftip allow Yannick and the characters inside. He explains that it is not for her to decide who may or may not seek the comfort or forgiveness of the gods. Leaftip immediately bows to his authority in the manner and vanishes.

Once she is gone and everyone is inside the church, Yannick tells what little he knows of his tale. Autzen Jemm is already familiar with the tale, and goes on about his business unless asked for advice.

"They first arrived weeks ago. I had other things on my mind then and barely registered their strange visit, but it was that sprite and one other who visited me at my shop and told me they were emissaries from Mirquinoc, and that I had incurred the wrath of the faerie queen of the Mirquin Shee!" Yannick shakes his head. "I've never even *been* to Mirquinoc! I have a client there, but every time I write to her — or to the queen — for more information, the sprites intercept my message on the way out of town. I have no idea how I could possibly have offended a faerie queen — only that I would never have done so on purpose."

He seems absolutely sincere.

"I've asked them for more information, but they only tell me I know what I've done, and that they're here to bring me to justice." He throws up his hands and drops them helplessly at his sides. "I'm not sure *they* know what I've done. The other one especially seems confused about the whole thing, whenever I see him."

Yannick goes on to explain that while the sprites have never seriously injured anyone — not even when they set Belena's hair on fire — their pranks and "punishment" have been escalating steadily. Not only is Yannick's business struggling, but he's starting to worry how far the fey might take this vendetta. Though no wounds have yet been serious, in the last two weeks there have been several minor injuries and other creepy, haunting-like events.

"None of the ghostly activity is much more than I could accomplish myself, with a bit of minor magic," Yannick admits, "but it scares the townsfolk well enough. If it gets much worse they might burn my shop down for my own good." He shudders. "And that's assuming the sprites don't go over the edge and start attacking innocent townsfolk. I'm just so confused about this. I . . . I have to talk to this Queen Twylinvere myself. That's why I'm asking for an escort. I need to travel to Mirquinoc without the sprites tripping me into a canyon or getting me eaten by a bear along the road. Preferably, I'd like to bring the queen a gift, to soothe whatever ire I've caused her. Will you accompany me?"

If the party offers other options, like carrying the gift for him or catching and interrogating the sprites before departure, Yannick would far prefer to simply head out to Mirquinoc as soon as possible. He's very convinced that this is the best plan for his circumstances. He *can* be convinced to stay

---

If Yannick Stays Behind

Here is a short list of ways to tweak encounters if Yannick isn't there:

The Pixies: These bored local fey pester the party for any conceivable reason. Perhaps they are aware that the characters were seen with Yannick and have decided that this is "crime" enough. Perhaps they don't like one party member's haircut. Perhaps they've decided that one character is attractive and are vying for that person's affection in the most annoying possible ways. They're very impulsive people and don't need much excuse for their behavior.

The Sprites: Leaftip is sufficiently volatile and confused to assume the party is working for Yannick, engaged in his nefarious plot to somehow threaten Queen Twylinvere. She still talks about Yannick to the party, but as their distant employer, rather than speaking to him directly. Cattail's interactions are a little harder to tweak, but if the first encounter with Cattail takes place as Yannick is bidding the party farewell, it can be used to establish Cattail's future interaction with them. Since Cattail's actions are so very dependent upon the party's response to him, it's best to play his character however makes sense for the circumstances following that initial meeting.

Oromirlynn and her thralls: Oromirlynn's response to the party has nothing to do with Yannick. His absence shouldn't change her behavior much at all.

Queen Twylinvere: If the party approaches her as messengers from Yannick, she may well decide that the situation has grown sufficiently out of hand to merit her direct involvement — including *teleporting* all involved parties to her. Thus, in the final scene with her court, Yannick may be present even without having made the journey. If Leaftip was mistaken about the party working for Yannick, the queen rewards them for Oromirlynn, just as described, and then offers additional treasure in apology for their trouble at her emissaries' hands. At GM's discretion, this may even be as generous a reward as if they really had been working for Yannick all along.

Yannick: If Yannick is left behind, he continues suffering at the pixies' hands for most of the time the characters are en route to Mirquinoc (other than during the period when the pixies follow the party instead). However, since the pixies are not nearly as formidable foes as the sprites were, Yannick's wizardry proves up to the task of protecting his shop and keeping his business afloat until Queen Twylinvere is finally made aware of his plight.

behind and let the characters carry a message and his gift for him, if they insist, but he would prefer to go, and the rest of the adventure assumes he is with the party. He sees no purpose in interrogating the sprites, since he suspects that the sprites don't know much more than he does. He thinks they're probably just blindly loyal to this Twylinvere, who Yannick hopes has merely mistaken him for someone else.

On the Road

Yannick is quick about getting ready to leave. His friends help him to box up most of his merchandise and belongings and store them in safe locations. He locks up his shop, hires a few local children to keep watch in case the fey set it on fire while he's gone, and packs bravely for the journey to come. Again, Yannick is happy to pay for any reasonable equipment the party needs for the trip, so long as it is available in Old Lawson Town in the time allotted.

Just as the group is leaving, Cattail the sprite nervously approaches Yannick. If any of the characters seemed especially hostile in the party's previous encounter with Leaftip, Cattail makes himself known to Yannick when those characters are elsewhere. He is polite and obviously ready to flee at the slightest provocation.

Cattail, Male Sprite Drd5 (circle of the land, forest): AC 17; **HP** 15 (6d4); **Spd** 10ft, fly 40ft; **Melee** scimitar (+6, 1d6+6 slashing); **Ranged** +1 shortbow (+7, 40ft/160ft, 1d6+7 piercing); **SA** heart sight, invisibility, spells (Wis+4, DC 12);

Yannick's Equipment

Yannick's pack mule is carrying any reasonable/plausible normal tool that he could have acquired under the circumstances and can fit on the little beast of burden (saving room for candles and his gift to Queen Twylinvere). However, the items are carefully packed and some may only be accessible in camp at night or after a significant pause to look for them. With any item Yannick might logically have, roll 1d4 each day to determine whether it is available at a moment's notice, such as during combat. On a 4, it can be easily accessed. (During camp in the mornings, Yannick can deliberately pack to keep some items available, at party request.)

In addition to his normal equipment, Yannick has brought candles he thinks might be useful (quantity and variety at GM's discretion, though not more than 2 dozen candles total, and no more than a handful of each type). These are in a separate box that is always easy to access. As long as characters can justify how a candle's use is relevant to the mission, Yannick offers it for free. The others he will sell at regular price should characters offer to buy.

Yannick's Spellbook

Yannick has a great many spells in his spellbook. He's not a powerful wizard, but he's been doing this a long time, and he's recorded many spells, always hoping to use them in his candlecraft. It is safe to assume that Yannick already has any given illusion spell of first or second level in his book. All other first- and second-level spells are present or absent in his book at GM's discretion, although he has sadly not yet learned *see invisibility, gust of wind,* or *detect thoughts.* If a party wizard wishes to teach him these spells, or any others he does not possess, he will do his best to learn while traveling.

Yannick of course has only spells of levels he can cast, but he's happy to share them with a fellow wizard and is quite humble about his collection. GMs should also feel free to have Yannick prepare a different group of spells than that given in his stat-block, below, if the party asks him to do so.

Str –4, **Dex** +4, **Con** +0, **Int** +2 (+4), **Wis** +2 (+4), **Cha** +0; **Skills** Perception +4, Stealth +8; **Traits** druidic, wild shape; **AL** LG; **CR** 1; **XP** 200.

Spells (slots): 0 (at will)—*druidcraft, mending, poison spray;* 1st (4)—*cure wounds, entangle, fog cloud, thunderwave;* 2nd (3)—*barkskin, beast sense, gust of wind, spider climb;* 3rd (2)—*call lightning, plant growth, sleet storm.*

Equipment: leather armor, shield, scimitar, +1 shortbow, 50 arrows.

If the group engages Cattail in conversation, he says:

"If I overheard rightly, you're setting out to apologize to the queen. I'll tell my companion that our mission is probably complete, but you be sure you do what you've said you will. We'll be watching." He sounds more like he's pleading with Yannick than threatening him.

Cattail won't stay around to chat, or to fight.

With that, the group can set out. Yannick brings a pack mule with useful items, including a selection of magical candles, and a box that he says is his gift for the faerie queen. He's an inexperienced and occasionally-naive traveler, but he had a more experienced friend help him pack, so he's more over- than under-prepared, and he's cheerful and curious, never complaining or getting in the way.

The Trek Begins

The journey from Old Lawson Town to Mirquinoc is about 140 miles along the Watershed Road southward to reach the King's Road, then another 50 miles west to Mirquinoc. The maximum possible speed on the Watershed Road is 10 miles per day due to constantly fording small streams, which exhausts the horses fairly quickly. Walking speed is about the same as riding, but it is less tiring to ride.

Make one encounter check per day (which is conveniently also once per hex on the map included with this adventure), using the encounter table for the King's Road in *The Lost Lands: Borderland Provinces*, Chapter 8: *Duchy of the Rampart* (if you do not have a copy of that book, use any appropriate encounter table for wooded and hilly terrain). Although the list of encounters is the same, the *chances* are different than on the King's Road itself. Use the following table:

01-50	No Encounter
51-85	Mundane Encounter
86-00	Dangerous Encounter

All encounters are at the Medium Risk Level, as shown in the encounter details in the Appendix of *The Borderland Provinces*.

The adventure indicates various other events that take place along the way in addition to any random encounters. These are shown on the map, although the exact location isn't required.

Back to the Loamwood

The forested Watershed Road remains mildly creepy, though never quite as bad as the night the party unknowingly crossed paths with Oromirlynn. Nevertheless, mischief dogs the expedition every single night from the moment they cross outside Old Lawson Town.

These are small (though not necessarily harmless) pranks, including (but certainly not limited to) the following:
• Tying together the bootlaces of whoever is on watch
• Stealing of food or (especially) alcohol
• Dipping all of the party's spare clothing in the stream, so that it's

From Old Lawson Town
to
The Free City of Mirquinoc

1 hex ~ 10 miles
(One day's travel)

N · W · E · S

Old Lawson Town

Loomwood

Istivoon River

x The Hunting Pack

Shorn Forest

x The Mysterious Stalker

x The Sprites Return

x Unlikely Quartet

x Parting Shots

Mirquinoc ◉

x The Campsite King's Road

strewn about in trees and soaking wet when found
 • Painting silly faces on party members in their sleep
 • Drugging party food with intoxicants
 • Bedecking the group's animals (or at least Yannick's pack mule) with flowers, feathers, and lewd or insulting banners
 • Stealing of party underwear and stuffing it into other party-members' bags
 • Tickling people in their sleep so they can't rest properly
 • Hanging important party treasures up high in trees
 • Leading Yannick's pony miles away
 • Using *sleep* or other spells to make life humorously difficult for whoever is on watch

All such efforts are subject to Dex (Stealth) checks as usual, so waking characters and characters being touched all have opportunities to catch the pranksters in the act. Sleeping characters may also wake if loud noises occur. During all such antics, the party sees no sign of Leaftip or Cattail. Instead, these pranks are being orchestrated by Leaftip's and Cattail's local pixie friends.

Pixie (5–7): AC 15; **HP** 1 (1d4–1); **Spd** 10ft, fly 30ft; **SA** innate spells (Cha +4, DC 12), superior invisibility; **Str** –4, **Dex** +5, **Con** –1, **Int** +0, **Wis** +2, **Cha** +2; **Skills** Perception +4, Stealth +7; **Traits** magic resistance; **AL** CG; **CR** 1/4; **XP** 50.
 Innate Spells: at will—*druidcraft*; 1/day—*confusion, dancing lights, detect evil and good, detect thoughts, dispel magic, entangle, fly, phantasmal force, polymorph, sleep.*

These pixies are no match for the party and have zero intention of fighting. However, the local Yolbiac Vale pixies are a bit wilder than usual. They lean more toward CG than NG, and some among their number may be CN in outlook. This particular group are also partiers, often intoxicated. They've been a very bad influence on Leaftip during her visit to the region, in part because they, in turn, have been negatively

influenced by association with the deceptively lovely Oromirlynn, who has given them weird ideas about the world. Though none of these pixies are evil or likely to engage in violent acts, if the party converses with them, several among the group say evil or bloodthirsty things, as if trying hard to sound "cool".

Though these pixies are friends of Leaftip and Cattail, they are harrying the party without the knowledge of either. If the party engages them violently, they scatter. If the party catches and interrogates one or more, they may learn the following through Cha (Intimidation or Persuasion). If the party has killed any of the other pixies, increase DCs accordingly.

DC 12
 • No one told them to do this. They're just having fun.
 • They *are* trying to do a favor for Leaftip, even if she doesn't know about it.
 • They have no idea why Leaftip doesn't like Yannick.

DC 15
 • All of them, including the visiting sprite emissaries, have been drinking a lot of Old Lawson Black Wizard Stout, which leaves the drinker more than slightly intoxicated for days afterward.
 • Old Lawson Black Wizard Stout is made with roasted local beans as well as ordinary ingredients, and tends to mix and garble a drinker's memories in a dreamlike manner.
 • Leaftip and Cattail are also friends with another local fey, of whom these particular pixies are in a kind of fearful awe.
 • While they don't know what Leaftip and Cattail have against Yannick, the pixies do know that the visiting sprites got their orders somehow confused.
 • Some of the sprites' treatment of Yannick may actually be based on their pixie friends' advice for how to bring a "miscreant" to "justice", rather than on the orders of their queen.
 • Some of the antics in Yannick's shop have been perpetrated by these pixies all along, "helping" Leaftip with her "justice", because it was funny.

DC 18

• Cattail has convinced Leaftip to leave Yannick alone for a while. The sprites intend to check back on him later. The pixies were just bored, and they've developed a taste for pestering Yannick.

• The pixies do not have access to more Black Wizard Stout, and are not wholly unwilling to barter for a pixie-sized barrel, maybe more (especially if none of them has been killed). It they *really* like the party, they'll warn the characters to only consume the beer in a safe place, with a spotter. Incidentally, this is not necessary; humans are not nearly as affected by the beer as fey creatures are.

• Leaftip probably suspects what the pixies are up to and hasn't stopped them, but she really, really didn't tell them to do this.

• Leaftip and Cattail are off spending time with their "other friend", who is very beautiful and named Oromirlynn. The pixies don't know any more than that about Leaftip and Cattail's activities.

DC 20

• Oromirlynn calls herself a wildshadow. This is a type of fey these pixies have never seen anywhere else, though Oromirlynn herself has lived here a long time. She's almost as tall as a halfling and has pretty, black moth wings.

• The pixies think Oromirlynn is really, really cool.

Keep in mind that this is a fey-rich forest, so if the pixies are bullied, stolen from, or otherwise mistreated, there should be a massive fey backlash against the party, unrelated to this adventure. Other local fey know that these particular pixies can be annoying, so a reasonable and proportional response will be ignored by the forest's "community", but excessive retaliation against the pixies will not be tolerated. Allow a DC 12 Int (Nature) check for a character to recognize this fact. (Local bards, druids, and rangers gain tactical advantage on this check.)

The pixies stop pestering the party after any of them are caught (assuming any proportional, just, or diplomatic response). Now that they've sobered up a bit further, these pixies realize they all nearly got themselves killed, annoying people much stronger than themselves. Particularly likable characters may elicit apologies or even gifts from the pixies, especially if none of the revelers/pranksters have died. Due to the nature of the encounter, experience should also be awarded more generously for parties who end the pixie problem *without* killing the pixies.

The Hunting Pack

After the pixies have stopped following the party, a new threat surfaces. Encountering the characters in the course of an extensive hunt through the surrounding forest, a pack of werewolves charges through the party.

These werewolves seek a pack mate of theirs who has gone missing. Some of the pack are loyal to their companion, while other members suspect a betrayal. In any case, the entire pack is looking for the missing werewolf, high and low through the forest. They were told by some pixies to check in this general direction, but they do not particularly suspect the party of having relevant knowledge. In fact, had they happened to encounter the characters while in human form, they might simply have asked a few questions and gone on their way. However, they instead blow through the party at high speed while in wolf form.

The werewolves make no attempt at stealth or courtesy. These are arrogant, hotheaded youths drunk on their own lycanthropy, and they don't even attempt to gauge the party's strength before rushing through. They simply assume that they can bully the party however they like without consequences, as they probably could with most travelers on the road.

Characters have every opportunity to notice a pack of wolves rushing toward them at speed, their behavior entirely lacking in a natural wolf's caution or shyness. The werewolves make no attempt at stealth, so barring whole-party Perception failures, the characters should not be surprised. A mere DC 8 Int (Nature) check reveals that this is not normal wolf behavior — and that these probably aren't normal wolves. Those who beat this check by 5 or more identify 3 members of the pack as **werewolves**, and the 2 larger members as **dire wolves**. Due to the thickness of the trees and the speed at which the wolves approach, Characters with a passive Perception of 12 or better have 3 rounds of warning as other animals

fall silent and they hear the sound of the approaching pack; while other Characters have only 2 rounds to prepare.

What happens next depends largely on the party. If they can hide fast enough, they might attempt to ambush the oncoming wolves or avoid the encounter entirely; in the latter case, assuming their Stealth checks beat the wolves' passive Perception, the pack rushes through and goes on its way.

Alternatively, the Characters might stand their ground. The werewolves cannot be engaged in conversation before initiative is rolled, as they are in a hurry and do not care what the party has to say.

If the party holds their ground on the road, 1d4 of the werewolves and/or dire wolves rush directly at party members; treat this as an attempt to "overrun."

Should the Characters still not react, the pack continues on its way. Any attack or hostile action on the part of a party member, however, inspires the wolves to stop and fight. (And let's be honest, not many Characters are likely to stand still and allow a pack of wolves — were-, dire, or otherwise — to run them over without reaction.)

Once combat begins, the wolves attempt to surround the party. One or two of the werewolves transform into hybrid form, hoping to shake the characters' morale. (They still haven't fully realized these are experienced adventurers, not normal travelers.) The werewolves intend to fight until the uppity Characters are dead (or surrender, at which point the lycanthropes lose interest). If, however, they began to fare poorly against the party, they're willing to reassess their efforts and might even withdraw; this pack is made up of violent hotheads, and none would win any battles of wits, but they are not suicidal.

Werewolf (3): AC 12; HP 58 (9d8+18); Spd 30ft, as wolf 40ft; **Melee** bite (+4, 1d8+2 piercing plus lycanthropy, DC 12 Con), claws (+4, 2d4+2 slashing); **SA** multiattack (bite, claws), shapechanger; **Immune** non-silver normal weapons; **Str** +2, **Dex** +1, **Con** +2, **Int** +0, **Wis** +0, **Cha** +0; **Skills** Perception +4, Stealth +3; **Senses** keen hearing and smell; **AL** CE; **CR** 3; **XP** 700.

Wolf, Dire (2): AC 14; HP 37 (5d10+10); Spd 50ft; **Melee** bite (+5, 2d6+3 piercing plus knock prone, DC 13 Str); **Str** +3, **Dex** +2, **Con** +2, **Int** −4, **Wis** +1, **Cha** −2; **Skills** Perception +3, Stealth +4; Skills Perception +3, Stealth +4; **Senses** keen hearing and smell; **Traits** pack tactics; **AL** U; **CR** 1; **XP** 200.

A werewolf who is captured and questioned reveals that the pack only seeks their missing friend. (Tthis is the werewolf who has been enthralled by Oromirlynn; see below). They were sent in this general direction by pixies who saw their friend with a beautiful fey woman.

While the players may well assume this is another pixie prank, in fact it is not. They really did see a werewolf with Oromirlynn, and they really did see her headed in this general direction. The characters were just in the wrong place at the wrong time.

The Mysterious Stalker

On a later night, after Yannick and his escort have left behind the fey-touched forest and are on the King's Road, a familiar chill feeling returns. It doesn't stay long, and only magically-sensitive characters feel it, but it's exactly like the chill the party felt near the road just outside Old Lawson Town.

This chill is, again, Oromirlynn, who has again stumbled upon the party while hunting for quality thralls. Though the encounter is by chance, it is not, however, truly coincidence. Oromirlynn has been convinced by Leaftip and Cattail to journey with them to Mirquinoc, where she believes the queen intends to hire her for services unknown. Thus, she is traveling in the same direction as the party, through the one and only reliable mountain pass. Though she left the Old Lawson Town area several days after the characters, her ability to fly has allowed her to catch up to them.

If they haven't already, some of the party members now take her fancy as potentially useful thralls. Oromirlynn begins to consider how to catch one or two. As before, however, she is not yet ready to engage in open combat and flees back into the night if detected. This is her choice, however; now that the characters are out of the Loamwood they are no longer protected by the ancient wards placed on that path.

The Sprites Return

On the day following the return of Oromirlynn's observation and accompanying chill, Leaftip and Cattail suddenly accost the party again. They approach the party invisibly and stealthily, but give themselves away in what sounds like a half-whispered argument before they can surprise the characters. Once they realize their presence has been announced, Leaftip (still invisible and flitting between the leaves of trees, up on the slopes of the pass) calls out to the party.

"We're still watching you, halfling! Whatever your plans, you'll never succeed! You feign repentance, but we are not fooled!"

Leaftip's tirade is interrupted by more loud whispers in not-quite-discernible Sylvan, coming from another direction. She responds in an angry hiss before continuing.

"Watch yourselves!" she warns, adding inexplicably, "Stay out of our affairs!"

Leaftip — based upon things Oromirlynn has said to her, as well as wild conjecture — is now under the impression that Yannick intends ill toward Oromirlynn and that he and his escort have, in fact, journeyed this way to lay an ambush for the wildshadow in the narrow mountain pass. However, Leaftip doesn't want to reveal where Oromirlynn might be, in case the characters don't know yet, so she is behaving in a cagey and, as usual, unintelligible manner. Depending on how the characters respond, this interaction could lead to further dialogue, to light combat, or simply to the sprites fleeing.

Dialogue is unlikely to sway Leaftip, but a particularly eloquent character might confuse her enough to retreat and rethink things. Should this happen, assume that a later conversation with the silver-tongued Oromirlynn re-convinces Leaftip to see Yannick and his bodyguards as a threat.

Cattail, however, could indeed be convinced that something strange is going on, since he has begun to suspect that Oromirlynn may not be a nice person. If characters have good arguments and can convince Cattail that they are decent people (which may or may not require a Deception check, if the characters are not, in fact, "decent"), GMs should permit them a Cha (Persuasion) skill check to entice him toward helpfulness. At this stage, such an endeavor is still difficult, even if the party have been courteous, and is at a DC 25. (Later, if the party attempts this after he's observed them for a longer time, the DC might fall to 20 or even 15, at the GM's discretion.) Should the party succeed, Cattail remains loyal to Leaftip as his commanding officer, but handled appropriately could be convinced to aid the party in subtle ways or to share what little he remembers of the garbled orders situation.

Visible Invisibility

If a party is particularly skilled at seeing invisible creatures, it may be difficult to orchestrate some of the scenes in this adventure. Here is a list of back-up plans:

• Leaftip is very sneaky at +11 Stealth. She is also tiny and thus able to hide behind almost anything. By keeping her in the treetops or up high on rocky slopes, she might be effectively invisible regardless.

• Cattail is not terrible at Stealth, with a +8, but he also has access to Wild Shape, allowing him to appear as an animal. If he transforms into a larger animal, Leaftip could even hide behind *him*. He can also prepare different druid spells at need. Not many at his level are useful for hiding, but *meld into stone* could be, especially in the mountains.

• Oromirlynn also has a +8 in Stealth and is quite fast. She, in addition, has access to several illusion spells, including *disguise self*. She might make herself appear to be a small, lost child, a halfling passer-by, or even Yannick (or other small-sized party members), should it be useful to her to do so.

• Cattail and Oromirlynn can both cast *fog cloud*.

If the confrontation leads to combat, Cattail acts only to protect Leaftip from harm or to execute her direct orders in as nonviolent a manner as possible. He helps far more enthusiastically if Leaftip chooses to retreat.

Leaftip engages in skirmishing tactics, avoiding being trapped or surrounded at all costs, attacking on the move, staying to the edges of the group or high on steep slopes above the party. If she feels she needs to and is given an opportunity, she takes Yannick or a party healer hostage in order to ensure her escape. She is not so much trying to defeat the characters here as to show off her battle prowess and demonstrate that she means business. She hopes to encourage the party to avoid her.

Between her own natural goodness and her understanding of Cattail's doubts regarding the party's guilt, Leaftip has no interest in killing the characters or Yannick at this time. If she comes close to doing so, she considers her point to have been sufficiently made and retreats, with perhaps a few parting insults/warnings.

Leaftip, Female Sprite Ftr7 (champion): AC 19; **HP** 44 (8d4+24); **Spd** 10ft, fly 40ft; **Melee** +2 *rapier* (+10,1d8+12 piercing); **Ranged** shortbow (+8, 40ft/160ft, 1d6+8 piercing); **SA** heart sight, invisibility, multiattack (rapier x2 or shortbow x2); **Str** –3 (+0), **Dex** +5, **Con** +3 (+6), **Int** +1, **Wis** –1, **Cha** +0; **Skills** Perception +2, Stealth +11; **Traits** action surge, fighting style (dueling), improved critical, remarkable athlete, second wind; **AL** NG; **CR** 7; **XP** 2900.
   Equipment: studded leather armor, shield, +2 *rapier*, shortbow, 50 arrows.

Cattail, Male Sprite Drd5 (circle of the land: forest): AC 17; **HP** 15 (6d4); **Spd** 10ft, fly 40ft; **Melee** scimitar (+6, 1d6+6 slashing); **Ranged** +1 *shortbow* (+7, 40ft/160ft, 1d6+7 piercing); **SA** heart sight, invisibility, spells (Wis+4, DC 12); **Str** –4, **Dex** +4, **Con** +0, **Int** +2 (+4), **Wis** +2 (+4), **Cha** +0; **Skills** Perception +4, Stealth +8; **Traits** druidic, wild shape; **AL** LG; **CR** 1; **XP** 200.
   Spells (slots): 0 (at will)—*druidcraft, mending, poison spray*; 1st (4)—*cure wounds, entangle, fog cloud, thunderwave*; 2nd (3)—*barkskin, beast sense, gust of wind, spider climb*; 3rd (2)—*call lightning, plant growth, sleet storm*.
   Equipment: leather armor, shield, scimitar, +1 *shortbow*, 50 arrows.

Yannick participates to defend himself if needed.

Yannick the Candlemaker, Male Halfling Wiz3 (illusionist): AC 17 (with *mage armor*); **HP** 16 (3d6+6); **Spd** 25ft; **Melee** dagger (+6, 1d4+6 piercing); **Ranged** sling (+6, 30ft/120ft, 1d4+6 bludgeoning); **SA** spells (Int+6, DC 14); **Str** +0, **Dex** +4, **Con** +2, **Int** +4 (+6), **Wis** +2 (+4), **Cha** +1; **Skills** Insight +4, Medicine +4, Perception +4; **Traits** brave, halfling nimbleness, lucky, stout resilience; **AL** NG; **CR** 1; **XP** 200.
   Spells (slots): 0 (at will)—*friends, mending, message, minor illusion*; 1st (4)—*alarm, longstrider, mage armor, shield*; 2nd (2)—*flaming sphere, mirror image, web*.
   Equipment: spellbook, dagger, sling, 30 sling-bullets, see text for more.

If it seems as if one of the sprites might inconveniently die here, several options exist for saving them that don't require a potentially player-frustrating exercise of GM fiat. Here are some examples:

• Cattail offers himself as a hostage so Leaftip can escape.

• Yannick asks the characters not to kill Twylinvere's emissaries, since he still hopes this is all a mistake, and he doesn't want to further anger the faerie queen.

• Oromirlynn decides to save the sprites by casting spells from hiding, should it amuse her to do so.

• Oromirlynn sends in a thrall or two to protect the sprites (see later sections).

• Some other fey, forest, or mountain creature chooses to involve itself on the sprites' behalf. After the sprites flee, the party might convince the creature that the sprites were in the wrong, at which point it might pursue the sprites and return later as a thrall of Oromirlynn, or run off in the direction of Mirquinoc to consult the queen before interfering further, etc.

If at any point Cattail becomes a captive or ally of the party, he sheepishly discloses the irresponsible way in which their orders for this mission were lost and confused. Convincing him that he and Leaftip made several mistakes in piecing together what they remembered of the queen's wishes is not terribly difficult, requiring only a DC 10 Cha (Persuasion) check if the characters offer a compelling argument. However, he remains remarkably stubborn that he mustn't disobey Leaftip as his superior officer. He's clearly agonizing over all of this. Lawful he may be, but he is emotionally still fey: passionate, extreme, and occasionally incomprehensible. He does not willingly talk about Oromirlynn, though a DC 10 Wis (Insight) check is all that's required to discern that he is hiding something, should the topic arise.

You've Seen One Bit of Forested Terrain . . .

You'll note the lack of maps associated with most of the combats in this adventure. This is deliberate. The various fey opponents lack the means and/or the disciplines to set up particularly intricate ambush scenarios, and the encounters occur in fairly simple forest or village terrain. As such, the battlegrounds are all relatively standard in terms of terrain, and random in terms of positioning, and have therefore been left to the GM's prerogative.

The Unlikely Quartet

Once beyond the Ghostwind Pass, Oromirlynn begins to give the sprites a bit of a run-around. She wants the best possible thralls for her appearance at Twylinvere's court, seeking a balance between brute strength and an appearance of civility. The party sees little direct evidence of this, but Oromirlynn's efforts accomplish two things.

First, though at least one of her thralls accompanied her all the way from the Old Lawson Town area (the werewolf), Oromirlynn might well have found herself unable to bring others through the pass without announcing her presence to everyone in the area. Low on servants, she begins a quest to acquire new ones the moment she and her guides dip back below the treeline on the Cretian Mountain slopes. Since the taking of slaves would bother the sprites, Oromirlynn must use her *charm* ability to its fullest, in order to keep them out of her hair while she hunts.

A time-consuming process, this thrall-hunt leads to the flying NPCs taking their sweet time through the foothills while the walking characters have a chance to catch up. The party might even hear rumors or see evidence of strange activities along the trail — reports of people behaving strangely or disappearing, or sightings of flying creatures almost invisible in the dark — giving the characters a few more bits of mystery to ponder surrounding that strange chill the magic users sometimes feel at night.

Second, Oromirlynn's thrall-hunt keeps the player characters fixed firmly in the forefront of her mind. Though they should seem too strong for her to tackle immediately, some of them would come across to her as the perfect balance of power and social grace that she seeks for her entourage. She *wants* the party to catch up to her, so that, once she's ready, she can enslave her favorite members.

Wishing to assess the characters' strengths and abilities, Oromirlynn eventually sends a few thralls against them. Sometime before they reach the Gaelon River, in a small, wooded area, four enthralled monsters attempt to surprise the party at Oromirlynn's bidding. Oromirlynn herself controls them from the shadows and does not participate in combat.

As soon as one thrall dies, she orders the others to retreat, but she will not save them, beyond, at most, casting *fog cloud* on their behalf. If she doesn't have confidence in a thrall's ability to heal in time to be of use again soon, she forces that thrall to stand its ground and die while the least-wounded thrall escapes instead. Oromirlynn does, however, place high value on her lizardfolk shaman's healing ability.

Should her thralls come near to killing a character that Oromirlynn thinks of as useful to her, her centaur may attempt to finish the character off with his *wild enchantment* weapons, depending on whether or not any of the other thralls has fallen. If Oromirlynn does enthrall a player character, she immediately casts *fog cloud* and withdraws with all of her thralls. See the **wildshadow** description for what happens if she at any point has more than four thralls.

Since Oromirlynn is present, invisibly watching this fight, her now-familiar, subtle chill rides the air.

Oromirlynn's thralls are in no way unusual for their species, other than being emotionally subdued and willing to fight alongside one another. Using *detect magic*, it is possible to discern that the thralls are under an enchantment. A DC 20 Wis (Medicine) check allows a character to determine that the thralls are somehow ill or intoxicated. If the *wild thrall* enchantment is broken, the thralls immediately take damage as outlined in the wildshadow description and (if still conscious/living) flee, confused and disoriented.

Note that Oromirlynn has had the lizardfolk shaman prepare spells differently than listed in the *MM*. His actions, as per Oromirlynn's will, are to serve primarily as support and healer for the others. The centaur mostly keeps well back from melee and fires arrows into the party.

Manticore: AC 14; HP 68 (8d10+24); **Spd** 30ft, fly 50ft; **Melee** bite (+5, 1d8+3 piercing), claw x2 (+5, 1d6+3 slashing); **Ranged** tail spike x3 (+5, 100ft/200ft, 1d8+3 piercing); **SA** multiattack (bite, claw or tail spike x3); **Str** +3, **Dex** +3, **Con** +3, **Int** −2, **Wis** +1, **Cha** −1; **Senses** darkvision 60ft; **Traits** tail spike regrowth (24 count); **AL** LE; **CR** 3; **XP** 700.

Werewolf: AC 12; HP 58 (9d8+18); **Spd** 30ft, as wolf 40ft; **Melee** bite (+4, 1d8+2 piercing plus lycanthropy, **DC** 12 Con), claws (+4, 2d4+2 slashing); **SA** multiattack (bite, claws), shapechanger; **Immune** non-silver normal weapons; **Str** +2, **Dex** +1, **Con** +2, **Int** +0, **Wis** +0, **Cha** +0; **Skills** Perception +4, Stealth +3; **Senses** keen hearing and smell; **AL** CE; **CR** 3; **XP** 700.

Centaur: AC 12; HP 45 (6d10+12); **Spd** 50ft; **Melee** pike (+7, reach 10ft, 1d10+5 piercing plus *wild thrall*), hooves (+6, 2d6+4 bludgeoning); **Ranged** longbow (+5, 150ft/600ft, 1d8+3 piercing plus *wild thrall*); SA multiattack (pike, hooves or longbow x2); **Str** +4, **Dex** +2, **Con** +2, **Int** −1, **Wis** +1, **Cha** +0; **Skills** Athletics +6, Perception +3, Survival +3; **Traits** charge, multiattack; **AL** NG; **CR** 2; **XP** 450.
> **Equipment:** pike, longbow, 50 arrows. This centaur's weapons are all very dark in color, as per the wildshadow trait, *wild enchantment*.

Lizardfolk Shaman: (lizardfolk form) AC 13; HP 27 (5d8+5); **Spd** 30ft, swim 30ft; **Melee** bite (+4, 1d6+2 piercing), claws (+4, 1d4+2 slashing); **SA** change shape, multiattack (bite, claws), spells (Wis +4, DC 12); **Str** +2, **Dex** +0, **Con** +1, **Int** +0, **Wis** +2, **Cha** −1; **Skills** Perception +4, Stealth +4, Survival +6; **Traits** hold breath; **AL** N; **CR** 2; **XP** 450.
> **Spells (slots):** 0 (at will)—*druidcraft, produce flame, thorn whip*; 1st (4)—*entangle, cure wounds*; 2nd (3)—*heat metal, spike growth*; 3rd (2)—*plant growth, protection from energy*.

Again, if any characters contract lycanthropy, Yannick is very knowledgeable about the condition.

If any of the thralls becomes a captive of the party without being cured of *wild thrall*, they die before they talk. If cured of the thrall as outlined in the **wildshadow** description, it may be possible to interrogate them.

The lizardfolk is the most likely to offer available information, but only speaks Draconic and has thus understood less of Oromirlynn's motivations.

The centaur's response depends on the party's behavior, as he is proud and wary. Handled carefully, he is the only one of the four who might be convinced to ally with the party to seek vengeance against Oromirlynn, but he is also eager to rejoin his own tribe, who are traveling in another direction. He speaks Elvish and Sylvan, and the latter may have given him more insights into Oromirlynn's relationships with the other fey, perhaps even more information than listed below, at GM's discretion.

The manticore is belligerent, stupid, insulting, and unobservant. It knows very little of the information below and shares less than it knows. If threatened or bribed (it likes gems, but would want them in a container it can carry), it will lie wildly to the party, inventing "information". It's not a good liar. It hates Oromirlynn, but cannot be recruited to the party's cause by any means short of magical compulsion. It speaks Common.

The werewolf, despite some annoyance at having been enslaved, finds Oromirlynn attractive and may thus be somewhat cagey on her behalf. Nevertheless, the werewolf has been with her the longest, all the way since Old Lawson Town. At GM's discretion and if properly motivated, this thrall too might turn out to know more than listed below. This werewolf is also a friend of those the party encountered in the Yolbiac Vale. The party's interaction with them may help or hurt their interaction with those werewolves' packmate, depending on what the characters choose to share. As with the others, Yannick does not recognize this werewolf (GM's discretion whether or not the party does, as above).

Here is information that one or all freed thralls might offer the characters:
• They acted against their will, fully under the control of an enchantment they don't understand.
• They were controlled by a beautiful fey-looking woman with black moth-wings.
• Their captor has smaller fey friends. (Describe individuals who resemble Leaftip and Cattail, but don't point out their identities if the players don't make the connection.)
• Those two friends are convinced that the thralls served willingly, out of personal devotion. In part, this is because their captor is a good liar, and in part because she could force her thralls to say anything she wished.
• Before they became controlled, the thralls were struck by unusually dark-colored weapons (just like the centaur's, whose weapons were not that color before she enslaved him).
• The thralls felt strange and hallucinated between being wounded by the dark weapons and becoming controlled.
• They all remember taking very serious wounds before becoming controlled, but that they didn't die.
• Their memories during the time they spent enthralled are fuzzy, but not missing.
• Their captor seeks more powerful thralls.
• Their captor is on the way to visit some queen.
• Their captor seems to have more than one means of controlling others through enchantment, considering observations they've made of interactions between their captor and her "friends".

If the party chooses to go hunting Oromirlynn, she makes herself very difficult to find. Yannick makes it clear that he would prefer to press onward toward Mirquinoc than to spend time tracking her down. He hopes that whatever has attacked them, it won't continue to follow them past the river, which the party should reach tomorrow.

Whether or not the party pursues Oromirlynn, they are accosted by Leaftip. Either Leaftip intercepts them while they hunt for Oromirlynn, or she stops them in a grove of trees the next day, just before a rocky ford over one of the small streams that seem to be everywhere through this area.

Parting Shots

Much of the following interaction varies greatly depending upon the party's behavior in previous scenes. Parties who killed or were otherwise cruel to the pixies, who behaved violently toward Cattail, or who gave Leaptip other reasons to believe they might be evil, are attacked outright by the sprite. She continues to avoid being surrounded at all costs. On the other hand, Leaptip merely remains invisible and shouts at aparties who won over the pixies or Cattail, or successfully freed the thralls from their enchantment.

Once her position is revealed, Leaftip threatens the party to stay away from Oromirlynn, who is, she claims, a relative of the queen's. Leaftip clearly believes that the party attacked Oromirlynn's "acolytes", rather than the other

way around. She seems totally unaware that any of Oromirlynn's thralls lacked free will. She is also more convinced than ever that the characters are headed toward Mirquinoc with intentions of harm toward Queen Twylinvere.

If it no longer makes sense for Leaftip to feel this way about the party, it is possible that Oromirlynn's *charm* ability has somehow inspired this tirade, or that Oromirlynn had some reason to use *suggestion* to goad Leaftip's behavior, or that the pixies left Leaftip with a flask of pixie dream cider, and she is once again influenced by the aftereffects of its intoxication.

Cattail's relative level of participation, especially if Leaftip decides to fight, depends entirely upon the party's previous interactions with him. In a best case scenario, from the characters' perspective, Cattail might join the fight on their side, seeking to subdue Leaftip without harming her. In a worst case scenario, the party's conflict with Oromirlynn's "acolytes" (the thralls he does not know lack free will) could convince him that Leaftip has been right all along — particularly if he too has been subjected to Oromirlynn's *charm* ability. He might fight alongside his superior.

Leaftip, Female Sprite Ftr7 (champion): AC 19; **HP** 44 (8d4+24); **Spd** 10ft, fly 40ft; **Melee** +2 *rapier* (+10, 1d8+12 piercing); **Ranged** shortbow (+8, 40ft/160ft, 1d6+8 piercing); **SA** heart sight, invisibility, multiattack (rapier x2 or shortbow x2); **Str** –3 (+0), **Dex** +5, **Con** +3 (+6), **Int** +1, **Wis** –1, **Cha** +0; **Skills** Perception +2, Stealth +11; **Traits** action surge, fighting style (dueling), improved critical, remarkable athlete, second wind; **AL** NG; **CR** 7; **XP** 2900.
> **Equipment:** studded leather armor, shield, +2 *rapier*, shortbow, 50 arrows.

Cattail, Male Sprite Drd5 (circle of the land, forest): AC 17; **HP** 15 (6d4); **Spd** 10ft, fly 40ft; **Melee** scimitar (+6, 1d6+6 slashing); **Ranged** +1 *shortbow* (+7, 40ft/160ft, 1d6+7 piercing); **SA** heart sight, invisibility, spells (Wis +4, DC 12); **Str** –4, **Dex** +4, **Con** +0, **Int** +2 (+4), **Wis** +2 (+4), **Cha** +0; **Skills** Perception +4, Stealth +8; **Traits** druidic, wild shape; **AL** LG; **CR** 1; **XP** 200.
> **Spells (slots):** 0 (at will)—*druidcraft, mending, poison spray*; 1st (4)—*cure wounds, entangle, fog cloud, thunderwave*; 2nd (3)—*barkskin, beast sense, gust of wind, spider climb*; 3rd (2)—*call lightning, plant growth, sleet storm*.
> **Equipment:** leather armor, shield, scimitar, +1 *shortbow*, 50 arrows.

Possible Outcomes:

• Leaftip is finally convinced to attempt her *heart sight* on Yannick or one of the characters (and to trust its results). Troubled and confused to learn she's been fighting "good guys", she excuses herself and takes Cattail with her to confront Oromirlynn for more information.
• Leaftip and Cattail flee to where Oromirlynn is hiding, more convinced than ever that she is their friend.
• Cattail *wild shapes* into an animal large enough to carry an injured or subdued Leaftip. He takes his leave and heads toward Mirquinoc at top speed, convinced that Oromirlynn can take care of herself, and that he and Leaftip must consult with the queen before taking further action.
• Leaftip retreats back to Oromirlynn while Cattail remains with the party. After using her *heart sight* on Oromirlynn, Leaftip later shows up to apologize to Cattail (not to the party) and to ask him to accompany her back to Mirquinoc, to clarify matters with the queen.
• If your group likes tragedy better than comedy and/or is playing an evil party, or if you've portrayed Leaftip in such a way that her death would be more satisfying than otherwise, this is a fine place for her to die. Cattail would then flee by himself toward Mirquinoc at top speed.
• Yannick interferes to keep the party from killing the sprites, insisting they be taken captive instead. He still hopes to make things right with Queen Twylinvere.

If the Sprites Are Captured

If only one sprite is captured, this is probably fine. Cattail or Leaftip would attempt to free the bound companion, but should this prove impossible, the free sprite would immediately set out for Mirquinoc.

Similarly, if either sprite can escape or be freed, even if the other cannot, only one is needed to get the message to Mirquinoc ahead of the party.

Oromirlynn *might* bother to rescue the sprites, if she thought it would be easy and consequence-free. Should she happen to do so during her later attack on the party, at least one sprite would head for Mirquinoc after that.

If necessary and possible, Yannick might release one or both sprites himself, explaining to the party that he'd made an agreement with them. Once released, they would head for either Mirquinoc or Oromirlynn.

If the party makes it truly impossible (outside divine or GM intervention) for either sprite to escape, assume that other long-range fey scouts from Mirquinoc, or local creatures loyal to Queen Twylinvere, have observed the party and brought news to the Mirquin Shee. Such scouts might even find secret ways to communicate with the prisoners and bring messages directly from Leaftip or Cattail.

It is assumed after this scene that the characters do not encounter Leaftip and Cattail again until Mirquinoc, but if they are held captive the scenes can still play out largely as written. The only really vital thing is that word reach Queen Twylinvere so that she is prepared to meet the party when they arrive.

If one or both of the sprites go to Oromirlynn, they subsequently use their *heart sight* on her for the first time and learn that she is evil (or

otherwise come across clear evidence of her cruel nature). With or without Leaftip's knowledge, Cattail then informs the party that he and Leaftip have decided to head back to Mirquinoc for clarification of their orders. If his relationship with the party is poor, he'll leave a terse note for them to find instead of approaching. Thus, for the sprites, so long as they are free to choose, all roads lead back to Mirquinoc.

Since the walking characters must deal with the vagaries of the foothills' geography, the airborne sprites arrive at Mirquinoc before they do. Oromirlynn can fly as well, and faster than the sprites, but without her guides she must stick to the meandering cart-tracks through the foothills or risk losing her way, so even if she chose to chase Leaftip and Cattail, the sprites beat her to Mirquinoc.

Shadow of the Wild

Oromirlynn is finally puzzling out that this invitation from Twylinvere isn't quite the opportunity she hoped. Between the sprites' strange behavior, their disappearance, and various other hints she's cobbled together, the wildshadow begins to understand that she may be in danger if she continues to Mirquinoc. She finds this realization exceedingly annoying after all the trouble she's put in, and she's sure all of this is somehow partially the party's fault. Looking for some way to make her trip worthwhile, Oromirlynn decides she might as well at least take one or two of the characters as thralls before she heads home.

Oromirlynn now plans the next fight carefully. Instead of rushing into anything, Oromirlynn takes a few days as the characters get to the King's Road to catch herself the finest new thralls she can, and she waits until the characters camp in just the right place. See map of the Campsite.

At this point, the characters are already on the King's Road and within a day of reaching Mirquinoc. There is a well-used campsite off the road, which (for simplicity) empty this evening.

All but the firepit and the center of the clearing are shaded by tree-branches. Some ground amongst the trees is full of roots and other minor

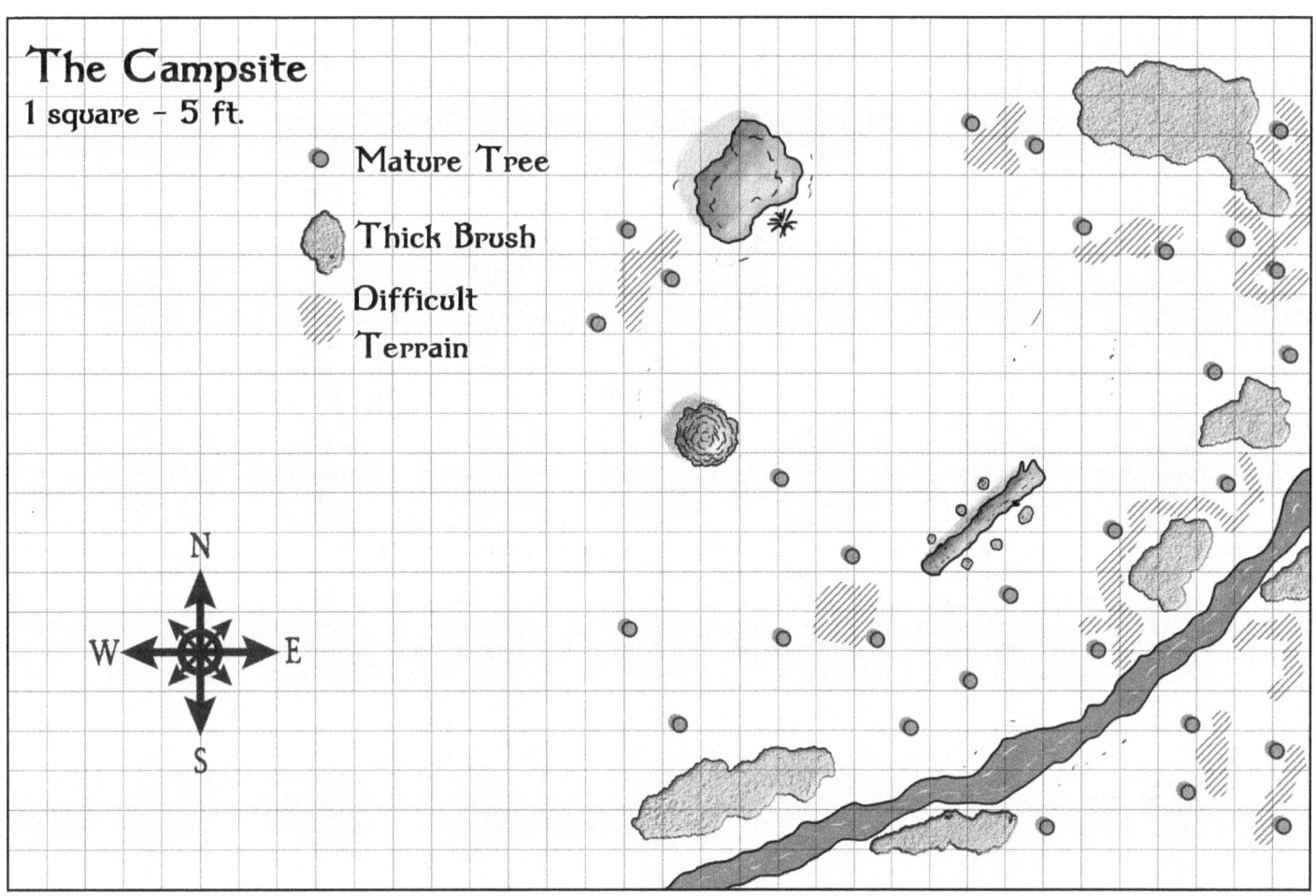

The Campsite
1 square - 5 ft.

• Mature Tree

Thick Brush

Difficult Terrain

N
W — E
S

tripping hazards, and constitutes difficult terrain. (Marked on the map.) The "thick brush" is very difficult to pass through — it requires 5ft of movement to move 1ft — and tends to be 4–7ft high, thick enough to provide cover. This is a well-used campsite, frequented by many travelers, probably over many decades. It looks pleasant and would be relatively defensible against common bandits or large predators.

Oromirlynn waits for night, and launches her attack from hiding if possible, preferring to have her thralls surround the party on all sides. She may use the unicorn as a distraction, approaching the party openly while other thralls sneak into position. This time Oromirlynn herself participates actively in the battle, though her tactics are always to avoid harm to herself at all costs, and she uses her *superior invisibility* to the utmost if she can.

If the werewolf survived the previous attack without being freed, Oromirlynn uses that thrall again here. Otherwise, another werewolf from the same pack (either one of those previously encountered by the characters or from another sub-pack who never encountered the party) has fallen under Oromirlynn's influence in the course of their hunt for their missing companion. She may well have picked up a second werewolf at the same time. (Remember, though, that Oromirlynn can only control 4 thralls at once, so she would not arrive with more than 3 for this fight — or any fight in which she hopes to enthrall someone more powerful than her current "acolytes").

It would be good if the players have enough information by this point to keep themselves prepared to break Oromirlynn's thrall. In part, this helps prevent the fight from becoming *too* much more difficult if Oromirlynn manages to enthrall a character. Consider, too, that if the characters cannot free the unicorn of its thrall, Oromirlynn can use the unicorn's 1/day *teleport* ability to escape if things go poorly for her.

On the other hand, if characters *do* come well-prepared to cure the *wild thrall*, the fight could suddenly turn too easyl thus, the option to include an extra werewolf if needed to bump up the difficulty.

As the unicorn is Oromirlynn's healer in this fight, she makes every effort to keep the unicorn safe and moves near to it if she becomes wounded.

Oromirlynn is *not* life-or-death invested in this fight. She just doesn't want her long trek away from home to turn out to be wasted effort, and she's developed an attachment to enslaving one or two of the characters. If she has reason to believe her life is seriously in danger, she flees. Should the fight come to that point and Oromirlynn's escape feels inappropriate, as long as the unicorn's *teleport* has been removed from the equation, it makes perfect sense for the wildshadow to inadvertently flee right into a group of warrior-sprites arriving from Mirquinoc to greet and/or escort the party.

Werewolf (1 or 2): AC 12; HP 58 (9d8+18); Spd 30ft, as wolf 40ft; **Melee** bite (+4, 1d8+2 piercing plus lycanthropy, DC 12 Con), claws (+4, 2d4+2 slashing); **SA** multiattack (bite, claws), shapechanger; **Immune** non-silver normal weapons; **Str** +2, **Dex** +1, **Con** +2, **Int** +0, **Wis** +0, **Cha** +0; **Skills** Perception +4, Stealth +3; **Senses** keen hearing and smell; **AL** CE; **CR** 3; **XP** 700.

Unicorn: AC 12; HP 67 (9d10+18); **Spd** 50ft; **Melee** hooves (+7, 2d6+4 bludgeoning), horn (+7, 1d8+4 piercing); **SA** healing touch (3/day), innate spells (Cha+6, DC 14), multiattack (hooves, horn), teleport (1/day); **LA** heal self (costs 3 actions), hooves, shimmering shield (costs 2 actions); **Immune** charm, paralysis, poison; **Str** +4, **Dex** +2, **Con** +2, **Int** +0, **Wis** +3, **Cha** +3; **Senses** darkvision 60ft; **Traits** charge, magic resistance, magic weapons; **AL** LG; **CR** 5; **XP** 1800.

> **Innate Spells:** at will—*detect evil and good, druidcraft, pass without trace;* 1/day—*calm emotions, dispel evil and good, entangle.*

Oromirlynn, Female Wildshadow: AC 15; HP 67 (15d6+15); **Spd** 40ft, fly 50ft; **Melee** rapier (+9, 1d8+9 piercing plus *wild thrall*), dagger (+9, 1d4+9 piercing plus *wild thrall*); **Ranged** dart (+9, x2, 20ft/60ft, 1d4+9 piercing plus *wild thrall*); **SA** charm, innate spells (Cha +7, DC 15), multiattack (rapier and dagger in melee, or dart x2 at range), superior invisibility; **Str** +1, **Dex** +5 (+8), **Con** +1, **Int** +1, **Wis** +3 (+6), **Cha** +4; **Skills** Deception +5, Perception +6, Stealth+8, Survival +6; **Senses** darkvision 120ft; **Traits** magic resistance, wild enchantment, wild thrall; **AL** NE; **CR** 5; **XP** 1800. **(Monster Appendix)**

> **Innate Spells:** at will—*dancing lights, mage hand, minor illusion, prestidigitation, vicious mockery;* 3/day—*disguise self, entangle, fog cloud, hypnotic pattern, major image, phantasmal force, silent image, suggestion;* 1/day—*confusion.*
>
> **Equipment:** rapier, dagger, 15 darts (all of Oromirlynn's weapons are subject to her *wild enchantment*).

This may be a difficult encounter, so if the party is struggling, remember Yannick's spells and candles, as well as the warrior-sprites from Mirquinoc mentioned above. If worst comes to worst, the latter can offer a rescue, possibly even with a sheepish Leaftip and/or Cattail among them.

The Faerie Queen

If you do not choose to have the escort of sprites show up at the end of the battle with Oromirlynn, a liveried honor guard of sprite warriors instead meet up with Yannick and his guards on the King's Road a mile to the east of Mirquinoc. These warriors, led by Captain Loganberry — an unreadable sprite of military bearing and an aura of casual competence — take custody of Oromirlynn if she was taken captive (as well as Leaftip and Cattail if they also are held captive), and invite Yannick and his companions to a small cluster of fantastical pavilions in the center of a massive circle of the oldest living oaks the characters have ever seen. Around the pavilion, fae and animals of all manner dance, play, sing, and cavort happily, while serious, uniformed sprites patrol the area.

The party is taken to one of the pavilions and invited to refresh themselves from their journey. Inside, the pavilion looks more like the inside of a *magnificent mansion*, as the spell. Characters may eat, bathe, change clothes, whatever they wish.

After about two hours, attendants come to summon the party into the queen's presence. While it would make sense for them to be required to leave their weapons behind, such a detail isn't very relevant to the adventure and should be insisted upon only at GM's discretion.

On a raised, outdoor dais, bedecked like an open gazebo with living vines in bloom, stands the faerie queen along with a few guards and courtiers. You are directed to bow before her and each of you is presented with a crown of fresh plants. The queen bids you to rise.

Queen Twylinvere is beautiful and elegant, graceful and surprisingly tall for a fey — though precisely what *sort* of fey she may be, you cannot quite determine. She is courteous and soft-spoken, with an ancient, almost alien wildness to her deep green eyes. Every subtle move she makes is hypnotic and lovely. Her voice sounds like a gentle, spring breeze. She wears implausibly fine clothing in gauzy pastels, and her hair shimmers as if each strand were a shining silken thread. Each of you sees her hair color differently, gold, copper, pearl white, jet black, or even more exotic.

She smiles at you and thanks you for bringing Yannick safely to her court.

Yannick, trembling and overwhelmed, says, "I-I've brought you a gift, your majesty. Will you accept it?"

Her smile widens in a manner both beautiful and wild. "Of course," she replies.

Her attendants take the box that Yannick's mule has carried all this way. They check the contents for safety and nod before kneeling to present the box to the queen.

She gasps in delight and lifts out a hand-carved wooden candle-holder in the shape of a tree, with intricately interwoven branches to hold the candles. It's impressive and delicate work, and it could not have survived such a journey without a wizard to cast mending after every bump and jostle.

"It's perfect," the queen says, "and it brings me to the purpose of this audience."

Queen Twylinvere explains her original intentions: to buy candles from Yannick and to hire him to make more for her, as well as for her emissaries to bring the evil Oromirlynn to justice.

Depending on how the characters have handled the various encounters on this mission, the queen proceeds in several possible ways.

If Oromirlynn was defeated:

If the wildshadow was slain or taken captive, each member of the party is rewarded with a magical item appropriate to that character (from table F). The fey are all more cheerful about this if Oromirlynn is alive and taken captive, but not angry or ungrateful if she was killed. Remember that, unless the GM wishes otherwise, Queen Twylinvere remains mysterious and secretive about her reasons for wishing Oromirlynn defeated.

Partial success: If Oromirlynn was injured but escaped, the party is courteously thanked for their aid in combating an enemy of the queen and each character is presented with a minor art object.

If no sylvan creatures were slain:

If the party spared the lives of all non-evil fey as well as the centaur and unicorn, they are invited to feast with the fey of the Mirquin Shee for as long as they like and declared friends of the Shee, each given a small, silver, flower-shaped pin to symbolize this.

In addition, Leaftip and Cattail step forward. Cattail oozes grateful and sincere apology even before speaking. He seems to feel much better about the world than at any previous point the characters have met him. He's almost *relaxed* as he thanks the party for succeeding where he failed. He appears interested in befriending the characters.

Leaftip is depressed, shockingly sober, and entirely humble. Her eyes are red and her voice thick as she apologizes and thanks the party. She declares publicly that she has arranged with the queen to do penance for her gross mis-execution of her duty. At GM's discretion she might take vows in the clergy of an appropriate deity, swear herself to Yannick's service as his personal bodyguard and servant for so long as he serves Queen Twylinvere, or even swear herself into the service of the party, should such an outcome be appropriate for this campaign. (If you have a fey-focused warlock in the party, or another caster interested in acquiring an exotic familiar, an oath to serve in that capacity might also be appropriate.)

Seeing as everything turned out basically all right, however, the ancient-eyed queen seems more amused than angry with Leaftip.

Partial success: If sylvan creatures were only slain by accident, and the party behaved in a mostly-compassionate-ish manner, they are invited to feast for the day, if not quite so emphatically. Leaftip and Cattail still apologize, though Cattail seems sad and Leaftip sick with rage and despair. She wears no weapons and plain, rough clothing. She says little and disappears soon afterward. If Cattail is questioned, he explains that Leaftip has chosen self-exile as her punishment for her failure and can never return to the Mirquin Shee after today. She has also vowed to give up violence forever. Cattail implies that he too has faced disciplinary action, though he doesn't want to talk about it and seems to prefer to put all this behind him.

Note: Depending on the details, feel free to use a sliding scale of responses between total and partial success.

If Yannick is pleased

If the party did a good job of keeping Yannick safe and were reasonably nice to him in the process, Yannick lauds the characters' skill and bravery to the queen. To make up for Yannick's heroic effort and expense in his quest to please her, Queen Twylinvere offers to cover all the costs of his journey, rewarding the party with more treasure than they were originally promised (perhaps even a hoard's worth, if they have impressed her; roll for money and gems, but not magic items, on the CR 5–10 treasure hoard chart), *and* vowing to send her own people home with Yannick whenever he wishes to return, at her own expense, so that the characters receive (at least) the full monetary reward for a round-trip journey even though they've only guarded Yannick the one way.

Partial success: If Yannick feels that the party basically upheld the contract, but that he has good reason to dislike or distrust most of the characters, he won't speak of them to the queen, but privately (using funds newly acquired from the queen) pays the characters just over the agreed amount for a one-way journey and releases them courteously from his service, explaining that he no longer needs an escort home, since the fey will provide one.

Note: It is assumed that Yannick survives to the end, given that most of the violent threats specifically target the characters rather than the candlemaker. However, it should be expected that the welcome of the faerie queen will be considerably less warm should the candle-artist she wished to hire have perished.

Total failure

If none of the above conditions are met, even partially, the fey take the party into custody, transporting them to a dungeon in the feywild, where they are imprisoned across the hall from Leaftip, for what could lead to many more grand, fey adventures.

The Mountain That Moved

For 4–6 characters of 7th level, *The Mountain That Moved* is a location-based adventure, involving strange occurrences in the northeastern reaches of the Cretian Mountains, a region with a sinister reputation for inbred communities, cannibals and mysterious disappearances. The rumors and stories have a strong base in reality, but the town of Yandek and the Mountain that Moved go well beyond even the wildest of those tavern-yarns.

The adventure should appeal to characters who enjoy investigation and discovery, but there's plenty of combat opportunities as well. The adventure allows for a great deal of flexibility in the structure of the encounters and potential outcomes.

Adventure Background

Hundreds of years ago, the glabrezu demon Metanual marauded through the foothills and outer peaks of the eastern Cretian Mountains (see maps in *The Lost Lands: Borderland Provinces*). His power drew worshippers from among the region's people, who contributed to Metanual's reign of terror. Lesser demons rampaged. Evil reigned. People died. This continued for several years. The glabrezu claimed the title "Demon Lord-Master Metanual" and began to boast about his future role in the Abyss. He wanted power and respect and sought the opportunity to improve his status among demons by causing havoc among humans.

He attracted ever great numbers of lesser demons who wanted to share in the destruction and chaos. He also attracted a few hundred human followers with evil alignments and intentions. He freely promised them many things: power, wealth, prestige. The gullible mortals took him at his word, foolishly believing that any demon might honor a bargain. Metanual enjoyed their worship, but would have gleefully killed these followers if they annoyed him or he grew bored. Fate intervened before either could occur.

Coming to the aid of the settlements in the area was a dwarven wizard known only as Obsidian. Using her significant arcane talents, she managed to defeat the demon. Calling upon a pact she had once made with an enormous creature of elemental might whose name roughly translated as GrindStone, she created a prison for Metanual, binding the glabrezu within the mountain-sized elemental. Deep inside the stone, she inscribed a series of protective runes, to bolster GrindStone's own not inconsiderable power and keep the demon in check.

The demon's human minions settled near their imprisoned lord, committing themselves to Metanual's return. They called their city Yandek, after their leader who had originally dedicated the cult to the demon lord. At first, they had a sharp clarity of purpose, and start digging to free the demon.

Centuries passed and the elemental slumbered, blending into the terrain of the Cretian Mountains. Trees grew upon the mighty creature, animals tromped paths into the scrub, and travelers in turn transformed those paths into trade roads.

Today

As generations passed, the demon cult's purpose blurred and faded. Today, the people of Yandek still dig in the mines for the "greater glory of our Lord-Master," but more out of tradition and habit than clear intent. The deeper they dig, the more the stone they extract exhibits strange characteristics (see the "GrindStone Granite" sidebar).

As it nears the demon's cavern, the mining has finally begun to disturb GrindStone. For several months, faint tremors have occasionally rattled the mountain and its surrounds, and the frequency and severity of those tremors continues to grow.

What's drawn the greatest attention from people living at the fringes, or passing through the area, is the abrupt disappearance of the Vulture Pass, which connects some mountain villages to the raft camps at the sources of the Gaelon River. Like the tremors and earthquakes, this is a result of GrindStone stirring.

GrindStone's movements have also eroded the runes imprisoning Metanual. While still lacking the power to free himself, Metanual has succeeded in attracting other demons back to the region.

Metanual is not one of the great lords of the Abyss. Compared to a Marilith or a Balor, he's insignificant. As during the days of yore when he terrorized the region, however, he has always chosen to position himself as the "big fish in a small pond," avoiding greater demons or areas that might interest them. He focuses instead on those weaker than he, serving as something of a "king of the rabble." Now, even imprisoned, he draws lesser demons to his aid through a mix of intimidation, inspiration, and reputation. These demons have been searching for their demon lord — and harassing travelers as they do so, adding another level of superstitious dread to people's view of the ever-growing tremors.

Location

This adventure centers on Vulture Pass, a mountain trail in the Cretian Peaks high in the foothills near the source of the Gaelon River, approximately 60 miles southwest of Deadfellows (see *The Lost Lands: Borderland Provinces*, Chapter 5: *Gaelon River Valley*, Deadfellows). It is a "false" pass, in that it does not cross from one side of the Cretians to another, but it does connect a few mountain villages, including the village of Yandek, to the "raft camps" near the river's main sources where they run down into the highest part of the foothills. These "raft camps" are little more than hamlets situated at good landings on the source-rivers, dedicated to making rafts that can survive down the rapid waters toward Deadfellows. Trappers and prospectors come to these camps to obtain a raft in exchange for some of their pelts, gems, or other bounty, and disappear aboard the rafts into the whitewater rapids, hoping to make it to Deadfellows intact with their loot. Experienced hunters and trappers know that even in a well-made raft, many of their fellows do not survive the journey downriver: some are lost every year. Those who try to make their own rafts with branches and rope? It's a fool's gamble. Few of these penny-pinchers ever arrive. The price of a professionally-built river raft is worth every copper piece.

In any case, the Vulture Pass is the easiest way between the mountain villages, such as Yandek, and the raft camps. There are a few other routes, but they are considerably more perilous.

Whisper and Rumor

News of the sudden disappearance of a mountain pass generates rumors, speculation, and discussion. Even if the characters are miles away, likely in Deadfellows, some version of the story will reach them. For greatest effect, deliberately seed reports of the event in the adventure you run before *The Mountain that Moved*.

The DCs given here represent deliberate investigation into the Cretian Mountains, assuming the characters wish to investigate further once they hear of the vanishing pass.

DC 10

The Cretian Mountains have a sinister reputation for small, hostile communities, dangerous roads, and missing travelers. (True)

The hamlet of Yandek was founded by a druid as a refuge for naturalists. (False)

The mines are infested with flesh-eating ghouls that prey on travelers. (False)

Seismic activity has disrupted the normal trade routes. (True)

An ancient curse causes people living in the mountains to be deformed. (False, at least in this part of the mountains)

The newest trend among the well-to-do is to build using exotic stone that generates its own comforting warmth. This stone is mined in only one spot in the Cretian Mountains. (True)

DC 15

Some of the villages in the Cretian Mountains have problems with inbreeding which results in deformities. (True)

A remote monastery in the Cretian Mountains trains professional assassins. (False)

Every new baby born in the village of Yandek is sacrificed on its first birthday. (False)

Previously reliable maps of the mountain pass through the Cretians are now unreliable. (True)

Some of the settlements in the mountains resort to cannibalism as a means of survival during hard times. (True)

DC 20

Travelers in the Cretian Mountains disappear into the realms of the fey by walking between a pair of standing stones. (False, these standing stones are almost a hundred miles from Vulture Pass)

The disappearances in the region center around the hamlet of Yandek. (True)

A halfling named Tovord who lives in the village of Yandek gets drunk every night and howls at the moon. (False)

A demon-worshipping cult thrives in the mountains. (True)

Adventure Hooks

As the Game Master, you know what best motivates your group. Some players favor doing good in the world: righting wrongs and protecting the weak. Others live to explore, while still others prefer treasure and personal gain. If the rumors of the region and its missing mountain pass aren't sufficient to draw them in, feel free to use multiple motivations from the list below, or create others that you know appeal to your players.

Mile By Mile

A cartographer in Deadfellows, who goes by the name of Mimsy (male human **scout**), wants to learn whether the rumors are true — that the established pass has disappeared — and to create a new map of the area if it they are. He offers the characters a choice of reward: 500gp or a map he was given that the previous owner swore led to buried treasure on a small island.

Lost Goods

A small band of mountain traders that had been traveling via the old roads lost their way, unable to find the established mountain pass, and was attacked by horrific, demonic creatures (see the "Balban and Manes" variable encounter). The guard captain was wise enough to order everyone to flee as the attack began, saving the entire band (other than herself). The merchant, Nial (male human **noble**) wants his goods recovered.

Find the Halfling!

A band of traveling halfling have put out a bounty, hoping to learn the fate of a relative who may have vanished in the area. Locating Tovord

THE LOST LANDS: ADVENTURES IN THE BORDERLAND PROVINCES

GrindStone Granite

The stone mined from the elemental near Metanual's prison has some unusual properties:
- It always feels warm to the touch.
- It has a magnet-like attraction to other GrindStone granite, but not iron.
- It glows faintly in the presence of demons. (Note that the bulk of the people building with it, or purchasing it as raw materials, are unaware of this last property, and might be rather disturbed by the implications if they knew.)

Older buildings in Yandek are made of regular granite. Some newer construction has the above properties, but most of recently-mined GrindStone granite has been sold.

Recently, this stone has become popular among wealthy estate owners who enjoy the warmth. In large flooring slabs or wall facades, it's more trendy and expensive than marble.

As you're building up to this adventure, consider having your PCs run across a new building in Deadfellows, made of this stuff. If you've introduced them to its properties, and made it clear the fad is spreading, that adds tension and motivation once they later discover that it comes from an area of sinister repute.

Traechi (male halfling **commoner**) and providing proof of his location and that he yet lives offers a reward of 2500gp. Proof that he's dead, and of what happened to him, pays 250gp.

Evil in the Rock

Savra Benarras (female half-elf **priest**) has come to believe the GrindStone Granite, that has become such a popular building material for the region's wealthy, has the taint of evil upon it. She requests the characters investigate, and assists them by providing 5 vials of holy water, 3 *potions of healing*, and scrolls with up to 5 cleric spells totaling up to 10 levels (with no single spell of higher than 4th level).

The Pen is Mightier, but Just In Case . . .

Already a famous author sensationalized and adventuresome autobiographical tales, Crawleigh (male gnome **noble**) wants to travel the Cretian Mountains for a month, due to their sinister history of cults, cannibals, and strange creatures. He offers the characters 100gp each plus expenses to accompany him, as well as the fame and prestige of being featured as his entourage in his next book.

Sub-Contracting

Rhyse (male human **noble**), currently the architect and builder of the Del'Ancy family's winter chalet, wants a large supply of GrindStone granite. He wants to buy directly from the mines to ensure the quality and quantity he needs for the project, and his extensive research indicates that someone named M'rar in the Village of Yandek is the person to contact. He wants the player characters to be his proxies to go negotiate a contract.

The Mountain

While there are many maps of the area available for the player characters to purchase, Grindstone's shifting makes all existing maps quite inaccurate. The mountain has quite literally moved.

GrindStone stirred because of the mining, essentially flinching from an irritation, unaware of the destruction and consternation it has caused. It just doesn't think about things on a human scale. It intended no malice or harm; the notion that creatures might have been hurt by its movement simply isn't part of its way of thinking.

The size of the creature also means it operates on a different scale of existence. Trees grow, sinking roots into it. Animals and humans walk on

Yandek Mutations

The tinker Tovord is the only person dwelling in Yandek who wasn't born there. All of the native inhabitants have one or more mutation due to their inbreeding and their many generations of life near the demon Metanual. Use the standard statistics for a resident of Yandek, but customize the look of the person with the following table.

1d20	Mutation
1	Hands with fingers that have grown together, the most excessive of these like lobster-claws
2	Feet that resemble ostrich feet
3	Reddish skin
4	Scaly skin
5	Open sores and lesions
6	Patches of chitin-like skin
7	Multiple moles with tufts of hair growing out of them
8	Excessively large body size
9	Excessively small body size
10	Extra nostril
11	Prominent lower jaw
12	Sloping forehead
13	Eyes that turn and move independently of each other
14	A small extra arm (or pair of arms) protruding from the person's chest
15	Spikey growths on the shoulders (40%), wrists (40%), or both (20%)
16	Small tiefling-like horns where at the front hairline
17	Oversized ears that are triangular in shape
18	Fang-like teeth jutting up from the lower jaw
19	Red eyes
20	Roll twice

it and live on it without notice. It is only the persistent, extensive mining, ever deeper into its "flesh," that has caused it to stir.

Time has a very different meaning to a creature like GrindStone. It doesn't have immediate needs like humanoids do. The time scale on which it thinks is that of eons, not hours. It doesn't get tired or weary, which is why Obsidian enlisted it as the guardian for Metanual in the first place. (Though how she ever managed to attract the attention of something like GrindStone, let alone bargain with it, remains a mystery unanswered even in the many tales of her exploits.)

As you travel deeper into the area, the land shows obvious signs of recent earthquakes and upheavals. Trees have toppled, trunks on the ground, roots exposed to the air. Off in the distance, an entire section of cliff face is sheared off; the unweathered wound in the rock looks raw and fresh, the rockfall a scattered pile at the base of the cliff. The banks and underbrush show where a small stream recently flowed, but the creekbed lies dry, and carrion birds pick at the dead fish that suffocated in the air.

During their travels, the characters witness many instances of destruction caused by the shifting land — including substantial carnage among the fauna, and possibly even a few (formerly thriving) mountainside communities. Be as discrete or macabre in describing these as suits your group's play style. Either way, though, make it clear that nature, and people, are suffering.

The party should encounter a couple of mild earthquakes, mere tremors, as they get closer to Yandek. The intention of these encounters is to raise awareness among the characters of the shaking of the mountain and also to presage the "Earthquake" variable encounter.

The songs of birds and insects abruptly cease, as though the sound were severed by a razored knife. The ground beneath you starts to shake — a quick tremor, the earth shivering for just a moment before it settles. The birds take a longer moment and then resume their songs.

Mounted characters need to make a DC 10 Wis (Animal Handling) check to keep control of their mounts.

Variable Encounters

This area of the Cretian Mountains is not a common destination, nor is it heavily-traveled, but there have always been a steady trickle of travelers through the area — trappers, prospectors, and some traders hoping to buy furs and gems at rock-bottom prices near the source. Most used the recently-disappeared pass to the villages, but some sought other options, hoping for a short cut. Due to the demons and cannibals in the area, many of these never reached their destination — and now that the pass is gone, the numbers of passersby on these less traveled, less safe, trails is only growing. And so, too, are the number of predators hoping to prey on them.

These encounters are not "random" in the traditional sense, in that it is entirely up to you as GM when and where they occur. (Or even *if* they occur, though we recommend you include them.) Feel free to create your own additional encounters to beef these up, and for additional excitement and challenge, consider combining more than one of these, running them simultaneously as a single event, such as a vrock attack during an earthquake.

Balban and Manes Packs

Metanual's long and lingering presence draws groups of demons to the region with a compulsion almost as strong as a genuine summons. The balban, with its ability to smash through inanimate objects, can greatly help to free the trapped Metanual.

While they do indeed want to find the demon lord, these are creatures of chaos, easily distracted by any opportunity for wanton destruction, mayhem and death — much to the chagrin of anyone passing through the area. Due to their long residency near Metanual, the Yandek natives are perceived as fellow demons, so the balban and manes don't attack them. Every resident of the hamlet and the surrounding area, except for Tovord (see below), is ignored by these Abyssal horrors.

A twelve-foot tall humanoid-shaped creature bellows and beats its broad, muscular chest. It has a squat, pot-bellied torso, massive arms, and columnar legs. Its slate gray skin hangs loose and leathery, paler on its face and belly, darker on its back and legs. Curving back from its head are four reddish black horns that spiral upward like an antelope's. The brute harries a pack of small, rubbery-skinned creatures whose hides are pocked with weeping sores. These foul beings charge forward, intent on attack.

Demon, Balban (2): AC 15; HP 143 (15d10 + 60); Spd 40ft; **Melee** slam (+6, x2, 10ft, 2d6+5 bludgeoning), gore (+6, 10 ft., 1d10+5 piercing); **SA** charge (15ft move then gore, plus 2d10 piercing, DC 16 Str or pushed 10ft and knocked prone), multiattack (slam x2); **Immune** lightning; **Resist** acid, cold, fire; **Vulnerable** radiant; Str +5, Dex +2, Con +6, Int −2 (+1), Wis +2 (+5), Cha +0; **Senses** blindsight 30ft, darkvision 120ft; **Skills** Athletics +10, Survival +5; **Traits** double damage against objects, magic resistance; **AL** CE; **CR** 5; **XP** 1800. (**Monster Appendix**)

Demon, Manes (8): AC 9; HP 9 (2d6+2); Spd 20ft; **Melee** claws (+2, 10ft, 2d4 slashing); **Immune** poison; **Resist** cold, fire, lightning; Str +0, Dex −1, Con +1, Int −4, Wis −1, Cha −3; **Senses** darkvision 60ft, tremorsense 60ft; **AL** CE; **CR** 1/8; **XP** 25.

Note: As the demons are killed, their bodies disappear and return to the Abyss.

Vrock-Fall

Like the balban and manes packs, the vrocks feel drawn to the area, and are delighted to pick off prey already off-balance or injured by the tremors. (And of course, as the vrocks spend much of their time flying, they needn't make checks if you choose to combine this with the Earthquake encounter.)

Large, feathered wings beat the air with a steady rhythm then a snap. A piercing shriek follows. Two dusky-hued, 8-foot tall vulture-like creatures fly into view. Their toothy beaks, sharp clawlike hands, and glowing red eyes distinguish them as unnatural, unearthly.

Demon, Vrock (2): AC 15; HP 104 (11d10+44); Spd 40ft, fly 60ft; **Melee** beak (+6, 2d6+3 piercing), talons (+6, 2d10+3 slashing); **SA** multiattack (beak, talons), spores (recharge 6, 15ft radius, poisoned, DC 14 Con repeat, then take 1d10 poison each turn), stunning screech (1/day, 20ft, stunned until end of vrock's next turn, DC 14 Con); Str +3, Dex +2 (+5), Con +4, Int −1, Wis +1 (+4), Cha −1 (+2); **Immune** poison; **Resist** cold, fire, lightning, normal weapons; **Senses** darkvision 120ft; **Traits** magic resistance; **AL** CE; **CR** 6; **XP** 2300.

Note: As the demons are killed, their bodies disappear and return to the Abyss.

Earthquake

The ground swells and undulates, rising under your feet like an angry sea, threatening to hurl you aside. You've felt tremors before, but this surge and shake is tremendously fierce in comparison.

The tremors and earthquakes operate like complex traps, and require a variety of ability checks.

• A successful DC 20 Wis (Survival) check offers just enough advanced warning that the characters have a +2 bonus on the following checks

• A successful DC 15 Str (Athletics) or Dex (Acrobatics) check is necessary to remain standing. Those who fail fall prone and take 1d6 bludgeoning damage as loose rocks and debris batter them.

• Any mounted character must make a DC 15 Wis (Animal Handling) check to keep control of his or her mount. A successful check also means that the animal does not need to make a Str or Dex check (as above) to remain standing. A failed Wis check requires the mount to make the previous check. If the animal fails, it falls and takes 1d4 bludgeoning damage. The rider takes 2d6 bludgeoning damage and is pinned prone beneath the mount. A successful DC 15 Dex saving throw halves that damage and allows the rider to roll out from beneath the falling mount.

• If the characters are inside one of the hamlet buildings or the mine when the earthquake occurs, the ceiling collapses. Any creature in the area must succeed on a DC 15 Dex saving throw, taking 2d10 bludgeoning damage on a failed save. Those already prone from failing the prior Strength or Dexterity check may become trapped beneath the debris. A successful DC 15 Str (Athletics) check allows a creature to free itself from the debris; a creature already free, working to free another, requires only a DC 12 check.

Gone Huntin'

This band is composed of members of the Blood family (see "Blood Boys' Ranch"), hunting meat for the village. Animal prey has been scarce recently, as the seismic activity has driven much of the fauna to flee. The regular paths used by humanoid travelers — the Blood family's other white meat — have also disappeared, so the Bloods have been out longer than usual on their hunt and are feeling bored, more likely to take chances and attack a larger group.

The baying of hounds rends the air. Ferocious and wild, they sound eager, having caught a scent and hotly in pursuit of prey. Large and brutal-looking, these fighting mastiffs — sporting sharp teeth and angry red eyes — approach from several directions.

A sharp whistle stops the hounds' advance. The baying changes mid-tone into an almost-pitiable whine.

"Down! Down! Heel! You mangy curs! Lookee wha' we got here, boys! Strangers. Strangers passin' through *our* huntin' territory."

A large man in worn buckskin clothes casually holds a spear. His body is overly large and muscular. One shoulder sits higher than the other. Moles and warts speckle his flesh.

Flanking him on either side, but a few steps behind are two other large men, who show a family resemblance to the first.

"That's right, pa! We need to teach them a lesson, don't we, Drouck?"

"I call dibs on the purty one. It's my turn, ain't it pa? Drumm can't have first pick ag'in! I like that mouth; bet it screams real nice."

Drumm, Drouck, and Duncle love hunting. They encourage their dogs to be exceptionally vicious. As they fight, they banter back and forth, boasting when they score a solid hit, egging each other on. They take particular delight in humanoids as prey, making their target suffer for as long as possible, even taking victims back to the Ranch for prolonged torture. Because of this, they avoid damaging someone who has dropped to 0 hit points and might even attempt to stabilize an unconscious creature if at no risk to themselves. Their family motto is "Fear adds flavor." After killing a creature, they'll butcher it and distribute the meat to the rest of the community, as their family's contribution to the mining town.

"Pa" Duncle: AC 16; HP 127 (15d8+60); **Spd** 30ft; **Melee** spear (+7, 2d8+5 piercing); **Range** spear (+8, 20ft/60ft, 2d6+5 piercing) or weighted net (+5, 10ft/20ft, 2d4+5 bludgeoning plus restraint, escape DC 15); **Resist** poison; **Str** +5, **Dex** +2, **Con** +4, **Int** −2, **Wis** +1, **Cha** −1; **Skills** Stealth +5, Survival +4; **Senses** darkvision 30ft, tremorsense 10ft; **AL** CE; **CR** 5; **XP** 1800.

Drumm and Drouck, The Blood Boys: AC 12; **HP** 125 (12d10+48); **Spd** 30ft; **Melee** hunting knife (+5, 2d8+4 slashing); **Range** weighted net (+5, 10ft/20ft, 2d4+4 bludgeoning plus restraint, escape DC 14); **Resist** poison; **Str** +4, **Dex** +0, **Con** +4, **Int** −2, **Wis** +0, **Cha** −2; **Skills** Medicine +3; Stealth +2, Survival +3; **Senses** darkvision 30ft, tremorsense 10ft; **AL** CE; **CR** 4; **XP** 1100.

Demon-Tainted Hunting Dog (4): AC 12; HP 22 (4d8+4); **Spd** 40ft; **Melee** bite (+4, 1d8+2 piercing); **Immune** poison; **Str** +2, **Dex** +1, **Con** +1, **Int** −4, **Wis** +0, **Cha** −3; **Skills** Perception +2; Stealth +3, Survival +3; **Senses** darkvision 60ft, keen sight and smell; **Traits** pack tactics; **AL** CE; **CR** 1/2; **XP** 100.

The Hamlet of Yandek

Many generations of living near Metanual and GrindStone, along with their insular and inbred ways, have warped and changed people here into an interlinked bloodline no longer entirely human. (See "Yandek Mutations.") As generations passed and the taint grew, people's longevity increased and the number of live births declined. What new children *were* born were progressively more warped and demon-touched. Very rarely, a child might be born with less taint, looking almost or entirely human, such as the perfect Sophi (see below). These "freaks" were often killed by their disgusted parents, but by the time Sophi was born, the birth rate had declined so severely, her family reluctantly chose to accept her. Currently, there are no children at all in the village; even the youngest inhabitant is fully grown.

Unlike in most small villages, all of the buildings in Yandek are made of stone. Older buildings are of ordinary granite from the older mines. Newer buildings — and in particular the newest, the Still — incorporate ever more GrindStone granite from the current, active mine.

Although the countryside thus far has been mostly mountain passes of breathtaking beauty and wilderness only lightly-touched by people, the exact opposite is true of this squalid little hamlet. Old-growth trees give way to barren soil, having been clear-cut for wood. The very air has a sharp tang to it, like rust. The road continues to climb.

During the day, every household works the mines. The only regular activity in the town itself is at Tovord's, the Chapel, and the Still.

Except for Tovord, every inhabitant starts with an Unfriendly Attitude toward any stranger and utterly refuses to help the player characters, sell them anything, or answer any questions unless the characters can improve the person's attitude. The typical resident is hostile and quite chaotic evil; however, they've enough cunning and sense of self-preservation to not attack a group of stalwart adventurers and to hide the worst of their vile behaviors from outsiders.

Unless otherwise noted, use the following statistics for the hamlet inhabitants. They actively investigate any noises and disturbances, coming to one another's aid.

Yandek Resident: AC 14; HP 60 (7d8+28); **Spd** 30ft; **Melee** club (+5, 1d10+5 bludgeoning); **Ranged** improvised weapon (+5, 2d4+2 bludgeoning) or spear (+5, 1d6+3 piercing); **Resist** poison; **Str** +3, **Dex** +0, **Con** +4, **Int** −1, **Wis** +0, **Cha** −2; **Senses** darkvision 60ft, tremorsense 10ft; **AL** CE; **CR** 2; **XP** 450.

Yandek Human Template

Foul, demon-tainted, and inbred, those born in Yandek are no longer quite normal humans. They tend to prefer physical classes such as fighter. Those few inclined toward spellcasting are typically clerics devoted to demons. Their characteristics include mutations (see "Yandek Mutations") and the following racial traits:

Physical Prowess, Mental Impairment: The inhabitant of Yandek gains advantage on all Str-based checks, but suffers tactical disadvantage on all Int-based *or* Cha-based checks (but not both). These apply *only* to checks, not to saving throws or attack rolls.

Senses: The inhabitant of Yandek gains darkvision 60ft and tremorsense 10ft.

Resistances: The inhabitant gains resistance to poison.

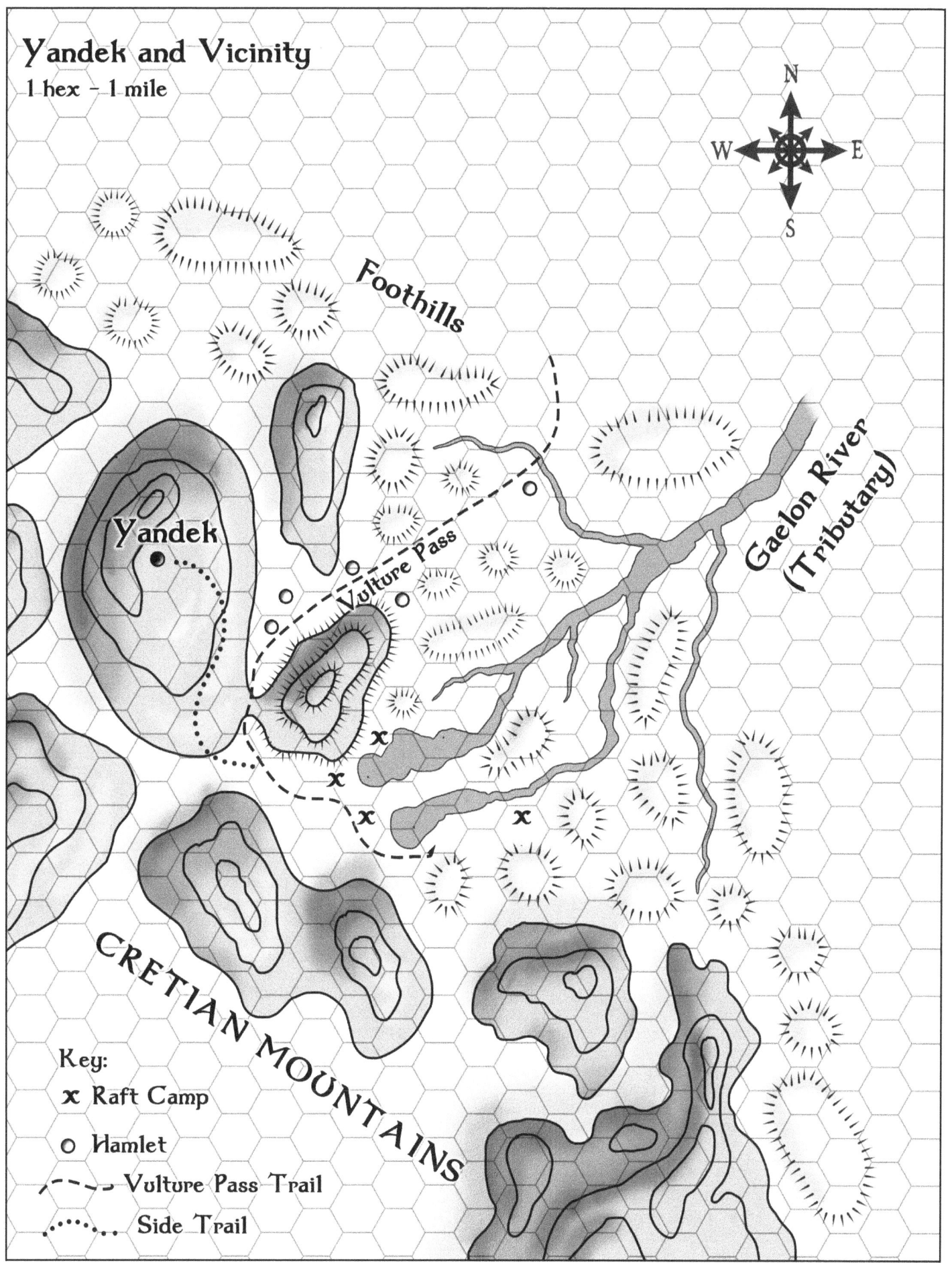

Yandek and Vicinity

1 hex – 1 mile

Foothills

Yandek

Vulture Pass

Gaelon River
(Tributary)

CRETIAN MOUNTAINS

Key:

x Raft Camp

○ Hamlet

- - - Vulture Pass Trail

••••••• Side Trail

A carved stone sign on the road announces that you have reached the "Village of Yandek." The mountain looms overhead as the road widens out among a handful of buildings clustered around a well. To the right is a general supply store, labeled "Tovord the Tinker: Store and Services" by a simple wooden sign. Straight ahead, just past the well, is an imposing building with ivy clinging to the stonework. It's simple in design, but occupies a clear position of importance.

Several other stone buildings, presumably homes, cluster in the general vicinity. In fact, all the buildings here, even the meanest, appear to be made of stone rather than wood.

Piles of rubble collect around entrances into the mountain. These locations, obviously mines, boast well-worn road leading to them.

Just a little ways from the other buildings in the distance is what appears to be a still. Indeed, a faint breeze reinforces that initial assumption, carrying the aroma of a strong distillation. Moonshine? Quite possibly, though at *that* potency, it could almost as easily be paint thinner or tanning solutions.

The tap of a hammer on metal returns your attention to the first building, the tinker shop. You can see someone sitting out on the porch.

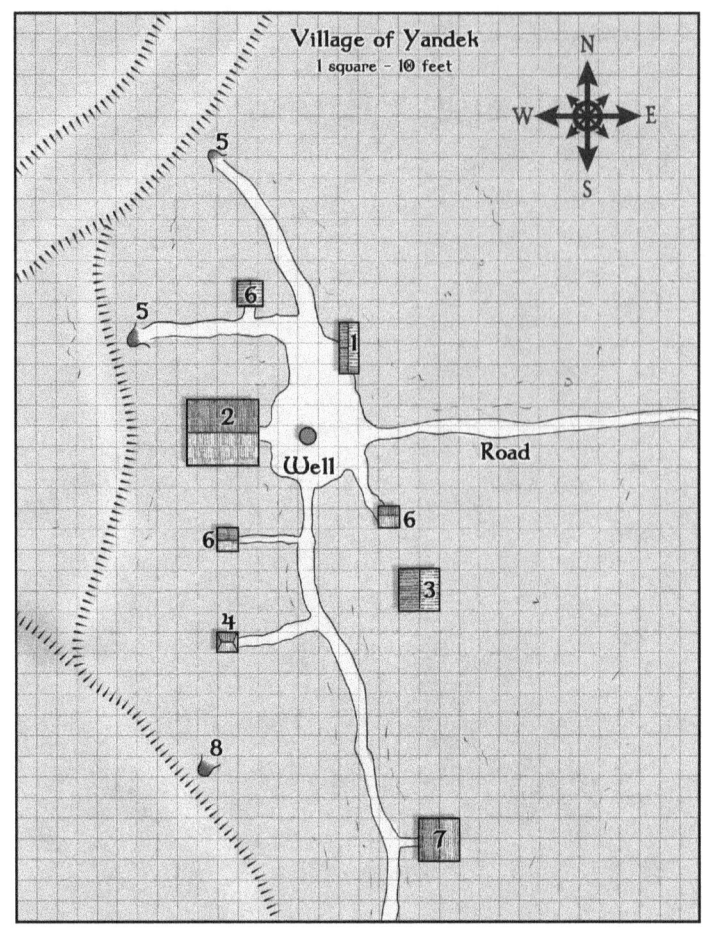

1. Tovord the Tinker – Store and Services

A somber halfling sits outside a modest-sized building that has a worn and flaking hand-painted sign proclaiming "Tovord the Tinker: Store and Services". The halfling patiently twists metal into shape, repairing a cooking pot handle.

He looks up at you and gives you a smile a weak smile and a small wave, as if unsure if you're friendly.

"Hey-a," he calls.

Tovord Traechi (male halfling **commoner**) starts with a Friendly Attitude toward the player characters. He's by nature a gregarious, social type, but no one in town spends time with him, and travelers have been even fewer than usual. He's lonely, full of remembrances of his dead wife, and eager to talk with agreeable people. Even the most simple of queries from a character produces a long, fond reminiscence.

If the characters are patient, they'll hear Tovord's story in full. Unless circumstances are appropriate for a long, drawn out tale, though, don't try to recite all this at once. Instead, intersperse the pieces of the halfling's anecdotes into conversation and interaction.

• I guess I'm not cut out for country living. I miss traveling from town to town and talking with people. Pretty much all my life, I've been a traveling tinker, working my trade along the road and over the mountain pass.

• Yandek isn't the most welcoming of places. Folks here are pretty stand-offish to outsiders, but everyone needs their pots and pans mended and a bit of this and that repaired. Yandek is strange, but not so strange that they didn't welcome a tinker. And unpleasant as it can be, my feet always found my way back here. I guess my heart was guiding them. Mine or Sophi's.

• The gods must have smiled when Sophi was born to the Blood family here in Yandek. The rest of the family isn't much to look at, but Sophi... She was beautiful. The only thing that might've put off another human was her size — she was only three feet tall, and that was standing straight — but that just made her even more perfect, if you ask me.

• We got to talking about, well, about nothing and everything. You know how it is when you're young and falling in love. She'd lived her whole life in Yandek. I'd tell her stories about other place, like the seashore or the big city. The next time I traveled through here I'd bring her a seashell or a sketch of the ramparts.

• I soon figured out that she felt about me like I felt about her. But Sophie didn't want anyone to know about us. She wouldn't let me ask her parents for permission to marry her. She didn't want me to bring my family here to meet her. She finally agreed to run off with me and get married, but we had to keep it a secret, even from my clan.

• After about a year, we were expecting a baby. Sophi had a change of heart and wanted to return to her home town to be near her kin. I agreed. I'd agree to whatever made her happiest. Oh! It wasn't easy coming back, though. After much debate and more than a bit of threatened violence toward me, the elders of Yandek permitted us to settle in town.

• We started to build some good memories here. Sophi was happy with me and being in her hometown with her kin. I never quite fit in with the town. I try, but it's clear that I'll never be welcome as one of their own. Didn't bother me at the time, though; my whole world was the two of us.

• But Sophi, she... And the babe... They died in childbirth, both of them. I... I miss her. I stay here to be as close to her and the life she chose for us. So I repair items and do some basic blacksmithing work. And I act as sort of a go-between for travelers and merchants wanting to sell things to the town or buy some of that new rock they're mining. I guess I think of myself as the town's welcoming committee.

Tovord truly doesn't know anything further about the town and its history. He is good-hearted, and offers fair prices for basic goods. He can shoe horses and do basic blacksmithing, but knows his skills are limited. He tries hard to be a good person and offers hospitality to travelers "Because that is what my beloved Sophi would have wanted."

He's very transparent with his emotions and his thought processes. It only takes a DC 10 Wis (Insight) check to verify that he's very genuine — as well as burdened with a deep grief.

Why doesn't Tovord leave? The town of Yandek is where his darling Sophi wanted them to live. It's where he feels he can be closest to her. And he's so deeply mired in his depression that it's virtually impossible for him to think of what would be a better tomorrow when he's doing the best he can to get through today.

If the heroes have come here for the adventure hook of reuniting Tovord with his family, he can be swayed to leave, but needs several days to pack, close up his shop, and set things in good order. As he explains this to the characters, a DC 5 Wis (Insight) check reveals that while good-intentioned, Tovord, is unlikely to follow through on leaving without character oversight.

The characters can buy any standard equipment, armor or armor — which in itself is a warning sign that something's amiss, as a village like Yandek and a tinkerer like Tovord should lack the requisite supplies or skills for crafting items such as high-quality weapons or heavy armor. And indeed, most of the weapons and armor are clearly secondhand, albeit in good repair.

It's an eclectic assortment. Tovord gets some of his inventory from trading with caravans or travelers passing through. The Blood family also provides a lot of the secondhand goods. Tovord thinks it's kind of them that they supply his store. It never occurred to him to ask where they get the armor, weapons, and supplies from.

Tovord can help the characters in several ways. If the characters are here to buy granite, he can negotiate a deal that makes everyone help. In addition, he knows the rhythms of the village and can help the heroes investigate places by acting as a lookout or decoy to help them go places undetected or chat with particular people — if he can be convinced it's the right thing to do.

2. The Chapel

Though founded by a demon-worshipping cult, the inhabitants of Yandek have very innocuous-seeming religious services each night, shortly after the miners return and have eaten their evening meals. Almost all the townsfolk perform these devotions out of tradition and habit, and lack insight into what the rituals really mean. Despite that ignorance, however, they're far from innocent. The townsfolk are at core chaotic evil, knowing opportunists and cannibals.

The leader of the town is Elder Tencher. At nearly 200 years of age, she's only a couple of generations removed from the original cultist settlers. Because of this, she doesn't have all of the subrace traits, lacking both darkvision and tremorsense. She can always be found in the chapel building, either in the apse or in the attached living quarters. She knows the purpose of the town and that they mine with the intention of freeing their Demon Lord-Master Metanual.

Tencher is absolutely the most cunning and charismatic inhabitant of the town. She has no immediately visible deformities (a few patches of chitin-like skin are well-hidden by her robes), and presents a friendly, affable persona to strangers. Intelligent, she knows that a group of adventurers can be much more trouble than they're worth, and that if people asking questions disappear, more people asking questions are likely to follow.

She wants to find out why the group has come to Yandek and how much of a threat they pose. If the party seems strong or influential, she'll do what she can to satisfy their needs and send them on their way. If the visitors seem weak and easy prey, she'll send the Blood family hunting party (see "Gone Huntin'") after them once they're outside the village.

Because of the rare occasions when an outsider could attend the nightly service, such as when Tovord joined the community, the words are generic and provide no overt clues that the ceremony is an honor of a demon, or anticipating his return.

Built with more architectural skill and care than its neighbors, this building evidences great age and importance. Heavy wood doors open into a large nave. The architecture is simple. Stone pews face a raised dais and lectern in a large room. The chamber itself is unadorned: No symbols, icons, statues or carvings interrupt the plain stone.

An old woman in simple robes over a plain chain shirt tends to the candles that illuminate this dim space.

She smiles in welcome.

"Come in. Come in. How may I be of service? Do you need some help? Are you here to worship?"

Elder Tencher appears friendly and expresses a keen desire to assist the characters. She'll amiably ask about their motives for coming to Yandek and how long they're staying. She invites the characters to attend the service that evening. If the player characters choose to do so, read the following:

Dusk has fallen. A dust-streaked lantern here, a shielded candle there... These sparks of brightness illuminate the Yandek townfolk as they gather from their homes and from the countryside, all converging on the large, stone chapel at the center of town.

The flickering flames create a welcoming atmosphere. Residents call out to each other by name — the greetings of kinfolks and long familiarity.

Homily of the Church of Yandek

We are the followers of our Lord-Master. We, only we, are the chosen: the devoted, the faithful.

• • •

The nearness of our Lord-Master changes us, makes us special. More than merely human.

• • •

We listen for our Lord-Master and work for the day of his return.

• • •

We labor for the sake of our Lord-Master.

• • •

Do not become too attached to the things of the world. Our Lord-Master will come again with fury and devastation.

• • •

The righteous keep apart from the unrighteous, as the lamb must be kept from the wolf.

The service itself is fairly simple. The townsfolk gather in the chapel. Elder Tencher enters, calls the congregation to order, invoking "Our Lord-Master," and leading the people with a call-and-answer style liturgy. She follows with a brief homily on the virtues of hard work and on faith in the return of the Great One, Our Lord-Master, when he rewards the faithful and wreaks devastation upon the nonbelievers. She closes with a remonstrance about associating with or accepting outside ideas.

Elder Tencher: AC 13; HP 49 (9d8+9); Spd 30ft; **Melee** mace (+6, 1d6 bludgeoning); **SA** demonic eminence (expend spell slot to deal extra 3d6 fire on a hit, +1d6 for each slot above 1st), spellcasting (Wis +6, DC 13); **Resist** poison; **Str** +0, **Dex** +0, **Con** +1, **Int** +1, **Wis** +3, **Cha** +1; **Skills** Medicine +7, Persuasion +3, Religion +4; **AL** CE; **CR** 7; **XP** 2900.
  Spells (slots): 0 (at will)—*guidance, light, resistance, sacred flame;* 1st (4)—*bane, cure wounds, inflict wounds, shield of faith;* 2nd (3)—*hold person, prayer of healing, spiritual weapon;* 3rd (3)—*bestow curse,*

dispel magic, spirit guardians; 4th (3)—*freedom of movement, guardian of faith, stone shape;* 5th (1)—*flame strike.*
Equipment: chain shirt, mace, *brooch of shielding, potion of greater healing, bag of holding,* book

Inside Elder Tencher's *bag of holding* is an old tome, written in cramped, spidery handwriting. Intended as both religious text and historical record, it describes the founding of the town, its fall, and its inevitable rise once more. Draw this information from the **Adventure Background** but note that the citizens of Yandek do not know about GrindStone. They know only that a dwarven wizard arrived and somehow imprisoned their demonic lord deep without the mountain. Thus, the book makes no mention of the gargantuan elemental.

Knowledge Questions

The players may ask what sort of knowledge they already have, or what conclusions they can draw, based on what they see or hear throughout the adventure. Use the following examples as guidelines. The characters, of course, have to know the right question to ask, so many of these are most likely to occur in specific order.

What's the difference between the older buildings and the newer construction?
With a DC 10 Int (Nature) check, the characters determine the stone from the older buildings came from the older mines which were further away from the influence that gives GrindStone granite its properties.

How old is the Chapel building?
A DC 10 Int (History) check discloses that the architecture makes it the oldest building in the area, approximately 250 years old.

What was happening in the area around 250 years ago?
Int (History) DC 25 recalls stories of a supernatural horror, possibly a demon, rampaging through the area, eventually defeated by a powerful dwarf wizard named Obsidian.

What was known about the monster/demon?
Int (History or Religion) DC 25 check reveals that the creature's name was Metanual. He sought to gain power and glory by blazing a path of destruction. While nobody is certain, the more detailed tales and legends of the time suggest Metanual may have been a sort of demon called a "glabrezu."

What's a glabrezu?
Int (Arcana or Religion) check DC 15 is enough to recall the basic description of a glabrezu. If the check is at least 20, it reveals typical glabrezu traits and abilities: 1) Innate spell-casting, often of substantial offensive power; 2) resistance to cold, fire, lightning; bludgeoning, piercing, and slashing from normal weapons; and 3) magic resistance.

3. M'rar's House

M'rar is the leader of Yandek's miners, and very knowledgeable about the history of the mines. It was under his guidance several years ago that the second mine was abandoned and the third location chosen. He knows how the GrindStone Granite from the newest mine is very different from the two that had been dug before and abandoned. He has an aptitude for magic and a greater sense of discipline and order than the other residents of Yandek. (M'rar is neutral evil, rather than chaotic). While he doesn't know that they're digging to free a demon lord, he does comprehend that the mining has a purpose and that they're getting close to completing it.

Unless the characters interfere with the working of the mines under M'rar's leadership, the dig breaches through to Metanual's chamber within a couple of weeks.

This building looks old, the stone showing age and weathering. Of particular note is that, instead of a lawn or plant garden, the house boasts a stone garden with sections of several different varieties of rocks. This landscape looks well-tended and regularly cared-for.

If the characters explore the property during the day, the door is locked and secured. If they look around very early in the morning or in the evening, M'rar is working in the yard.

A diminutive but broad-shouldered man works among the rock, rearranging several stone that had shifted. As he looks up at you, you notice his skin and eyes both have a reddish hue. "Aye-ah. You lookin' for me?" he asks.

M'rar has a natural aptitude for and genuine interest in geology and his hobby is the rock garden. Like the rest of the town, he starts with a Hostile attitude toward the characters, but engaging him on the topics of geology, rock collecting, or mining automatically shifts his attitude to Neutral.

What can M'rar tell the party?

If motivated, he can tell the characters that the purity and quality of the stone increases toward the northeast section of the current mines and that's where he's focused the diggers' efforts.

He knows the areas of the mines where rock creatures (galeb duhr) have attacked his miners. Their solution has been to abandon those tunnels and dig through other areas.

M'Rar: AC 12 (15 with *mage armor*); **HP** 40 (9d8); **Spd** 30ft; **Melee** dagger (+5, 1d4+6 piercing); **Ranged** dagger (+5, 20ft/60ft, 1d4+6 piercing); **SA** spellcasting (Int+6, DC 14); **Resist** poison; **Str** +4, **Dex** +2, **Con** +0, **Int** +3, **Wis** +1, **Cha** +0; **Skills** Arcana +3, History +6; **Senses** darkvision 30ft, tremorsense 10ft; **AL** NE; **CR** 6; **XP** 2300.
> **Spells (slots):** 0 (at will)—*dancing lights, light, message, true strike;* 1st (4)—*feather fall, fog cloud, mage armor, shield;* 2nd (3)—*darkness, levitate, shatter;* 3rd (3)—*haste, protection from energy, slow, stinking cloud;* 4th (3)—*fabricate, stone shape, stoneskin;* 5th (1)—*telekinesis.*
> **Equipment**: clothing, 2 daggers, *gauntlets of ogre power* (attuned).

Inside the house are simple furnishing, an assortment of books, samples of interesting rocks (worth 100gp total), and M'rar's spellbook.

4. The Still

Set somewhat apart from the cluster of buildings stands a structure that looks more recently built. The blocks of stone are sharp-edged and have little weathering. The new construction feels primitive, though, created without much skill or artistry.
The breeze shifts, bringing with it the distinctive smell of distilling liquor. Without a doubt, this is a moonshine still.
The place is manned by a large man with a hunched shoulder, wearing threadbare homespun clothes covered by a thick hardened-leather apron, gloves and boots. He works

vigorously at the tubing, making multiple adjustments as he adds grain hash at one end and banks a cooking fire. His eyes are milky white and red rimmed, but he seems very aware of the area around him.

"Eh?" he says. "Who's there? Don't you all know better than to bother a man at 'is work?"

Like most everyone here, the fellow is unfriendly; he grudgingly introduces himself as Piet. Between the fumes from the still and the regular consumption of the moonshine, Piet is "hard-of-seein'" (vision limited to 30ft), a disability that's earned him the moniker "Blind Piet."

Piet is deadly if attacked in the area of the still. Though his vision is limited, he knows his still and this side of town very well.

Yandek Moonshine

Very Rare Alchemical Item

Blind Piet makes incredibly potent moonshine from a secret formula known only to him. The moonshine intoxicates the drinker for 1 hour (tactical disadvantage on all ability and skill checks), but also bestows the following ability:

After drinking this potion, a character can use a bonus action to exhale burning, caustic fumes in a 30ft cone. Each creature in that area must make a DC 13 Dex saving throw, taking 7d6 acid damage on a failed save, or half as much damage on a successful one. The effect ends after the character has exhaled the fumes three times or when 1 hour has passed.

The still has 6 vials total.

The building is new because the old still blew up a few years ago.

If anyone is asked about why the still is in plain sight, the response is a confused "Why wouldn't it be?' The hamlet hasn't had a tax collector or government official dare to enter it in decades.

Blind Piet: AC 15; **HP** 78 (12d8+24); **Spd** 30ft; **Melee** quarterstaff (+7, 1d6+3 bludgeoning plus 7d6 poison, DC 15 Con half); **SA** sneak attack (1/turn, 4d6 damage), *Yandek moonshine*; **Resist** poison; **Str** +3, **Dex** +0, **Con** +2, **Int** −1, **Wis** +0, **Cha** −2; **Senses** darkvision 30ft, tremorsense 10ft; **Traits** blind beyond 30ft, assassinate (on first turn, advantage on attack rolls against creature that hasn't taken a turn, and any hit against a surprised creature is a critical hit), evasion (when subject to an effect that allows a Dex save half, takes no damage on success and only half on fail); **AL** CE; **CR** 8; **XP** 3900.
  Equipment: studded leather, club, 3 vials of poison, 6 vials of *Yandek moonshine* (see sidebar).

5. Abandoned Mines

The original mine is the one located nearest to the chapel. After several generations working it without drawing any closer to their goal, the cult stopped digging in that direction and opened the northernmost mine.

Again, after hauling ton after ton of rock from the mine, the cult eventually determined that it didn't lead them closer to their goal and abandoned it.

Judging by the rubble outside this opening into the mountain, you would guess that this was once a functioning mine. The weeds growing thickly outside the entrance, though, suggest that it's been many years since this particular mine has been worked.

The abandoned mines are extensive and yield nothing of interest. If the characters choose to explore them, they likely pass enough time within to come out in the early evening when M'rar is working in his yard, or at night when the town gathers for their nightly services.

6. Typical Yandek House

If the player characters investigate any of the houses during the day, no one is home; everyone works at the mines.

The residents of Yandek do lock their houses — they may all know one another, but they're suspicious and surly by nature — but the locks aren't very complicated, nor do the residents trap their houses or living areas. A simple DC 10 Dex check, with thieves' tools, is sufficient to break into any of the houses.

In addition to the houses marked on the town map, others stand scattered around the mountain, as the founding cultists preferred some space between their house and their neighbors'. Several buildings are empty, left abandoned as the population dwindled.

During the day or during evening when chapel services are held, read the following.

A ramshackle stone building shows little care in its design and neglect in its upkeep. No one appears to be home at this time.

At other times, this is the scene awaiting the characters.

A bad-tempered woman shouts at you: "Get off my property! We don't like outsiders around here. Leave us alone."

If the player characters search a house, roll 1d6 times on the following table for items of interest:

1d20	Item
1	Bucket
2	Clothes, common
3	Crowbar
4	Flask of moonshine
5	Grappling Hook
6	Haunch of meat. Wisdom (Medicine) DC 15 check reveals that it's human.
7	Hammer
8	Hammer, sledge
9	Iron Pot
10	Iron Spikes (5)
11	Lamp
12	Lantern, bullseye
13	Lantern, hooded
14	Oil, flask
15	Pick, miner's
16	Rope, hempen (50ft)
17	Rope, silk (50ft)
18	Shovel
19	Torches (5)
20	Waterskin

7. The Blood Boys' Ranch

tOne of the few non-mining households, the Blood family raises livestock and hunts, providing meat to the town of Yandek. The family handles all aspects of the animals from raising and feeding them, to slaughtering, to tanning the hides.

It's a large family for the town. The heads of Blood household are the matriarch/mother/aunt Momant, and the patriarch/father/uncle Duncle (whom the characters may have already encountered). Their only daughter, Sophi, left to marry Tovord. Of the five sons/nephews, Harval, Yanoush, and B'than are at the Ranch with Momant. Drumm and Drouck are out hunting with Duncle (see "Gone Huntin'").

You start to smell this place long before you see it. A reek of farm animals, manure and tanning fumes fills the air. Soon, the sounds of unhappy beasts add to the atmosphere. Primitive wood, wire, and stone fences pen in a variety of livestock. Different enclosures confine cattle, sheep, goats, and chickens. All look sickly and poorly treated, and several even show wounds or scars from beatings.

The farmhouse, barn, and outbuildings are of the same stone that dominates the architecture in the area.

As you approach, three burly men step out into the yard — and in this case, "burly" means "larger than most humans."

"What do you want?" shouts the first, grabbing a nearby pitchfork. The spikey growths protruding from his shoulders don't seem to impede his muscular movements.

"Strangers ain't welcome here," warns the second beady-eyed hulk, brandishing an axe.

"Clear out if you know what's good fo' ya," says the third with an odd lisp; his jaw may be notable deformed, but his flexing, oversized fists appear to work just fine.

The Blood family is actively hostile to any intruders on their land. If the characters insist on approaching the house, they attack.

The following family members are at the ranch on a continuous basis. They don't work at the mines; providing meat is their contribution to the cult's efforts. They also don't bother attending services. For them, every time they capture, torture, and kill someone, it's an act of worship. Their mantra is "Fear Adds Flavor." It was a saying from the earliest days of the cult as a devotion to Metanual.

Harval, Blood Boy: AC 13; **HP** 125 (12d10+48); **Spd** 30ft; **Melee** pitchfork (+5, 2d8+3 piercing); **SA** multiattack (pitchfork x2); **Resist** poison; **Str** +3, **Dex** +0, **Con** +4, **Int** –2, **Wis** +0, **Cha** –2; **Senses** darkvision 30ft, tremorsense 10ft; **AL** CE; **CR** 4; **XP** 1100.

Yanoush, Blood Boy: AC 13; **HP** 113 (12d10+36); **Spd** 30ft; **Melee** battleaxe (+5, 2d8+4 slashing); **SA** multiattack (battleaxe x2); **Resist** poison; **Str** +4, **Dex** +0, **Con** +3, **Int** –2, **Wis** +0, **Cha** –2; **Senses** darkvision 30ft, tremorsense 10ft; **AL** CE; **CR** 4; **XP** 1100.

B'than, Blood Boy: AC 13; **HP** 137 (12d10+60); **Spd** 30ft; **Melee** slam (+7, 2d8+5 bludgeoning); **SA** multiattack (slam x2); **Resist** poison; **Str** +5, **Dex** +0, **Con** +5, **Int** –2, **Wis** +0, **Cha** –2; **Senses** darkvision 30ft, tremorsense 10ft; **AL** CE; **CR** 4; **XP** 1100.

In response to sounds of combat, the matriarch of the Blood family, Momant, joins the combat in 1d4 rounds. She had been in the farmhouse cellar having "fun" with Kit, their latest prisoner.

As the fight progresses, a woman rushes from the farmhouse, a bloody dagger clutched in her hand. She is a large woman with tufts of hair sprouting at random along her chin line. She wears an odd mix of clothes that seems to have been taken from a variety of individuals — and the occasional dark stain suggests the donations weren't willing. A wild assortment of colors, fabrics, and textures, few of the clothes fit well.

"You leave my boys alone!"

Momant: AC 12; **HP** 40 (9d8); **Spd** 30ft; **Melee** pact blade longsword (+5, 1d8+5 slashing); **SA** dark one's blessing, dark one's own luck, eldritch invocations (devil's sight, repelling blast), pact of the blade, spells (Cha +3, DC 11, 2 slots, 5th level slot); **Resist** poison; **Str** +2, **Dex** +0, **Con** +0, **Int** +3, **Wis** +1 (+4), **Cha** +0 (+3); **Senses** darkvision 120ft, tremorsense 10ft; **Skills** History +6; **AL** CE; **CR** 6; **XP** 2300.

Spells (known): 0 (at will)—*blade ward, eldritch blast (repelling blast), poison spray*; 1st —*expeditious retreat, protection from good, witch bolt*; 2nd—*darkness, ray of enfeeblement*; 3rd— *fear, vampiric touch*; 4th— *blight, dimension door*; 5th—*hold monster*.

A search of the house reveals an unhidden trapdoor in the kitchen. A ladder leads down into Bloods' "recreation room" a torture chamber. Kit Del'Ancy (male human **noble**), their current "guest," slumps amid gruesome devices, blood stains on the floor, and hooks on the ceiling. Kit is trussed up in a harness and gagged, thus making escape or even calling out for help impossible. He is somewhat wounded, but suffers more from the mental anguish he endured than the physical punishments. (Kit currently has 2 hit points, rather than his normal 9, due to various wounds.)

The Del'Ancy family is minor nobility, owning extensive vineyards known for producing quality wine. At a mere eighteen years of age, Kit is the youngest of their seven children and was keen to see the world and travel. He had chosen to accompany a caravan transporting some of his family's wines over the mountains. The Blood Boys attacked the caravan several days ago. Kit and one guard survived and were brought here for the Bloods' amusement. The guard died yesterday, leaving Kit as the only survivor.

While he doesn't have any valuables currently, if he survives to be reunited with his family, he'll ensure that the characters receive a 1000gp reward. Of course, the characters can keep any of the items remaining from the caravan. (The Bloods have not yet disposed of those.)

Treasure: The Blood family's hunting of animals and humanoids produces a regular, valued supply of meat for the village. The travelers and adventurers they've killed in the process had reasonable equipment, with most functional items, such as coins, gems, rope, lanterns, and rations, distributed out to members of the community. Any surplus was given to Tovord for sale.

The loot from the most recent caravan attack remains at the farmhouse. It includes:
• 6 cases of wine (100gp/case)
• 4 bolts of fine silk (50gp/bolt)
• assorted armor, weapons, and equipment from the guards (500gp total value).

A few additional items belonged to Kit: a mithral chain shirt and *+1 rapier*. These are family heirlooms, in addition to being useful items, but while he would appreciate their return, he doesn't insist on it. He's just grateful to be alive.

If and only if the characters offer to return those items — without pressing for additional payment or trade, without promise of further reward — Kit provides them with even greater items upon their return to civilization: a mithral breastplate and a *+2 weapon* of a type appropriate for one of the characters.

Many items requiring higher-order thinking (scrolls, books), or magic items requiring attunement were simply discarded in a trash heap behind the barn. A methodical search of the heap of discards unearths the following, one each after 10–30 minutes of digging:
• a *figurine of wondrous power (serpentine owl)*

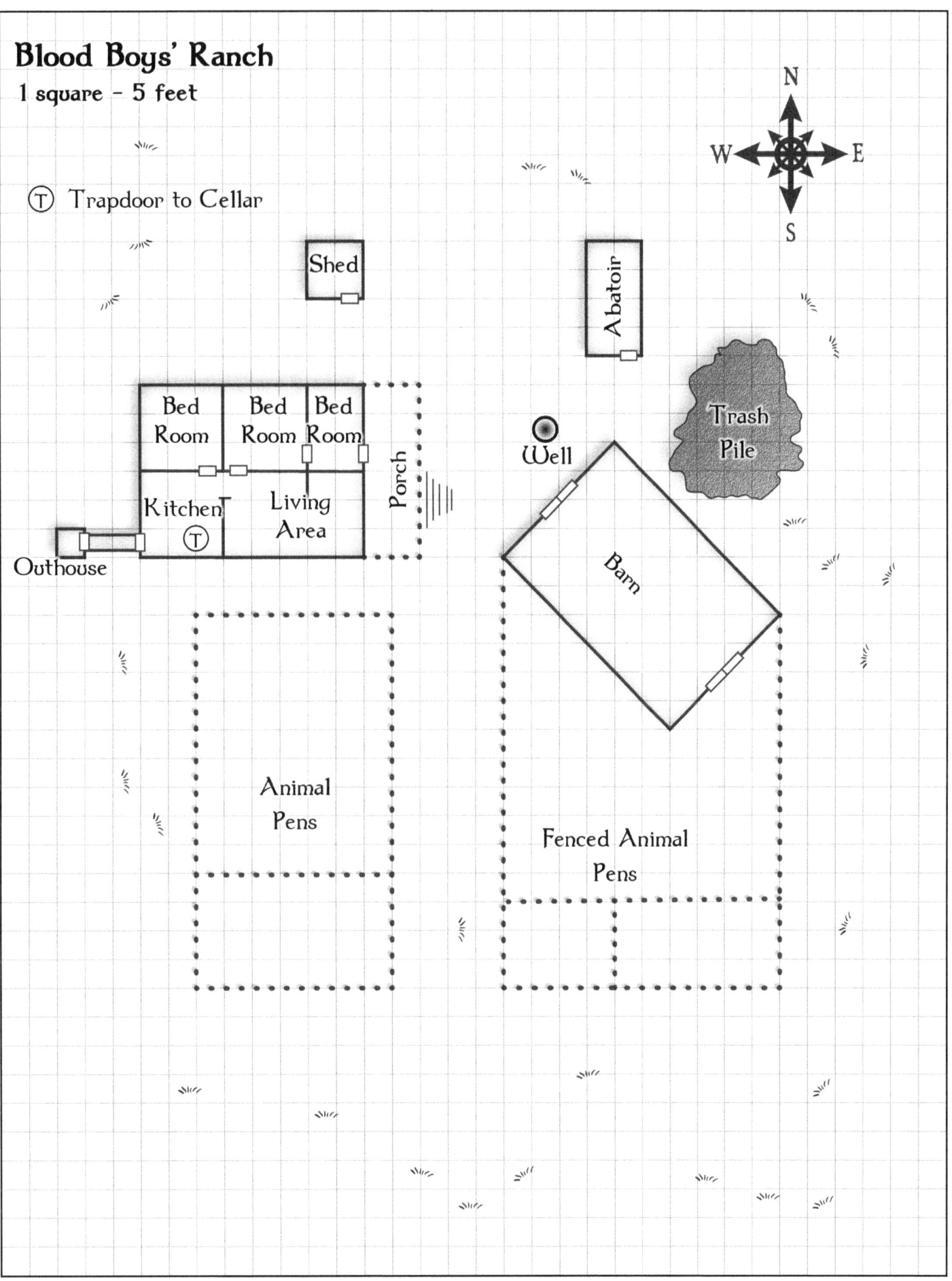

Blood Boys' Ranch

1 square - 5 feet

(T) Trapdoor to Cellar

Shed

Abatoir

Well

Trash Pile

Bed Room

Bed Room

Bed Room

Porch

Kitchen

(T)

Living Area

Outhouse

Barn

Animal Pens

Fenced Animal Pens

N
W   E
S

- a *deck of illusions* (clubs only)
- a *scroll of protection (fey)*, a *scroll of spiritual weapon*
- a *scroll of mage armor*.

The player characters can also find varied trinkets that can help identify several unlucky souls who went missing in the mountains and ended up as victims of the Yandek cannibals. These items have a negligible monetary value but can serve as adventure hooks for future sessions.

8. The Active Mines of GrindStone

The many years of mining by the village of Yandek has created a complex set of twisting and turning tunnels. Not the most competent of miners to begin with, the inbreeding of the community increased their lack of expertise. Even so, they've been excavating long enough that they were bound to find their goal eventually.

About a year ago, a passing trader noticed the warmth of the GrindStone granite. Recognizing a potential fad, he's paid premium prices for the stone ever since. No malice or evil intent on the part of the trader: The warmth makes desirable as a home construction material in cooler climates, and a fascinating oddity for those wealthy enough to afford fascinating oddities. But his opening of this new market did have the side effect of concentrating the Yandek miners' efforts on the earth elemental, near the chamber of Metanual.

Its slumber disturbed, GrindStone shifted and moved, causing the well-known trails and mountain pass in the area to disappear. As the irritation continued, GrindStone also detached part of itself in the form of two earth elementals that now patrol the depths of the mines.

> Unlike the other mine shafts nearer the village, this one definitely remains in continuous operation. The path to the mine opening is hard-packed earth, pressed firm from the regular passage of workers. The rubble outside the shaft seems to be a somewhat different stone, too. As you walk on, over, and around the waste rock, you notice that it's warm underfoot. Not hot — there's no danger of being burnt — but definitely and unnaturally warm.

If the characters investigate during the day, 3d6 miners (see stats for Yandek Resident) work to break rock, primarily in the Northeast area of the mine, load it into baskets, tote them to the mine entrance, and dump them. Directing the work is the mine overseer, M'Rar (see area **3**). The miners don't initiate combat, but do physically block the mine and call for M'Rar who orders the characters to leave. Failure to comply results in an attack.

Rewarding Player Innovation

If the players want to do something unusual, such as trying to contact GrindStone with a ritual or an unusual combination of spells, let them! The incredibly large earth elemental has had contact with humanoids in the past, and is only here due to whatever pact or favor it owed the dwarf wizard Obsidian. Consider GrindStone to have average intelligence and a starting attitude of Indifferent. If the players can shift GrindStone to a Friendly Attitude, the elemental might be convinced to shake itself so that the mine tunnels collapse, ensuring the demon's prison is reburied. If the players can explain in a way that a friendly GrindStone can understand, a DC 15 Int (Nature) check instructs the elemental how to restore the mountain pass.

The Mines

At set points in the earth around the glabrezu's prison are galeb duhr, set to stand an endless watch as guardians. Occasionally, the Yandek find one as they tunnel, and every time, the galeb duhr attacks the minders, defending its assigned territory. The people of Yandek have responded by abandoning the tunnels within the galeb duhr's area and digging others, hoping to go around the sentinels. These galeb duhr are marked on the map with a **G**. They protect an area of 30ft around them, attacking any creatures digging in or otherwise intruding upon the area. The galeb duhr speak only Terran, but are intelligent and able to communicate with each other, the earth elementals, and GrindStone. How well the characters can convince them that they aren't the enemy is entirely in their hands (and quite possibly in their ability to pantomime if they can't cast the proper spells to communicate).

Read the following when the characters approach an area labeled **G**.

> This area of the mine doesn't seem to be in current use. Rocks litter the tunnel floor with no signs of recent foot traffic. Here and there a few tools lie among the rubble.

The tools are in useable shape, abandoned by the miners when the galeb duhr attacked. The tools can be collected and sold to Tovord for a total of 100gp.

Galeb Duhr: **AC** 16; **HP** 85 (9d8+45); **Spd** 15ft, (30ft when rolling, 60ft when rolling downhill); **Melee** slam (+8, 2d6+5 bludgeoning); **SA** animate boulders 1/day, rolling charge (+2d6 bludgeoning DC 16 Str save or knocked prone); **Immune** poison; **Resist** normal weapons; **Str** +5, **Dex** +2, **Con** +5, **Int** +0, **Wis** +1, **Cha** +0; **Senses** darkvision 60ft, tremorsense 60ft; **AL** N; **CR** 6; **XP** 2300.

G. Avatars of the Earth Elemental

In addition to the galeb duhr set as guardians long ago by Obsidian, if GrindStone perceives a threat, it can create two earth elementals each week, maintaining up to a total of four at any one time. GrindStone controls these elementals telepathically and can see what they see, even speak through them if given reason.

What would instigate GrindStone creating these elemental avatars?
Casting divination spells within the active minds draws GrindStone's attention, as this was how Obsidian typically communicated with and instructed the elemental. This occurs if the focal point of the spell (such as the sensor of a *clairvoyance* spell) is within the mine, even if the spell is cast elsewhere.

If the player characters try to communicate with GrindStone through the galeb duhr, GrindStone chooses to use an earth elemental as a more direct method of talking.

If anyone breaches Metanual's chamber, GrindStone creates elementals to investigate the situation. As mentioned earlier, GrindStone's thinking process is slower than most humanoids'. The elementals appear and begin their search about 10 minutes after the chamber is entered.

If the elementals manifest for any reason, read the following.

> Mighty footsteps rumble and echo throughout the mine, steadily, inexorably approaching.

The characters have plenty of time to react and prepare.

The earth elemental manifestations/avatars of GrindStone have been sent to be the eyes and ears of the massive, mountain elemental. They attack on sight if Metanual has been freed from his prison; otherwise

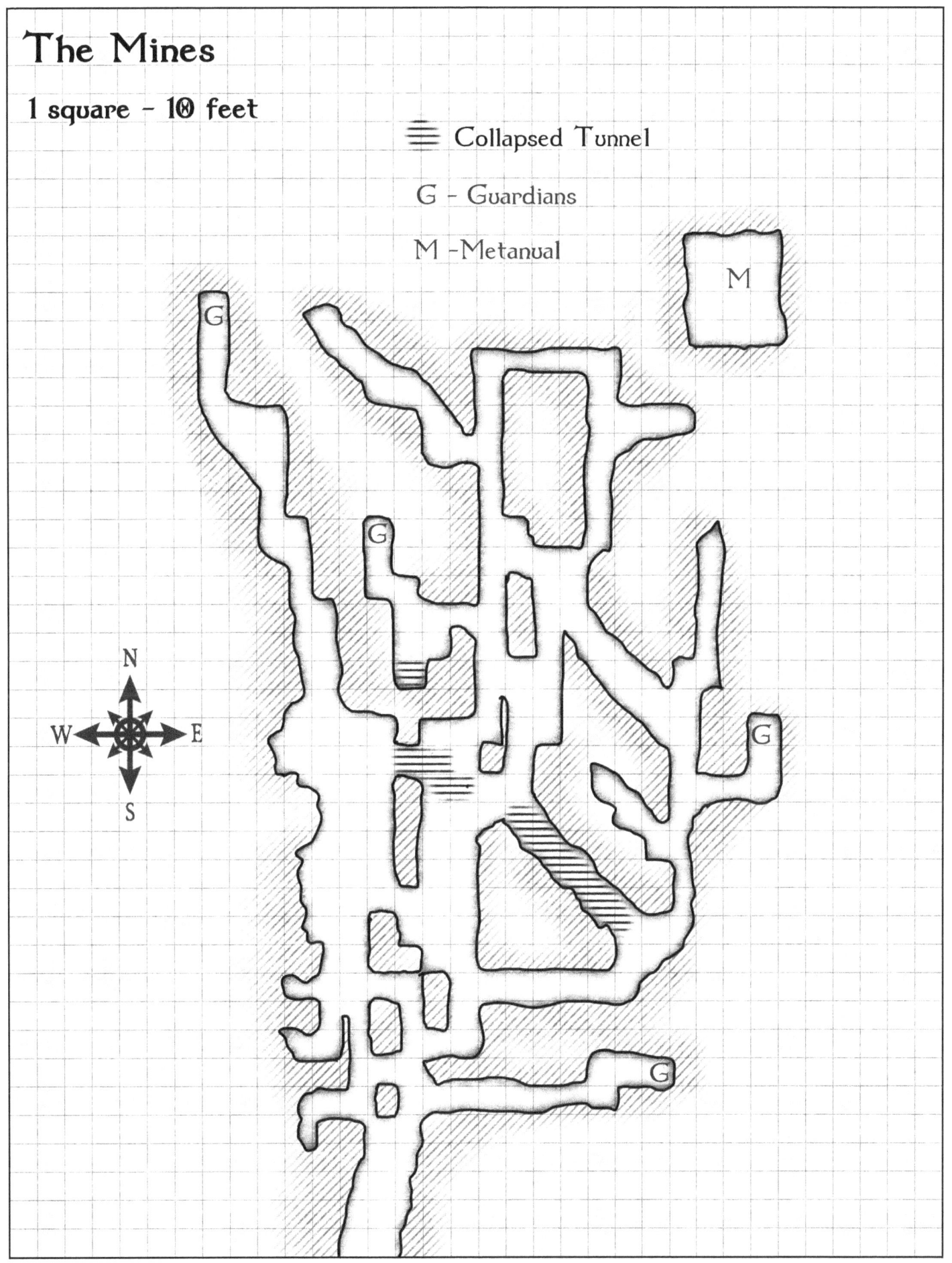

The Mines

1 square – 10 feet

≡ Collapsed Tunnel

G – Guardians

M – Metanual

GrindStone looks around through them, tries to understand what is happening, and attempts to communicate, but isn't very adept at thinking or talking on a human-scale.

Earth Elemental (2): AC 17; HP 126 (12d10+60); **Spd** 30ft, burrow 30ft; **Melee** slam (+8, 10ft, 2d8+5 bludgeoning); **SA** multiattack (slam x2), earth glide, siege monster; **Immune** poison; **Resist** normal weapons; **Str** +5, **Dex** –1, **Con** +5, **Int** –3, **Wis** +0, **Cha** –3; **Senses** darkvision 60ft, tremorsense 60ft; **AL** N; **CR** 5; **XP** 1800.

Activist Earth

One of the galeb duhr is older and more experienced a creature than most of its kind, having spent many years on the Material Plane in a variety of locations. It learned to understand and speak Common, as well as several other languages, and has developed an affection for humanoids. It partnered with several people over the millennia, most recently helping Obsidian enlist several of its kind as guardians. This broad experience causes it to take a more expansive interpretation of its duties as guardian. In response to the recent stirring by GrindStone and the very real likelihood of the miners breaching the chamber and freeing the demon lord, this galeb duhr decided that it needed to take some active steps to ensure Metanual doesn't escape. Dubbing itself "DemonBane," it left its post in the mines and seeks a means of real change. It has noticed the characters as strangers in the area.

In its camouflage form of a boulder, it observes the characters and decides to enlist their aid.

DemonBane approaches the characters at some point after their initial exploration of Yandek, when there aren't any town residents around.

A nearby rock moves, bending at its middle and then straightening up again, as if bowing.

A deep, resonating voice speaks in Common.

"I have been keeping the watch for adventure-spirit humanoids like you. I need many helps."

DemonBane tells the characters that long ago, a wizard named Obsidian imprisoned the glabrezu demon Metanual inside an enormous, mountain-sized elemental named GrindStone.

Recently, the village mining has begun to irritate GrindStone as it nears the demon's cavern.

For several months, faint tremors have occasionally rattled the mountain and its surrounds, and the frequency and severity of those tremors continues to grow. The miners are getting closer to their goal of the demon chamber. Even worse, the elemental's restlessness has damaged the protective wards that help to seal the demon within. (In essence, give the characters the remainder of the **Adventure Background** section at this time.) The galeb duhr wants the characters' help to prevent this.

DemonBane, Greater Galeb Duhr: AC 16; HP 85 (9d8+45); **Spd** 15ft, (30ft when rolling, 60ft when rolling downhill); **Melee** slam (+8, 2d6+5 bludgeoning); **SA** animate boulders 1/day, rolling charge (+2d6 bludgeoning, DC 16 Str or knocked prone); **Immune** poison; **Resist** normal weapons; **Skills** History +5, Insight +5, Perception +5; **Str** +5, **Dex** +2, **Con** +5, **Int** +2, **Wis** +2, **Cha** +0; **Senses** darkvision 60ft, tremorsense 60ft; **AL** N; **CR** 7; **XP** 2900.

Innate Spells: 1/day—detect magic, dispel magic, protection from energy, stoneskin.

DemonBane speaks Common fairly well (some idioms do give it trouble — like "keeping watch" or "what time is it?" are mis-stated as "keeping the watch" or "how is your time?"). More importantly, it understands humanoid norms and ways of life. It can also communicate directly with GrindStone and act as a liaison between the characters and the mountain-elemental.

Note that while DemonBane might actually join with the characters to explore the mine — in which case you should feel free to increase the number of miners who oppose them — it cannot order the other galeb duhr to do the same; it holds no particular authority over them, and they interpret their instructions far more literally and strictly than DemonBane does.

M. The Chamber of the Demon Lord-Master

Occasionally, an adventuring group may choose to resolve a course of action without ever entering this area. Burying the mine under tons of rock is a viable option.

Many groups want to see the plotline through to the end, gaining resolution through personally assessing the threat. The most thorough of good-intentioned heroes seek to reinforce the wards. (The most selfish or evil-intentioned want to meet the demon lord himself, Metanual for their own motivations.)

Seeking out the Chamber

If the player characters pursue a visit to the demon, the encounter likely focuses on roleplaying and persuasion. Metanual does whatever he can to convince the characters to free him and then betrays them by attacking. He's the epitome of chaotic evil, power-seeking demonhood.

Note: Unless the characters have tampered with them, the runes are still strong enough to keep the demon imprisoned for several more years, so they can easily avoid an encounter if they wish. On the other hand, that's just putting the region's problems off for three or four years — or less, since Elder Tencher or one of the other cultists might well choose to try to destroy the glyphs.

With no small amount of effort, you manage to continue the mine tunnel. In this part of the mine, the rock feels warm and emits a reddish glow. You see a brighter glow emanating from the rocks ahead of you. Your goal must be near: The chamber of the demon lord Metanual.

There are several dozen feet of rock between the most current tunnel and the demon's chamber as the characters start the adventure. There are many different ways that the rock can be excavated.

If left unimpeded, with a few weeks of mining, the miners uncover the chamber.

While the *stoneshape* spell only enables the manipulation of a chunk of stone less than 5ft in diameter, there are a variety of magics including *disintegrate* that can enable quick access. Even something as commonplace among adventurers as a *bag of holding* can help immeasurably with the process of rock removal.

DemonBane, or a DC 20 Int (Investigation) check, can tell the characters in what direction they must continue tunnel in order to reach the demon's chamber. (DemonBane must be convinced that the characters seek the chamber to reinforce the runes or destroy the demon before it will provide this information.) Otherwise, they'll have to dig blindly, as the cultists were.

The last of the rock breaks away, revealing an uneven cubical chamber. The walls seem almost to post with an unnatural warmth, one that felt comforting in smaller quantities but here feels almost like the touch of a ravaging fever. All around the chamber are inscribed lines of blue, silvery runes.

Within the chamber stands a large, hulking creature with horns, jutting teeth, muscular arms ending in pincers, and two smaller additional arms ending in fists. He looks at you quizzically, evaluating and assessing. Only a thin, line of the blue runes separates you.

"Welcome," he says as he opens his two pairs of arms in greeting. "I am very happy to see you."

He smiles at you.

"I've waited here for a very long time, thinking about how to reward those who free me. Tell me, are you the sort who appreciates gold and treasure? Or would you prefer glory and minions to sing your praises?"

Metanual cajoles and promises the characters great power and treasure if freed. The barrier trapping him within GrindStone has prevented him from returning to the Abyss. Of course he doesn't have any intention of keeping his promises and attacks the characters if they break the barrier.

No magic, creatures, or physical items can cross the runes.

Search: A close examination of the runes with a successful DC 15 Int (Arcana or Investigation) check shows that the shifting mountain has abraded several of the runes.

Promises, Temptations, and Threats

Metanual uses his Deception +7, which can be opposed by characters' Insight. In addition, because he lies, there are many parts of his spiel that vary from the history and accounts that the characters learned. Here's a sampling of dialogue for him. He starts off supremely confident of gaining his freedom. He'll wait for the characters to respond and tries a variety of tactics to play on the character's desires.

If persuasion and temptation fail, Metanual attempts to goad them into breaking the runes to combat him directly. He uses his Insight skill to find an approach likely to work: challenging their honor, duping them into thinking they can truly kill him, or pretending fear that they'll destroy the runes.

If he succeeds, he stops talking and attacks. If he fails, he grows increasingly desperate.

• You're my saviors, my champions. I shall reward you with a king's ransom in gold and gems. I'll give you each a diamond as large as a chicken egg.

• Or I can ensure your fame. A hundred bards will write a thousand songs in praise of you. Just imagine as word of your great deeds spreads! Crowds gathering as word spreads of your approach to their humble town. How they bow and scrape for your attention.

• Would you rule? We can start with Yandek. I hereby give you the town and all its denizens to do with as you wish. From Yandek a small seat of power, then the mountains, then the region, the kingdom, the world? I can give that to you.

• Power, true power, to have your own coterie of minions. A veritable army from the Abyss that I can summon and have bound to you to do your bidding. They can crush your enemies!

• No? What about knowledge? Don't you want to know the true story of all this? How a vile dwarf summoned me here, and trapped me, purely for her own amusement?

• You know that this prison won't hold me forever. I see you. If you don't free me now, I shall hunt you down, have you watch as I torture those closest to you, and then imprison you in a tomb such as this one. I tingle with anticipation. Free me now or pay later.

• Ah, sweet success. You're leaving me in peace. I've been here for hundreds of years. I can wait hundreds more. Here, I am immortal, safe from the small danger that such heroes like you pose.

• Of course, I see that you're too cowardly to envision freeing me. Your fear tastes spicy to me. Pure seasoning. You tremble on the other side of this barrier, too scared to face me directly. Someday, perhaps, a real champion will come.

• Wait! Consider the possibilities. I can fulfill your every desire. Just tell me what you want.

Restoring the Runes: The worn parts of the text could be restored to refresh their binding magic with a DC 20 Int (Arcana) check.

Destroying the Runes: A little effort can obliterate the runes and free the demon with a DC 15 Str check.

Once the barrier is gone, Metanual fights without fear. After all, even if the characters "kill" him, he knows he'll just remanifest in the Abyss, free as he hasn't been in centuries.

Metanual, Glabrezu Demon: AC 17; **HP** 157 (15d10+75); **Spd** 40ft; **Melee** pincer (+9, 10ft, 2d10+5 bludgeoning), fist (+9, 2d4+2 bludgeoning); **SA** multiattack (pincer x2, fist x2), innate spells (Int +4, DC 16); **Immune** poison; **Resist** cold, fire, lightning, normal weapons; **Skills** Deception +7, Insight +6, Perception +6; **Str** +5, **Dex** +2, **Con** +5, **Int** +4, **Wis** +3, **Cha** +3; **Senses** truesight 120ft, telepathy 120ft; **Traits** magic resistance; **AL** CE; **CR** 9; **XP** 5000 XP.

    Innate Spells: (at will)—*darkness, detect magic, dispel magic*; 1/day—*confusion, fly, power word stun*.

Reburying the Chamber

If the player characters want to make it more difficult for others to reach the chamber, there are a few possibilities.

If they've communicated with GrindStone and established a friendly rapport, GrindStone localizes an earthquake on the mines and causes them to collapse, burying the room under many tons of granite.

The characters can also make a DC 20 Int (Investigation or Nature) check to find some weaker points in the mine and devise a way to make the mine cave in.

Concluding the Adventure

If the characters collapsed the mine or at least stopped the village from continuing their mining, Metanual rots in his prison, locked away from the world he *almost* managed to touch once again.

If the Blood family's predations have been stopped, travel becomes easier and trade goods more readily available. The hamlet of Yandek disappears over the next generation. Without any concrete motivation to stay and continue mining, and with their most steady supply of food stopped, Yandek residents drift away to pursue lives elsewhere, typically joining bands of bandits or trying their luck in Underdark communities more suited to their deep-mine experiences and more accepting of their deformed physiology.

Over the next few weeks, GrindStone settles back into its former customary position, returning to its long, slumbering vigil. The pass through the mountains is restored and trade resumes.

If, on the other hand, Metanual escaped his prison, after a few months, Grindstone realizes its guard duty has ended and leaves the Material Plane. Its absence creates a large, smooth valley between other mountains that serves as an easy pass-through.

Either way, the availability of GrindStone granite tapers off and architects recommend heated pipes beneath wood floors as the next status symbol for the wealthy and fashionable.

If Tovord survived the adventure, the characters are sure to meet him again, making a new, happier life on the road.

The Two Crucibles

In *The Two Crucibles*, a party of 4–6 adventurers averaging 8th level has the opportunity to not only witness, but fully partake in the seldom seem (and even more rarely understood) world of internal barbarian politics in the wild regions north of the Wilderland Hills. As a scenario, this adventure combines three general arenas of roleplaying challenge into a single tight arc — deductive investigation, social maneuvering and politicking, and dungeon crawling — all the while showing off a wilder region of the Borderland Provinces that might otherwise go unexplored.

The Vanigoths are a semi-barbarian people who dominate the plains of southeastern Suilley, an area where the Suilleyn King exerts virtually no real authority and is not widely acknowledged as a king at all. Rather, the Vanigoths have their own king in Aen Vani, a town in the eastern part of the Wilderland Hills. See, **The Lost Lands: Borderland Provinces**, Chapter 9: *Kingdom of Suilley*. Aen Vani is located in the south of the Vanigoth realm, and the farther north one goes, the less loyal are the Vanigothic nobles to their nominal king.

Most of the action takes place in the middle of the Vanigoth territory, roughly 100 miles north of Aen Vani itself, where the barbarian moot called the "Crucible of Blood" musters itself, the first crucible of the adventure's title. The player characters must race against time and piece out clues to a puzzle, all while being the tenuous guests of hundreds of the most dangerous mortal humans in all the Borderlands.

Adventure Background

To the civilized men and women of Suilley, Keston, and Exeter, the name of the Vanigoth people is a familiar and often bone-chilling one. It was only 10 years ago that the Wilderlands Clan War wreaked havoc across Keston Province, and that memory is fresh in the minds of both the civilized locals and the barbarians who retreated back into the hills to lick their wounds at war's end — so fresh, in fact, that today those collective tribes are on the precipice of allowing from within their ranks a new incursion so devastating that it could not help but be the first salvo in an all-out war between the Vanigoths and the Kingdom of Suilley.

It all comes down to what transpires at the Crucible of Blood.

The Crucible

As a people, the Vanigoth have ever been divided between Highland Vanigoths and Lowland Vanigoths, although all Vanigoths have, at times through their long history, bent the knee (however nominally) to a single "overking" of their own. After a decade of rebuilding, and of increasing levels of infighting about the future, the lowland nobles seek to re-institute an event they haven't observed in centuries: a seven-day gathering of tribes called the Crucible of Blood. During this extended moot, the barbarians engage in all manner of contests alongside more traditional feasts and politicking, all leading to the answering of some important question or establishment of a new order. In this case, they aim to elect one of their most powerful Rohalacs (hereditary chieftains) to the ancient title of the "Warhalac," a warlord independent of the King, with the authority to command Vanigothic warriors from many tribes as the army for a specific war. All Vanigoths present at the Crucible are pledged to follow the elected Warhalac.

The election of a Warhalac would be a bad outcome for two quite different groups of people: the Kingdom of Suilley, and the Highland Vanigoths. For the Kingdom of Suilley, it would mean war within its southeastern borders, an expensive proposition that could conceivably bankrupt the Suilleyn king and topple his rule. For the Highland Vanigoths, the election of a Lowland Warhalac would represent a direct challenge to the King in Aen Vani, currently Saldevic II, a Highland Vanigoth.

Historically the election of a Warhalac often precedes the removal of the King and his replacement by the Warhalac. Thus, if the Vanigoths elect a Warhalac, the entire area north of the Wilderland Hills could erupt in simultaneous wars: civil war among the Vanigoths, and a territorial war with the Kingdom of Suilley.

Not all the local tribes respond to the call for moot — a few find it overly defiant of their ostensible king. Most of them choose to participate, however, for they all want a say in how the collective future of the Lowland Vanigoths will unfold.

This massive social event is the theater and backdrop for much of the action in this adventure.

The Outsider Chieftains

Beyond the motives of the barbarian tribes, but intimately connected to their activities, two other chieftains (of a sort) have turned their schemes toward the Crucible of Blood.

One of these is Fortress-Commander Sir Oessum Keenblade (EE-sum). Sir Oessum is the commanding officer of Stronghold Hjerrin (JAYR-in), the great Suilleyn border-fortress in the eastern Lorremach. Through various informants, Sir Oessum knows the Crucible has been declared, and desperately wants to get someone inside it to see what the barbarian tribes are up to, and what they might decide regarding an incursion into Suilley. For this reason, he puts into motion a plan that carries his will into the Crucible — on the backs of the characters.

The other chieftain is an oni named Zemicek, and he is the pure villain of the piece. Addled in service to the demon prince Fraz-Urb'luu and plagued by delusions of grandeur, Zemicek is trying to use one of the three top candidates for the crown of Rohalac to demolish an entire barony and kick off another war between civilized men and an allied army of furious Vanigoths, ogres, and ogrillons (half-ogres), led by himself. See below for more on Zemicek and the Cauldron of Dreams.

Adventure Synopsis

While traveling in the southeastern part of the Kingdom of Suilley (probably on the Traders Way), the characters come upon a grisly scene: a merchant caravan attacked and pillaged on the road, with dozens butchered and a priestess of Freya missing from amongst the dead. After the local authorities call upon the party for help, the characters head north into the mountains to effectively "crash" the most significant barbarian socio-political event in decades. While a guest of the Vanigoths, the party observes and even participates in various games of skill, sport, and chance, all while trying to figure out what is really going on at the event and hopefully locate the missing priestess.

While the Crucible is under way, the three leaders involved are all making their own moves, culminating in the murder of the Shadowguard spy who accompanied the party. With the Cs' help, the tide of barbarian favor is hopefully turned against Zemicek's traitorous ally, who is forced to quit the event and ride with what remains of his men for safety.

Zemicek's scheme is his trump card in the game of war. By sacrificing to Fraz-Urb'luu's earthly stain a priestess who was true in her faith, but deceived into offering prayers to (and receiving blessings from) a false god, and by doing it right in the moment of her revelation and horror, Zemicek will empower all those who carry his standard — his army of demonically empowered tribes — and the Kingdom of Suilley will be in a fight for its life. Only by stopping Zemicek and his allied barbarians can the characters hope to forestall another full-on war like the Wilderlands War 10 years ago — this time aimed directly at the kingdom.

50

Caerboar Hall

Caerboar Hall is a fortified manor house located at the very southeastern tip of the Kingdom of Suilley, nestled in the intersection of the Forlorn Mountains and the Wilderland Hills — an area riven with deep, forested canyons and honeycombed with extensive caverns. Characters whose players can make relevant checks might recall or discover the following information about it:

DC 12: An ancient ranger bloodline built a fortified manor house a hundred or more years ago on the site of a ruined Hyperborean fort, and managed to clear out a small fiefdom, forcing numerous beasts and monsters into the mountains and hills.

DC 15: Since that time, a hamlet of a few families has clustered around the manor, gaining protection from the region's fell beasts, since members of the isolated family owning the manor are considered to be brutal, murderous foes in battle.

DC 18: The Bristleback family only has three or four of their "bloodline" rangers in residence at any given time, but the place is considered a refuge for traveling rangers and other wayfarers of honest intent. The Vanigoths consider the Bristleback rangers to be dangerous foreigners in their territory, a nest of wasps. On more than one occasion, the Bristlebacks have interfered with the actions of Vanigoth Chieftains, and this has usually led to the death of the Chieftain, not in nice ways. It is impressive that the Vanigoths consider the Bristlebacks to be unusually savage and brutal, since Vanigoth standards for savagery and brutality are really quite high.

Adventure Hooks

One can get the characters into the adventure via a number of means. Consider the following as possible ways of slotting the party into the story.

Family Matters

One of only two survivors of the wreck of Paster Sturgess' caravan is a tragically misled woman of faith named Matilder (female human **commoner**). When they hit the caravan, Zemicek's men kidnapped her and took her from the scene (after leaving the evidence just as Zemicek wanted it to appear). Depending on the make-up and specific circumstances of the party, it may work better to have a local relative of Matilder's — her father Fergus (male human **commoner**) — entreat the characters for help in finding her, and if possible, bringing her (or her body) back home. Fergus doesn't have much money, but he can offer the party 200gp (his life's savings) for the safe return of whatever remains of his beloved daughter.

Paid Patrols

The characters may already be part of the Fortress-Commander's plans for the security of the southeastern border marches. The Kingdom's forces are spread too thinly in this area, and the Stronghold has leave from the crown to offer modest sums to bands of proven adventurers, provided they operate with discretion and are unlikely to stain the military reputation of the Kingdom. Most of these jobs are informal, and in most cases involve little more than the Stronghold providing a tip to a local adventuring party as to where a particular problem or problem area might reside, and providing notice that anyone who resolves the problem or clears out that particular area will be paid a reward.

Serendipitous Concurrence

The simplest way to involve the characters is to have them come upon the scene of the wrecked caravan in the natural course of whatever business brought them to or through this part of Suilley. In this event, they'll have just enough time to survey the wreckage for themselves before any Suilleyn authority arrives and reluctantly takes charge. The GM could certainly combine this hook with either of the other two; in one case Matilder's father would entreat the characters after they've found the wreckage (or do so upon arriving on scene with the soldiers, perhaps), and in the other case the party would come upon the scene in the course of their regular patrol duties. Either way, the adventure truly begins at the scene of a horrible crime.

The Wreck of Paster Sturgess

The characters are traveling on the Trader's Way, arriving at the rocky ground where the road enters (or leaves, depending on the direction of their travels) the northern side of the Wilderland Hills. The ground here is not infertile, but it is rocky and uneven. The road, which is in extremely poor repair here, runs roughly north to south into the hills. Travel is slow, for the stone-paved road is broken in some places, and uneven in many as it makes the steep ascent toward the hills.

The horses huff their way to the crest of yet another climb, but rather than pick up speed for leveling off, they suddenly whinny and snort to an unexpected stop. Scattered before them and you, filling your field of view, is a visual lesson in why people are nervous about traveling far from their homes in this area.

Ahead of you the road winds downward and cuts sharply to the west, around a steep rock face in the terrain, ascending again as it bends out of sight. Everything between here and there... is a blood-soaked abattoir.

Among the overturned wrecks of three caravan wagons lie the remains of at least two dozen people and animals. Mangled bodies poke out from holes in canvas, or from beneath other mangled bodies; some of them, seemingly whole at first glance, reveal themselves now to be little more than collections of torsos and heads, their lost limbs scattered about the area. And rising up behind it all, that bare rock face — now so spattered with gore as to resemble the artistic ravings of a madman.

At the head of the doomed caravan, slumped over his fallen horse, rots the figure of a man you assume to be the caravan master. One drooping hand holds a blade, its tip a jagged break in the steel, and his other hand is gone entirely. A lone black crow stands perched atop his head, eyeing you with an inky disregard, a trail of glistening sinew dangling from its beak.

Characters who make relevant checks might discover the following information:

DC 10: The caravan was obviously ambushed from both above and behind in a brutally effective lightning attack. The deceased were killed by way of direct physical damage; cuts and blows.

DC 12: The caravan master and all the caravan attendants are present and accounted for (if perforated badly), but the merchants in the log are missing, as well as the priestess of Freya.

DC 14: Paster Sturgess himself put up one hell of a fight, clearly wounding or killing at least one attacker, as did Peraulto Vaen. No attackers' bodies remain at the scene, however.

DC 16: All the bodies present are missing their tongues. Attempts to use

---

The Caravan of Paster Sturgess

Contingent:
- Caravan Master Paster Sturgess (male human)
- 3 wagons, 6 oxen, 1 yak-beast
- 3 dogs
- 6 cavalry (non-military), 6 warhorses
- 3 teamsters
- 3 archers
- 3 merchants (gone, but noted in manifest): Bromley Fitzhubert (male human), Gillia Tenberry (female human), Peraulto Vaen (male human)
- 1 guest (gone, but noted in manifest): Matilder the Fair (female human)

Cargo (gone, but noted in manifest): 1 wagon of hazelnuts (500gp), 1 wagon of cloth tapestries (2000gp), half-wagon of cheap spices (700gp), half-wagon of leather shoes (500gp).

Coin Box (gone, but noted in Sturgess' logbook): 316gp in coins of various denominations.

---

speak with dead or the like on any of the deceased fail, regardless of roll or power. "Contact" appears successful, but it registers to the spellcaster/user as though the dead simply have nothing to say.

DC 18: Among the wreckage is an idol of St. Hildemar, a saint revered by the clergy of Freya.

DC 20: Although a number of loosed arrows pepper the area, they all flew from the dead men. (GM's note: The assailants used javelins, just as the Vanigoth do, but removed them all from the scene.)

Any character who thinks to scrape off the paint on the idol discovers a second face underneath — one that looks a lot less like St. Hildemar and a lot more like a leering imp or gremlin-thing. Unless that character has specific prior experience with the cult of Fraz-Urb'luu in the region, thinking to do such a random thing should be a DC 20 check in itself, at the very easiest.

The Strategos' Offer

At this juncture Fortress-Captain Sir Kenan Parnordh (male human **Clr7** of Vanitthu). Kenan is the captain of a survey patrol from Stronghold Hjerrin, tasked to evaluate the defenses of the few castles along the edge of the Lorremach Highhills and make recommendations to the Fortress-Commander. Kenan arrives on the scene with his escort, about 2 dozen elite soldiers (male and female human **Ftr3**). How exactly to play this out depends on which set-up the GM decided to go with:

If the characters were hired by Matilder's father to find her, then they have just received confirmation that she's been taken by some marauding band when the Fortress-Captain arrives. If they were already hired by the crown, or by Stronghold Hjerrin to perform some service, then this is where they debrief and where the Fortress-Captain offers them a new assignment on behalf of Sir Oessum, the Fortress-Commander of Hjerrin Stronghold. If they happened upon the scene by coincidence, he will see their appearance for the opportunity it is, and proceed accordingly. (While there's room for a brief misunderstanding, it's clear to any professional military officer that the characters aren't responsible for the carnage.)

Sir Kenan is a severe-looking man, not too tall, but powerfully broad across the middle, dressed in breastplate armor with tabards of the Kingdom of Suilley affixed to the front and back, quartered with a tower (the symbol of Hjerrin's forces). Whether he's met the characters before or not, the terms of his situation and offer remain the same and are as follows:

- To his eyes and mind, this attack is pretty clearly the work of the Vanigoths, who had been known in decades past for just this sort of raid: The use of terrain, the wanton killing of both man and beast, the pillaging of all coin and cargo... all hallmarks of a Vanigoth raid. A Vanigoth raid this far to the west is unusual, but becoming more common recently.

• He needs a group of independent agents — capable people, but not soldiers or anyone else who can be traced back to Suilley — to provide cover for a lone spy to get inside the most important Vanigoth tribal event in years: The Crucible of Blood, a great moot established in a temporary camp-town deep in the "Kingdom" of the Vanigoths.

• The primary purpose in this mission is to determine what the Vanigoths are up to and what their plans for troublemaking are. It would also be nice to find out who raided the caravan, and where the missing merchants are.

• The Fortress-Captain has the key any such operatives will require to participate in a Vanigothic moot: An actual Vanigoth expatriate who knows the location of the event. The cover story he suggests is that the characters rescued this man from the evils of a Suilleyn baron, and that he now owes them a blood debt for saving him and returning him to his people. Sir Kenan knows the Vanigoths always honor a blood debt and will give the characters safe passage on those grounds.

• If they agree, Sir Kenan will give each of them 500gp and a letter of marque from Stronghold Hjerrin. It will also likely result in additional work from the Stronghold if the characters decide to remain in that area. In addition, the Fortress-Captain assures them they're free to keep just about anything else they find.

Note: While this isn't an issue if the GM chose the adventure hook in which the party is already working on Suilley's behalf, it otherwise might seem a bit off that Sir Kenan is so ready to trust the characters, and to hire them for such an important mission. The fact of the matter is that Sir Kenan, a devout follower of Vanitthu, god of guardians, has been riding directly toward the characters for the last two days, following a series of minor omens and divine guidances toward the only group nearby that could feasibly complete the mission. He already suspects that he is being guided toward the people he needs, and unless the characters demonstrate unreliable or vicious personalities, he will have no concerns about putting the mission into their hands. He has already encountered and recruited Halvor, and now he has the other half of the expedition standing in front of him. There definitely isn't a surplus of adventurers of the party's level just walking around ready to be hired.

Other Party Members

Accompanying the characters to the Crucible are the aforementioned Shadowguard agent, Evienne, and their Vanigoth guide, Halvor.

The slender, raven-haired woman the adventurers know as "Evienne" was born Raula Piyette in a small hillside village about 10 miles from Caerboar Hall. The Vanigoth and their allies wiped out half her family during the rampages of the Wilderlands Clan War, and she has since dedicated herself to serving the Kingdom of Suilley as a member of the country's secretive "Shadowguards." "Evienne" has worked very hard simply for the opportunity to put her own life in great jeopardy, but she wouldn't trade it for the world. Nothing is more important than making sure that no one else suffers as she did at the hands of savages.

Evienne, the Shadowguard: AC 14; HP 33 (6d8+6); **Spd** 30ft; **Melee** shortsword (+5, 1d6+3 piercing); **SA** cunning action (dash, disengage, or hide as bonus), multiattack (shortsword x2), sneak attack (1/turn, 2d6 damage); **Ranged** hand crossbow (+5, 30ft/120ft, 1d6+3 piercing); **Str** +0, **Dex** +3, **Con** +1, **Int** +2, **Wis** +2, **Cha** +3; **Skills** Deception +5, Investigation +5, Persuasion +5, Sleight of Hand +5, Stealth +5; **AL** N; **CR** 1; **XP** 200.
    Equipment: leather armor, shortsword, hand crossbow, 30 bolts, backpack, thieves' tools

The party's only hope for winning entrance to the otherwise private event that is the Crucible of Blood resides in the personage of a traitor. Halvor is a Vanigoth himself, but one who no longer wants to live the life of a highland barbarian. While looking for work in Pfefferain, the local authorities picked him up on a minor offense and upon discovering his heritage, delivered him to Sir Kenan, who was already on his way to the town, following his trail of divine hints. Halvor's news of the Crucible of Blood immediately led Sir Kenan to communicate by carrier pigeon with his commander at Stronghold Hjerrin, informing the Fortress-Commander of the developments in the Vanigoth region. Although Sir

Kenan didn't really grasp the significance of the news, Sir Oessum, the Fortress-Commander, did. A fast-courier rode from the Stronghold to Pfefferain with new orders for Sir Kenan: to make an offer to Halvor, and to assemble a group of capable veterans to accompany. If Halvor can get these adventurers into the Crucible and back, the Fortress-Commander will grant him amnesty for past offenses, citizenship rights within the kingdom, and honest work in Pfefferain. All the red-headed warrior wants is a fresh start, and he's willing to take a very big risk to get it.

Halvor, the Expatriate: AC 14; HP 67 (9d8+27); **Spd** 30ft; **Melee** greataxe (+5, 1d12+3 slashing); **Ranged** javelin (+3, 30ft/120ft, 1d6+3 piercing); **Str** +3, **Dex** +1, **Con** +3, **Int** +1, **Wis** +1, **Cha** +0; **Traits** reckless (gain tactical advantage on melee during turn, but any attack suffered has tactical advantage until start of next turn), unarmored defense; **AL** CG; **CR** 2; **XP** 450.
    Equipment: greataxe, 4 javelins.

Aen Fathorr

(Een FAH-thor)

After days of hard traveling with your two new companions, you push through the last fringes of a massive copse of trees and see the landscape open up before you. Spread out across acres of relatively flat land is a massive camptown surrounded in a wooden log wall. Smoke drifts up in lazily climbing spirals here and there across the camp, and the sounds of rough men shouting, sparring, and working fill the air.

A single modest path, little more than a worn-out stretch of grass, winds its way from the nearest scrabble roadway towards an ad-hoc wooden gate in the side of the log wall. At relatively even intervals, pairs of spikes driven into the earth rise up on either side of the path. Atop each spike is a severed head — some old and all but rotted out, others fresh and red.

This is Aen Fathorr, a Vanigoth town that only exists while the Crucible of Blood is underway. Each time they call for the event, participating tribes send men ahead of the event to build the camptown, making it ready for the arrival of their kinsmen and assembled retinues. The severed heads are a simple but effective warning: KEEP OUT.

Naturally, the characters are supposed to do the very opposite, according to their guide Halvor, who heads directly for the gate. Getting inside shouldn't be very difficult, as Halvor is a proven Vanigoth with the look and ritual scarification to prove it, in addition to a solid story to provide the guards at the gate. Good as their cover story is, however, the guards still order the group to report their arrival to at least one of the Rohalacs in attendance once they are admitted.

This is the party's first chance to meet and encounter Karemoryc, who is the chieftain to whom Halvor presents them (and the most socially gracious, at least outwardly). During this encounter, Karimoryc is the very model of the noble savage, listening intently as Halvor recites his tale and nodding when he gets to the part about the blood debt he owes the characters. Although accommodations in the camptown are meager (the Rohalacs' personal tribes do live a bit better than the rest, in simple log cabins as opposed to just collections of camp tents), Karimoryc sees to it that Halvor finds his closest kinsmen at the event, and that his indebted guests have a place to set up shop for the duration.

This conversation, which occurs in a great, high-beamed wooden hall before the eyes of many assembled barbarian warriors, can play out in whatever manner best suits your campaign. If the characters prefer to simply get on with the adventure, you can breeze through it with the prior description. If they prefer more in-depth roleplaying, feel free to expand it into a prolonged conversation, with many shouted questions and savage threats from the onlookers before their story is accepted, followed by an invitation to feast and drink.

At some point during the conversation, Karimoryc tells them, "Be warned that, as a guest at the Crucible, you are expected to bear witness to the trials and the tests. That means standing alongside us even when we face danger to life and limb, and while the trials are not yours, you may on occasion share in that danger. This is our way, that even our guests must prove their courage. If you cannot accept this, you must leave, blood debt or no!"

What Karimoryc doesn't say, of course, is that he's more than a little worried about the characters' presence, and while he may be outwardly welcoming and polite, adhering to the Vanigothic traditions of debt and hospitality, he's already concocting ways to get these foreigners out of the way before they can interfere with his plans.

The Three Contenders

Once inside the grounds it doesn't take the characters long to discover that although there are more than three Rohalacs in attendance, only three are true contenders for the title that the gathered Vanigoth tribes are obliged to bestow upon one chosen leader at the close of the event. These three Vanigoth leaders are named Idugo, Winvani, and Karimoryc, and are detailed as follows.

Idugo, the Unchained

For some in attendance, Idugo is the presumptive favorite for the prize of regional Rohalac, thanks largely to his renowned prowess as a warrior and his powerful tribal totem (black bear). But others suspect he's not up

---

The Barbarians of Aen Fathorr

Although the characters will find a wide variety of specific traits and abilities among the tribes present for the Crucible, a time might come when the GM requires statistics to serve as exemplary of the broader body of attending barbarians. In such an event, use the following stat block.

Vanigoth Barbarian: AC 14; HP 67 (9d8+27); Spd 30ft; Melee greataxe (+5, 1d12+3 slashing); Ranged javelin (+3, 30ft/120ft, 1d6+3 piercing); Str +3, Dex +1, Con +3, Int −1, Wis +0, Cha −1; Traits reckless (gain tactical advantage on melee during turn, but any attack suffered has tactical advantage until start of next turn), unarmored defense; AL CN; CR 2; XP 450.
Equipment: greataxe, 4 javelins.

---

to such a demanding role, intellectually or socially, as the ogrish blood is strong in him. He stands nearly 7ft in height, and looks like a cross between a bear-pelted berserker and an ogrillon. Zemicek tried to engage Idugo first, using the Cauldron of Dreams (see below) to approach him in his sleep, but Idugo's subconscious rejected the overture and the ogre mage had to move on to other possible foils. Ever since then, Idugo has carried a quiet and unsubstantiated suspicion regarding his rival Karimoryc, and although ideas are not what he's known for, on this one he happens to be dead right.

Idugo: AC 17; HP 142 (15d10+75); Spd 40ft; Melee greataxe (+10, 2d12+9 slashing); Ranged javelin (+10, 30ft/120ft, 1d6+9 piercing); SA multiattack (greataxe x2 or javelin x2); Resist all damage except psychic; Str +6, Dex +2, Con +5, Int +0, Wis +0, Cha −1; Skills Investigation +2, Medicine +2, Nature +4, Perception +4, Religion +2; Traits brute (extra die of damage on melee attacks, included), rage (+3 on Strength-based weapon damage, included), reckless (tactical advantage on all attacks, but all attacks against Idugo have tactical advantage), tactical advantage on initiative, Dex saves and Str checks, unarmored defense; AL CN; CR 9; XP 5000.
Equipment: bear pelt, fur boots, greataxe, 4 javelins.

Winvani, the Unheralded

The second contender for the tribal crown is perhaps the "dark horse" (if there is one), based on the fact that he is the smallest of the three, standing barely 6ft in height, and of the three, probably the weakest warrior in one-on-one combat. What people outside his own family tribe don't realize is that what he lacks in martial size and prowess, he more than makes up for in cunning and focus, and when all is said and done he is the likeliest to end up with the crown. Unlike the other two, Winvani hasn't a drop of ogrish blood in him, which makes him effectively immune to Zemicek's long-distance charms, but he's not a very social or personable man and his effective charisma and leadership among those who don't already know his caliber suffer for it.

Winvani: AC 18; HP 98 (15d8+30); Spd 40ft; Melee scimitar (+10, 1d6+9 slashing); Ranged dagger (+10, 20ft/60ft, 1d4+9 piercing); SA cunning action (dash, disengage, or hide as bonus), multiattack (scimitar x2 or dagger x2), sneak attack (1/turn, 6d6 damage), uncanny dodge (reaction, half damage when hit by attack); Resist bludgeoning, piercing, slashing; Str +2, Dex +6, Con +2, Int +2, Wis +1, Cha +0; Skills Arcana +6, History +6, Insight +3, Religion +6; Traits, dexterous rage (+3 on Dexterity-based weapon damage, included), eagle totem (opportunity attacks against Winvani have tactical disadvantage), evasion, unarmored defense; AL CN; CR 9; XP 5000.
Equipment: stealthy clothes, scimitar, 4 daggers, backpack, thieves' tools

Karimoryc, the Unwary

The final contender is a tragic figure in our story. Although he has just about as much ogrish blood in him as does the bear Idugo, Karimoryc doesn't look the part — and indeed, passes for completely human. He stands over 6ft tall, with broad (but not ogrish) shoulders and deep-set, piercing green eyes. After Zemicek failed to connect with Idugo's blunt and uncooperatively simple subconscious, the ogre mage found much more fertile soil romping around the dreamscape of the already ambitious and frustrated tribal leader Karimoryc. Zemicek has been incredibly cunning and persuasive, convincing Karimoryc in his dreams that this is the right thing not only for him, personally, but for the people who will follow him into battle. Karimoryc is ambitious, yes, but he genuinely feels he's doing the right thing for his tribe. With his secret mentor guiding him, Karimoryc intends to bend the Crucible of Blood to his will, and once he has control over all the gathered tribes, he will order them to battle against the rangers.

Karimoryc: AC 17; HP 98 (13d8+39); Spd 40ft; Melee *+1 battleaxe* (+9, 2d8+9 slashing); Ranged longbow (+4, 150ft/600ft, 1d6+1 piercing); SA multiattack (battleaxe x2 or longbow x2); Resist bludgeoning, piercing, slashing; Str +5, Dex +1, Con +3, Int +1, Wis +1, Cha +2; Skills Investigation +2, Medicine +5, Nature +2, Perception +5, Religion +2; Traits brute (extra die of damage on melee attacks, included), frenzy (Karimoryc makes a battleaxe attack as a bonus action every round until end of combat, but gains a level of exhaustion at combat's end), rage (+3 on Strength-based weapon damage, included), reckless (tactical advantage on all attacks, but all attacks against Karimoryc have advantage), tactical advantage on initiative, Dexterity saves, and Strength checks, unarmored defense; AL CN (E); CR 8; XP 3900.

Equipment: clothes, heavy boots, *+1 battleaxe*, *+1 shield*, longbow, 20 arrows.

Although the characters arrive in the afternoon of the second day of the event, for clarity's sake this adventure will reckon things from their perspective from here on out, starting with "Day One."

Day One

Although they have been welcomed as guests, not everyone is thrilled to see outsiders present during the Crucible. A number of the Vanigoth give the characters the stink-eye throughout the evening and the following morning. Insults are thrown and the characters may, at your discretion, find themselves involved in a brawl or two. Winvani doesn't appear to care much that the characters are here, but Idugo angrily berates Halvor for bringing them, and takes every opportunity to snarl at the party, reminding them that they're here only on their hosts' sufferance and had better not make a nuisance of themselves.

On the morning of day one, the characters emerge from their guest huts to find the Vanigoth already engaged in all manner of contests of strength. While the competition between the three chieftains is obviously paramount, other members of the tribes are also engaged in various games and rivalries. Here, a pair of burly warriors wrestle with violent abandon, each attempting to pin the other. Over there, two teams of Vanigoth youths engage in a tug-of-war — with a flexing, bearded barbarian, his arms outstretched, serving as the rope!

The chieftains themselves are engaged in a caber-toss, each hefting a massive log upright and hurling it as far along a measured field as he can. It's an incredible display of might, with good-sized boles tumbling down-field, accompanied by hefty grunts and savage cries. Everyone's giving their all, but there can be no doubt that Idugo's got the edge in this particular contest.

(Characters cannot compete against the chieftains, but they're welcome to challenge any of the other Vanigoths. Some accept such a challenge in a friendly manner, others are pridefully eager to show up the outsiders, but either way the characters can build up some social currency with a good showing, if they don't mind enduring some rude taunts in the process.)

These, however, are all just prelude to the day's true challenge to come.

The Running of the Boars

At around midmorning, warriors of the tribes begin to gather, preparing to head out. Everyone seems to already know what's going on, but if the characters can find a Vanigoth who's not particularly hostile to them — Halvor, if nobody else — they can get an explanation.

> "We hunt," the barbarian tells you, "but it is more than a hunt. Within the trees roam packs of boar, massive and wild. Each of the Rohalacs and his handpicked companions will run the boars, driving them and pursuing them for many

miles to prove their endurance and hunting prowess. Then and only then will they take the prey in glorious bloodshed, the winner determined by how many boar they bring down, the average size of the beasts, and how far they ran to keep up with their prey.

"Good luck keeping up, my 'civilized' friends!" he adds with a laugh.

What follows is several hours of dirt, sweat, and tears. The characters and their allies are, indeed, expected to keep up with the hunting expedition.

For the first few hours, this involves stalking through the woods, hunting signs of boar. The characters don't need to actually do the tracking, as that is part of the challenge for the chieftains, but they *are* expected not to interfere. Have the party make DC 12 Dex (Stealth) checks (individually or as a group check, as you prefer). On a failure, the characters make enough noise to prolong the hunt, drawing disdainful and hateful comments from Idugo and many of the others.

Eventually, the Vanigoths discover their prey and drive the boars into a dead run with a cacophony of screams, shouts, and the banging of weapons on shields. Everyone, characters included, breaks into a dead run through the forest, the chase punctuated by porcine squeals and snorts.

At this point, each of the characters must make a DC 10 Con check. (If the earlier Stealth check was failed, this Con check is instead DC 12, as the characters are already a bit more tired than the otherwise would be.) Characters who fail this check suffer 1 level of exhaustion at the end of the chase.

As the chase goes on, the Rohalacs and their companions peel off, each pursuing a different group of wild boar, eventually leaving Halvor and the characters on their own in the middle of the woodlands. (If the characters attempt to keep with the last of the three chieftains, Halvor tells them to hang back, that interfering with the actual kill is forbidden.)

> As you finally come to a halt, gasping for air after the seemingly endless run, you realize that your party is one short! At some point during the mad dash, Evienne has vanished — perhaps doubling back to gather intelligence back at Aen Fathorr?

Whether the characters choose to remain where they are or to go back and search for her is irrelevant, for only moments later…

> Your brief silent respite is broken by more shouting, more clashing of metal on metal, starting at a distance but growing steadily nearer. And then that manmade chorus is drowned out by the scream of bestial fury and the thunder of hooves and shattering branches!"

The characters have a single round in which to prepare before a sounder of **6 giant boars** tear out of the forest and charge them.

The boars aren't trying to escape; they've been whipped up into enough of a fury to attack! At least one of the boars makes a beeline for Halvor; the man's no pushover, but if the characters don't help him, it's entirely possible that he'll perish in this encounter.

Giant Boar (6): AC 12; HP 42 (5d10+15); Spd 40ft; Melee tusk (+5, 2d6+3 slashing); SA charge (move 20ft then attack, tusk deals extra 2d6 and target must make DC 13 Str save or fall prone); Str +3, Dex +0, Con +3, Int −4, Wis −2, Cha −3; Traits relentless (1/encounter, if boar takes 10 damage or less than would reduce it 0 hp, it is reduced to 1 hp instead); AL U; CR 2; XP 450.

Halvor, the Expatriate: AC 14; HP 67 (9d8+27); Spd 30ft; Melee greataxe (+5, 1d12+3 slashing); Ranged javelin (+3, 30ft/120ft, 1d6+3 piercing); Str +3, Dex +1, Con +3, Int +1,

Wis +1, **Cha** +0; **Traits** reckless (gain tactical advantage on melee during turn, but any attack suffered has tactical advantage until start of next turn), unarmored defense; **AL** CG; **CR** 2; **XP** 450.

Equipment: greataxe, 4 javelins.

The boars are enraged enough to fight to the death. Once they're dead, allow the characters to attempt a DC 15 Wis (Perception or Survival) check. On a success, the character realizes that the sounds they heard driving the boars — the screams, banging, and so forth — were very specifically moving in this direction. There's no way to say for sure, but it's almost as though someone *deliberately* drove the boars their way!

(Indeed, this was Karimoryc's first attempt at getting them out of the way, though of course they can't know that.)

Celebrating the Hunt

The mood is tense that evening. Everyone has gathered in the main hall to celebrate the end of the hunt and this second day of the Crucible. All attention *should* be on the three chieftains, each of whom made a respectable showing, and particularly on Idugo whose kill count clearly marks him as the day's victor. Instead, however, many of the eyes are upon your own party, the outsiders who slew half a dozen of the giant boar. While some of the Vanigoth look upon you with newfound respect, others are furious at your "interference." That your "hunt" was conducted in self-defense doesn't seem to make a difference in their eyes. Indeed, Rohalac Idugo himself is infuriated, and you're fairly certain that only the quick words of the other chieftains, and several of Idugo's own men, have prevented him from resorting to violence in his anger.

Still, the bulk of the Vanigoths — even those seemingly unhappy with how things turned out — continue to treat you as welcome guests.

After an hour or so of feasting, the three Rohalacs rise and recite the names of the those who fell in battle with the giant boars — including Halvor, if he's dead — and burst into a heavily martial paean to the gods and the spirits of the fallen. It's certainly a loud and heartfelt tribute, if nothing else, and is followed by additional rounds of drinking.

Again, how much or how little you choose to roleplay through this scene is entirely up to you and the needs of the campaign. At some point during the drinking, however, Evienne takes a seat next to one of the characters. (If she's developed a particular friendship with any of them, choose him or her; otherwise, she chooses whichever character has shown the most signs of intelligence and subtlety.)

"While you were out waging war against angry pigs," she says, "I was able to do a bit of asking around. You might be interested to know that things were a bit unfriendly around here even before we stuck our outsider noses into things. The Vanigoth tribes aren't always best buddies, but apparently there's been some particular tension between Idugo and Karimoryc — and it's more than just the competition. Nobody's come out and said it this way, but I get the impression Idugo's been surlier and shorter tempered than usual, which is kind of like saying a vampire's thirstier than usual. I don't know what's behind it all, but let me know if you hear anything relevant, would you?"

The characters are welcome to question her further, but that really is all she's learned. If pressed, though, she'll admit that she's starting to suspect Idugo's tribe of being responsible for the raid on the caravan. It is, however, *just* a suspicion.

Day Two

Again the Vanigoth are awake and active with the rising of the sun, and whether or not the characters *meant* to awaken that early, they most certainly will. This time, the sounds are not of wrestling, hurling, and similar feats of strength, but of hammers, nails, shovels, and logs.

Just beyond Aen Fathorr, a massive project is underway beneath the graying skies and the chilly early morning drizzle. Dozens of men and women, of all the major tribes, seem to be erecting wooden fences across several acres of open field and the sides of several hills. If there's a plan to this construction, it's not immediately obvious; they appear to be forming random rooms, hallways, and courtyards, rather than any particular structure.

The characters can earn a bit more social capital if they offer to help with the manual labor, but otherwise there's nothing for them to do, or really even to see, until midmorning.

War Games

As before, it's not hard for the characters to find someone willing to explain the day's trials. As yesterday was a test of strength, stamina, and personal combat prowess, today is a measure of leadership, teamwork, and tactics. The open chambers and twisting passages of the fencework serve as a battleground and game board, wherein the three Rohalacs will guide their forces toward the achievement of various objectives. One game is simply a variety of "capture the flag," for instance, while another involves moves in careful sequence far more complex than a life-sized version of three-way chess, and a third is simply a grand melee where the winner is the chieftain who has warriors still standing at the end.

The characters, along with the rest of the observers, may stand atop one of the nearby hills, where the bulk of the field is visible to them.

Here, of course, the characters have nothing to do but watch, and for the bulk of the day, that's what they do. (It's possible for one or two characters to slip away at a time, if they have other activities they'd like to attempt, but the party as a whole is expected to remain.)

As the hours pass and this side or that claims a victory, it becomes quite clear that this is a contest between Karimoryc and Winvani. Idugo is no fool, but he simply can't match the quick-thinking and tactical acumen of the other two.

And their tactics are good indeed. For all their barbaric reputation, the Vanigoth are warriors bred, and all three Rohalacs show a solid grasp of how to use the terrain to their advantage, of group formations, and other rudiments of warfare.

And that, of course, is when the characters find themselves involved despite themselves. Fill in the bracket in the text box below with the name of the toughest/strongest-looking character.

You've no warning at all. Between one breath and the next, one of the Vanigoths watching the games alongside you suddenly spins and throws a hard right cross across [character name]'s face!

A **trio of Vanigoths** instigate a brawl with the three most physically oriented characters. It's sudden and violent, but it *is* a brawl, not a genuine melee; no weapons are involved unless the characters draw first, at which point *everyone* nearby dives in to break things up. (And the characters will have lost face in the eyes of every man and woman present.) On the incredibly unlikely chance that the barbarians manage to drop a character to zero hit points, they strike to knock out, not to kill.

You can treat this as a genuine combat if you like, rolling initiative and the works, or you can run through it purely descriptively.

Vanigoth Barbarian: AC 14; HP 67 (9d8+27); **Spd** 30ft; **Melee** greataxe (+5, 1d12+3 slashing); **Ranged** javelin (+3, 30ft/120ft, 1d6+3 piercing); **Str** +3, **Dex** +1, **Con** +3, **Int** −1, **Wis** +0, **Cha** −1; **Traits** reckless (gain tactical advantage on melee during turn, but any attack suffered has tactical advantage until start of next turn), unarmored defense; **AL** CN; **CR** 2; **XP** 450.
Equipment: greataxe, 4 javelins

3 rounds after this brawl begins, Karimoryc and several of his men step out from within the winding fences of the battleground. *"What is this?!"* the Rohalac bellows, is voice cutting through the sound of the fight. "I demand to know what—!"

At which point a team of Idugo's tribesmen also leap from within the fences, falling upon Karimoryc's people and striking them down.

For this was, indeed, a ploy of Idugo's. Outsiders may not be permitted to participate in the war games, but nowhere in the rules of the contest does is specifically state that they cannot be *targeted*. Anticipating that Karimoryc, as the chieftain who first granted the characters their guest status, would break from the game to determine what was going on, Idugo planned this brawl as a tactical diversion. After a great a deal of argument, the consulting of tribal elders, and several more punches thrown, it is determined that Idugo's victory stands. Although he has clearly lost the day, he is awarded this one particular competition.

Celebrating the Games

Despite the results of the grand melee, it was Rohalac Karimoryc who was declared the overall victor, with Winvani a close second: four games to three, with Idugo taking one. The mood at the feast is celebratory, Karimoryc's tribe celebrating their chief's victory, the others content with contests well won. A few remain troubled by the unorthodox involvement of the characters, but as it made no substantial difference in the game's results, most of the Vanigoth have chosen to let it pass.

Most, but not all. Karimoryc himself seems subdued, far less jubilant than his victory should suggest. He eats but little, and avoids any efforts the characters might make to sit with him or speak to him.

In fact, Karimoryc is beginning to panic. Yes, he won, but his margin of victory was razor-thin. Even when they weren't trying to interfere, the characters' presence very nearly cost him. Between that and the suspicions Zamicek is feeding him in his dreams, Karimoryc is growing ever more paranoid about their presence. He retires early that night, ostensibly to prepare for the morrow but in fact to plot over what to do.

Evienne makes no particular effort to speak with the party, and if one of the characters should question her, she tells them simply that she was able to learn nothing new that day — she's learned all she can from casual gossip or light snooping — and is going to have to resort to riskier methods if she's to discover any more useful intelligence.

Day Three

At this point, it should come as no surprise to the characters that the day's activity begins at, or even before, the rising of the sun. What they may find odd, however, is that the three Rohalacs, as well as a great many of the Vanigoth, are already fully ensconced in the feasting hall. Drinks and plates are passed, shouts and roaring laughter fills the air. Other tribesmen and women come and go, but the chieftains remain — sometimes seated, sometimes making the rounds of the crowd, but never departing. The characters are welcomed to join, to observe, to eat and drink their fill. It certainly appears, initially, as though the day is one of revelry rather than competition.

Wit and Wariness

As the characters observe, however, they'll slowly begin to pick up on an ongoing pattern. The tone of the conversations may be friendly and jovial, at least to start with, but the content certainly isn't. The Rohalacs are constantly commenting on the past histories of the people to whom they speak — prior successes, prior failures, even parentage and families. These frequently turn into taunts and insults, stinging observations on shameful anecdotes. The other Vanigoth, in turn, send verbal barbs back at the chieftains to whom they normally show such respect, accusations and insults that the three candidates parry and riposte with further jabs.

It finally dawns on you precisely what's happening here. Every comment, every insult, requires that Kureth, Winvani, or Idugo display not only knowledge of the personal history of the Vanigoth they're addressing, but also a sense of what sorts of observations will get under his or her skin. Especially considering that they aren't limiting their verbal barbs to their own tribesmen, but to warriors of the other tribes as well, it's a startling display of awareness and social acumen.

The contest — for you can see, now, that this is exactly what it is — goes far beyond even that. The Rohalacs also have to address the failures and defeats they reference, explaining (in the form of bragging or taunting) how they or their own people might have done better, *and* they must prove quick-witted enough to defend against the accusations, and the knowledge of their own past failures, that are thrown their way in turn. Every Vanigoth who enters the hall, replacing one who has departed, presents both a new target and a new potential social threat. It's an almost dizzying display of social maneuvering, broad knowledge of the Vanigoth nation, and clashing wits.

Of course, these are Vanigoth, and even in this test of social and mental acumen, physical prowess has a part to play. Now and again — perhaps driven by a particularly brutal insult, or possibly simply as part of the test — one of the feasters moves to attack this Rohalac or that, swinging a fist or occasionally a wooden flagon. In every case, the assault ends as soon as its target reacts, whether by avoiding the blow or striking down his attacker, but you've no doubt that the speed of the response, and the chieftain's ability to sense the danger, also factors into the contest results.

It is, in its own way, the most fascinating of the trials you've witnessed during your time in the Crucible.

The Rohalacs are, of course, not expected to spend *every* waking moment engaged in this social melee. Every now and again one of the three leaves the hall for a few moments to rest his voice, relieve himself, or handle a question of government. (They *are* the leaders of their tribes, after all.) No rules limit the amount of time a chieftain can be absent; he simply loses any opportunity to increase his standing in the trials while he's away.

Characters who spend the bulk of the day observing this trial learn a great deal about the Vanigoth, particularly tribal and personal histories. They gain a permanent +1 bonus to any future Intelligence (History) checks that involve the Vanigoth tribes.

Over the course of the day, it becomes apparent that Winvani's going to come out ahead on this one. His shrewd mind and quick wits eclipse Igudo almost immediately, and even Karimoryc seems unable to keep up with him. As the hours pass, Karimoryc grows more and more sullen, a reaction obvious even to observers — such as the characters — who don't know him well.

What the characters cannot yet know is that a slow panic is starting to set in. Karimoryc's certainty has been badly shaken; he's starting to face up to the very real possibility that he won't be selected to lead the assembled Vanigoth tribes.

Which is why, when he's briefly pulled from the hall that evening and informed that one of the outsiders was caught snooping around his personal hut, his panic flares and he reacts with brutal violence.

Gruesome Discoveries

When the characters return to their guest quarters that night, Evienne is nowhere to be found. Of course, she's often out doing her own thing, so don't bring this up unless the characters ask. If they do, they're welcome to go out searching for her, in which case they'll locate her in the dark, early hours of the morning.

If they *don't* go out searching, they are instead awakened a few hours after midnight by one of the Vanigoth, who claims he was sent to fetch them and demands they accompany him.

In either event, read the following.

Even the dim light of the cloud-smeared moon and stars cannot cloak the horror of the sight before you. In the grasses beyond the edge of town, among the fences that haven't yet been taken down, lies the crumpled body of your missing companion. Several large stab wounds mar Evienne's body, but far more disturbing is the drying blood that cakes the skin around her gaping — and empty — mouth. Her tongue is gone, apparently torn out at the root!

Depending on who discovered the body, some of the Vanigoth may already be assembling here when the characters arrive; otherwise, they start to do so not long after the party discovers Evienne's body. In either case, all three chieftains show up soon after. Following a quick flurry of questions and demands, the Rohalacs promise that they will begin asking around among their tribesmen, trying to figure out who murdered their guest — and that once the moot is concluded, they will make that investigation their priority, though until then, they still have other duties that will occupy much of their time. (Even Idugo seems furious at this violation of hospitality, though he still isn't particularly friendly or sympathetic toward the outsiders.) The characters are welcome to ask questions in the interim, but they haven't the right to subject anyone to full-on interrogation, magical examination, or the like. Karimoryc suggests that the characters return to their quarters and get a good night's sleep — perhaps setting watch to ensure that none of them suffer the same fate.

Players Are Stubborn

It's possible that the players decide not to return to their quarters, but to investigate through the remainder of the night. If so, the Vanigoth object to being awakened (or kept from their beds), but under the circumstances are willing to answer a basic array of questions. All of them, however, express ignorance as to what happened or who is responsible. Any attempts at spellcasting or in-depth interrogation without one of the chieftains present are met with hostility.

If the characters don't go to sleep, they can't awaken to discover that Karimoryc and many of his warriors have left. In that case, feel free to let them witness the Rohalac and his men riding off, along with some of the other Vanigoth.

If they attempt to pursue, half a dozen to a dozen of Karimoryc's men attack them, seeking to buy time for their chief to make his exit. If nothing else, this should keep the characters from leaving long enough for Idugo and Winvani to be awakened and to demand answers and discussion from the characters as they try to determine what's just happened. At this point, continue with "Day Four" as written.

Day Four

The penultimate day of a Crucible of Blood is supposed to be the day when the important decision (in this case, the establishment of a new regional Rohalac) is brought to order and voted upon. This done, the Vanigoth will hold a massive evening celebration called the "Mootfeast" to officially ring in the new order; in this case a giant barbarian party in the new Rohalac's honor.

That is what's *supposed* to happen on the penultimate day of the event.

Instead, everyone wakes up to find Karimoryc and all the warriors he could muster gone from camp; those who saw them depart report that they were headed east. He knows he has overplayed his hand, and in so doing, lost his bid to win the title of Rohalac legitimately (he is behind even Idugo at this point in the proceedings). One final dream consult with Zemicek has convinced him that the only thing he can do is take his men and ride hard for Caerboar Hall and Zemicek's cavern complex, nearby. Karimoryc knows that once the ogre mage's latest ritual sacrifice is complete, and the rangers are no more, and the Hall is theirs… well, it won't matter who the gathered tribes have declared as their new regional Rohalac.

He's going to take it all.

Without the additional men Karimoryc would have had at his command had he won the title himself, the battle is going to be that much harder, but he's convinced that his is a life of destiny and that together with the help of Zemicek's forces and magics, they can only prevail over the rangers.

And if the characters don't find out what's happening and convince the remaining barbarian tribes to ride out against their own cousins, they almost certainly will.

The Ogreblood's Tale

Since it's highly unlikely that a player character has learned what's been going on in Karimoryc's private dreamspace by now, there's really only one way to reliably confirm for the characters not only what's really been happening the whole time, but also where Karimoryc and his men have just gone:

Idugo.

Outside of Karimoryc's own kin, one of the only people in the world who knows about Karimoryc's ogrish blood is Idugo. In addition, Karimoryc wasn't the first ogre-blooded chieftain Zemicek "approached" in his sleep. Idugo was. And during those brief exchanges, before Zemicek gave up and moved on to Karimoryc, Idugo learned a great deal more than the ogre mage realizes.

If and when the characters think to ask Idugo about Karimoryc's loyalties or whereabouts, he will demur if questioned directly. (He still doesn't like or trust them.) If they convince Winvani to approach Idugo, however, that will prove much more successful, as Idugo certainly trusts and respects his fellow tribal chieftain (*even if he is a little small for a Vanigoth leader*, thinks Idugo).

Getting information from the slow, ornery, and not remotely talkative (and likely hungover) Idugo is difficult, but with Winvani's help, the collected group can get the following out of him. (It's not required, but if the GM wants to call for relevant social skill checks during this process, these pieces of information can be offered up as results of those same rolls.)

DC 10: Some sinister force came to Idugo in dreams some time ago, entreating him to bring glory and honor to his people, who have lived in shame lo these many years since the battle at Broch Tarna which ended the Wilderlands Clan War. This being seemed to speak directly to his blood, and did indeed stir his passion to raise the Vanigoth.

DC 12: Being "no fool" (his words), Idugo pressed this being for a sense of what he wanted to conspire to accomplish, specifically. The being responded by showing him a momentary image of a citadel in a valley between two mountains, and whispering the words, "It begins here."

DC 14: During their second dreamtime exchange, Idugo asked the being how it intended to help the Vanigoth beyond selecting targets for them that might be considered militarily problematic. The being pointed out their connection as proof of its power, and further offered to help Idugo claim the title of regional Rohalac, which would put numerous additional tribes at his command.

DC 16: He wasn't being testy with Karimoryc just because they were rivals for the title of Rohalac. Once his own dreamtime visitations ceased, he started to wonder if maybe Karimoryc hadn't also been approached. (He never saw anything that could be construed as proof, but he has strong gut feelings.)

DC 18: During their final dreamtime exchange, Idugo challenged the being to tell him how it could help the Vanigoth ride to victory over the men of the plains when they failed years before. The being whispered, "Just as your kin will rally to your bloody banner, so too will mine rally to mine. Together, we shall all ride out from the mountains like an avalanche of human suffering." At this, Idugo stole a brief glimpse of a wind-scarred cliff face, a yawning opening in its side. The look of the rock was very similar to that which he saw framing the citadel in his vision.

All of this, together with the fact that Karimoryc and his men all rode east, which is the direction of Caerboar Hall, should be enough to clue the characters in on what's about to happen.

For his part, Idugo is finished with Karimoryc, believing him a fool. ("If he wants to go throw himself at Caerboar, let him. He'll be a dead man.") He is therefore stridently against any intervention in Karimoryc's plan, as he believes it will have no blowback on him or his people; indeed, he thinks the only way to avoid guilt by association is to stay out of it entirely, and let Karimoryc and his tribe take the blame.

No one but Karimoryc knows of Zemicek's plans for his latest ritual, which makes the prospect of heeding Idugo's advice that much more perilous. Thankfully, Winvani doesn't need to know that extra bit of bad news to know that his people stand the best chance of coming out of this unscathed and uninvaded by kingdom forces if they ride out and actively stand with the rangers of Caerboar. Winvani is worried that Stronghold Hjerrin will use the incident to martial a wider-scale assault on the Vanigoths from the Kingdom of Suilley, and he's likely right. And it doesn't hurt that Winvani is both enraged at Karimoryc and eager to prove himself in battle — the final remaining test for him as a worthy regional Rohalac.

Caverns Forlorn

Just as Idugo described it, there's a mountain with a wind-swept cliff face not too far from the valley where Caerboar Hall lies. During the ride from Aen Fathorr to the valley, Winvani suggests the following plan of action:

Winvani and his men will ride on to Caerboar Hall, catching the traitorous Karimoryc and his men in a pincer and forcing them to fight a war on two fronts against the Hall's defenses *and* their kin. Meanwhile, the adventurers will make their way to the cavern complex of which Idugo spoke, hoping to rid Karimoryc of whatever arcane assistance/malady has been driving his ambition the whole time. If both groups are successful, the threat will be ended and Caerboar Hall will remain secure.

1. Sinister Adit

The ascent to the entrance to Zemicek's cavern complex isn't too difficult, especially for those who have any climbing gear whatsoever. The closer they get to the mouth of the cave opening, however, the more ill at ease they'll feel — especially characters of pronounced faith (e.g., clerics, paladins, monks, druids). There's no particular feel or flavor to this unease ("Hey, what smells like demon?"), but that only serves to make them more uneasy. Once they get within a few yards, it becomes clear that the adit appears as a leering face, the opening like a gaping mouth twisted into a grimace by the shape and weight of the surrounding stone. The characters have never seen anything like it, and each one who passes through this otherwise unguarded and untrapped opening must make a DC 14 Wis save (characters of pronounced faith suffer a –1 penalty to their roll.) Failure imposes a –1 penalty to all attack rolls and saving throws for as long as that character remains within. Receiving a *remove curse* spell will alleviate this effect.

2. The Forlorn Doormen

This yawning cavern represents the inner sanctum's first line of defense. It contains a **pair of cyclopes** — the first of many, if Zemicek has anything to say about it — who were drawn to the ogre-mage's growing court after the latter sacrificed his own eye to the Cauldron of Dreams. The giant-kin's names are Othu and Urral, and they are loyal on a level that most intelligent beings could never even comprehend.

Othu and Urral are pledged to the defense of the chamber at the entrance of which they stand guard, and intruders will descend that tunneled stair only and literally over their dead bodies.

Cyclops (2): AC 14; HP 138 (12d12+60); **Spd** 30ft; **Melee** greatclub (+9, 10ft., 3d8+6 bludgeoning); **Ranged** rocks

(+9, 30ft/120ft, 4d10+6 bludgeoning); **SA** multiattack (greatclub x2); **Str** +6, **Dex** +0, **Con** +5, **Int** −1, **Wis** −2, **Cha** +0; **Senses** poor depth perception (tactical disadvantage on ranged attacks beyond 30ft); **AL** CN; **CR** 6; **XP** 2,300. **Equipment:** greatclub, 3 big rocks.

3. Grim Larder

Spinning off from the darkened tunnel is a chamber better left unseen by human eyes. This is where Zemicek and his ogre-blooded men deposit their various non-monetary winnings from raids and the like. Inside the cavern floor is slick and sticky. Organized into loose sections composed largely of piles are the remnants of the cargo from Paster Sturgess' caravan (now mostly ruined or eaten), as well as whatever food has yet to be eaten, but which isn't kept in **Area 5: Animal pens**. In this case, that means the remnants of two of the caravan's merchants: Gillia Tenberry and Peraulto Vaen. The former is dead, but still largely coherent in form; her body rests on a cold stone slab, for better keeping until her killers can cut it up into sections for meals. Of the latter, however, there isn't much left. They've already started in on him, and what remains of Peraulto Vaen (head, one limb, lower torso) has been stuffed haphazardly into a wooden barrel in the corner. Characters who run in this room must make DC 12 Dex saves or fall prone.

4. Oubliette (not shown on map)

In addition to being dank and dark, this cavern does not smell good. In fact, it's pretty wretched. The cavern floor is slick with who-knows-what, making footing difficult. Characters who move faster than a slow walk must make DC 12 Dex saves or fall prone.

At the far end of the chamber, set into the cavern floor with a groove for run-off, is a roughly 15ft radius shallow grave for those unfortunate enough to meet their ends at the hands of Zemicek and his hungry kin. This grim collection of human bone, blood, viscera, and effluvia includes the bloated remains of those the ogre mage drowned or otherwise gave up in offering to the Cauldron of Dreams (see below) — bodies fished out, their purpose served, and dumped here thereafter.

Literally inside and amongst the remains are **4 insect swarms**. Fattened on the tainted flesh and blood of those claimed by the Cauldron, these swarms are also considered **fiendtouched**. Those disturbing the remains in any way get swarmed, as a flood of locusts and a carpet of poisonous centipedes emerges to embrace them, and the same thing happens if anyone fails a Dexterity save and falls anywhere in the chamber.

Two of the swarms are locust swarms (a new swarm variant) and two are centipede swarms. Each swarm has the statistics listed in addition to its own insect type-specific characteristics. (For more on the Fiendtouched template, see sidebar.)

Fiendtouched Insect Swarm (4): AC 12; HP 138 (12d12+60); **Spd** 30ft; **Melee** bite (+3, one target in swarm's space, 4d4 piercing [2d4 if swarm has fewer than half hit points]); **Resistance** bludgeoning, fire, piercing, slashing; **Immune** charm, fright, paralysis, petrify, poison, prone, restraint, stun; **Str** −4, **Dex** +1, **Con** +0, **Int** −5, **Wis** −2, **Cha** −5; **Senses** blindsight 10ft., darkvision 120ft; **Traits** fiendish adaptation (see sidebar), swarm; **AL** NE; **CR** 1/2; **XP** 100.

Centipede Swarm (2): A creature reduced to 0 hit points by a swarm of centipedes is stable but poisoned for 1 hour, even after regaining hit points, and paralyzed while so poisoned.

Locust Swarm (2): A swarm of locusts has a walking speed of 5ft, a flying speed of 20ft, and no climbing speed. A creature hit by a locust swarm's bite attack only suffers 1d4 damage, but is sickened by plague for 1 hour and can't regain hit points during that time unless it succeeds on a DC 11 Con saving throw.

Technically, there's a second way out of this chamber — the trap door in the ceiling through which Zemicek dumps new remains — but it's only

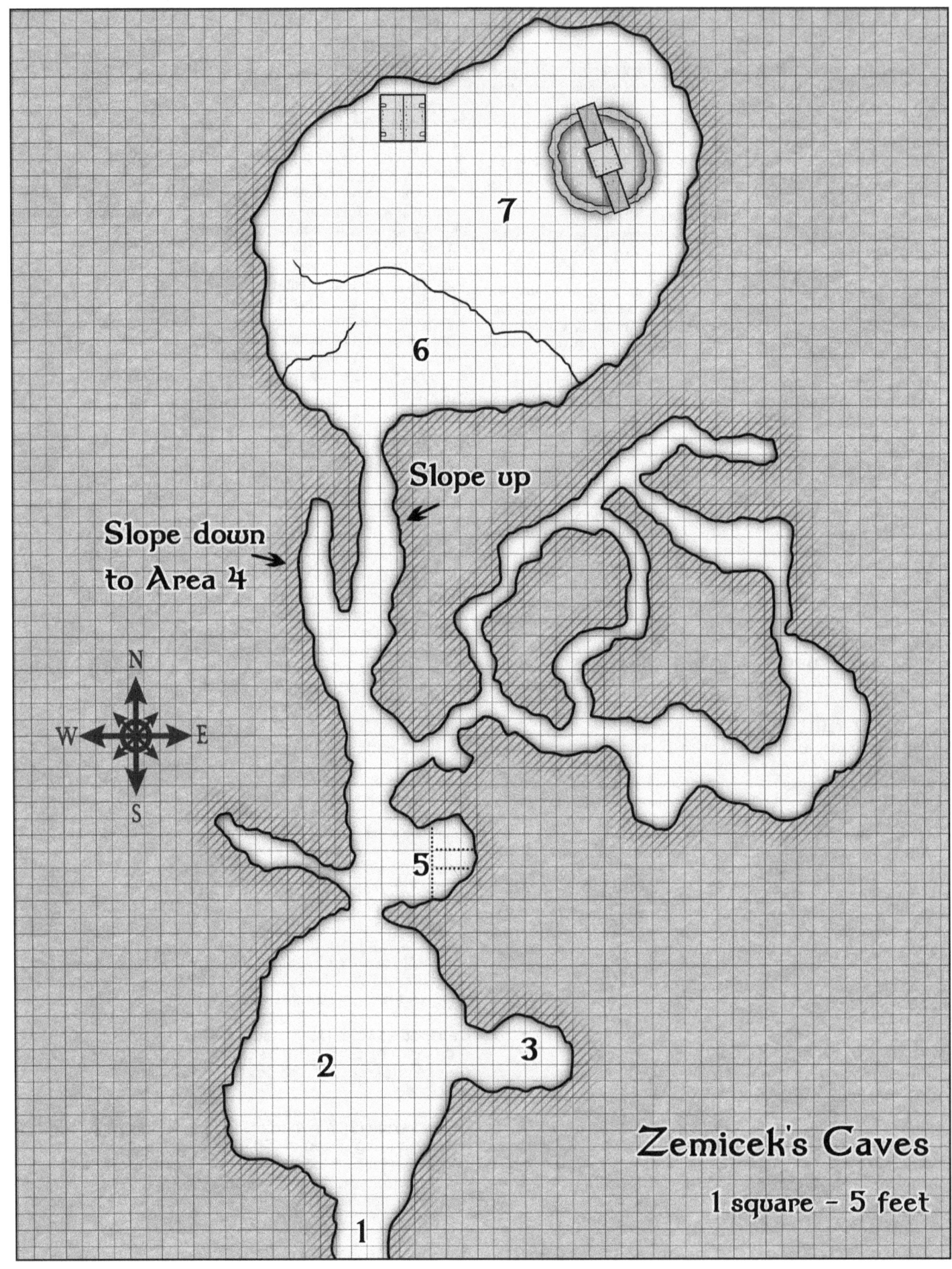

Slope up

Slope down
to Area 4

N
W E
S

7

6

5

2

3

1

Zemicek's Caves

1 square – 5 feet

New Template: Fiendtouched

An aberration, beast, humanoid, giant, monstrosity, or plant can potentially become fiendtouched. When a being becomes fiendtouched it retains its statistics except as noted below.

Senses: The creature gains darkvision with a radius of 120ft.

Resistance: The creature gains resistance to any one of the following damage types: cold, fire, lightning, or psychic.

Immunity: The creature gains immunity to the poisoned condition.

Language: If the creature uses language, it speaks either Abyssal or Infernal (depending on the nature of its fiendishness) in addition to any other languages it knows.

New action: Fiendish Adaptation (recharge 6): The creature gains resistance to one of the attack forms listed under **Resistance** (to which it is not already resistant) as a reaction to being hit with an attack that would do damage of the appropriate type. This resistance lasts for the duration of combat, or until this ability recharges and changes to a different type.

accessible and unlockable from above. Forcing the issue from the ceiling of this room requires not only that someone be able to exert strength while floating/perched right under the gate, but also succeed in a DC 25 Str (Athletics) check.

5. Animal Pens

This chamber contains some of the only actual interior structure or real design the characters have yet seen. Moving into the cavern, which has the same cold but slick look and feel as most of the rest of the place, they observe that a long iron grate has been set up all along one side of the chamber, effectively cutting it off from the rest of the cavern and the complex beyond. Within this space additional smaller grates have been driven into the floor and ceiling, trifurcating the area into three distinct cells.

One of these cells is empty. The second contains the body of a dog, recently dead from some combination of exposure and mistreatment. The third cell contains the final captive from Paster Sturgess' doomed caravan — Bromley Fitzhubert (male human **noble**) — who is very much alive. As a corpulent merchant with no weapons and no combat skill, he is of course terrified out of his mind, knowing he is merely awaiting his grisly death and consumption by monsters.

What old Fitzy doesn't know is that what little water he's been given by his captors so far was water ladled directly from the Cauldron of Dreams. The man isn't evil (yet), and no amount of interrogation (mundane or arcane) will reveal anything untoward about the sweaty merchant, but if the characters release him and bring him back to civilization without seeing him taken to a temple or other holy group for copious ritual blessing and curse removal, he will almost certainly go on to become one of the most powerful and zealous heretical clerics of Fraz-Urb'luu the kingdom's ever seen.

For now, though, he's just a frightened man who is delighted to see a friendly face.

6. The Dreaming Guard

If the characters have gotten this far they're a real threat to Zemicek. He has ordered his personal cadre of **fiendtouched ogrillon** enforcers, called the Dreaming Guard, to hold the line here, hoping they'll dispatch anyone strong enough to win through to him. Since all of the one-eyed members of the Dreaming Guard can see in pitch darkness, that's the state of affairs when the characters arrive. The GM is encouraged to use this to the ogrillons' best advantage during the inevitable combat.

Fiendtouched Half-Ogre (11): AC 14; **HP** 30 (4d10+8); **Spd** 30ft; **Melee** axe (+5, reach 5 ft., 2d8+3 slashing or 2d10+3 if two-handed); **Ranged** javelin (+3, 30ft/120ft, 2d6+3 piercing); **Resistance** fire; **Immune** poison; **Str** +3, **Dex** +0, **Con** +2, **Int** −2, **Wis** −1, **Cha** +0; **Senses** darkvision 120ft.;

Traits fiendish adaptation (see Fiendtouched sidebar); **AL** CE; **CR** 1; **XP** 200.

Equipment: hide armor, axe, 3 javelins; 1 ogrillon (leader) has a *ring of regeneration*.

A search of the room and the bodies yields 63gp, 21sp and 25cp. Apart from the ogrillon leader's magic ring, there is nothing else of value or interest in the cavern... excepting, of course, the lone cavern entrance to Zemicek's private chambers.

7. Chamber of Dreams

The first thing you notice about this chamber is the steam. It's everywhere, but seems to rise from a centrally located source toward the back of the cavern space. It's exceptionally warm in here, and something about the place makes the hair on the back of your neck stand on end.

Peering into the chamber, you see now that the source of the steam is what looks like a hot fracture spring, taking the shape of a roughly circular pool of mist-covered water with a five-foot-high rim of stone encircling it.

Rising from opposite sides of the natural pool is what appears to be an iron framework of some kind, forming two awkward gangways that meet in the middle on either end of a metal platform, seven feet in length, some eight to ten feet over the steaming waters. Laid carefully, almost reverently, atop this suspended plane is the body of a woman dressed in dark blue robes. Her blonde hair cascades down over the side of the dais, as though reaching for the water below.

When the player characters enter the chamber, **Zemicek** is both *invisible* and ducked down behind the lip of the pool, near a hidden release mechanism for the suspended apparatus. Ideally, one or more of the intruders ascend the frame and attempt to examine or recover Matilder's supine body, but if none of them braves the ascent (or whenever a character touches or enters the waters, whichever comes first) the ogre mage forces the issue by triggering the release lever. The characters have just enough time to register what's happening before his *darkness* ability drops, bathing the entire chamber in magical darkness (which of course he and his familiar can see through). When this happens, the DM can read the following secondary text to the players.

Suddenly, the entire apparatus gives way, and with a squeal of metal, plunges into the steaming waters below! There's just enough time to see the priestess' supine form slip fully beneath the surface before everything goes dark.

Any character actually on the platform with Matilder's body when it plummets may attempt a DC 24 Dex save to leap to the edge of the pool, and thence to the solid ground beyond. Any character on the frame but not yet on the dais itself can make a more manageable DC 16 Dex save to do the same. (For the complete effects of taking a dip in the Cauldron, see the "Drowning in Dreams" sidebar.)

Regardless, once the frame has collapsed and Matilder's body (and hopefully one or more characters) is submerged, Zemicek takes advantage of the chaos to launch his offensive against any party members who stand free of the steaming waters. If he can catch one or more characters standing atop the grate that covers the oubliette chamber (room **4**), he'll trigger that lever, too, sending those characters down into the muck below unless they succeed in a DC 16 Dex save to get clear.

Starting in the second round after the oni engages directly, his mephit familiar **Hiss** emerges from hiding and blasts as many party members as it can with its *steam breath* power. (It spends the first round casting *blur*.) The round after that, it summons 2 more **steam mephits** from the mists to harry the adventurers. These two mephits cannot in turn summon more

61

The Cauldron of Dreams

The Cauldron of Dreams is the second "crucible" of the adventure's title, the source of the ogre mage's great power, and the source of his great woe.

At first Zemicek mistook it for a simple hot spring, bubbling up from the darkness of the mountain's underbelly and warming the network of caverns above. At first he mistook the absence of monstrous and mortal competition for these otherwise desirable living conditions as a sign of certitude in his newfound purpose, of the rightness of his arrival as destiny made manifest. Soon enough, however, the experienced occultist recognized that the swirling pool of misty water was not only a great deal more than it seemed, but also the reason why every other living thing for leagues chose to steer clear of that particular network of caverns.

Put plainly, the true nature of the Cauldron of Dreams is a disturbing thing.

Some places in the world are effectively windows looking out upon vistas of eternal evil in the Ginnungagap — not active and open portals, but rather what one might regard as the next best/worst thing: places of powerful sympathy with a specific demonic force or demonic influence. This particular site reeks with the sympathetic potency of deception and insidious influence, and is the means by which the demon prince Fraz-Urb'luu can extend his reach, his ineffable will, and considerable demonic power into the stuff of the Material Plane.

Faces in the Mist

When Zemicek performs his rituals before the Cauldron, the steam rising from its surface intensifies and eventually produces visions — sometimes of the shadowy face of his demonic liege, but often of whatever person the oni wishes to observe. Before long he found that the more he called upon (and gazed into) the Cauldron's mists, the stronger his oracular power grew, and it soon became apparent to him that the nature of the phenomenon allowed a skilled arcanist to work the pool like a well, plumbing its darkened depths for buckets of golden power.

And this, Zemicek did, and to great success… for a time. Soon enough, his breakthrough occurred and he accepted the fact that if he were to grow any more powerful — if he had a chance of growing as powerful as he and his minions would *have* to grow in order to accomplish what a larger number of his kind could not accomplish a decade before — the relationship between himself and the Cauldron would have to change. Sacrifices would have to be made.

The Cauldron's Power

When he offered up a cave rat, scalding it in the mists before drowning it, Zemicek gained for a time the ability to scry (by way of those mists) areas of his own cavern network, even when there was no soul on which to home in. When he offered up some of his own blood to the Cauldron, spilled in steaming droplets across its surface, he discovered he could enter the dreams of any creature with even a drop of ogrish blood — could watch those dreams unfold in real time, for a time. And when he sacrificed his own eye in offering, scraping it out and leaving a scar trailing from just below the eye socket to the side of his forehead near the temple, he gained the ability to not merely enter the dreams of any being with ogrish blood, but to actually *interact* with that being there, in its dreams. And for his permanent sacrifice, he gained this ability permanently.

Immediately after confirming the power of the bargain he'd struck, Zemicek called in what remained of his loyal tribal followers — a couple dozen ogrillon and half as many ogres — and one by one, performed upon them a ritual intended to honor the same bargain, and thereby increase the power of his house-in-exile. They are all marked by its power now, all manifesting the same loss of an eye and livid diagonal scar through its socket.

As reflected in his statistics block, the Cauldron has made Zemicek both moderately tougher than the average ogre mage and a slightly more potent natural arcanist. In addition, he and all of his men received the Fiendtouched template (see sidebar), which renders them immune to poison, resistant to fire, and adaptive to other fiend-related sources of injury.

The Cauldron cannot be cleansed, exorcised, or destroyed. As the local inhabitants learned long ago, the best course of action is to make sure anything sentient steers well clear of it. Forever.

---

mephits, and if they are still around 10 rounds later, they spontaneously wink out of existence in a puff of steam.

Zemicek, Greater Ogre Mage (Oni): AC 17; **HP** 178 (17d10+85); **Spd** 30ft, fly 30ft; **Melee** claw (+10, 1d8+6 slashing), glaive (+10, reach 10ft, 2d10+6 slashing, or 1d10+6 slashing in Small or Medium form); **SA** innate spells (Cha+9, DC 17), multiattack (4 claw or glaive) **Immunity** poison; **Resistance** fire; **Str** +6, **Dex** +0 (+4), **Con** +5 (+9), **Int** +2, **Wis** +1 (+5), **Cha** +5 (+9); **Skills** Arcana +6, Deception +9, Perception +5; **Senses** darkvision 120ft; **Traits** change shape (as an action, Zemicek polymorphs into a Small or Medium humanoid, Large giant, or back to his true form), fiendish adaptation (5–6), magic weapons, poor depth perception (tactical disadvantage on ranged attacks beyond 30ft), regeneration (regains 10 hit points at the start of his turn if he has at least 1 hit point); **AL** LE; **CR** 11; **XP** 7200. (**Monster Appendix**)

 Innate Spells: at will—*darkness, fire bolt, invisibility*; 1/day—*charm person, cone of cold, gaseous form, misty step, sleep*.

 Equipment: *fetish necklace of Zemicek,* skin armor, glaive.

Hiss: AC 12; **HP** 21 (6d6); **Spd** 30ft, fly 30ft; **Melee** claw (+3, 1d4 slashing plus 1d4 fire); **SA** steam breath (15 ft cone of steam, 1d8 fire, DC 10 Dex half); **Immunity** fire, poison; **Str**

+0, **Dex** +2, **Con** +0, **Int** +0, **Wis** +0, **Cha** +1; **Skills** Perception +4, Stealth +6; **Senses** darkvision 60ft; **Traits** death burst (explodes in cloud of steam on death, hitting adjacent creatures, 1d8 fire, DC 12 Dex negates), innate spell (Cha), summon mephits (1/day, summons 2 steam mephits within 60ft); **AL** NE; **CR** 1/4; **XP** 50.

 Innate Spells: 1/day—*blur*

Dropping Zemicek below 17 hp triggers his survival instinct, and the oni tries to make good his escape via a combination of flight, *darkness, invisibility,* and *misty step.*

Treasure: Once the ogre mage and his mephits are gone, the party can search the room. Zemicek was no fool, and he hid the bulk of his wealth in a sealed cask affixed to the wall inside the pool; if the characters want to drag it out (or attach something to it by which they might accomplish same), someone has to reach into the water. Inside the cask are 300cp, 900sp, 850gp, and 420pp; 12 gems (200gp each), a *potion of supreme healing,* a *ring of fire resistance,* and a *+2 battleaxe.*

Concluding the Adventure

If the characters kill or remove Zemicek from his cavern complex for any length of time, the particular threat he posed to the lands of civilized men ends, too. Without having a chance to fully partake in the Cauldron's power (and give up an eye in the process), and bereft of the mystical

Drowning in Dreams

The Cauldron of Dreams is bad news for souls who merely come in contact with those who have been in its *presence*. For those who actually fall into its waters? The nightmare is something else.

If any part of a character not bound to the Cauldron (e.g., Zemicek) is submerged in the pool during a round, that character suffers 2d10 damage (half fire damage, half psychic damage). In addition, that character must make a DC 16 Wis saving throw. What happens as a result depends on whether or not the character is already a priest of some kind (cleric levels count, certainly, but levels in druid, monk, and/or paladin would likely count, too).

Priest: If a priest of faith touches the steaming waters, that person has a vision of coming face to face with his deity, spirit, or other divinity. This deity or force chastises the character for his impiety, intemperance, weakness in the face of evil — whatever guilt will work the best). If the priest makes the Wis saving throw, nothing happens to his soul. If he fails, he loses a single spell slot (or point of ki) from his total for one week thereafter, as those blessings are instead transferred as sweet ambrosia to the waiting maw of the demon prince Fraz-Urb'luu.

Non-priest: When a non-priest is submerged in the Cauldron's waters, that person also experiences a vision of coming face to face with a benevolent or neutral divinity of that player's choice. This deity or force tells the person of the great evil loosed in the world, and exhorts the person to get involved, to walk a righteous path of faith and service. If the person makes the saving throw, nothing happens to his soul. If he fails, he feels a calling to the priesthood, one that intensifies after he leaves the Cauldron's presence; the more failed saves, the stronger the calling. This calling urges the character to take on cleric levels in the name of whatever deity or force appeared to him; if he does, he'll gain all the usual traits and spells, but he'll be a *heretical cleric* — one whose prayers actually go toward nourishing and empowering a demon prince.

Note that this saving throw must be repeated every round a character remains submerged, whether drowning or not, and effects accumulate. If a character dies while submerged the effects are permanent, even if the character is later brought back to life. At that point, only a *wish* will return the resurrected soul to its former state.

support it would have given them, the remnants of Karimoryc's tribe are routed by Caerboar Hall's forces fighting alongside Vanigoths loyal to Winvani. Whether Karimoryc himself dies, surrenders to the Bristleback rangers, or escapes to fight another day remains in the GM's hands. What is almost certain is that the assembled Vanigoth name Winvani as their new regional Rohalac, and depending on how everyone plays it, he could become either a shrewd ally or a formidable foe to the people of Suilley down the line.

For their part, the characters have just done not one, but two favors for the government and people of Suilley (in foiling Zemicek's scheme and in gathering days' worth of valuable intelligence and social data on the Vanigoth), and neither Stronghold Hjerrin nor the Shadowguards are likely to forget any time soon — which could, of course, lead to further adventures in and around the Kingdom of Suilley.

It's too late to save Matilder's life, but if the party cares enough it can retrieve her corpse and bring it to an actual temple of Freya (or even just any lone cleric of Freya the characters can find). Once her soul has been blessed by same, it is no longer tainted by the deception of Fraz-Urb'luu and is free to enjoy its afterlife in peace. Actually going through this process should earn each player character an unexpected bonus of 500 XP for doing the right thing by the priestess.

The War of the Poppies

The War of the Poppies is a politics and intrigue-based adventure intended for 10th-level characters. It is likely to take several sessions, though it could be completed in one or could be extended into an entire campaign in its own right. The story centers on the simple, greedy plan of a drug dealer to sell magically-fortified opium in the kingdom of Suilley, and the unintended consequences that result.

Adventure Background

Brilliant blue poppies sway in the breeze, innocent of the havoc they wreak on the streets of Manas, the capital and economic center of the kingdom of Suilley. Bloodthirsty gangs fight over the opium trade, vying to control the flow of the poppy paste, but as with all situations of chaos, it is those who can see the patterns who manage to rise above the fray.

One such man is Monjerrat the Bookkeeper, a quiet, clever opium merchant. Realizing that no one in Manas has the resources or knowledge to bring together the various warring factions, Monjerrat has contacted the Friendly Men, a much larger organized crime syndicate with experience in such matters. He has formed a partnership with Sir Brodovic of Tilny, their chief agent in Manas, in an effort to bring the opium trade under a single organized front. Brodovic has contracted the services of the Smoky Flowers, a local group of thugs, to do the dirty work of the organization. The Smoky Flowers eliminate or cow Monjerrat's rivals, provide a protection racket, and perform other unsavory duties. Brodovic manages their practical affairs, while Monjerrat keeps track of the books.

Had Monjerrat and Brodovic been content to limit their interests to the sale of legal opium — along with illegal, but standard, protection rackets — they would not likely have drawn much attention. They took a step over the line, however, when they decided to cultivate a magical strain of poppy that produced a much more addictive form of opium. This drug has been named "blue angel" due to the blue-gray veins that pulse like wings on either side of the eyes of its users, as well as in the flowers themselves. Some addicts descend into delirium after only a few uses, useless husks, devoid of the will to live.

The distant Palatine County of Toullen cares little about opium dealings in the Kingdom of Suilley, or they would, if it were not for the recent disappearance of three young Toullenese nobles. This is where our adventure begins.

The Tournament of Lilies in Tertry (capital of the Palatine County of Toullen), ended approximately two months ago. The Tournament is the most prestigious jousting event in the Borderland Provinces, and the sponsors of victorious jousters gain significant political, social, and economic clout when their champions become famous. The tournament consists of a number of separate competitions (for specific details of the competitions, see **The Borderland Provinces**, Chapter 10: *The County of Toullen*), the most prestigious of which are the Crown of Lilies and the Count's Tournament. The former is a competition open to those of any realm, whereas the latter is an elite, local affair.

Following the Tournament, three of the most successful participants went on a celebratory "tour" of the nearby realms — an opportunity to sow wild oats before taking on important responsibilities, and also a chance to learn about the County's neighboring regions. What is particularly important is that the youths were not just of the nobility — they are from the very pinnacle of Toullenese nobility, related directly to some of the most powerful and influential people in the realm.

The youths made their way north from Tertry, stopping at various taverns, inns, gambling halls and the like. Although they are generally good natured, it is important to keep in mind that these are, nevertheless, teenagers, and their judgment can prove lacking. Along the way, they learned of an opium dealer in Manas by the name of Monjerrat the Bookkeeper. In the city of Olaric, they managed to slip away from the knights and soldiers escorting them and rode for Manas, assuming new names and trying to make themselves look like ordinary folk (not with much success, but enough to foil the pursuit by their protectors). With assumed names and lots of coin, they found their way quickly into the seedy underworld of drugs, drinking, and gambling in Manas — including the Five Cups, the largest of the blue angel opium dens controlled by Monjerrat the Bookkeeper. Within a matter of days, all four youths were out of money, for the "blue angel" was incredibly expensive and its abusers often have little control over or awareness of money.

Monjerrat the Bookkeeper, the mastermind behind the development of the blue angel strain, knew that some obviously incognito nobles were asking about opium, but left town for Sir Brodovic's manor during the nobles' first night in Manas, to inspect the poppy fields. In point of fact, he specifically gave Luther Smile, the owner of the Five Cups Inn, instructions to cut the nobles loose to avoid trouble. Even though Monjerrat didn't know the extreme high rank of the three foreign youths, he knew they were high enough in the nobility to cause trouble if anything happened to them. Missing young nobles are followed by people with swords and lots of experience using them. Smile ignored the order, bearing a grudge against all nobles and now having some about to fall into his power. He wished to see the youths brought low by the opium, knowing that the Smoky Flowers would take them without question as soon as they ran out of money.

That is exactly what happened. The four youths ran out of gold, and, separated from their escorts, were unable to avoid their fate. They were rounded up by the Smoky Flowers, along with several other addicts, and taken off to work the opium fields in the Tilny Hills, the site of Sir Brodovic's manor. Before sending them, Smile made sure to strip all the accoutrements of their noble lives. They appeared no better than the average street urchin: filthy, emaciated, sunken, and starved. For the past several weeks, they have been housed in an outbuilding next to Sir Brodovic of Tilny's manor house in the Tilny Hills.

Smile is now the only individual who knows the fate of the three youths. Monjerrat and Sir Brodovic are completely unaware that three of the filthy opium workers happen to be the rich nobles they saw weeks ago in Manas. Neither Monjerrat, Brodovic, nor any of the Smoky Flowers knew the real identities of the nobles, who were traveling under assumed names.

Two months have passed since the youths embarked on their celebratory tour following their victories at the Tournament of Lilies, and their escorts have returned after a frantic search, to report that they lost touch with their charges in Olaric. Cyrilinde the Lance, sister of Count Luthien, has realized she needs to track them down, for they are politically important individuals (one, indeed, is her own god-daughter). If they were kidnapped, the ransoms would be very large, and although the young scions of the high nobility probably know very little about their various family politics, what they do know could certainly be embarrassing, or even useful to enemies of the Palatine County. She has started inquiries into the disappearance of the young jousters using the varied resources of Ruthenvais the Fair (High Priest of Thyr in the City of Tertry), the underworld contacts of Parale Greenguild (Guildmaster of Thieves in Tertry), the law enforcement and military connections of Lord Parzalon Mothcandle, as well as the considerable political resources of her own, to track down the three wayward youths.

This group already knows that the youths got safely to the city of Olaric, in the County of Vourdon, and assume that they headed toward the city of Manas, capital of the Kingdom of Suilley, since divinations indicate that they are somewhere in that Kingdom. These divinations reveal that the youths are still alive, but not in good health and in significant danger. High Priest Ruthenvais insists that something is clouding his ability to locate them.

GMs are advised to read the entire adventure thoroughly before running it. The two ultimate objectives of the adventure are to bring the youths

---

Experience

This adventure is quite freeform, and thus can prove challenging for GMs to adjudicate in terms of experience. If the PCs perform well, they should advance the equivalent of a full level. Assuming that the PCs started the adventure one-quarter of the way between 10th and 11th level, and the party was deemed successful, they should finish the adventure one-quarter of the way between 11th and 12th (adjust starting and ending points based on PCs' actual experience totals). For exceptional roleplaying, creativity, and discretion, they might receive more experience, and for the opposite, they might receive less. In this regard, you are encouraged not to keep track of individual encounters during this adventure, but to treat each objective or accomplishment as a milestone of sorts.

---

back safely and possibly to influence the regulation of opium in the Kingdom of Suilley. It is possible that the PCs might come up with an entirely different solution than any presented here. The most important thing for GMs to be in this adventure is flexible. It is not best solved by brute force, a few powerful spells, or magic items, though there are times when these prove useful.

Many of the social encounters in this adventure are presented as a series of commonly asked questions. This is not meant to indicate that the encounters are entirely scripted. These exchanges are simply there to provide answers to questions PCs are likely to ask. Use the background provided by the NPCs to engage the PCs in a three-dimensional conversation, and adapt the encounter as you see fit.

Part 1: Tertry

The adventure starts in Tertry, the capital city of the County of Toullen (see **The Borderland Provinces** Chapter 10: *County of Toullen*). Cyrilinde and her allies are growing frustrated. They are an extraordinarily powerful group of people both politically and personally, but this is also the reason they cannot just go searching through a foreign countryside for three teenagers. The matter is also sensitive, requiring a great deal of discretion, something that their asking questions in other lands would make difficult. They need help from an outside party, and one resourceful, powerful, and discrete enough to get the job done without exposing them to potential scandal.

This adventure assumes that the PCs have come to the attention of Cyrilinde and/or other members of the court, due to their valor, power, influence, and deeds. The party should be passing near the jousting grounds outside Tertry at the start of the adventure when they come across jousters in a dire predicament. The purpose of this encounter is to interject a combat opportunity into this relatively combat-light encounter, as well as to make the Lady Cyrilinde aware of the PCs as she considers a group to help solve her problem.

Brilliant early afternoon sunshine streams through thick, swaying poplars that line the road leading to Tertry. A quick resupply after your recent endeavors would do you good, and Tertry has a reputation as a pleasant city. As you stop to admire the jousting fairgrounds, a whooshing wind ruffles your cloaks as a large red shape flies above you.

Creatures: Hovering over the jousting grounds is the **young red dragon, Daraktrikash the Scourge**, about to unleash a gout of flame on two bumbling, battered knights. The knights are father and son, **Sir Bervald** and his son **Sir Baragond**, who were responsible for slaying the dragon's mate, Tempateyroth, and commissioning her hide into *red dragon scale mail*, which Sir Baragond now wears. When they attacked her, they were with a larger group, they caught her sleeping, and the confined space was to their advantage. Daraktrikash wants revenge and has tracked them to this field, where he intends to destroy them, or die trying. The dragon is extremely verbose, taunting and threatening the knights, screeching about how they callously wear "his lover's hide" as he breathes on them and viciously mauls them. Until and unless the PCs intervene, assume the two knights are primarily taking the Dodge action, struggling simply to survive until some hope presents itself.

Daraktrikash the Scourge; AC 18; **HP** 178 (17d10+85); **Spd** 40ft, climb 40ft, fly 80ft; **Melee** bite (+10, reach 10ft, 2d10+6 piercing plus 1d6 fire), claw x2 (+10, 2d8+6 slashing); **SA** fire breath (recharge 5–6, 30ft cone, DC 17 Dex half, 16d6 fire), Multiattack; **Immune** fire; **Str** +6, **Dex** +0 (+4), **Con** +5 (+9), **Int** +2, **Wis** +0 (+4), **Cha** +4 (+8); **Skills** Perception +8, Stealth +4; **Senses** blindsight 30ft, darkvision 120ft, passive Perception 18; **AL** CE; **CR** 10; **XP** 5,900.

Sir Bervald: AC 18; **HP** 52 (8d8+16); **Spd** 30ft; **Melee** greatsword x2 (+5, 2d6+3 bludgeoning); **Ranged** heavy crossbow (+2, 100ft/400ft, 1d10 piercing); **SA** Multiattack; **Str** +3, **Dex** +0, **Con** +2 (+4), **Int** +0, **Wis** +0 (+2), **Cha** +2; **Senses** passive Perception 11; **Traits** Father son spirit (as long as both Sir Bervald and Sir Baragond are conscious and adjacent to each other, they gain a +2 bonus to their AC; **AL** LN.
  Equipment: scale mail, club, light crossbow, 20 bolts, 20 gp.

Sir Baragond: AC 19; **HP** 52 (8d8+16); **Spd** 30ft; **Melee** greatsword x2 (+5, 2d6+3 bludgeoning); **Ranged** heavy crossbow (+2, 100ft/400ft, 1d10 piercing); **SA** Multiattack; **Resist** fire; **Str** +3, **Dex** +0, **Con** +2 (+4), **Int** +0, **Wis** +0 (+2), **Cha** +2; **Senses** passive Perception 11; **Traits** Father son spirit (as long as both Sir Bervald and Sir Baragond are conscious and adjacent to each other, they gain a +2 bonus to their AC), advantage vs. Frightful Presence and dragon breath weapons, discern location of dragons; **AL** LN.
  Equipment: *red dragon scale mail,* club, light crossbow, 20 bolts, 20 gp.

The knights, assuming they survive, bend over backwards in thanks to the PCs, insisting on presenting them with the most valuable item from the dragons' horde, as their "share" of the treasure, the suit of *red dragon scale mail.* The knights then depart, after making another round of vociferously flowery pronouncements of gratitude.

The Invitation

By the time the PCs reach the city, the battle with the dragon has attracted the attention of the Lady Cyrilinde, who sends a messenger to invite them to an audience. Anyone who could best a red dragon is worthy of consideration in the difficult task she has before her.

A messenger in the livery of a Toullenese servant approaches your group bearing an ornate envelope sealed with a red shield. A preserved pale pink lily is affixed into the wax, creating the impression of a lance crossing a heraldic crest. The servant inclines her head slightly in respect handing a note to [the PC with the highest Charisma score in the party]. She waits for your response.

The document is a short invitation on heavy, expensive paper, written in an elegant yet simple script, in slate gray ink.

Dear [insert character names here],
I have heard of your great deed slaying the red dragon

Daraktrikash the Scourge. It would please me greatly if you would join me at tea time in the Garden of the Ducks. I have a matter of significant import to discuss with you.
  Sincerely,
  Lady Cyrilinde of Tertry

The PCs can make DC 12 Intelligence (History) checks to recognize the heraldry and name of Lady Cyrilinde, a famous warrior, champion jouster, and sister of the Count of Toullen. From nobility at this level, "It would please me greatly" is essentially the command at the level of royalty. Her reputation indicates that she is a woman of honor, who would not entreat the PCs to perform a task for her without reason and sincerity. If the PCs require significant motivation beyond this, the servant confirms that the lady is prepared to make it "worth their while." Assuming they agree to meet with Lady Cyrilinde, the servant speaks before departing. Feel free to interrupt the box text between the servant's dialog and the PCs' approach to the palace, to allow the PCs to prepare, purchase equipment, or do whatever else they need.

After you give your assent, the servant says, "Please approach the guards at the east gate of the palace at tea time. You will be escorted to the Garden of the Ducks for your meeting with the Lady Cyrilinde." She nods to you, and then turns to go back toward the city.
  As you continue toward the palace, you can't help but feel that the city seems fatigued. The massive jousting field outside the walls is mostly empty, though there are some diehard combatants training. Merchants hawk their wares and townsfolk go about their business, weaving between the many skywalk-linked towers and more humble thatch-roofed wooden homes. It is a reasonably large city, but one that revolves around a single yearly event that passed a few months back.
  The guards at the east gate of the palace seem prepared for your arrival. The one to the right holds out his hand as if expecting to see the invitation. After he reviews the invitation, he gives a signal and the gates open. You are escorted by a pair of similarly attired guards to a sedate garden surrounding a small duck pond.
  A tall woman in a simple gown of rich fabric looks up from a book she is reading, saying to one of the guards, "That'll be all, Alric. I'll be fine from here." All the guards and all but one of the servants retreat to corners of the garden. The woman possesses a distinctly military bearing, perhaps more at home on the battlefield than in court.
  "Please sit and enjoy the refreshments," says the woman. "We have much to discuss." Beneath a veranda, a large table is set with trays of sweets, a tea set, fresh fruit, and cheese. It is situated in front of a pond of ducks and swans, koi, tiny black-speckled red frogs, turtles, and egrets. Several small foot-bridges cross the pond, and a white swan boat sits at a small dock a few feet beyond the table. Pathways meander throughout the gardens, allowing strollers to bask in the scents of the many varieties of fragrant rose, lily, and dahlia.

This is the Cyrilinde the Lance, sister of the Count, and the godmother of Vivica, one of the missing tournament winners. Cyrilinde is relatively young, but obviously very intelligent for her years, and has an imposing presence. Given that she is not only a fighter of legendary stature, but also a person that anyone in Toullen would die to defend, that sense of presence is not unjustified.

The remaining servant pours tea for each of you as well as for Cyrilinde, and then steps away respectfully to join the others. Cyrilinde smiles at you, but it is a grim smile, not reflected in her eyes. "Two months ago, after minor victories in several of the events at the Tournament of the Lilies, three young Toullenese nobles went on a victory tour to celebrate their achievements. This was meant to be a last hurrah before assuming a greater role in their social and familial responsibilities. They traveled to Olaric, and then to Manas, but after that we have been unable to determine their whereabouts. We expected them back home several weeks ago and have received no word from them.

Before we go any further, I must emphasize how important discretion will be in the matters we are about to discuss. I will not be asking you to do anything evil, immoral, or reprehensible, but you will need to be discrete. The lives and reputations of many may be involved. Can I count on you to do everything in your power to protect the honor of those we discuss?"

She looks each of you in the eye to judge your response.

Common questions and answers are below. Again, remember that the PCs do not need to ask all of these, and that the conversation shouldn't come across as an interrogation. The information is presented in this fashion for ease of reference, but you should present it as best fits the flow and role-play of the scene. Cyrilinde can volunteer information to common and obvious questions as part of the flow of conversation. For example, she will volunteer the information about the youths and transportation if the PCs don't ask.

Questions and Answers with Cyrilinde

Question: What can you tell us about the young nobles?

Answer: They are the Lady Vivica, my god-daughter; Sir Trincalium Mothcandle, son of Lord Parzalon Mothcandle who is Commander of the Guard of Tertry; and Lady Parnasaal, a young cousin to Ruthenvais the Fair, who is the High Priest of Thyr here in the city. Vivica won the Crown of Lilies in the last Tournament, and many believe her to be one of the Borderlands' greatest jousters. Trin was fourth to Vivica in the Crown of Lilies and they are good friends. [She holds up a portrait of the three teenagers in tournament regalia, obviously painted at some time during the closing ceremonies]. Parnasaal didn't participate in the jousting, but won a number of other contests, including archery and athletics. She hasn't inherited her father's religious zeal. They're all good kids, for the most part. Occasionally foolish, as most youth can be, but none of them is particularly trouble-prone. I suppose Trin sometimes gets a little tongue-tied, but what 18-year-old boy doesn't?

Question: What steps have already been taken to locate the youths?

Answer: We have investigators out looking for them. We have contacted the authorities in major cities in Suilley and the largest towns on the South County Road. Our divinations have shown that they are still alive, but not in good health and in significant danger. Something seems to be interfering with the magic involved. We know they are somewhere in Suilley, but cannot narrow it down any further. Lord Parzalon has contacted Orlando Cormont, head of law enforcement in the City of Manas, alerting him to the situation in case the youths reached Manas before they disappeared.

Question: Would anyone wish to harm the youths?

Answer: Not for any reasons I can imagine. Certainly Lord Parzalon, Ruthenvais, and I have a few enemies of our own, but there is nothing in particular linking us together other than our children having been successful in the recent tournament. I suppose it's possible that someone could be disgruntled at losing in the tournament, but no one seemed that upset at the time.

Question: Can you provide assistance with transportation to Manas?

Answer: Of course. We would have no difficulty finding someone to assist you in this. Once in Manas, if you speak to Orlando Cormont, Commander of the Corps of Wardens in Manas, he can arrange for transportation within Suilley during your investigation.

Question: Why should we help you?/What's in it for us?/Will we be compensated?

Answer: I assumed that individuals of your caliber would benefit more from political favors and influence than material possessions. If something more specific is what you want, may each pick an item from the Count's treasury after successfully bringing back the youths.

A Second Conversation

Cyrilinde doesn't know much more than what she has shared with the PCs, but the same cannot be said of Parale Greenguild, who has suspicions about the nature of the disappearances. The nobles have called in favors to get the assistance of the Thieves Guild of Tertry in this matter, but when Parale undertakes a task, she pursues it fiercely.

After Cyrilinde finishes answering their questions, Parale approaches the gathering, intent on having her part in the proceedings. Cyrilinde is aware that Parale is conducting her own, more "covert" investigations, and given Parale's position as head of the Thieves Guild, prefers to be left out of such discussions. The dialog for Parale below is quite long, and it is quite possible that the PCs might interrupt her, and that is fine. Allow them to make inconsequential small talk with her, though she won't discuss the matter at hand until she's finished with everything she has to say.

Just as the Lady Cyrilinde has answered the last of your questions, another woman glides up to the table. She provides a striking contrast to Cyrilinde. Whereas Cyrilinde is simple of dress and obviously dangerous, the newcomer is richly garbed, beautiful, and has an enchanting smile. Cyrilinde stands and turns to look at the newcomer. "Please allow me to introduce Parale Greenguild. She may have some additional matters to discuss with you. For now, I must take my leave. Good luck." She walks off, her back and shoulders rigid, and Parale sits down. When she begins to talk, your extensive travels and experience suddenly give you a strong impression that this well-dressed noblewoman might actually be far more of a stone-cold killer than Cyrilinde the Jouster.

"I imagine my Lady of the Lance has explained to you the basics of what has happened, so I will skip to what she hasn't told you — either out of a misplaced sense of propriety or genuine ignorance. For months, Manas has been plagued by a war of gangs fighting over control of the opium trade coming out of the Tilny Hills. My sources in the city believe that factions in the underworld there have grown a new strain of the drug infused with magic, making it significantly more potent and more addictive. This, of course, changes the entire balance of power in their underground struggle, for obvious reasons.

In Olaric, they talked to a traveling peddler named Honest Pyet. Pyet has a connection to the opium trade, and our three idiots slipped the leash the day after talking to him. The captain of the escort didn't overhear the conversation with Pyet, and when I asked the Olaric thieves guild to look for him, he had disappeared. I don't think dead, since no body turned up, but if he's traveling the back roads of the County of Vourdon it will take a long time to find him. We might not have that time. This tells me, and everyone else disagrees, that this disappearance has something to do with opium. Why they couldn't get it in Olaric, I don't know. Probably because of the escorts being there.

This is why discretion is so important. It means they are dealing with dangerous people, not just drinking in taverns under assumed names. It means that Toullen might be forced to take issue with the Kingdom of Suilley if these fools die, or get addicted. It means they are much more likely to spill some kind of information to someone who can use it, and who knows what secrets they've learned from their parents and uncles and aunts about diplomacy in Toullen. It could lead to the Kingdom of Suilley trying to regulate the opium trade more closely, possibly make the stuff illegal."

At this she frowns, and drums her fingers on the table,

suddenly thoughtful, looking off into the distance. Then she collects herself.

"Oh, and it would ruin their lives, too, I expect. That would also be a shame."

So I would add one additional request on behalf of ... another organization here in the city. Feel out the political climate in Manas surrounding the opium war. If possible, try to moderate it. This magically-enhanced opium is a problem, but the complete criminalization of normal opium would interrupt lots of mercantile activity, not to mention a valuable painkiller. There will be those arguing for both extremes. If you can act as a moderating force, keep the city to the least extreme path, you'll have done a great service to a certain group of organizations—official and, ah, "informal," both.

These "organizations" are the thieves guilds of several cities and towns in the western provinces, guilds that would like to see the violence of the opium wars decrease, and possibly even have the substance regulated enough to come under their own influence. On the other hand, they have no desire to see the entire trade disappear, or to have their cities start digging around in the affairs of criminal underworlds looking for opium dealers. The cities might find things the thieves guilds would prefer stay secret.

Parale is willing to stay and answer questions, though she does not wish to reveal too many of her own secrets. The questions below are ones she will answer in addition to what she's already said. Everything else will result in the same answers the PCs already have.

Questions and Answers with Parale

Question: Who are you?

Answer: Not anyone important. Let's say that I'm someone with friends. Lots of friends. I'm offering you my friendship, too. Isn't that wonderful? We can all be friends. I suggest it. I wouldn't have so many friends if it weren't such a good idea to be my friend. In fact, if you run into trouble in Manas, ask for a fellow named Casmir Dark. He's the guildmaster of thieves in Manas. He's a friend of mine.

Question: What can you tell us about the young nobles?

Answer: I think my sister covered most of the important details. I can confirm that they weren't involved in anything anyone would consider the least bit questionable prior to leaving Tertry.

Question: What are you doing to find them?

Answer: I have means at my disposal that my sister does not, which you may have surmised. I am conversing with people, and will continue to do so.

Question: Would anyone wish to harm the youths?

Answer: I highly doubt it. It is far more likely that they were in the wrong place at the wrong time.

Question: What's in it for us?

Answer: There are many rewards that might be of interest to individuals of your caliber. Of course, I could offer you monetary reward or objects of magical power. Perhaps you would prefer a favor from the less savory "powers" of the Borderlands? In the event that you should find yourself in trouble with the wrong sort of people, such a favor might come in handy.

Part 2: Manas

The PCs are provided with good horses if they need any, and a letter of authority signed by the Count Palatine of Toullen. This letter will get them through virtually any legal difficulty all the way from Tertry to Manas. It also allows the PCs to change horses at most large inns along the way, and their overland speed from Tertry to Manas will be doubled as a result. They also have a letter from the Ruthenvais the Fair, High Priest of Thyr

in Tertry, to Besondar the Cognate, High Priest of Belon the Wise (a god of knowledge), in Manas.

The rambling urban expanse of Manas extends before you, a city bursting at the seams. It is a stark and strange clash of prosperity and dire poverty: nobles step over emaciated homeless children; merchants on expensive horses glance away from destitute lepers; and gaudy, bejeweled bully boys collect the shirts off the backs of cloudy-eyed opium addicts. Hawkers cry out their wares, trying to drown out occasional wails of pain coming from alleys, clip-clopping hoof beats, shouted arguments between wagoneers, ringing bells, and a thousand other deafening urban sounds. As you begin to look around, planning your next move, a feverish looking elderly man in rags comes up to [choose a random PC], grabbing [that PC's] arm. Something is terribly wrong with his face.

"You must help me!" screams the man as he grips your arm with the strength of the dead — and die is exactly what he does, for he falls to the ground, all life having left his eyes.

Bright bluish veins glow on the skin around his eyes, appearing like wings curling up his bald temples. His clothes are rags, though they were once fine. At first, he appeared to be elderly, but closer examination suggests he may actually be far younger than he looks. His fingertips are stained blue-gray, almost like he had dipped them in ink that had long since dried.

No one seems to care very much about what just happened, though one of the nearby merchants does call for guards to come for the body.

From here, the PCs have a number of options, all of which they are encouraged to follow up on based on what Cyrilinde has told them. These options can be chosen in any order, though it's probably easier on the PCs if they investigate the Underworld first. It should be possible for PCs to discover information in any number of ways, and this is only meant to provide a loose framework to eventually lead the PCs to the whereabouts of the youths.

• Investigate the underworld and drug scene, possibly with the authority of Casmir Dark, the guildmaster of thieves.

• Speak with Orlando Cormont, Commander of the Corps of Wardens, and learn about the legal situation of opium.

• Speak to Besondar the Cognate, the High Priest of Belon the Wise, for divine assistance.

While traversing the city, and especially the underworld, the PCs may attract unwanted attention if they ask too many questions. At the GM's discretion and wherever dramatically appropriate, they may be jumped in dark alleys or otherwise accosted. The thieves will leave them alone if they have contacted Casmir Dark, but the opium wars have spawned a violent new underworld that dislikes people who ask questions about opium. You can use the Smoky Flower NPCs listed under the Five Cups Inn to represent local underworld thugs.

Casmir Dark

If the PCs begin with Casmir Dark, contacting the city's thieves and obtaining an appointment with the guildmaster, he will meet them in a nameless tavern in the poor quarter, one that has been emptied of patrons for the meeting. A number of hooded thieves will file into the room after the characters are seated, checking for any traps and requesting that the characters place their weapons on the far side of the room for the interview. If the PCs do not comply, they will have no meeting with Casmir.

Casmir is of average height, with brown hair, and wears a fur-trimmed black cloak over leather armor. As he talks to you, the features of his face seem to shift, and by the time the interview is finished he looks like an entirely different person. It is disturbing to watch.

THE WAR OF THE POPPIES

The guildmaster of thieves asks the characters to describe the woman who sent them to him, and they are able to give a good description of Parale Greenguild. He nods, and says:

Let me be clear, I have no desire to see you, I have no desire to talk to you, and as far as I'm concerned we never met each other. I want no connection to the opium trade while it's a business where people kill each other over a few coppers or a street corner. I'm a peaceful man in the business of peacefulness: I keep things orderly, I keep things calm, and everyone wants things to be calm and orderly. Everybody wins. Everybody has a share.

I could point you to lots of opium dealers here. Most of them are one-man operations buying opium from Pfefferain, marking it up, and selling it on street corners next to people who sell meat pies and secondhand clothes. There are some bigger fish out there, and since one of them isn't very peaceful like I am, I'll tell you where to fish. It might not be the operation you want, but it's a start, and it's all I'm going to give you.

Find a place called the Five Cups.

Casmir isn't interested in answering any further questions. "How can I answer your questions if you never met me? One day I hope to make your acquaintance, perhaps when this is all done. I'm a good person to meet. As I said, everybody has a share. Some shares are bigger than others, though."

He leaves, remaining polite but firm that he will not provide more information, followed by his bodyguard.

The Five Cups Inn

Anyone with the Criminal, Guild Merchant, or Urchin background, or a similar background (GM's discretion), can automatically determine that the Five Cups Inn is the best source of opium in Manas. All others must make DC 15 Charisma (Persuasion) checks to learn that the tavern is a criminal haven and opium source. Failing or repeating the search on multiple days should attract notice by the underworld community, which could trigger combat encounters with the Smoky Flowers.

To get any useful information at the Five Cups Inn, the PCs will need to go there at night, when it is open for business and busy. During the day, the staff are obviously so far down the chain of command that they are useless as information sources.

As they are traversing the seedier area of the city, read the following (or, if you prefer, play out the events described therein during the course of the PCs' investigations):

Plumbing the depths of the underworld has led you to some very close calls. A frothing pair of street youths with blue-angel-wing veins extending from their eyes tried to shake you down for opium. The leper on the corner of the plaza assured you that if you asked even one more question, it would not be *his* fingers that went missing. Nevertheless, careful and deliberate searching has eventually led you to the city's best source of opium: the Five Cups Inn.

The building itself is a narrow, wedge-shaped structure in a disused portion of the warehouse district. The block has a derelict air about it, and few walk its streets other than the occasional beggar, prostitute, leper, or junky. Little marks it apart from the surrounding warehouses other than a flimsy hand-written sign that says "Five Cups Inn," with a badly-painted picture of five cups.

After pushing open the doors, it takes a few moments for your eyes to adjust to the light. Even then, it is difficult to see through the haze of smoke wafting through the room. The Five Cups Inn is a large, open, room with eight tables, almost completely full of drinkers, gamblers, and other unsavory sorts. An unsurprising number of thugs lounge lazily about the room, chugging ale, throwing darts, and making general asses of themselves. A door on the right side of the room remains closed and beyond it, near the back corner, is a ladder, leading to what looks like a loft with storage rooms. Lazy curls of smoke waft from the left, where the sliding doors to an open den lie slightly ajar.

A profoundly ugly pig of a man stands behind a large rounded bar at the back of the room, cleaning glasses haphazardly. His face is branded with a mark that usually means disrespect for a noble, which is often considered a criminal offense in the countryside, although not generally in cities. The bartender's yellowish eyes follow you as you walk in, but he makes no move to greet or welcome you. A couple of disinterested serving women pick up drinks and bring them to customers, collecting empty glasses on their way.

A single empty table, close to the door, is free of patrons.

"Right this way, Gentlefolk," says one of the serving women, indicating the empty table.

Area 1: the Tavern

The PCs can order drinks and participate in games of dice and cards, though there is no food served in the tavern other than bar snacks. If the PCs start any trouble, the Smoky Flowers are ready to deal with them. The other patrons know nothing of note.

Creatures: present in the tavern are a **Smoky Flower assassin, Smoky Flower mage, and (5) Smoky Flower thugs**. Sitting on a stool behind the bar, glaring at the entire bar with jaundiced eyes, is **Luther Smile**.

What do the Smokey Flowers know?

It's important that the PCs have multiple opportunities to learn of Sir Brodovic's manor house in the small barony of Tilny, where he keeps opium workers (including the three youths). The PCs are likely to have a number of run-ins with different combinations of Smoky Flowers throughout this adventure. While the thugs do not know that the nobles in question are currently at the Tilny manor, they are aware that Brodovic and Monjerrat keep addicts who fall into debt out there to produce opium. They can speculate, especially under the threat of torture or the pressure of intimidation, that the youths might have been rounded up, and also that everyone starts to look the same after taking too much blue angel.

Smoky Flower Assassin: AC 16; HP 66 (12d8+12); **Spd** 30ft; **Melee** rapier x 2 (+8, 1d8+4 piercing); **Ranged** light crossbow (+7, 80ft/320ft, 1d8 piercing); **SA** Multiattack; **Str** +0, **Dex** +4 (+8), **Con** +1, **Int** +1 (+5), **Wis** +0, **Cha** +0; **Skills** Acrobatics +8, Deception +4, Perception +4, Stealth + 12; **Senses** passive Perception 14; **Traits** assassinate (1st turn, has advantage on attacks against creatures that haven't acted, and hits against such creatures are critical hits), evasion, sneak attack (1/turn, 4d6 damage); **AL** NE; **CR** 8; **XP** 3,900.
   Equipment: studded leather armor, rapier, light crossbow, 20 bolts, 50 gp.

Smoky Flower Mage: AC 12 (15 with *mage armor*); **HP** 49 (9d8+9); **Spd** 30ft; **Melee** dagger (+5, 1d4+2); **SA** spells (Int+6, DC 14); **Str** −1, **Dex** +2, **Con** +1, **Int** +3 (+6), **Wis** +0 (+4), **Cha** +0; **Skills** Arcana +6, History +6; **Senses** passive

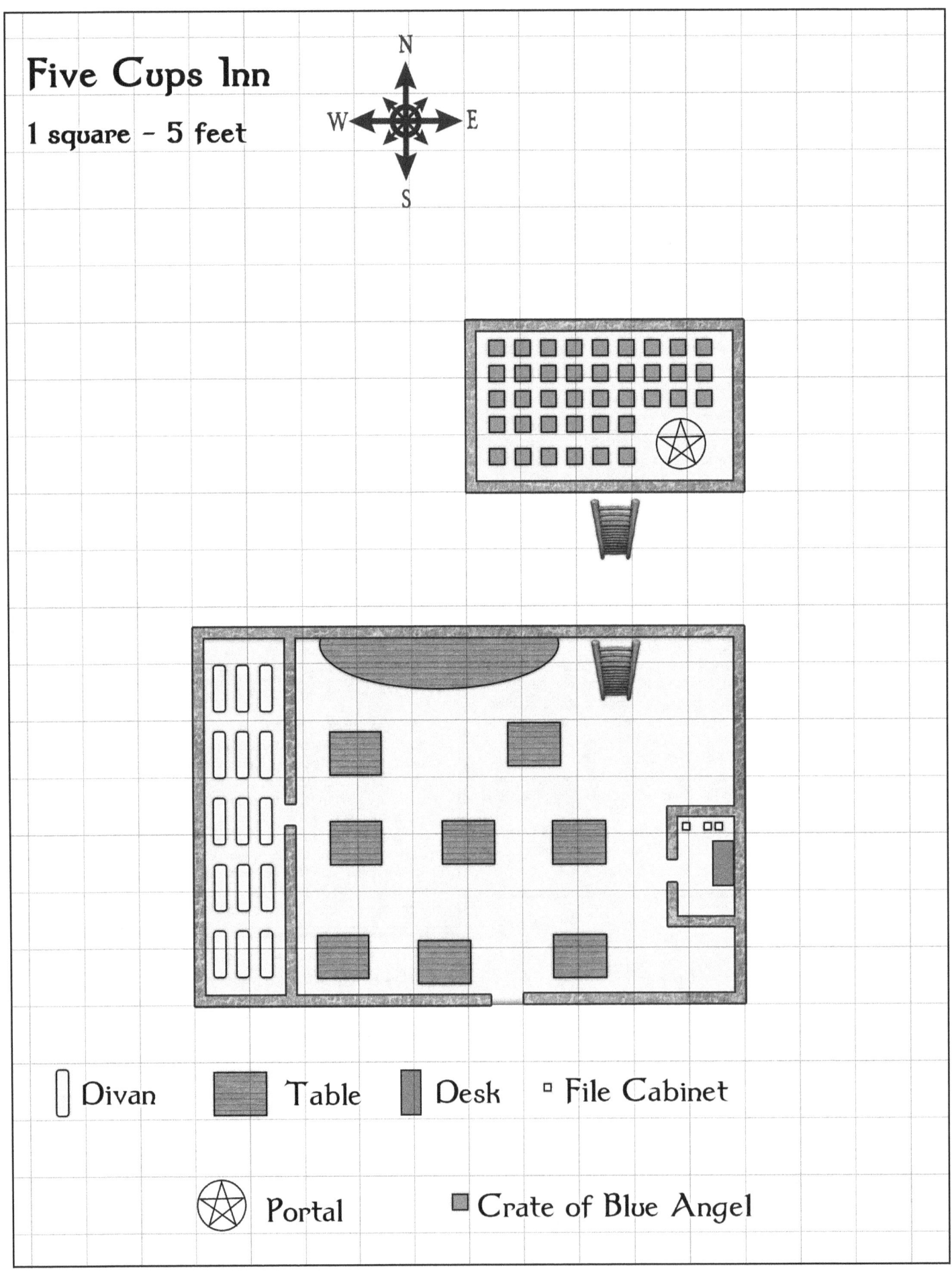

Five Cups Inn

1 square – 5 feet

| Divan | Table | Desk | □ File Cabinet |

| ⬟ Portal | ■ Crate of Blue Angel |

Perception 11; **Traits AL** NE; **CR** 6; **XP** 2,300.
Spells (slots): 0 (at will)—*acid splash, light, mage hand, message;* 1st (4)—*detect magic, expeditious retreat, mage armor, magic missile;* 2nd (3)—*hold person, web;* 3rd (3)—*dispel magic, fireball, fly;* 4th (3)—*dimension door, greater invisibility;* 5th (1)—*cone of cold*
Equipment: dagger, spellbook (containing all prepared spells, plus whatever other spells GM wishes), 30 gp.

Smoky Flower Thugs (5): AC 14; **HP** 54 (9d8+18); **Spd** 30ft; **Melee** club x 2 (+6, 1d6+3 bludgeoning); **Ranged** light crossbow (+5, 80ft/320ft, 1d8 piercing); **SA** Multiattack; **Str** +2, **Dex** +2, **Con** +2, **Int** –1, **Wis** +0, **Cha** –1; **Skills** Athletics +5, Intimidation +5; **Senses** passive Perception 11; **Traits** Pack Tactics (the thug has advantage on an attack roll against a creature if at least one of the thug's allies is within 5ft of the creature and the ally isn't incapacitated); **AL** NE; **CR** 3; **XP** 700.
Equipment: studded leather armor, club, light crossbow, 20 bolts, 20 gp.

Luther Smile is a vile human being. He would sell his sister for a few gold pieces, if he hadn't already done that at the age of 15. Once a serf in some countryside barony, he was branded for disrespect to the baron, and later escaped to the city of Manas, where he took employment with Monjerrat the Bookkeeper. He cares for nothing but money and no one but himself. Luther, or "Lute" as the Smoky Flowers call him, much to his annoyance, regularly robs strung out junkies in the opium den (which he calls a lounge) beyond a sliding-panel door at the side of the inn.

This is Luther's establishment, but it's really been commandeered by Monjerrat, Brodovic, and the Smoky Flowers — a fact that Smile deeply and viciously resents. Because Smile is such a detestable person, Monjerrat and Brodovic haven't realized how big a liability he is to them. Keep that in mind in all dealings with him. If they knew what he had done with the nobles, they'd get rid of him immediately.

Luther Smile: AC 11; **HP** 28 (4d8+12); **Spd** 30ft; **Melee** dagger (+5, 1d4+2 piercing); **SA** Poison (if Smile has advanced warning, he applies scorpion venom to his dagger, 3d8 poison damage, DC 13 Constitution save for half damage, lasts for 1 minute); **Str** +0, **Dex** +1, **Con** +3, **Int** +1, **Wis** +0, **Cha** +1; **Skills** Deception +5, Intimidation +6, Persuasion +6; **Senses** passive Perception 12; **Traits; AL** NE; **CR** 2; **XP** 450.
Equipment: 3 doses blue angel opium, 2 doses scorpion venom (300 gp each dose).

Should the PCs get into a confrontation with Smile, his main goal is to avoid facing them on his own. He'll seek the greater numbers of the Smoky Flowers, run away, or hide in an upstairs or side room. He doesn't want to fight and has no loyalty to anyone other than himself.

Questions and Answers with Smile

Question: Where do we find opium?
Answer: Speak to Monjerrat the Bookkeeper in the side office. He can hook you up. He's a weird one, if you catch my drift. Feel free to "relax" in the lounge once you have what you came for.

Question: What is Blue Angel?
Answer: Looking for the good stuff, eh? Discerning tastes, eh? That stuff is way better than your standard stuff. Once you go blue, you won't ever want the boring regular crap anymore. I call the regular stuff "oldpium," get it?

Question: Who runs the opium trade here?
Answer: That'd be old Monjerrat in the other room. He's fighting with a bunch of other gangs, but he's a man with a plan. He's got some fancy noble, Sir Brodovic of Tilny's his name, out north of the Lorremach Highhills. Brodovic is in and outta here, bossing around the Smoky Flowers, those thuggish louts you see lounging around. Sir Brodovic hired out the Smoky Flowers and grows the opium on his manor lands in

Tilny. The Smoky Flowers do Monjerrat's dirty work, but they answer to Brodovic and he puts the coin in their pockets.

Question: Where is Tilny (or Brodovic's manor house)?
Answer: Not sure exactly, somewhere on the west edge of the Lorremach Highhills. Maybe 150 miles southeast of Manas, as the crow flies.

Question: Who do you work for?
Answer: I only work for me. All the gangs, syndicates, guilds, and such, they may come in and outta here, throw their weight around, but this place is mine and I don't work for none of 'em. I think they forget that sometime.

Question: Have you seen three noble kids?
Answer: Nah. What sort of noble would hang out in a dump like this? This place is for ruffians, whores, and drunkards. **[GM's Note:** PCs can role Insight vs. Smile's +5 Deception to know that he is lying]
Answer (If bribed with 20 gp, Intimidated DC 15, or Persuaded DC 15): Yeah, I seen 'em. Came in a few weeks ago looking to have a good time, like they all do. Real fancy clothes. Old Monjerrat in the other room got 'em hooked right quick and soon enough they was broke. They couldn't pay for the habit no longer, so they had to go to the poppy fields in Tilny to pay off their debt.

Question: Where do they store the opium around here?
Answer: That's worth more money than you have.
Answer (If bribed with 200 gp, Intimidated DC 20, or Persuaded DC 25): They keep it in the storage lofts up the ladders in the back of the room, but I wouldn't go up there if I were you. The Smoky Flowers will be up your behinds until you hightail it out of Manas.

Area 1A: Monjerrat the Bookkeeper's Office

Inevitably, the PCs will decide to pay a visit to Monjerrat the Bookkeeper, who is, along with Smile and Brodovic, the cause of this mess. Monjerrat is more of an accountant than a thug, and had he been raised by more loving parents, he may have grown up to perform a more beneficial role in society. As it stands, his mother never loved him and his father favored his more athletic brothers, leaving Monjerrat to his own devices. He fell in with bad crowds, who tolerated him little more, but appreciated his head for numbers. He picked up a variety of less savory skills and his associations have hardened him in ways that would likely never have happened had fate left him to a more pleasant life. However, as a creative and resourceful criminal, Monjerrat was contacted by Sir Brodovic of Tilny, who was looking for an investment in the opium trade in Manas.

Sir Brodovic of Tilny is now Monjerrat's partner in the effort to take control of the opium trade in Manas. He provided the initial money and

What if Monjerrat the Bookkeeper Learns that the Nobles are in the Lodge?

If the PCs find out from Smile that the nobles were sent to the lodge, they may end up revealing it to Monjerrat. Fortunately for the PCs, Monjerrat doesn't have a means of teleportation or magical communication. There is a portal in the storage loft area of the Five Cups Inn that goes to the manor house, but only Sir Brodovic knows the command word to open the portal. If the code word is known, the portal can be activate as often as desired, and stays open for one minute. Nevertheless, if the PCs don't kill Monjerrat, and he believes that they are searching for the nobles and interfering with his business plans, he will step up attacks on them by the Smoky Flowers, especially if they tarry in city.

still provides a safe location for Monjerrat to grow his magically-fortified opium, receiving a share of the operation's profits.

While Brodovic cares little whether Monjerrat lives or dies, he is, at least for the nonce, a useful tool. Should he prove a liability, Brodovic would cut him loose in an instant. For now, he appreciates Monjerrat's combination of creative intelligence, ruthless efficiency, and honest bookkeeping.

Most of Monjerrat's days consist of careful bookkeeping in the side room in the Five Cups Inn, organizing the efforts of minor dealers and selling opium to individual customers. He takes occasional trips out to the poppy fields and Brodovic's country estate to inspect affairs, but finds such excursions somewhat distasteful, preferring the insulation of his legers. He finds the dirty, criminal world somewhat odious in general, and has little taste for the drugs themselves, but relishes creatively moving sums of money around. He is not afraid of blood or violence, but finds them boring and boorish. He is more prissy than wimpy, but when cornered, can be a hissing viper.

Monjerrat the Bookkeeper: AC 15; **HP** 54 (9d8+18); **Spd** 30ft; **Melee** *dagger of venom* x 2 (+8, 1d4+4 piercing); **SA** Multiattack; **Str** +0, **Dex** +4 (+8), **Con** +2, **Int** +2 (+5), **Wis** +1, **Cha** +1; **Skills** Deception +6, Sleight of Hand +5, Stealth + 4; **Senses** passive Perception 11; **Traits** evasion, sneak attack (1/turn, 4d6 damage); **AL** N (evil tendencies); **CR** 6; **XP** 2,300.

> **Equipment:** *dagger of venom* (DC 15 Con save or +2d10 poison on first hit during encounter), *ring of protection*.

When PCs enter his office off the right side of the inn, read the following:

The door off the side of the tavern opens into an office that could not be more different from the large room of the tavern. Where the tavern is grimy, smoky, dim, and reeking of a variety of unpleasant aromas, the office is spotless, clear, bright, and warm. An antique desk sits in the center of the small space. Several dark wood cabinets sit against the left wall, and candles burn in filigreed sconces providing bright illumination.

Behind the desk sits a short, wiry man with stooped shoulders and the pinched face of one who spends his days staring at ledgers. This is most certainly Monjerrat the Bookkeeper, the opium merchant. His exceedingly ornate red velvet overcoat is embellished with gold thread and an abundance of lace. He resembles a wealthy merchant that slithered into the local pimp's lair and never slithered back out again.

"Who are you?" says the man, his voice cold and full of distaste at the interruption.

Monjerrat is engaged in the same sorts of routine tasks he does every day. No opium, blue angel or other illicit substances are kept in the room. All are on the second floor loft. The Smoky Flowers go to fetch the drugs and give them to buyers, who take them into the opium den through the sliding door in the inn.

Below are common answers to questions the PCs might ask him. If they beat his Deception roll anywhere mentioned, they know he is hiding something, and, where specified, can attempt to Intimidate him into answering more.

Should the PCs manage to search the room (perhaps by sneaking in late at night, using *invisibility* or employing other trickery), they can piece together the plans of Monjerrat, Brodovic, and the Smoky Flowers (see **Adventure Background**).

It is possible that the PCs may wish to arrest Monjerrat. Should they recover the documents in his room, they may have sufficient cause to do that, though this is will depend heavily on how they go about things.

Questions and Answers with Monjerrat

Question: Where do we find opium?

Answer: That depends on what you are looking for. Of course, you could purchase garden variety opium from a variety of hoodlums, scoundrels, ruffians, thugs, criminals, and ne'er-do-wells, but I only sell medical grade opium for healing matters. I assume that is the reason you are here. Such discerning folk as you could not possibly be here for illicit purposes.

Question: What is Blue Angel?

Answer: Is that what the riffraff are calling it? Like with any substance, I suppose there will be side effects among those who take too much. My suppliers only harvest the purest poppies, and perhaps some partake of them too much. It is not my responsibility to police such things. Opium is, after all, legal. I am not their nanny.

Question: Who runs the opium trade here?

Answer: No one can really claim to run that trade. There are many competing entrepreneurs seeking their fortune, and there is enough bounty for all. While I only deal in higher-end merchandise, there is undoubtedly a product that fits every taste and budget. I'm sure I can find something that suits your needs, and if I can't, I've heard that there are some lepers down the street with a few pouches for sale. (**Insight** vs. his **Deception**+6)

Answer (Intimidation DC 25): If the PCs Intimidate him (bribes and persuasion won't work), he reveals that he is working with Sir Brodovic to slowly put the other opium dealers out of business. They created blue opium to addict people so they wouldn't want other kinds of opium anymore. The Smoky Flowers enforce their efforts and are local thugs, contracted by Sir Brodovic.

Question: Have you seen three noble children?

Answer: I saw a few noble youths several weeks. They enjoyed themselves for an evening and went on their way.

GM's Reminder: He's actually telling the truth here. He hasn't seen the nobles since, and has no knowledge of their disappearance. He may be responsible for the larger opium crisis, but only Luther Smile can claim direct responsibility for the nobles.

Question: Where do you keep the opium?

Answer: Why would I tell you that?

Answer (Intimidation DC 30): On the second floor, in the storage loft. But if I were you, I'd leave well enough alone, assuming you value your skin.

Blue Angel Poppies and Opium

Blue Angel is a particularly virulent strain of poppy that produces an extremely potent narcotic paste. Monjerrat the Bookkeeper discovered a small handful of the flowers growing in the Tilny Hills, and decided to cultivate them with the assistance of a hired alchemist and a minor wizard, both of whom later perished under strange circumstances, which is unknown to Monjerrat. The flowers are identical to standard poppies, except for two significant differences. Where ordinary poppies are known for their shocking red color, the blue angel strain is almost neon blue, with pulsing blue-gray veins radiating from the central eye of the flower like wings.

Cultivation of opium from blue angel poppies is performed in much the same way as standard opium, though those picking the flower must take extra precautions when handling them, due both to the difficulty in removing the deep blue stains that result, and to the intoxicating effect of the sappy paste within the bulb.

Smoking a single dose of blue angel opium results in a brief euphoric high, followed by a devastating crash. For ten minutes following the inhalation of the drug, the user is immune to all conditions and penalties imposed by fear, sickness, fatigue, pain, or morale, and has a +2 bonus on attack rolls, damage, ability checks, and saving throws. This is a treated as a poison.

The high of blue angel lasts for only about ten minutes, followed by a crash in which the user experiences fatigue and dehydration. 4d6 hours later, the user is possessed by a powerful compulsion to seek out more blue angel, doing whatever is necessary to acquire the drug. This compulsion can be resisted with a DC 10 Wisdom saving throw (poison). If the save fails, the user will perform desperate, even violent acts to satiate the addiction, completely unaware of personal morality and completely willing to take the lives of others or break any law or custom to get what the addict craves. After the addict quells the craving, the unfortunate person falls into another stupor for another 4d6 hours, then begins the cycle anew.

Each time the cycle starts over, the save DC increased by 1. Furthermore, if the DC rises high enough that the addict only succeeds on a natural 20, the addict has disadvantage on the save. This is not a mind-effecting effect, but rather is a form of physical addiction, and any resistance or bonuses against poison will help.

Even if an individual succeeds on a save, or is cured of addiction using *neutralize poison* or a similar spell, should the user take another dose of blue angel in the future, the save DC starts at whatever the highest save DC that the user has ever suffered. Nothing short of a *heal, wish, miracle* or magic of a similar power level can permanently remove the addiction. Even then, if the individual should ever try the drug again, the process of addiction begins again, though at the base DC of 10. For the few users who have survived a blue angel addiction, memory of their addiction is an insane and tortured blur.

There is only one treatment for blue angel other than powerful magic: standard opium. For some reason, normal opium counteracts the effects of blue angel, though only temporarily. If a user smokes standard opium, the normal effects of the blue opium crash are suppressed for the rest of the day, leaving the user dopey, but not manic. The user regains the compulsion to search for blue angel the following day, however, unless they smoke more standard opium. If a user takes another dose of blue angel, the neutralizing effects of standard opium end.

Unfortunately, most blue angel addicts would never think to seek out standard opium because of their craving for blue angel, and dealers of standard opium are unaware of its ability to temporary counter a blue angel addiction. This is how Monjerrat and Brodovic keep their opium pickers functional. They distribute standard opium to their pickers, keeping them placid and docile. If the authorities in Manas were to learn of this — especially the religious authorities — they would likely be able to use this as part of a treatment for blue angel.

In addition, blue opium makes those who use it difficult to affect with divination spells that answer questions or determine location, such as *augury, divination, commune, contact other plane*. While such spells do work, the information they return is less specific, cloudy, vague, and imprecise. It is up to the GM to adjudicate how much information is gained by such spells. Spells that locate objects or creatures automatically fail when targeting users of blue opium.

It is not surprising that users of blue angel often die of overdoses. The compulsive effect that occurs during the crash typically renders the users incapable of restraining themselves when they come upon supplies of the drug. Like a starving man coming upon food, they gorge themselves on the drug. Should a user roll a natural 1 on a Wisdom save against the drug's addictive effects, the user dies (though often not until one last, manic episode).

Area 1B: Opium Den

This area is full of nothing but blue angel addicts on divans, smoking opium.

Area 2: Storage Loft

This loft has numerous crates full of blue angel opium, ready to be smoked. If the drug is ever criminalized, and the guard knows that this is where it is stored, they move to seize it. The loft also contains a teleportation circle leading to Sir Brodovic's manor house. Only Brodovic knows the sigil's proper sequence, though there is a diagram of it in a painting in the lodge.

The Law

In order to investigate the legal issues surrounding opium, the PCs need to speak to Orlando Cormont. No special knowledge or background is required to find Cormont, though he isn't at the Headquarter of the City Wardens when the PCs locate him. He is observing the final stages of cleanup of an incident at the Damozel Square marketplace at midday. Guards are hauling off a knot of writhing and kicking vagabonds in filthy rags, each bearing the angel wing veins identifying him or her as a blue angel addict. The area nearby is in absolute chaos, with flour streaming through the air, melon splattering expensive silk shawls, sacks of grains spilled and mixing with split casks of ale.

Cormont is a stoic, normally imperturbable man, but this opium crisis has tried his last nerve. While a strict adherent of the law, he is normally a live and let live sort. Today, however, he's having trouble seeing any upside to allowing opium to remain legal, even though it is only the addicts of this new strain that are causing problems.

The PCs may need to revisit him a number of times throughout this adventure. They might return to him to report on what they find at Sir Brodovic of Tilny's estate, or to seek assistance in transportation.

You approach the man the guards pointed out as Orlando Cormont, Commander of the Corps of Wardens. A man in his middle years, he is graying at the temples, but there is nothing the least bit soft about the commander. He is watching a cleanup after some sort of scuffle in the marketplace. He projects a solid, unshakeable presence that makes it clear how he rose to his current rank. Nevertheless, cracks seem to be forming in his stony facade: he swats away flies that buzz around his face, seeking honey that splattered from a knocked over a stand; his once-spotless surcoat is stained with exploded tomatoes, and his shoes are scuffed.

Questions and Answers with Orlando Cormont

Cormont will speak to the PCs, courteously and — despite the scenario — with only a mild hint of exasperation. He has received the request for help sent by Lord Parzalon, and has been on the lookout for the PCs.

Question: What happened here?
Answer: I'm honestly not sure. Some opium addicts looking for the drug in the marketplace went wild. The drug makes people hallucinate, so maybe that's what set them off. It's really impossible to know.

Question: What is Blue Angel?
Answer: It's a new kind of opium being sold in the worse parts of town. We're not exactly sure who is selling it, though we suspect a group called the Smoky Flowers, a local group of thugs. I'd check out the Five Cups Inn if I were you. Opium is legal, so I have no reason to raid the place.

Question: Do you think opium should be illegal?
Answer: I'm not sure. I know that the normal stuff isn't that big a deal. Sure, it can ruin a man, but that's his choice. But this new strain, it's different. It doesn't just ruin you; it makes you crazy. Addicts go mad looking for the stuff, robbing and killing each other and innocent people. It would be hard to criminalize just one kind of opium because then the criminals would just alter their recipe a bit. I'm open to suggestions, frankly. **What do *you* think we should do?**

Cormont is asking the PCs for their honest, current opinions, since they are not only powerful individuals but apparently some sort of unofficial envoys from the County of Toullen. They can offer any number of possible solutions. See the "What Should Be Done About the Opium Problem" sidebar for some of the possibilities.

Question: Who runs the opium trade here?
Answer: It's a bunch of gangs, all killing each other. The thieves' guild seems to be waiting around to see who wins. I'm not sure who is going to come out on top, but whoever it is, they'll be a force to be reckoned with. I have heard rumors about a minor noble who's involved, a fellow named Sir Brodovic of Tilny. He owns a manor in the Tilny Hills near the Lorremach, but he's in the city quite a bit. A lot of the opium crop is grown around those hills. You might check out his manor house to look for more leads on your youths, if you want to make the trip.

What Should Be Done About the Opium Problem?

Several influential individuals are interested in hearing what actions the PCs think should be taken to mitigate or stop the opium problem. Below are a number of possible solutions, though the PCs can come up with other ones.

• *Criminalize all opium:* While it's regrettable that some are ruining things for all, opium is considered by many to be an odious habit that ruins lives. If the PCs choose to advocate this option, all opium sale, use, and production would be criminalized. This, of course, says nothing about rehabilitation and assistance with drug addiction, which may or may not be included in prosecution.

• *Criminalize only blue angel:* Why ruin things for everyone when it's only a few people causing trouble? Criminalize blue angel and create a standing king's order that any similar substances will be reviewed and may also be criminalized if found to be similarly destructive. Normal opium remains legal, though a closer eye will be kept on sellers and users.

• *Leave things as they are:* People will hear how destructive the drug is, and likely avoid it. This may be wishful thinking, but some merchants of neighboring communities advocate it. Unusually for the mercantile interests in the city, who normally prefer minimal government interference in commerce, the local traders and merchants are actually *not* advocating this position. They feel that the new strain hurts more honest, standard business and may eventually lead to criminalization of all opium, even if it remains legal for the time being.

• *Provide drug addiction programs and assist in rehabilitation:* This option can be combined with any of the other options and is the primary interest of Besondar. Various temples in Manas offer to help those addicted to blue angel and other drugs to kick their addictions.

• *Tax, regulate, and inspect all opium coming into Suilley:* By increasing oversight, the kingdom increases revenue, but also safety, at least in theory. This can be combined with banning blue angel.

• Another solution the PCs think of that hasn't been covered here.

Question: Do you have any information on the three missing noble kids?

Answer: I wish I could say I knew something, but I don't. No one has seen them, and I have people looking. I'll let you know if we find anything. Should you require any assistance in transportation, I can connect you with guides through the countryside. Otherwise it's a maze of little country roads and trails. Lord Parzalon is an old soldiering friend of mine; I want to see his son returned as much as anyone.

Church of Belon the Wise

The opium crisis has not gone unnoticed by the faiths of Manas. While the city has many temples and shrines, the Church of Belon is the one they have an introduction to, in the form of a letter given to them in Tertry by the High Priest of Thyr. Belon is a god of knowledge and magic, and the church's power is on the rise. Besondar the Cognate is the High Priest of the temple in Manas, and the PCs may go to him for assistance. Although the High Priest has no interest in how the opium trade is eventually addressed, he knows that his advice will be sought, and wants to get as much information as he can. Besondar is a man of subtlety and nuance, open to many possible solutions to the problem.

Besondar is outside in a meditation garden when the PCs track him down.

You approach the garden the parishioners pointed you to, near the entrance to the temple to Belon the Wise. The High Priest, Besondar, sits at noon each day in a meditation garden, considering things he has learned and deciding what

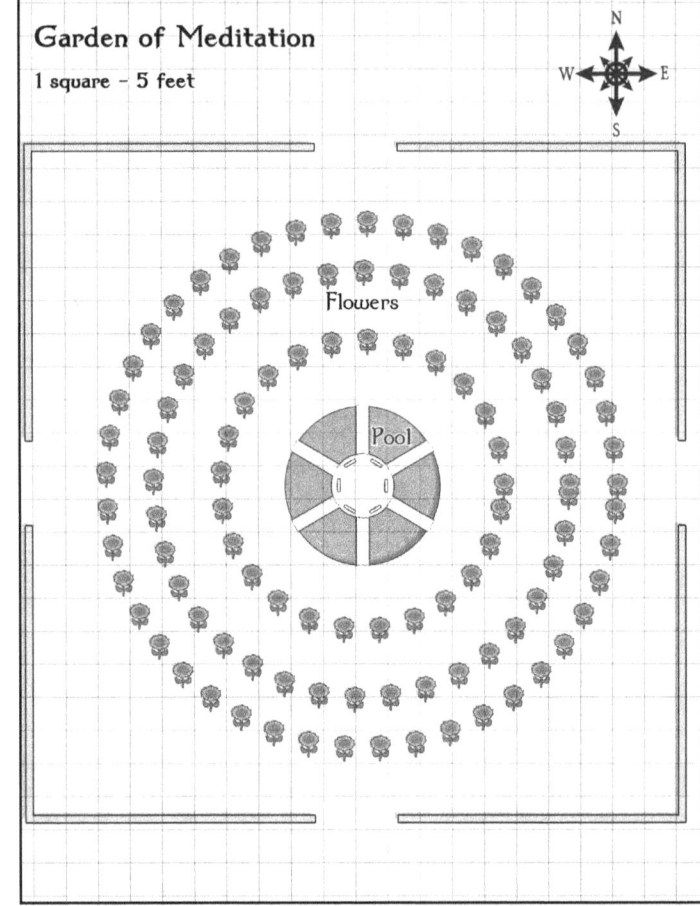

Garden of Meditation

1 square - 5 feet

Flowers

Pool

to do about them. The garden is essentially a small park, with a small pond at its center. Foot bridges lead to an island at the center of the pond, where a sun dial sits, surrounded by rounded benches. Extended out in concentric rings from the pond are circles of vibrant sunflowers, swaying in the gentle breeze, exultant in the brilliant radiance of the noonday sun.

A small number of people are strolling among the sunflowers in the garden, but there is only one person on the island, and he seems to notice you the moment you walk into the garden. He stands, motioning you to join him. As you walk the footbridges, coming closer, you see a strong, nobly-featured man in his middle years, wearing a white robe, like the other priests you have seen in the temple area.

"Welcome, welcome. I have been expecting you. I have heard troubling things and seen omens. I believe you are here to help this fair city rise from a dark shadow."

Besondar will speak to the PCs warmly, though distantly and distractedly. As a spiritual conduit with the god of knowledge, he constantly receives bits and pieces of information, most of them unconnected with anything else, "overheard" from distant oracles, statues of the god, and other sources like a jigsaw puzzle of cryptic clues. One of his tasks is to assemble as much of these scattered facts as possible into meaningful information that can be offered to the god in the nature of an offering. Certainly not all priests of Belon find themselves in this relationship to the deity — indeed, it is rare — but Besondar is one of these. The constant flood of disconnected images, words, and symbols intruding into his mind means that Besondar is constantly mentally occupied, and despite the fact that he is a brilliant person, it can be difficult for him to focus for too long on what is happening around him. Few of Belon's priests that are "blessed" with this divine connection reach high office in the Church: they are obviously singled out with a great gift and responsibility, but they are seldom able to do much else. The growth of Belon's popularity in the Borderland Provinces has left the Church of Belon with a shortage of true

High Priests, so Besondar is currently, temporarily, assigned to Manas until a more-political and less-holy successor can be found for the post.

Like elsewhere, the conversation with Besondar is structured as commonly asked questions, but you should weave them organically into the discourse with the NPC.

Questions and Answers with Besondar

Question: We've heard that there are issues with divinations used on people affected by blue angel. What do you think is happening?

Answer: I can't be certain. The drug seems to interfere with the divine conduit, though I've heard that it is equally effective in blocking arcane divination. I'm not able to test that. Either way, it makes answers to divinations vague. And given that we cannot perform divinations on a given subject multiple times in rapid succession, it's difficult to learn much about the whereabouts of the poor missing youths.

Question: Have you learned anything more about the whereabouts of the missing youths?

Answer: Alas, I haven't learned much. What I sent to Ruthenvais still holds true. They are still in Suilley, still alive, and still in danger. I have been seeing visions of blue poppy fields near a lumber-built hall or lodge of some sort, a large wall surrounding it. I don't know if that helps in any way.

Question: Where is Tilny Manor (or the Tilny Hills)?

Answer: Give me a moment. [Besondar takes out some parchment and a quill, then appears to drift into a reverie for a moment. He then draws a map, his eyes still closed, showing a complex series of roads and trails leading southeast from Manas. Halfway through, he writes the words: "would lead to a bad harvest," but crosses them out and says, "Sorry, that's something different."] This map should get you there on the most direct route through the countryside. It shouldn't take much longer than traveling on a high road, as long as you don't go off this particular way. [Despite the fact that he can apparently draw a precise map to an unknown location, he can tell the PCs nothing about Tilny Manor itself. He has never been there, and never heard of it.]

Question: Do you think opium should be illegal?

Answer: Perhaps… perhaps. In the end, I will support the side that comes up with the best plan to mitigate the harm my people and my city suffer. If the solution helps to restore the addicts, I will endorse it, whether the drug remains legal or becomes completely criminal. The legality is irrelevant to the actual problem.

I am curious. **What do *you* think should be done?**

Besondar is asking the PCs for their honest, current opinions about what should be done. They can offer any number of possible solutions. See the "What Should Be Done about the Opium Problem" sidebox for some of the possibilities. The PCs can also come back to him, should they change their minds, discover more information leading to other conclusions, or come up with new ideas. If the PCs present him with a reasonable plan for drug rehabilitation at any point in the adventure, he will support their position when they make their final recommendation to Cormont, who has the ear of the king.

Acolytes approach on the footbridges, appearing eager for their high priest's attentions. Besondar turns to you, "Ah. I fear I have other appointments to attend. Please take some time to meditate on what I have said and consider the problems of rehabilitation." He points to a slim, sun-darkened man tending a sunflower, who smiles at you. "Dorias will be around to assist you with anything you should need."

Besondar and all of the acolytes, excepting Dorias, go back to the temple, leaving the PCs to contemplate the issues in the garden. Give them some time to talk through the issues before proceeding to the next text box.

You spend some time discussing the conundrum posed to you by Besondar and enjoying the tranquility of the

Rehabilitation and Prevention

Besondar is asking the PCs to present him with reasonable options for rehabilitating drug addicts and curbing drug crime. While he and his clerics might be able to cure the addicts of their addiction with clerical magic, it is in no way realistic to heal all addicts of their ailments this way. Furthermore, it may not be possible. What's to stop a user from going right back to the drug after being cured of the addiction?

Any of the following might be considered a reasonable solution, and some might be combined as multi-part treatments:
• Research alchemical solutions to help ease withdrawal symptoms.
• Seek herbal remedies that bolster willpower to help resist cravings for the drug.
• Create minor magic items that help ward against drug addiction, or perhaps that ruin or disrupt the effects of the drug.

---

meditation garden. It is easy to imagine the high priest and acolytes coming here to contemplate their philosophical questions.

The peaceful afternoon serenity is interrupted by a commotion at the entrance to the gardens. Six frothing, raving people begin running around the gardens, howling "where is the angel? I know you've got her? Take me to her!"

Dorias, the acolyte who had been tending sunflowers calls to you. "Please, restrain them, but don't hurt them! And for Belon's sake, try not to destroy the gardens!"

As you move to try and stop the raving lunatics, Dorias begins to shoo the other patrons out, lock the gates, and secure the area.

Creatures: The **six addicts** aren't really a significant danger to the PCs. The challenge is rounding them up without hurting them, without causing significant damage to the gardens, and within a reasonable amount of time. It is unclear why they think there is blue angel in the garden. Perhaps they associate the PCs with the drug, having seen them in the Five Cups Inn. The longer the addicts are loose the more damage they cause. If they want Besondar's support on any matter, significant damage to the garden makes this harder to obtain.

Blue Angel Addict (2): AC 10; **HP** 4 (1d8); **Spd** 30ft; **Melee** club (+4, 1d4+2 bludgeoning); **Str** +2, **Dex** +2, **Con** +2, **Int** +2, **Wis** +2, **Cha** +2; **Senses** passive Perception 10; **Traits** blue angel high (see sidebox Blue Angel Poppies and Opium) **AL** N; **CR** 1/8; **XP** 25.

If the PCs round them up in 1–3 rounds, without harming the addicts, the priests take the addicts to the temple, where they will be cleansed of the poison. The guards will not be called. If the fight takes longer than 3 rounds, or harm any of the addicts, the priests call the guards.

Part 3: Tilny Manor

Traveling to the western edge of the Lorremach Highhills from Manas does not take any longer than traveling along a high road when the characters have a guides and a letter from the Commander of the Corps of Wardens in Manas, or a map from the High Priest of Belon. Roll encounters as if the PCs were traveling on the Flatlander Road, but treat any encounters as High-Risk. (see **Borderland Provinces**, Chapter 9: Kingdom of Suilley, *Flatlander Road*, and *Appendix C: Encounter Quick-Reference*).

If the PCs do not travel directly to the manor, their delays endanger the captives and could even lead to arriving after they have died. Normal travel times, even though they are fairly long, do not endanger the youths.

The Manor and Surrounds

The PCs eventually approach Sir Brodovic of Tilny's manor house and properties which, as Luther Smile said, are roughly 150 miles southeast of Manas, on the edge of the Lorremach Highhills. Brodovic owns a much larger estate, as well, where we makes his home most of the year, but his main castle and lands are quite distant from the Tilny Manor, and do not appear in this adventure.

When the PCs arrive, read or paraphrase the following:

Neatly-planted square fields of brilliant blue poppies flank the road leading to a compound that you've been told contains the manor house. Dazed workers harvest poppy pods in the harsh sun, loading them into wheelbarrows and carting them to the compound. Every one of them smokes on a small pipe, the curls of smoke drifting into the air. The compound is protected by a 10-foot-tall stone wall with a sliding wrought iron gate. The gate is flanked by two burly guards, who are inspecting the crop. They seem satisfied and call for the gate to be open. You can just make out sentries with crossbows standing atop a structure within the compound. If you're not careful, they'll spot you.

Unless the PCs are stealthy, the sentries spot them as they approach. (Note the sentries' passive Perception of 16.)

While opponents are listed in a number of separate locations, the scene is effectively a single large battle, occurring in waves and over multiple terrains where combatants can hide, take cover, or otherwise take advantage of their environment. This battle can be quite deadly if the PCs do not fight strategically.

Trap: The wyvern mages have inscribed the wall with a magical trap. Anyone who sets foot on the other side of the wall without passing through the gate (including via flight or teleportation) sets off a keening alarm and is sprayed with conjured blue angel sap. A DC 15 Wisdom (Perception or Intelligence (Investigation) check detects the runes that make up the trap. Determining their function requires a DC 17 Intelligence (Arcana) check, and disabling them requires a second such check. The alarm alerts the wyvern mages, who immediately give treats containing blue angel opium to each of the wyverns, who then fly off to attack the PCs. If the alarm isn't set off, the mages give the wyverns the treats if and when they are made aware of intruders.

Areas F1 and F2: Poppy Fields

Healthy blue angel poppies grow in a field flanking the road leading to the lodge.

Creatures: (40) noncombatant poppy pickers (male and female mostly human commoners) work in the fields, hauling poppy pods in wheelbarrows to the gate.

Area F3: the Gate

Two burly guards inspect wheelbarrows of poppy pods before giving the go ahead for two of their brethren to open the gates.

Creatures: (2) guards watch the poppy pickers at the gate.

Guard (2): AC 16; **HP** 52 (8d8+16); **Spd** 30ft; **Melee** shortsword x 2 (+7, 1d6+3 piercing); **Ranged** heavy crossbow (+6, 100ft/400ft, 1d10 piercing); **SA** Multiattack; **Str** +3 (+5), **Dex** +2, **Con** +2 (+4), **Int** +0, **Wis** +0, **Cha** +0; **Senses** passive Perception 16; **AL** NE; **CR** 3; **XP** 700.
> **Equipment:** scale mail, shortsword, heavy crossbow, 20 bolts, 22 gp.

Area F4: Gate Crank

Two more guards stand here pulling a winch to open and close the gates.
Creatures: (2) guards open and close the gates.

Area F5: Storage Building

Two more guards are off duty here, playing cards before their shifts, ignoring the dopey poppy pickers unloading pods.
Creatures: (2) Off-duty guards relax as the pickers unload. They are not wearing armor.

Off-Duty Friendly Men Compound Guard (2): AC 12; **HP** 52 (8d8+16); **Spd** 30ft; **Melee** shortsword x 2 (+7, 1d6+3 piercing); **Ranged** heavy crossbow (+6, 100ft/400ft, 1d10 piercing); **SA** Multiattack; **Str** +3 (+5), **Dex** +2, **Con** +2 (+4), **Int** +0, **Wis** +0, **Cha** +0; **Senses** passive Perception 16; **AL** NE; **CR** 2; **XP** 450.
> **Equipment:** scale mail (not worn), shortsword, heavy crossbow, 20 bolts, 22 gp.

Area F6: the Manor

This is the manor house, a small building that has been in Sir Brodovic's family for centuries. At one point it actually was a manor house, though all traces of that function have been stripped from it. Now, it is just a simple wood barrack with eight wood beds, a sturdy rectangular table and the basic belongings of the guards. A portal is inscribed on the floor near the back of the room. Only Brodovic knows the sequence of code words that must be spoken to activate it, but those in the room should make Intelligence (Arcana), DC 18 checks to decipher the code. If successful, the PCs figure out the words that let them activate the circle to transport themselves and all of the workers back to Manas through the Five Cups Inn. The circle can be activated as often as desired, and stays open for one minute.

Creatures: (3) crossbow sentries sit on the roof of the lodge.

Crossbow Sentries (3): AC 15; **HP** 52 (8d8+16); **Spd** 30ft; **Melee** shortsword (+6, 1d6+2 piercing); **Ranged** heavy crossbow x 2 (+7, 100ft/400ft, 1d10 piercing); **Str** +2 (+4), **Dex** +3 (+5), **Con** +2 (+4), **Int** +0, **Wis** +0, **Cha** +0; **SA** Rapid Reload; **Senses** passive Perception 16; **AL** NE; **CR** 3; **XP** 700.
> **Equipment:** studded leather, shortsword, heavy crossbow, 30 bolts, 22 gp.

Area F7: the Sleeping Hovel

This outbuilding contains the sleeping pallets of the 40 poppy picking drug addicts enslaved by Sir Brodovic. There is nothing else in here; certainly nothing of value.

Area F8: Wyvern House

The outbuilding houses two trained wyverns addicted to blue angel. Their caretakers are two mages specialized in wyvern training, who have had them from the egg. Because they are addicted to blue angel, the wyverns seek out the PCs if/when the characters are sprayed with poppy sap. Unsubtle as they are, the wyverns try to kill the PCs, believing that they can take the drug from them. The mages can also order them to attack the PCs, though they are even more ferocious when driven by their lust for blue angel.

Creatures: There are **2 drug addicted wyverns** and **2 wyvern mages** in the wyvern house, though they do not likely remain there. The wyverns bear the pulsing blue-gray angel wing markings of blue angel addicts. Blue angel is already factored into their statistics. After 10 minutes are up, they continue to fight, though they will lose the +2 to attack, damage, saves, and ability checks, as well as any immunities derived from the drug. The wyvern mages mostly focus on helping the wyverns by attacking PCs who seem to be hurting them.

Blue Angel Addicted Wyvern (2): AC 13; **HP** 110 (13d10+39); **Spd** 20ft, fly 80ft; **Melee** bite (+9, reach 10ft, 2d6+6

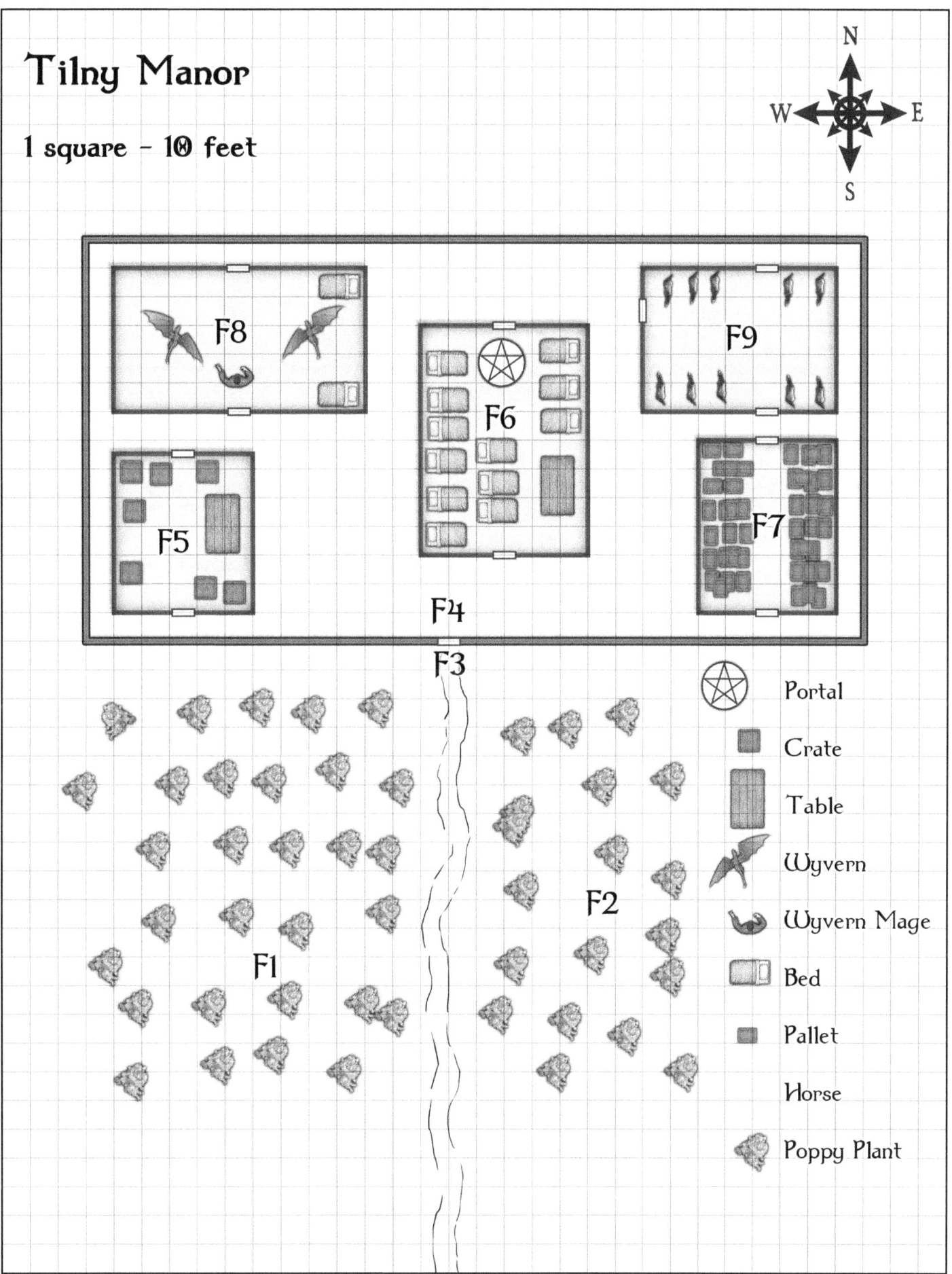

Tilny Manor

1 square – 10 feet

⬟	Portal
▪	Crate
▬	Table
🦅	Wyvern
	Wyvern Mage
🛏	Bed
▪	Pallet
	Horse
🌸	Poppy Plant

piercing), claw x2 (+9, 2d8+6 slashing), stinger (+9, 2d6+6 piercing and 7d6 poison, DC 15 Con save for half); **Str** +6, **Dex** +0, **Con** +5, **Int** −1, **Wis** +3, **Cha** +0; **SA** Multiattack (the wyvern makes two attacks: one with its bite and one with its stinger. While flying, it can use its claws in place of one other attack); **Immune** fear, sickness, fatigue, pain, or negative morale; **Skills** Perception +6; **Senses** darkvision 120ft, passive Perception 16; **AL** N **CR** 7; **XP** 2,900.

Wyvern Mage (2): **AC** 12 (15 with *mage armor*); **HP** 58 (9d8+18); **Spd** 30ft; **Melee** dagger (+4, 1d4+1); **SA** spells (Int+6, DC 14); **Str** −1, **Dex** +2, **Con** +2, **Int** +3 (+6), **Wis** +1 (+4), **Cha** +0; **Skills** Arcana +6, History +6; **Senses** passive Perception 11; **Traits**; **AL** LE; **CR** 6; **XP** 2,300.

    Spells (slots): 0 (at will)—*dancing lights, mage hand, mending, ray of frost*; 1st (4)—*detect magic, burning hands, mage armor, magic missile*; 2nd (3)—*alter self, scorching ray*; 3rd (3)— *fireball, fly, haste*; 4th (3)—*ice storm, wall of fire*; 5th (1)—*wall of force*

    Equipment: dagger, spellbook (containing all prepared spells, plus whatever other spells GM wishes), 36 gp.

Area F9: the Stable

There are **(10) horses** here for use by the guards and overseers. These are not war-trained horses and are not meant to be used as combatants.

Aftermath: Assuming the PCs are able to defeat the guards, wyverns, snipers, and mage, they find the youths among the poppy pickers after a small amount of conversation. The three nobles are somewhat ragged, but are alive and can be reunited with their families after some time with Besondar at the temple of Thyr. The PCs return to Manas without difficulty. What remains is for the PCs to resolve the legality of opium and discuss possibilities for rehabilitation.

Part 4: Audience with the King

The PCs must return to Manas with the three youths to see to their health, before the three nobles travel on to Tertry to reunite with their families. While the PCs may have potent magical healing as part of their skillset, Besondar wants his clerics to examine the youths before they are

sent back to Toullen, and to see the result of the Blue Angel on the other opium workers (which seems to be more a matter of curiosity). The PCs must also report to Orlando Cormont.

Report to Besondar

Assuming they agree to do so, the PCs report to Besondar. Read the following upon their arrival in the gardens:

Besondar sits on the same bench on the island in the garden where you met him before, feeding breadcrumbs to greedy ducks. He looks up, and welcomes you to join him. "I'm pleased to see that you've returned. The three youths, as well as all of the other workers, are being cared for by our healers, and all are doing fine. I'd appreciate it if you could tell me the full story of what happened. I'd also like to hear your final recommendations concerning opium itself.

If the PCs have presented a reasonable solution or combination of solutions to Besondar, he supports whatever position they take regarding the legality of opium. He then speaks privately to Orlando Cormont, advising him to support the PCs. Cormont has the ear of the king and the king will listen to his word above all when making his decision. Besondar's recommendation to Cormont results in the PCs gaining advantage on their roll when dealing with the commander.

Debrief with Orlando Cormont

Orlando Cormont requested that the PCs meet with him after they locate the youths. If they have forgotten this (and even if they have not), be sure to remind them by having him send a messenger to them inviting them to a debriefing at the guardhouse.

Sometime later, after you've had a bit of time to rest and recover from your adventures, a messenger from the city guard approaches you, requesting that you follow him to a debriefing with Commander Cormont.

[Assuming they follow, continue:] The messenger leads

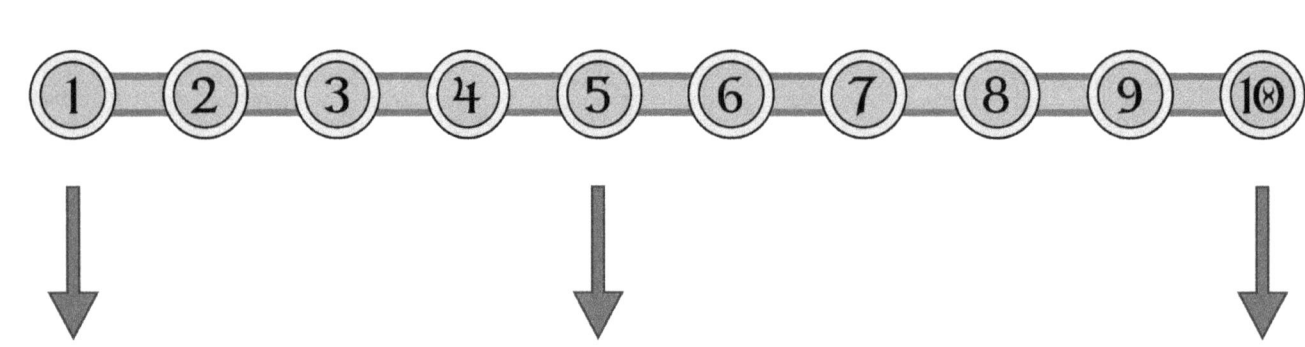

Use, sale and production of all forms of opium is illegal.

Use, sale, and production of blue angel opium, as well as other new forms of opium, is illegal, but existing 'standard' opium remains legal.

Use, sale, and production of all forms of opium remain legal, though users are liable for any crimes they commit while under the influence.

you to the Caerronde, the city's massive citadel tower, where you ascend the seemingly endless spiral staircase, passing numerous landings filled with guards engaged in training, recreation, and paperwork, before stopping at an office. Orlando Cormont looks up from a report, beckoning you to join him.

"Please, tell me of what has transpired. I've heard that things went well, but I wish to know the details."

After he hears the accounts, Cormont asks the PCs again to make a recommendation regarding the legality of opium. Before they state their case, determine Cormont's current position on Opium. Assume that Cormont starts the adventure at a neutral position (5 on the opium legality scale, below). Move the scale one position to the left for each negative incident related to opium that has occurred since the PCs first met him, including, but not limited to the marketplace, the gardens at the Temple of Thyr, the rescue of the noble youths at the manor house, and any other attacks that have occurred. The scale *cannot* go below 1. If an attack is never discovered by the watch or Cormont, do not include it.

Give the PCs an opportunity to sway Cormont's opinion. They can make a single Charisma (Persuasion) check, DC 15 (possibly with advantage, if they convinced Besondar). If they make a 15, they can move Cormont's opinion by 1 spot in either direction. For every 5 by which they exceed 15, they can move it an additional spot (2 spots at 20, 3 at 25, and so on). After the check, record Cormont's final position. Of course, as mentioned before, should the PCs come up with a better solution that does not fall on the scale below, Cormont is willing to consider it.

Concluding the Adventure

The PCs eventually discover the results of their discussions with Cormont, who makes his recommendation to the government of Suilley and to the King. His arguments might or might not affect the King, but the recommendations are put into place, at least temporarily, in the City of Manas itself. While the PCs may feel some personal satisfaction (or dissatisfaction) from the result, it is unlikely to affect them much personally. If they had argued for a reward from Cyrilinde, they can visit Tertry to claim a single Rare magic item from the treasury of Count Luthien (GM's discretion as to what is available, but presumably something of use to each PC). The PCs may wish to visit Tertry anyway, if just to check on the youths and the satisfaction of Cyrilinde. If they didn't ask for a physical reward, they still have a favor they can call in.

As to experience, follow the guidelines outlined in the Experience sidebar. Evaluate if the PCs managed to rescue the youths while exercising discretion wherever possible, and were engaged and roleplayed in regard to the opium legality issue. The matter of discretion is difficult to adjudicate, as it is impossible for the PCs to avoid asking questions. The best gauge of this if the PCs bungled their way in the underworld, or if they got attacked by the Smoky Flowers an excessive number of times for asking too many questions, too often. Large, messy, uncontained fights in the city also qualify as lacking in discretion.

As to Monjerrat, if the PCs didn't kill him and he wasn't arrested, his ability to consolidate the opium trade in Manas is finished. He will likely rise to criminal prominence again, based on his abilities, but for the time being he is no longer a danger to society. Sir Brodovic is mostly untouchable, though he might have to keep away from Manas for a while. The fate of Luther Smile heavily depends on what happened during the adventure, though if the PCs didn't kill him, he is probably still glaring at ruffians in his bar, while patrons smoke opium (legal or not) in the lounge to the side.

A Most Peculiar Hunt

Monster-hunting is the bread and butter of many an adventuring career. When the horrors of the wild threaten civilized lands — or sometimes even before they have the chance — brave mages and warriors set out to lay them low. It's a tale as old as adventuring itself.

Only this time, the heart of the problem isn't the monsters. It's the monster hunters.

A Most Peculiar Hunt is an adventure for 4–6 characters of 12th level. Set primarily in the wilds of the Unclaimed Lands, along the border of Aachen Province, this is a somewhat "sandboxy," non-linear adventure, one that may take the characters days or weeks of game time to work through.

Adventure Background

The so-called "Unclaimed Lands" consist largely of untamed wilderness; thick woodlands, rolling hills that hide whatever lies beyond, broad grasslands through which all manner of dangers crouch. For all that, though, the region is far more heavily populated than some believe. Countless tiny provinces dot the landscape, ruled by would-by barons, dukes, lords, and kings. And for every one of these minuscule fiefdoms of a few hundred people, half a dozen tiny hamlets of a few dozen souls stand between them. The average "kingdom" of the Unclaimed Lands is a town or two with outlying farms, but each has its own identity, and each ruler has his or her pride and ambitions.

Some while back, three of those communities not terribly far from the Aachen border — the "Duchy" of Avrandt, the "Barony" of Corvul, and a small province called Vath — all nearly went to war. The cause was

Where Are the Neighbors?

Although few and far between, the Unclaimed Lands do have a few genuine powers above and beyond the petty lords who claim dominion over scattered territories. The Pirate-Count of Turpin, for example, keeps a weather eye on everything going on in and around Avrandt, Corvul, and Vath. These other petty lords watch, however, only for threats to their own interests; they certainly have no intention of involving themselves unless they must. As such, with the exception of a few unfortunate river pirates — see encounter **E** — Turpin has no involvement in the adventure as written. (The key phrase is, of course, "as written." If you as GM wish to include them, they would certainly make for fascinating additions to the adventure.)

That's not to say that these other entities have *no* impact on what's happening, however. The defensive power of Turpin and the peculiar powers of the Court of Loom Ché are among the primary reasons that so many of the monsters are moving south toward Aachen Province, rather than further into the Unclaimed Lands.

nothing of import; some territory or lost livestock to which all three laid claim. Their solution, however, was noteworthy.

Rather than spend lives and resources in a war none of them could afford, they engaged in a spot of competition.

Playing in the Sandbox

A Most Peculiar Hunt is written to be very freeform. While the characters do need to find their way through a handful of clues/ questions to the individuals at the center of the trouble, the events and encounters can occur in almost any order. Encounters occur as and when the characters find them, as opposed to one leading directly into the next.

Any one of the first four encounters — encounters **A** through **D** — can kick off the adventure. Some involve the party stumbling into ongoing events, while others have them more deliberately hired to solve the problem. Choose the one you like best, or that best fits your characters' current locations. (encounter **D** is particularly appropriate if you want to fully emphasize the "backwards" nature of the adventure. What better way to start a tale where the monster hunters are the problem, than to have the heroes hired by a monster?)

Once the adventure has begun with whichever of those four scenes you've chosen, the characters should understand that they need to investigate the Unclaimed Lands, searching for clues as to what's driving the monsters south. They may wander the wilderness, they may head directly for one of the towns, but either way further encounters (possibly including the rest of the initial four; you can still use them, even if they're not starting the adventure) occur as and when the characters come across them. Only after days or weeks of searching, and multiple encounters, are the characters likely to have pieced together enough information to get to the heart of things. (And players who are inclined to resort to combat no matter what, rather than speaking when an opponent is capable of it, are going to have a harder time.)

A few points to be aware of when running *A Most Peculiar Hunt*:

• The GM is encouraged to reward experience points by milestone, rather than per encounter; otherwise, more careless parties are likely to acquire *more* experience than those who carefully think things through. Use the following as major milestones:

• Gaining the "What's Happening?" information (see **Learning the Whole Story**).

• Gaining the "Why Is It Happening?" information (again, se **Learning the Whole Story**).

• Learning Sir Habahn is one of the nobles responsible for the monster hunt.

• Learning Baroness Ruvaka is one of the nobles responsible for the monster hunt.

• Learning Duke Fiodmar is one of the nobles responsible for the monster hunt.

• Convincing Sir Habahn to abandon the hunt.

• Convincing Baroness Ruvaka to abandon the hunt.

• Defeating Duke Fiodmar (see encounter **Q**).

• In addition to all the above, consider throwing in a few minor milestone rewards — if, for instance, the characters go out of their

way to rescue bystanders from the monsters, or come up with some particularly clever plans for hunting or luring said monsters — in order to raise the XP value of the adventure high enough to gain 13th level at its conclusion if so desired.

• You can play through the traveling/exploration of the Unclaimed Lands wilderness in as much or as little detail — with as few or as many side-quests and random encounters — as you prefer. There's no right or wrong way to do it, but brush up on the exploration and environmental rules first if you're planning to go into any great detail.

• We encourage the GM to alter the environmental description — weather, time of day, ambient sounds — of each encounter. Since the adventure takes place over weeks or months, characters will doubtless participate in some of these encounters at very different times, or in very different circumstances, than others.

• If the players come up with interesting plans to do more than travel around searching, by all means let them. Villages and small hamlets may provide rumors as to the locations of nearby monsters — all with fairly easy efforts, such as DC 10–15 Int (Investigation) or Cha (Persuasion) checks — allowing characters to go straight to them rather than wandering. If they try to tail another group of hunters, more power to them. If the characters try to set bait for flying monsters, drawing the encounters to them, give them at least a chance of success. (As written, many of the encounters can be run unchanged even if they don't happen in precisely the locations given.) In other words, let the freeform nature of the adventure work both ways, and reward clever thinking with at least potential results. Similarly, the divination spells characters of this level can access — such as *commune with nature*, *contact other plane*, or *divination* — shouldn't be enough to give them an immediate answer to the mystery, but *should* provide them with additional means of locating their quarry, or narrowing down their list of suspects once they have one.

• Speaking of towns, you'll note several unnamed communities marked on the map, in addition to Avrandt, Corvul, and Vath. These are other Unclaimed Lands "kingdoms" — again, usually little more than a town or two and some farmland — where the characters might stop and investigate, or at least recuperate. Additional hamlets stand scattered throughout, unmarked on any map. These have no direct bearing on the plot, but provide additional opportunities for role-playing, information-gathering, and the like. Use them, or not, to whatever extent you prefer. (And see the "Other Fiefdoms" sidebar for more suggestions on *how* to use them.)

• Finally, note that most of the combat encounters in *A Most Peculiar Hunt* are absolutely deadly, in terms of difficulty. This is quite deliberate. On a gameplay level, it makes up for the fact that characters are likely to have a day or days to heal and recover between encounters; and on a thematic level, it drives home the threat that these monsters pose to civilized lands.

Specifically, trophy collecting. The lord who could collect the most numerous and the most interesting exotic trophies would be declared the victor. And by "exotic," of course, they meant "monsters."

The competition quickly took on a life of its own, and continues now for its own sake. Of even greater consequence, the three lords have begun hiring professional adventurers as monster hunters, turning what was initially only a nuisance to the local bestial population into a genuine threat.

And because it's a genuine threat, the monsters — and even though this hunt is limited to only a small portion of the Unclaimed Lands, there are many — have begun to move.

Most have moved south. Toward the Great Amrin River, and toward Aachen, beyond.

Playing Politics

Thus far, the displaced beasts haven't crossed the river, but they *have* interfered — sometimes dramatically so — with travel on the Amrin itself.

The inland city of Bard's Gate, which uses the waterways for an enormous portion of its trade, sends demand after demand that Aachen do something about the situation. The Regional Governors and Landsgrafs of Aachen, of course, delightedly refuse to comply, or even to look into the matter, for the tariffs on Bard's Gate trade are high, and if the Amrin becomes unusable, the merchants have no option but to use Aachen's roads. It's a shortsighted response, at best, but certainly in keeping for most of the province's nobles and politicians.

This, then, is the current situation. Trade suffers. Tensions mount. The nobles of the Unclaimed Lands, and their hirelings, continue their hunt.

And the monsters press ever nearer to civilization.

The Real Story

It's worth noting that while all three petty lords participating in the competition are involved due to the conflict between their domains and the personal pride now at stake, two of the three also have additional, ulterior motives. Only Sir Habahn the Gray, Lord of Vath, is involved *only* for the prestige among his peers. A fairly despicable human being hiding behind a veneer of honor, he nonetheless can be persuaded — or, at worst, bribed — to cease his troublesome activities.

The Lady Ruvaka, Baroness of Corvul, seeks the same ends — but she *also* has her people searching for a very specific monster, hoping that the ongoing hunt will eventually drive it into the open. If the characters can assist her in gaining more information about this particular creature, they'll find her much more amenable to the idea of calling off the competition. (See encounter **O**)

The third of the trio, alas, is likely to prove far more troublesome, for his motives aren't merely selfish, but malicious. Duke Fiodmar of Avrandt is a doppelganger — an abnormal one, an "impure" one, with power far above most of his ilk and bitter hatred to match — who understands full well the repercussions of everything going on. He's very deliberately hoping to use the hunt and the forced monster migration to set Aachen and Bard's Gate at each other's throats, even while the monsters of the Unclaimed Lands penetrate ever deeper into the civilization to the south. In the end, he wants nothing less than to see Aachen — or even the entirety of the Borderlands — overrun with beasts and blood. (See encounter **Q**)

Fame and Fortune . . . and Foolishness

Obviously, no matter how broad one might prefer it to be, any adventure must make certain assumptions. One of the assumptions *A Most Peculiar Hunt* makes is that a party of 12th-level characters has developed a widespread reputation, and can be treated as such.

A second assumption is that the characters didn't reach 12th level without gaining *some* understanding of how things work. That they are mature and experienced enough to know that, as powerful as they may be, they have to take political considerations into account. They cannot just strong-arm rulers and nobles — even the rulers of small communities such as those found in the Unclaimed Lands — into obedience. They must negotiate, must be diplomatic; not necessarily to *excess*, not to the point of groveling, but to the full extent that manners and international relations dictate.

If you worry that your players may *not* understand this, feel free to have one of the Aachen military commanders (see encounters **A–D**), or an equivalent NPC, point out that making enemies of prideful sovereign rulers, however tiny their dominions, can have serious repercussions not just for the characters, but potentially for all of Aachen Province.

Learning the Whole Story

As the characters work their way through these events, they'll slowly — or not so slowly — discover the people and problems at the heart of everything. They can, however, come to each "stage" of information from multiple directions, by battling or speaking to multiple different monsters and people. As such, the basics of what the characters discover are presented here, in a single location, rather than scattered and repeated (and repeated, and repeated) throughout the various encounters. Any encounter where the characters can learn some of this directs you back here, and explains which portions of this information to provide.

Remember not to simply read this to the players as an "info-dump." Present it as appropriate to the role-playing of a given scene and NPC, depending on where and how the characters acquire it. (Feel free to spice this up with a bit more detail, as given in the **Introduction**, above; just be sure not to give away knowledge the characters shouldn't have yet.)

What's Happening?

Monsters are moving south from the hills and forests of the Unclaimed Lands in numbers never seen before. They're already interfering with travel and commerce along the rivers. Bard's Gate is getting ever angrier, but the Governors and Landsgrafs of Aachen are doing nothing; they *like* the river becoming dangerous to travel, as it means Bard's Gate merchants are forced to pay tariffs to use Aachen's roads. Tensions are starting to rise, and — while politicians choose to ignore this fact — there's no real reason to think the monsters will stop at the river, since nobody knows why they're migrating in the first place.

Why Is it Happening?

Several "kingdoms" in the unclaimed lands nearly went to war, but instead began competing with one another for the most interesting and most numerous "exotic" trophies. What started as a mere nuisance to the region's monsters has become far more serious, for the competition has taken on a life of its own and the participating lords have hired professional adventurers and monster hunters to scour the area. Now a great many monsters are fleeing the region, and most of *them* appear to be moving south.

Who's Causing It?

While other lords have gotten involved around the edges of the hunt, participating here and there, the competition is driven by, and primarily between, these three:

• Duke Fiodmar of Avrandt.
• Baroness Ruvaka of Corvul.
• Sir Habahn the Gray, of Vath.

A. Scuffle on the Bridge

The characters find themselves near the Great Bridge, or perhaps within the town at Gretspaan Citadel, when a mercantile and political dispute threatens to break out into a riot.

It's been an uneventful if beautiful morning. Beams of cloud-filtered sunlight brush the backs and shoulders of passersby, glint off the walls of shops and homes, paint dappled and dancing patterns across the surface of the Great Amrin River.

The constant rough song of the waterway, however, and the constant muttering of the town as it goes about its business, are slowly chipped away by a rising chorus of frustration and anger from the Gretspaan side of the Great Bridge.

If the characters aren't the sort to investigate such things on their own initiative, you can have one of the local guard captains recognize them — by reputation if not personally — and ask them to step in, just in case things turn ugly. In either case, once they reach the bridge, continue with the following.

Gathered near the gates on the massive stone expanse is a fairly large caravan. Multiple wagons, their horses and mules rolling their eyes and fidgeting at the raised voices, are packed together at the rear of a small but growing crowd. While several blustery fellows in the fancy garb of inland merchants stand at the forefront of the throng, a great many of the men and women gathered behind them wear the battered armor and stern expressions of swords-for-hire.

Facing them are a roughly equal number of Gretspaan's soldiers, and while they're doing a decent job of keeping a calm façade, even from here you can see white knuckles clenched on hilts, hear the angry creaking of leather and grinding of teeth. It's difficult to make out precisely what's being said—shouted, really—but it's something to do with a disagreement over tariffs. The topic's hardly surprising, but the vehemence, and the lurking pall of rage and violence, seem abnormal.

Both forces, the Bard's Gate caravan guards and the Gretspaan soldiers, consist primarily of male and female human **guards**, with a handful of **veterans** and **knights** representing officers and commanders.

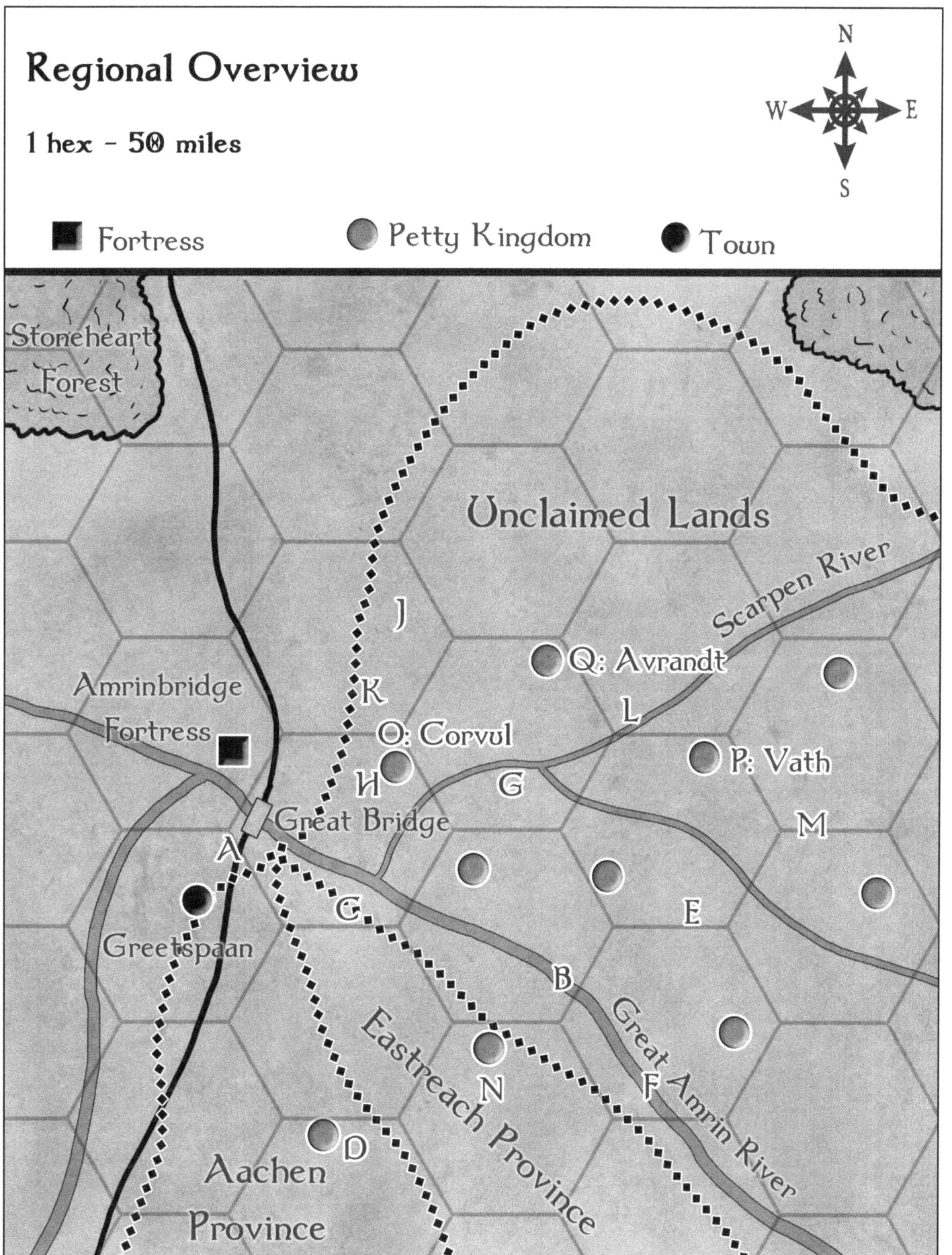

Regional Overview

1 hex – 50 miles

■ Fortress   ● Petty Kingdom   ● Town

N
W E
S

Stoneheart Forest

Unclaimed Lands

Scarpen River

J

Amrinbridge Fortress

K

O: Corvul

Q: Avrandt

L

P: Vath

H

G

M

A

Great Bridge

Greetspaan

C

E

B

Eastreach Province

N

F

Great Amrin River

D

Aachen Province

This isn't really a combat situation, though it's vaguely possible the characters might have to restrain or "soften up" a few loudmouths. For the most part, the party's reputation — and the fact that nobody here has gotten *quite* angry enough to want a genuine diplomatic incident — should be enough to quell the growing furor. Once the characters gain everyone's attention, a DC 15 Cha (Intimidation or Persuasion) check is enough to calm everyone. The DC drops to 10 if the characters can throw their muscle around a bit without actually harming anyone or making anyone fear for their lives first.

Once things are calm, the characters learn that the caravan represents a number of merchants from Bard's Gate. They feel that, since travel on the river has become unsafe, Aachen should lower the tariffs for use of the roads for trade. The Aachen soldiers, obviously, have neither the inclination nor the authority to do so. Either the guard captain (human **knight**) or Obral Dulas (male human **noble**), the lead merchant of the caravan, can give the characters all the information presented in the "What's Happening?" section, above. This is hopefully enough to get the characters interested in investigating, but see the "What's In It For Us?" sidebar, if necessary.

B. Bugbears on the Banks!

Your wanderings along the banks of the Great Amrin River have been peaceful and pleasant. The sun is bright without growing too hot, the clouds and the birds cast gentle shadows, and the river itself rushes and gurgles its part of the conversation as you walk.

All that changes, however, as you round a bend, the sights and sounds of battle striking you at once!

Up ahead, a shallow-keeled boat, likely a merchant of some sort, struggles against a pull far more dangerous than the current. A number of heavy ropes have been harpooned to the ship, and a sizable crew of furry, heavily muscled goblinoids is slowly dragging the vessel ever nearer the northern bank! Additional bugbears — for those are, indeed, what the foul creatures must be — swim out into the rushing waters, powerful strokes carrying them toward the listing boat. Several guards rush to the rails, loosing crossbow bolts at the oncoming marauders, but they're very clearly outmatched — to say nothing of literally off-balance.

At the characters' level, a band of **bugbears** is no great threat, but the circumstances make them a bit more than the nuisance they otherwise might be. The party may have to cross the river before they can engage, unless they're already on the north side for some reason or have particularly long-range spells prepared, as the river stands well over a 100ft wide at this point. The merchant vessel is considered difficult terrain, due to the constant tug of the ropes, and battling in the water is never easy. Fortunately, if the characters manage to engage the bugbears on shore, the remainder move quickly to join the combat.

There are **12 bugbears** total; **6** on the shore, **3** in the water between bank and boat, and **3** that had just reached the boat and were about to start climbing when the characters arrived. Assume those nearest the boat require 2 rounds to reach the bank, while those halfway can reach it in 1.

Bugbear (12): AC 16; HP 27 (5d8 + 5); **Spd** 30ft; **Melee** morningstar (+4, 2d8 + 2 bludgeoning); **Ranged** javelin (+4, 30ft/120ft, 2d6 + 2 piercing); **SA** surprise attack (extra 2d6 damage on first attack in first round against surprised opponent); **Str** +2, **Dex** +2, **Con** +1, **Int** −1, **Wis** +0, **Cha** −1; **Skills** Stealth +6, Survival +2; **Senses** darkvision 60ft; **Traits** brute (melee weapon deals extra die of damage, included above); **AL** CE; **CR** 1; **XP** 200.

> **Equipment:** hide armor, shield, morningstar, 6 javelins.

If nine of the bugbears are slain, the remainder attempt to flee. Questioning captured bugbears, or the captain of the merchant vessel (female human **noble**), provides the characters with the information from the "What's Happening?" section, above.

C. The Natural Order

The characters might be traveling the bank of the Amrin or the roads running along the Aachen border.

Screams and shouting shatter the peace of the day. Up ahead, at the very outskirts of one of the region's many towns, an angry crowd stands gathered. Most are clutching weapons — some genuine, such as bows and swords, others makeshift, like pitchforks and cudgels — and all are shouting and swearing, trying to push forward but held back as though by an unseen barrier.

The source of their anger is obvious. Standing before them, facing down the entire crowd, is a graceful, silver-haired woman in worn leathers. Feather-and-bone tokens dangle from bracelets on both arms and from combs in her hair; even from here she looks exhausted, covered in the dust and grime of the road, but she shows no sign of faltering.

Behind her, sprawled in the dirt and clearly injured, is a scaled, leathery reptilian thing. It's only as you draw slightly nearer, that you recognize it as a wyvern!

The woman, Annohka (female human **Drd10**) is, like the monsters themselves, recently displaced from her home in the forests of the Unclaimed Lands. The rest of the folks here are just frightened villagers. The wyvern is too injured even to defend itself and is not a viable threat or combatant.

The characters' arrival is enough to calm things down, and both Annohka and Calin (male human **scout**), the town's chief hunter and head of the angry mob, are willing to talk to them. When portraying the characters, Annohka is calm, determined, but weary and at the edge of her patience; Calin is angry at her interference, but at heart just wants to protect his home and his people.

Over the course of conversation, the characters learn what happened, and it's simple indeed. The town was attacked by the wyvern, who threatened both people and livestock. The people banded together to fight it, and were just about to finish it off when "this interfering druid!" arrived.

Annohka admits that she stopped them from killing it (she was interposing herself and her *antilife shield* between the villagers and the wyvern when the characters arrived), but only because it was already trying to flee. She points out that it, too, has been driven from its home, and has clearly learned not to bother this village any longer.

The characters can decide whether to let the wounded wyvern go or allow the townsfolk to finish it off. (Or even do so themselves.) As neutral outsiders — and powerful, respected ones — both Annohka and the villagers abide by their decision.

Regardless of how it turns out, Annohka will then share with the characters the background information presented in "What's Happening?" If the characters look as though they'll demand a reward, she has none to offer, but you might have a contingent of Aachen soldiers arrive a bit later to investigate the disturbance. This allows you to move on to the "What's In It For Us?" sidebar.

D. Wyrm Food!

This is a good encounter to begin the adventure if the characters are further from the border (you can choose a village in a different spot than marked on the map), or to emphasize the monster/monster-hunter switch, as suggested above.

Your first sign of trouble is the sight of several panicked people fleeing toward you, past you. They are clad in the loose, worn garb of field workers, but from the looks on their faces, they've just encountered something rather worse than a rotting crop or an infestation in the soil.

One points a trembling finger, scarcely even slowing, and now you can see why.

It circles in the sky around a small farming town, occasionally bathing the ground beneath it in caustic, poisonous fumes. The sun gleams an almost sickly green from its scales, and its outspread wings cast a fearsome shadow over the land as it soars in its wide arc.

Dragon.

None of the villagers are out trying to fight *this* monster, and as the characters draw near, they discover the town cloaked in a disturbing silence. Fortunately, this isn't the pall of death, just a whole lot of people trying very hard not to attract attention.

As the characters near, a DC 12 Int (Investigation) or Wis (Perception) check reveals that the dragon actually *isn't* attacking the town. Thus far, while it has poisoned some crops and a few examples of livestock that didn't run quite fast enough, it has very specifically kept its breath angled *just* far enough out that no villagers were endangered.

As the characters near, the wyrm banks upward, coming to a halt, wings spread wide — and then lands with an earth-shaking *whump* some dozen yards before the party.

"I AM KHYTHONTORRYX, CALLED TREE-BLIGHT, CALLED THE WOODLAND KING, CALLED THE EATER-IN-DUSK." The creature's voice is the clash of thunder, the splintering and collapsing of ancient trees. Even the faint trace of fumes carried on its breath as it speaks is enough to make your eyes blur and burn, your lungs to scream in pain. "AND I HAVE BEEN WAITING FOR YOU."

Allow the party to make DC 10 checks (any Int or Wis skills that sound remotely viable to you) to recognize that Khythontorryx (**adult green dragon**) is possibly beyond their abilities. If they attack anyway, the dragon is happy to battle for a few rounds, all while explaining that they're wasting their time, and possibly their lives.

Assuming they do eventually talk, the dragon explains that its seeming attack on the village was meant to attract their attention, or someone like them. He provides them with the "What's Happening?" information (in his own arrogant, condescending way), and also that he has reason to believe the local humans are somehow involved in what's happening (though he has no further details). He demands that the characters put a stop to it.

When the players ask (and they will) why he cares, read the following.

The dragon lacks the ability to mimic most human expressions, but you'd almost get the impression he's just the tiniest bit... embarrassed?

"THE WOODS TO THE NORTH WERE MY TERRITORY SOME TIME AGO, IN SLIGHTLY YOUNGER DAYS, AND I WAS... ADVENTUROUS IN MY ASSIGNATIONS. SEVERAL OF THE BEASTS AND BLOODLINES THAT HAVE BEEN DISPLACED ARE OFFSPRING OF MINE. I WOULD SEE THEM RETURNED HOME.

"AND SPEAKING OF..." Khythontorryx lowers his head, as though to meet you at eye level, even though said eye is larger than your *own* heads. "I ACKNOWLEDGE THAT SOME MAY GIVE YOU NO CHOICE IN THE MATTER, BUT WHERE POSSIBLE, YOU *WILL* DO YOUR BEST NOT TO SLAUGHTER ANY OF MY CHILDREN. IF YOU MUST, SO BE IT. IF YOU DO SO WHEN YOU HAD OTHER OPTION, I WILL BE... DISPLEASED."

What's In It For Us?

Several different factions can potentially offer the characters a monetary reward for looking into these events.

While the bulk of Aachen's nobles are quite happy to ignore future repercussions in favor of the new status quo, in terms of the danger to commerce on the Amrin, a few of the local Landsgrafs and Foerdewaith military leaders are more forward-thinking. Thus, while they can't be too public about it, they're willing to pay under the table for someone to investigate the monster migrations. If the characters interact with an Aachen guard captain (encounters **A**, **B**, and possibly **C**), the officer can slip them an offer of 2000gp per character and the gratitude of several local nobles.

The merchants of Bard's Gate, of course, have a vested monetary interest in making the river safe again. The merchants (encounters **A** or **B**) are willing to offer a larger reward — 3000gp per character — but this also earns the party some measure of distrust, moving forward, from Aachen's nobility. (Note that the Aachen guard captain revokes his offer if the characters accept the merchant's.)

If the characters press Khythontorryx for a reward, he actually offers one (mostly out of an amused respect for their gumption). The dragon's offer is a flat 10,000gp and the party's choice of *one* of the following: a *staff of frost*, a *helm of brilliance*, or a *spellguard shield*. He suggests, if the characters raise the topic, that they not ask where he got these.

Note that, in all cases, the rewards are presented only after the characters' succeed, never in advance.

As is to be expected with a green dragon, Khythontorryx isn't telling the entire truth. Oh, he does have offspring who have been displaced by the hunt, and all things being equal he'd rather not see most of them homeless or dead, but he really doesn't care all that much. No, his interest is in making certain that one particular child of his — one who has grown in power enough to suggest he may one day match his father, and whom the dragon now sees as a potential threat or rival — comes out second-best in conflict with the characters. This particular child Khythontorryx *does* want dead, but he won't say so outright; he simply trusts that the heroes will have no choice. See encounter **Q**.

Random Encounters

The spread of monsters throughout the region isn't remotely limited to the areas marked on the map. While the characters are in the Unclaimed Lands, roll 1d6 three times per day: early in the day, late in the day, and middle of the night. On a roll of 1, a random encounter occurs. Not every encounter needs to lead to combat, though; the characters might be able to spot and avoid trouble if they prefer, should the circumstances allow it. (If you roll an encounter in an inappropriate environment — giant crocodiles nowhere near water, for instance — feel free to either reroll or treat as no encounter.)

Monster Hunt Random Encounters

1d20	Encounter
1–2	1d6+2 **basilisks**[2]
3–4	4x1d4 **dire wolves**
5	1d4 **green dracolisks**[1, *]
6	1d4+1 **giant crocodiles**
7–8	1d8+8 **gnolls**
9	1d8+8 **bugbears**
10–11	2d8+4 **goblins**
12	1d8+2 **manticores**[2]

1d20	Encounter
13–14	1d8+8 **ogres**
15	2d4 **owlbears**[2]
16	1 **quickwood**
17	1 **two-headed troll** and 1d4 **trolls**[2]
18	1d4+1 **wyverns**[1]
19–20	2 **young green dragons**[1, *]

[1]Encounters marked with a superscript 1 can only occur once. Treat rerolls as "no encounter."

[2]Encounters marked with a superscript 2 can only occur twice. Treat rerolls beyond the second as "no encounter."

*Creatures marked with an asterisk are offspring of Khythontorryx, the green dragon. If the characters already know Khythontorryx's name, they can use it to intimidate the offspring into standing down, but only once they're already reduced to below one-quarter hit points. If the characters are instead attempting to *learn* the dragon's name, the offspring can be pressured into revealing it in exchange for their lives; again, this requires they be below one-quarter hit points. In either case, this requires a DC 15 Cha (Intimidation) check. (If made against the sole survivor of an encounter, the check has tactical advantage.)

Basilisk: AC 15; HP 52 (8d8+16); **Spd** 20ft; **Melee** bite (+5, 2d6+3 piercing plus 2d6 poison); **Str** +3, **Dex** –1, **Con** +2, **Int** –4, **Wis** –1, **Cha** –2; **Senses** darkvision 60ft; **Traits** petrifying gaze (30ft, restrained then petrified, DC 12 Con repeat); **AL** U; **CR** 3; **XP** 700.

Bugbear: AC 16; HP 27 (5d8+5); **Spd** 30ft; **Melee** morningstar (+4, 2d8+2 piercing); **Ranged** javelin (+4, 30ft/120ft, 1d6+2 piercing); **Str** +2, **Dex** +2, **Con** +1, **Int** –1, **Wis** +0, **Cha** –1; **Skills** Stealth +6, Survival +2; **Senses** darkvision 60ft; **Traits** brute, surprise attack (extra 2d6); **AL** CE; **CR** 1; **XP** 200.

Crocodile, Giant: AC 14; HP 85 (9d12+27); **Spd** 30ft, swim 50ft; **Melee** bite (+8, 3d10+5 piercing plus restraint, escape DC 16), tail (+8, 10ft, 2d8+5 bludgeoning plus knocked prone, DC 16 Str, target not restrained by bite); **SA** multiattack (bite, tail); **Str** +5, **Dex** –1, **Con** +3, **Int** –4, **Wis** +0, **Cha** –2; **Skills** Stealth +5, **Traits** hold breath (30 min); **AL** U; **CR** 5; **XP** 1800.

Dracolisk, Green: AC 17; HP 114 (12d10+48); **Spd** 30ft, fly 60ft; **Melee** bite (+8, 2d8+5 piercing), claws (+8, 3d8+5 slashing); **SA** poison breath (recharge 5–6, 30ft cone, 4d8 poison, DC 15 Con half), multiattack (bite, claws), petrifying gaze (30ft line of sight, restrained then petrified, DC 15 Con repeat); **Immune** paralysis, poison, petrify; **Str** +5, **Dex** +1, **Con** +4, **Int** –2, **Wis** +1, **Cha** +1; **Skills** Perception +4; **Senses** darkvision 60ft; **AL** U; **CR** 7; **XP** 2900. (*Fifth Edition Foes* 85)

Dragon, Young Green: AC 18; HP 136 (16d10+48); **Spd** 40ft, fly 80ft, swim 40ft; **Melee** bite (+7, 10ft, 2d10+4 piercing plus 2d6 poison), claw (+7, 2d6+4 slashing); **SA** multiattack (bite, claw x2), poison breath (recharge 5–6, 30ft cone 12d6 poison, DC 14 Con half); **Immune** poison; **Str** +4, **Dex** +1 (+4), **Con** +3 (+6), **Int** +3, **Wis** +1 (+4), **Cha** +2 (+5); Skills Deception +5, Perception +7, Stealth +4; Senses blindsight 30ft, darkvision 120ft; **Traits** amphibious; **AL** LE; **CR** 8; **XP** 3900.

Gnoll: AC 15; HP 22 (5d8); **Spd** 30ft; **Melee** spear (+4, 1d6+2 piercing) or bite (+4, 1d4+2 piercing); **Ranged** longbow (+3, 150ft/600ft, 1d8+1 piercing); **SA** rampage (reduce target to 0hp with melee, bonus to move half speed and make a bite); **Str** +2, **Dex** +1, **Con** +0, **Int** –2, **Wis** +0, **Cha** –2; **Senses** darkvision 60ft; **AL** CE; **CR** 1/2; **XP** 100.

Goblin: AC 15; HP 7 (2d6); **Spd** 30ft; **Melee** scimitar (+4, 1d6+2 slashing); **Ranged** shortbow (+4, 80ft/320ft, 1d6+2 piercing); **SA** nimble escape (bonus, disengage or hide); **Str** –1, **Dex** +2, **Con** +0, **Int** +0, **Wis** –1, **Cha** –1; **Skills** Stealth +6; **Senses** darkvision 60ft; **AL** NE; **CR** 1/4; **XP** 50.

Manticore: AC 14; HP 68 (8d10+24); **Spd** 30ft, fly 50ft; **Melee** bite (+5, 1d8+3 piercing), claw (+5, 1d6+3 slashing); **Ranged** tail spike (+5, 100ft/200ft, 1d8+3 piercing); **SA** multiattack (bite, claw x2 or tail spike x3); **Str** +3, **Dex** +3, **Con** +3, **Int** –2, **Wis** +1, **Cha** –1; **Senses** darkvision 60ft; **Traits** tail spike regrowth (up to 24); **AL** LE; **CR** 3; **XP** 700.

Ogre: AC 11; HP 59 (7d10+21); **Spd** 40ft; **Melee** greatclub (+6, 2d8+4 bludgeoning); **Ranged** (+6, 30ft/120ft, 2d6+4 piercing); **Str** +4, **Dex** –1, **Con** +3, **Int** –3, **Wis** –2, **Cha** –2; **Senses** darkvision 60ft; **AL** CE; **CR** 2; **XP** 450.

Owlbear: AC 13; HP 59 (7d10+21); **Spd** 40ft; **Melee** beak (+7, 1d10+5 piercing), claws (+7, 2d8+5 slashing); **SA** multiattack (beak, claws); **Str** +5, **Dex** +1, **Con** +3, **Int** –4, **Wis** +1, **Cha** –2; **Skills** Perception +3; **Senses** darkvision 60ft, keen sight and smell; **AL** U; **CR** 3; **XP** 700.

Quickwood: AC 14; HP 149 (13d12+65); **Spd** 10ft; **Melee** bite (+8, 3d8+5 piercing), root (+8, 30ft, 1d10+5 bludgeoning plus grapple and 15ft closer, escape DC 16); **SA** fear aura (reaction, 30ft radius, with a damaging spell save, spell absorbed and released as *fear*, DC 12), grasping roots (if grappled, additional attacks made with tactical advantage, escape or destroy root with AC 14, HP 10); **Immune** charm, lightning, psychic, stun, unconscious; **Resist** bludgeoning, piercing; **Vulnerable** fire; **Str** +5, **Dex** –2 (+1), **Con** +5 (+8), **Int** +0, **Wis** +1, **Cha** +0; **Senses** darkvision 60ft, remote sensing; **AL** N; **CR** 8; **XP** 3900. (*Fifth Edition Foes* 190)

Troll: AC 15; HP 84 (8d10+40); **Spd** 30ft; **Melee** bite (+7, 1d6+4 piercing), claw (+7, 2d6+4 slashing); **SA** multiattack (bite, claw x2); **Str** +4, **Dex** +1, **Con** +5, **Int** –2, **Wis** –1, **Cha** –2; **Skills** Perception +2; **Senses** darkvision 60ft, keen smell; **Traits** regeneration (10hp/turn); **AL** CE; **CR** 5; **XP** 1800.

Troll, Two-Headed: AC 15; HP 105 (10d10+50); **Spd** 30ft; **Melee** bite (+7, 1d8+4 piercing), claw (+7, 2d6+4 slashing); **SA** multiattack (bite x2, claw x2); **Str** +4, **Dex** +1, **Con** +5, **Int** –1, **Wis** –1, **Cha** –2; **Skills** Perception +5; **Senses** darkvision 60ft; **Traits** regeneration (5hp/turn), two heads, wakeful; **AL** CE; **CR** 6; **XP** 2300. (*Fifth Edition Foes* 235)

Wolf, Dire: AC 14; HP 37 (5d10+10); **Spd** 50ft; **Melee** bite (+5, 2d6+3 piercing plus knock prone, DC 13 Str); **Str** +3, **Dex** +2, **Con** +2, **Int** –4, **Wis** +1, **Cha** –2; **Skills** Perception +3, Stealth +4; **Skills** Perception +3, Stealth +4; **Senses** keen hearing and smell; **Traits** pack tactics; **AL** U; **CR** 1; **XP** 200.

Wyvern: AC 13; HP 110 (13d10+39); **Spd** 20ft, fly 80ft; **Melee** bite (+7, 10ft, 2d6+4 piercing), claws (+7, 2d8+4 slashing), stinger (+7, 10ft, 2d6+4 piercing plus 7d6 poison, DC 15 Con half); **SA** multiattack (bite, stinger or in flight, claws for one attack); **Str** +4, **Dex** +0, **Con** +3, **Int** –3, **Wis** +1, **Cha** –2; **Skills** Perception +4; **Senses** darkvision 60ft; **AL** U; **CR** 6; **XP** 2300.

E. Between a Roc and a Hard Place

> Rolling grasses crunch underfoot, waving in the soft breeze. All around you, soft undulations in the earth create an swelling ocean of greenery.
>
> Greenery that abruptly goes dark as an incomprehensibly huge shadow falls over you, accompanied by the soul-shriveling shriek of a hungry, *massive* raptor.

You can run this as a straightforward combat, in which case the **2 rocs** — who are simply out hunting — swoop and attack.

On the other hand, if you want to make things a bit more complicated, continue with the following.

> Screams of a far more human tone sound from up ahead, accompanied by a terrified whinnying and the creak of wood. A small wagon, presumably the property of a single family, thunders over the rolling plains, the horses clearly panicked and out of control. Fleeing for their lives, a handful of individuals flee in all directions, leaving themselves perfect prey for the rocs!"

This family (7 human **commoners**) was getting out of the way of the monster migration. They chose a really, *really* bad route. Assuming the characters aren't complete bastards, they now have to not only defeat the rocs, but lure them in or otherwise protect the fleeing family as well.

Roc (2): AC 15; **HP** 248 (16d20+80); **Spd**20ft, fly 120ft; **Melee** beak (+13,10ft, 4d8+9 piercing), talons (+13, 4d6+9 slashing plus grapple, escape DC 19); **SA** multiattack (beak, talons); **Str** +9, **Dex** +0 (+4), **Con** +5 (+9), **Int** –4, **Wis** +0 (+4), **Cha** –1 (+3); **Skills** Perception +4; **Traits** keen sight; **AL** U; **CR** 11; **XP** 700.

If both rocs are reduced to 25 hit points — or if one is slain and the other reduced to 40 — it/they attempt to flee. Should the characters succeed in protecting the refugees, the terrified souls can provide the characters all the information in the "Why Is It Happening?" section of **Learning the Whole Story**, they don't know if it's truth or rumor. (They do not, however, have any sense of *which* lords are responsible for the hunt.)

F. Ribbit?

> Something horrible has emerged from torrent of the river up ahead. An enormous rubbery shape — glistening and croaking, bristling with grasping tentacles and a writhing eyestock above a maw that seems to go on forever — has risen from the water. The current thrashes around it like new-formed rapids, but not so loudly that you cannot hear the rending of wood as the beast tears into what was once a river-worthy craft.

As the characters draw nearer, they can make out more detail, including the fact that the boat was shallow-keeled, built for speed, and equipped with ballistae that apparently did them no good in defending themselves. A fish speared on a trident adorns the flag that snaps atop the broken and tilted mast; a DC 12 Int (History) check reveals this to be the symbol of Count Jonas Ranquin of Turpin —

and *that* suggests that the victims of the monster's attack are likely river pirates.

The **froghemoth** doesn't know or care about any of that. It's just hungry and angry.

This isn't a difficult battle for the characters, in terms of challenge rating, but circumstances conspire to make things a bit tougher. First, the froghemoth remains in the depths of the river, requiring characters to boat or swim out to it if they want to attack at melee range. Second, only 3 pirates (male and female human **bandits**) survive, and they won't likely last long. If the characters want to talk to or question them, they'll have to act fast; the froghemoth attacks whoever's closest (unless it's just been attacked, in which case it focuses on the attacker). And right now, the pirates are a lot closer than the characters.

Froghemoth: AC 15; **HP** 200 (16d12+96); **Spd** 20ft, swim 30ft; **Melee** tentacle grab (+11, reach 15ft, 1d7+7 bludgeoning damage plus grapple, escape DC 17), tentacle crush (automatic hit, targets one creature already grappled by a tentacle at the start of the froghemoth's turn, 1d10+7 bludgeoning and the target remains grappled), tongue (+11, reach 30ft, 1d6+7 bludgeoning plus grapple and restrain, escape DC 17), bite (+11, targets one creature grappled, 15ft, 2d8+7 piercing and swallowed, DC 18 Dex); **SA** multiattack (tongue, tentacle x4, bite); **Immune** lightning; **Resist** fire; **Str** +7, **Dex** +0 (+4), **Con** +6, **Int** –4, **Wis** +1, **Cha** +0; **Skills** Perception +5, Stealth +4; **Senses** darkvision 60ft; **Traits** all-around vision (attackers never gain tactical advantage or bonus damage from presence of nearby allies), slowed by electricity (slowed for 1 round whenever it would otherwise take lightning damage), swallow (swallowed creature is blinded and restrained, takes 1d8+6 bludgeoning plus 2d8 acid damage at the start of the froghemoth's turn, can escape using 10ft of movement after froghemoth is dead); **AL** U; **CR** 11; **XP** 7200. (*Fifth Edition Foes* 107)

The froghemoth attempts to flee if reduced to 30 hit points. (Which could be troublesome if anyone's been swallowed.)

If the characters *do* manage to question a surviving pirate, they learn everything in the "Why Is It Happening?" section, but the pirate can also tell them the name of one of the three lords responsible for the hunt. (GM's choice as to which of the three he reveals.)

Should the characters ask why Turpin isn't involved in what's going on, the pirate can explain that Count Jonas is taking a "watch and wait" approach, and has no interest in interfering if he doesn't have to.

G. A Terrifying Amount of Teeth

This encounter can occur anywhere near the fork of the two Amrin tributaries marked on the map. The monsters in question are perfectly happy in the water, on the dry land near the banks, or in the thick marsh in and around the fork itself. In the description to follow, choose the first option if the characters are on the river or on the bank; the second if they're in the marsh.

> The constant chorus of the [birds of the fields/insects of the bog] cease in mid-chirp. You don't need to be an expert in the signs of the wilderness to know that something's not right.

The characters have 1 round to take any preparatory actions they wish. Then…

> The waters of the [rushing river/shallow marsh] spray outward, propelled by countless thrashing, serpentine forms. What sounds like a thousand hissing screams drowns out the splash and patter of the torrent!

There's not actually a thousand hissing screams, of course. Just, oh, 15 of them.

The characters have stumbled into the new hunting grounds of a truly terrifying family grouping of **3 hydras**. A couple of them are normal — fearsome enough — but the third is another offspring of Khythontorryx. This half-dragon is just smart enough to direct the other two in rudimentary tactics, making them even more dangerous than ever. The hydras initially attack the party from two or even three different directions at once, and they do their best to stay at least a few yards from each other, making it difficult to catch more than one in an area effect without also catching a character.

The half-dragon likely breathes in the first round, if several characters are clumped. Once the other hydras engage, it usually restricts itself to bite attacks, so as not to catch the others of its "pack."

Don't immediately inform the players that one of the three hydras is different from the others. As the first round or two of combat pass, however, describe the unusual green glint to its scales, the tint of red in its eyes, or the faint acrid wisps drifting from this maw or those nostrils as it breathes.

Half-Green Dragon Hydra: AC 15; **HP** 172 (15d12+75); **Spd** 30ft, swim 30ft; **Melee** bite (+8, reach 10ft, 1d10+5 piercing); **SA** multiattack (as many bites as remaining heads), poison breath (recharge 5–6, poison gas in 30ft cone, 12d6 poison damage, DC 14 Con half); **Resist** poison; **Str** +5, **Dex** +1, **Con** +5, **Int** –4, **Wis** +0, **Cha** –2; **Skills** Perception +6; **Senses** blindsight 10ft, darkvision 60ft; **Traits** hold breath (1 hour), multiple heads (starts with 5 heads; tactical advantage on saving throws against blind, charm, deafen, frighten, stun, or unconscious while it has multiple heads; loses 1 head when it takes 25 or more damage in a single turn, dies if it loses all heads; at the start of its turn, grows 2 heads for each 1 lost since last turn unless it has taken fire damage since last turn; regains 10 hit points for each head regrown), reactive heads (extra opportunity attack for each head beyond 1), wakeful (1 head always awake); **AL** U; **CR** 8; **XP** 3900.

Hydra (2): AC 15; **HP** 172 (15d12+75); **Spd** 30ft, swim 30ft; **Melee** bite (+8, reach 10ft, 1d10+5 piercing); **SA** multiattack (as many bites as remaining heads); **Str** +5, **Dex** +1, **Con** +5, **Int** –4, **Wis** +0, **Cha** –2; **Skills** Perception +6; **Senses** darkvision 60ft; **Traits** hold breath (1 hr), multiple heads (starts with 5 heads; tactical advantage on saving throws against blind, charm, deafen, frighten, stun, or unconscious while it has multiple heads; loses 1 head when it takes 25 or more damage in a single turn, dies if it loses all heads; at the start of its turn, grows 2 heads for each 1 lost since last turn unless it has taken fire damage since last turn; regains 10 hit points for each head regrown), reactive heads (extra opportunity attack for each head beyond 1), wakeful (1 head always awake); **AL** U; **CR** 8; **XP** 3900.

The two normal hydras are beasts of pure rage and appetite, and thus fight to the death. The half-dragon can be intimidated into fleeing *if*
• It is down to two heads permanently (due to fire damage) and has fewer than 30 hit points, *or*
• It is down to three heads permanently (due to fire damage), has fewer than 50 hit points, and the other two hydras are dead.

This requires a DC 20 Cha (Intimidate) check, or DC 15 if the character making the check speaks Draconic. (The hydra, more intelligent than most, understands a few words in that language.) If the characters know and invoke the name of Khythontorryx, this Cha (Intimidate) check has tactical advantage.

If the characters do *not* know the dragon's name, they can learn it from the half-dragon hydra. The hydra must already be Intimidated and prepared to retreat, and the characters must specifically ask it about the dragon's name (or "your sire's name," or something similar) in Draconic, or under the effect of magic such as *tongues*.

H. The Really Odd Couple

You can either run this encounter at the outskirts of Corvul (see encounter **O**), while the characters are waiting to see Baroness Ruvaka, or you can run it at one of the small towns near to Corvul. In either case, as written, the encounter assumes the characters are already within the town, but you can alter it so that it occurs as they're approaching.

> Cries of anger and fear, the pounding of feet, the clamor of bells, all make it sound as though full-scale war has erupted! And as you approach the edge of town, it looks almost as though it has. A small phalanx of militia have formed up to face an invading force that towers not only over the defenders, but over some of the buildings standing alongside!
>
> Grotesque, lumbering brutes, each the height of a house, stomp and tromp up from the countryside, hefty logs dangling from their fists and uncured hides tied across their loins and shoulders.
>
> At the head of the column, floating forward as though standing on some invisible platform, are two creatures of blue skin and bone-white hair, easily as tall as the ogres they lead but far more slender of build. Their eyes gleam an evil yellow and they cackle madly as they near, barbed pole-arms clutched in their clawed fists.

The characters have just had the misfortune to meet Udruusik and Zassabar, 2 **oni** — a mated pair, in fact — and their 10 **ogre** minions. (As the characters draw nearer, you can make it more clear that one of the oni is male, the other female. Even during the attack, they're fawning over and pawing each other like hormonal teens; to what degree you want to go into describing that is entirely up to you and the sensitivities of your players.)

Allow the characters to attempt DC 15 Int (Investigation or Nature) checks. On a success, the character recognizes that these two are fairly young as oni go. They're full-grown adults — and just as powerful as any others — but perhaps somewhat less disciplined and mature in their behavior.

If the characters just charge into combat, Udruusik, Zassabar, and the ogres are happy to oblige; fighting is why they're here. And indeed, if the characters do nothing, the invaders attack anyway. It's a winnable fight for the characters, but a brutal one. More to the point, there are going to be a *lot* of casualties. The town militia, or at least the portion that's arrived thus far, consists of 10 human **guards** and a pair of **veteran** officers. They're *ridiculously* outmatched, and that's not even counting the countless **commoners** who are still attempting to flee the area. (If the characters engage the invaders, the town militia focuses on getting the civilians to safety, rather than participating directly in the battle.)

People are going to die if this turns bloody; make that absolutely clear to the characters.

But if they think of it, the characters do have another option. The oni may be evil, but unlike many of the monsters the party may have faced thus far, they're intelligent and quite capable of communicating.

And they're young. This makes them outwardly brash, but internally less sure of themselves than they otherwise might be. And the truth is, they have no business being here. They're just looking to use the monster migration and general chaos as an excuse to work out some bloodlust.

If the characters call out, wave a flag of parley, or otherwise take any noticeable steps at attracting the oni's attention, read the following.

> The first of the vile creatures screeches at you, his words sounding like fingernails on slate. *I am Udruusik!*

"And I am Zassabar!" screams the second, her voice that of a cat impaled on a hot spike.

They pause after their announcement to trade a deep, passionate, and — even from this distance — utterly revolting kiss, lips flopping together like dead fish, their intertwining tongues resembling a pair of giant dancing maggots.

"We have come here," Udruusik shrieks again when they're finally done, twin lines of spittle dangling from is mouth, *"seeking vengeance!"*

If the characters can keep the oni talking — and it's not difficult to do so; so long as nobody's attacked the invaders yet, it requires only a DC 12 Cha (Deception or Persuasion) check — continue with the following.

Zassabar takes over the conversation — well, the tirade — once more. *"For too long you humans have tormented our brethren, those you would insultingly call 'monsters,' and this great hunt of yours is the final offense! No more will you be allowed to slaughter us with impunity! No more will you drive us from our homes and hunting grounds! No more..."*

As the litany of sins continues, allow any characters involved in the conversation to attempt a DC 18 Wis (Insight) check. Those who succeed begin to suspect that oni are playing to an audience. They're putting on a performance of some sort, as opposed to actually believing the speech they're giving. These characters also realize at this point that Udruusik and Zassabar are being as much like adolescents as adults, far less subtly (and frankly less intelligently) than "normal" oni.

Nor is this the only clue the characters have that something's a bit off.

"These are but the first!" the oni continues, gesturing back at the ogres who follow. *"We have come from the untamed wilds, where we have lived in hardship with our 'monstrous' brothers and sisters, so that we might wreak our revenge upon you and all who—"*

Her rant is interrupted by a confused mutter — which, from the mouth of an ogre, might as well be a bellow, so loudly and clearly can you hear it. "Wilds? Thought we from Ché's place." He turns to poke his nearest fellow ogre in the arm. "Wasn't us from Ché's place?"

The oni turn and begin screaming abuse (in Giant) at their dimwitted followers, and the characters make another skill check. Any character who succeeds in a DC 15 Int (History) check recognizes the reference to "Ché's place" as the Court of Loom Ché. (Characters native to the Unclaimed Lands or the northern reaches of Aachen gain tactical advantage on this check. If a player makes the connection on his or her own, with a die roll — and assuming the player's character has actually had dealings with the Court, as opposed to the player just remembering it from reading the **Borderlands Provinces** — no skill check is required.)

Once a check has succeeded, share with that player the basics of the Court as described in the sourcebook: Loom Ché's alien nature, the monstrous inhabitants of the Court, and so forth. Make a point of mentioning that the Court survives by *cooperating* with human civilization, that it has tight economic ties with multiple communities, and so forth. Make it clear, as well, to anyone who succeeded in the earlier Wis (Insight) check, that these two oni are obviously brash youngsters simply looking for an excuse to shed some blood, as opposed to actual victims of the hunt or champions of the "oppressed" monsters.

At this point, it's in the player's hands to figure out how to use that knowledge. If the characters correctly deduce that the oni couple's behavior would *not* meet with the approval of the Court — or the other oni therein — and might even cause political friction between Loom Ché and his partners, they can make that argument to Zassabar and Udruusik.

Once they've done so, it requires only a DC 15 Cha (Intimidate) check to make the oni stand down, to retreat back into the wild with the ogres at their back and tails tucked between their legs.

Trying to intimidate the oni to back off without using Loom Ché's displeasure as a threat requires a DC 25 check, and failure results in immediate combat — as, of course, does any effort on the part of the characters to defend themselves or the town with violence of their own.

Udruusik and Zassabar, Oni (2): AC 16; HP 110 (13d10+39); **Spd** 30ft, fly 30ft; **Melee** claw (+7, 1d8+4 slashing) or glaive (+7, 10ft, 2d10+4 or 1d10+4 slashing in S/M form); **SA** change shape, innate spells (Cha, DC 13), multiattack (claw x2 or glaive x2); **Str** +4, **Dex** +0 (+3), **Con** +3 (+6), **Int** +2, **Wis** +1 (+4), **Cha** +2 (+5); **Skills** Arcana +5, Deception +8, Perception +4; **Senses** darkvision 60ft; **Traits** magic weapons, regeneration (10/turn with at 1hp); **AL** LE; **CR** 7; **XP** 2900.
> **Innate Spells:** at will—*darkness, invisibility;* 1/day— *charm person, cone of cold, gaseous form, sleep*
> **Equipment:** chain mail, glaive.

Ogre (10): AC 11; HP 59 (7d10+21); **Spd** 40ft; **Melee** greatclub (+6, 2d8+4 bludgeoning); **Ranged** javelin (+6, 30ft/120ft, 2d6+4 piercing); **Str** +4, **Dex** –1, **Con** +3, **Int** –3, **Wis** –2, **Cha** –2; **Senses** darkvision 60ft; **AL** CE; **CR** 2; **XP** 450.
> **Equipment:** hide armor, greatclub, 4 javelins.

If the two oni are each reduced to 30 hit points or fewer and at least seven of the ogres are dead, they order a retreat (but might return at some future date to avenge their humiliation). If one of the oni is slain, however, the other fights to the death in grief-stricken fury. The ogres fight to the death unless ordered by an oni to fall back.

Once the oni are driven off or defeated, the villagers can offer the characters the information from the "Why Is It Happening?" section, as well as the knowledge that Baroness Ruvaka is one of the primary nobles behind the monster hunt.

I. Throwing a Party

This encounter has no fixed location, but instead occurs as and when the GM chooses. Optimal placement is some time after the characters have experienced several monster encounters and are fully engaged in the adventure, but before they've learned who is responsible for the hunts. (If you prefer to make it random, rather than choosing, you can do that. Once the characters are deep into the Unclaimed Lands, when you roll a d6 for random encounters, any time the result is a 1, roll the d6 again before rolling the d20. If that second d6 comes up a 1 or 2, this encounter occurs rather than one from the chart. This only happens once.)

Whether you choose or roll randomly, adjust the descriptions accordingly for environment, time of day, etc. At the start of the encounter, Imriss (female human **assassin**) is stealthily observing the party. Should they detect her — which requires a DC 21 Wis (Perception) check — she sheepishly reveals herself and waves for the rest of her group to join her. If she remains undetected, her group instead reveal themselves by popping up around the characters, mocking them about being careless. In neither case do they initiate hostilities, though they'll defend themselves if attacked (all while trying to convince the characters that they're not enemies).

However it comes about, eventually read the following:

The figures skillfully materializing around you out of the wilds look remarkably familiar. Not in the specifics, no — you don't know these people personally — but in *type*. The slender, hawk-faced man in traveling wools and a heavy over-robe; the stealthy figure in worn leathers; the burly pair armed with spear and shield. Oh, you definitely recognize a fellow adventuring party when you see one.

This isn't just some group of wannabe monster hunters, but rather one of the professional adventuring companies who have been engaged in this hunt for months—and thus one of the primary reasons the entire affair turned from a mere nuisance to a potential local calamity. Along with Imriss, this group consists of Dovrath (male human **archmage**) and the brother-sister team of Torval and Yndra (male and female human variant **gladiators**). It doesn't take much interaction for the characters to recognize that Dovrath — in addition to being somewhat smug and arrogant — is also the team leader.

The group initially assumes that the characters are hired monster hunters like themselves, working on behalf of one of the three nobles; assuming the characters don't attack them or otherwise interrupt, they begin by bragging of their latest kill (a family of manticores), and asking the characters about their own victories. If the players think to maintain the charade, acting the part and subtly digging for information, they can learn a great deal. Have the players roleplay accordingly, then allow them to make group DC 12 Cha (Deception) checks.

• If the check succeeds, the characters can learn everything in the "Why Is It Happening?" section.

• If the check succeeds by 5 or more (17 or higher), the characters also learn that this particular group of hunters is working for Duke Fiodmar of Avrandt.

• If the check succeeds by 10 or more (22 or higher), the characters can also gain the name of one of the other two nobles involved in the hunt — either Baroness Ruvalka, of Corvul, or Sir Habahn, of Vath, GM's choice as to which.

Eventually, however, Dovrath and the others realize that they've been played, that the characters aren't fellow monster hunters and have some *other* interest in what's going on. If the above check fails, this happens immediately. Otherwise, it slowly dawns on him after the characters have obtained their information that something's amiss. (If one of your players accidentally lets something slip in conversation while roleplaying, that can be the trigger, though you should still let them obtain all the information they've earned first.)

Once that happens, the monster hunters turn hostile. They don't attack, but they do proceed to threaten the characters, promising all sort of ugly retribution if they interfere with the hunt (which is one of the more profitable ventures Dovrath's group has had in a while.) After making their feelings quite clear, they storm off back into the wilderness.

Note, however, that if the characters instigate violence, the hunters respond in kind, rather than trying to talk the characters down as they did earlier. Otherwise, however, this remains a noncombat encounter. (See encounter R for the adventuring party's stats, if combat *does* break out.)

J. Big Decisions

Here, in a rocky portion of the hills on the borders of the Unclaimed Lands, a gathering is occurring, one that could have severe consequences for the entire region. A **cloud giant**, one of the nobles and leaders of the region's giant community, is meeting with 3 **stone giants**, emissaries of their own people who speak with the authority of their own chieftain. The four of them are currently debating whether to wage open war on the local human communities, in response to the monster hunts (which have claimed several giant lives already). Other types of giants dwell in the area — hill giants, in particular, as well "lesser" giant-kin like ogres, ettins, and trolls — but these four know that where the cloud and stone giants lead in this matter, the others will follow.

It's entirely possible for the characters to simply stumble into this encounter if they're exploring the hills. The giants are meeting in a small valley in the hills and trying to keep their presence secret, but "quiet" for giants is still more than loud enough to hear from a distance. Alternatively, though, the characters might learn about this meeting from other giants they encounter. Several of the region's random encounters are with giant-kin of various sorts, and some of the ogres accompanying the ogre mages in encounter **H** might also have heard something. In either case, conversation during combat or questioning survivors afterward could, at your discretion, alert the characters that something important is happening here in the hills.

The rumble is so low, so pervasive, that at first you wonder if you're feeling a mild earth tremor. Only as you draw nearer do you realize you're hearing *voices*, inhumanly deep and potent.

Inside a small valley, a depression in the rocky hills that appears even smaller thanks to them, stand a quartet of humanoid figures so large it's difficult to fathom. Three of them appear almost made of stone, their flesh rocky and hairless and all sharp angles. Each is thrice as tall as an average man, yet the fourth towers over even them, and by an additional human's height! She appears to be flesh, not stone, but her skin is a peculiar violet and stretched taut over obscenely bulging muscles."

If any of the characters speak Giant (or have *tongues* or similar magic affecting them) they can determine that the giants are, as mentioned above, debating the merits of declaring war on all of local human civilization in retaliation for the hunt. It sounds as though they're leaning toward deciding to do it.

If the characters attack, or make themselves known without any attempt at communication, combat ensues and the giants fight to the death. (This may result in the giants launching attacks on nearby communities later on. That's your call as GM, and beyond the scope of this adventure.)

If the characters talk fast, however, the giants are willing to hear them out.

The obvious approach is for the characters to explain:

• That only a few select human leaders — not everyone nearby — are behind the hunt. (If the characters point out that what the giants are doing now, in terms of meeting to make a unified decision, is more advanced and enlightened than how local human lords operate, grant the characters a +2 bonus on the upcoming check.)

• That the characters themselves are currently working to *stop* the monster hunts.

Of course, players are creative, and might choose an entirely different approach. If so, decide for yourself if the arguments they put forth have any real logic behind them and would make sense to the giants.

Once they've made their case, and perhaps roleplayed through some discussion or argument, allow one of the characters to make a DC 22 Cha (Persuasion, or other if their choice of approach suggests something else) check. If you really feel as though the argument or approach the characters chose wouldn't make sense to the giants — appealing to their sense of mercy, for instance — this check has tactical disadvantage. If the characters are willing to toss in a suitable bribe (and the giants won't be subtle in hinting that their patience can be bought), they gain a cumulative +1 bonus on the check for every 1000gp-worth of the bribe.

If the characters succeed, the giants agree to hold off making any decisions for a fortnight (plus one additional day for each point by which the check result exceeded the DC). Once that deadline has passed, however, the characters had better have succeeded in ending the hunt. Otherwise, the giants will consider attacking, as mentioned above (which, also as mentioned above, can lead to further adventures but is beyond the scope of this one).

Cloud Giant: AC 14; HP 200 (16d12+96); **Spd** 40ft; **Melee** morningstar (+12,10ft, 3d8+8 piercing); **Ranged** rock (+12, 60ft/240ft, 4d10+8 bludgeoning); **SA** innate spells (Cha+7, DC 15), multiattack (morningstar x2); **Str** +8, **Dex** +0, **Con** +6 (+9), **Int** +1, **Wis** +3 (+7), **Cha** +3 (+7); **Skills** Insight +7, Perception +7; **Traits** keen smell; **AL** NE; **CR** 9; **XP** 5000.
    Innate Spells: at will—*detect magic, fog cloud, light;* 3/day—*feather fall, fly, misty step, telekinesis;* 1/day—*control weather, gaseous form.*
    Equipment: morningstar, rocks.

Stone Giant (3): AC 17; HP 126 (11d12+55); **Spd** 40ft; **Melee** greatclub (+9, 15ft, 3d8+6 bludgeoning); **Ranged** rock (+9, 60ft/240ft, 4d10+6 bludgeoning); **SA** multiattack (greatclub x2); **Str** +6, **Dex** +2 (+5), **Con** +5 (+8), **Int** +0, **Wis** +1 (+4), **Cha** −1; **Skills** Athletics +12, Perception +4;

Senses darkvision 60ft; **Traits** rock catching (reaction, DC 10 Dex save to catch rock without taking damage), stone camouflage; **AL** N; **CR** 7; **XP** 2900.
Equipment: greatclub, rocks.

K. Dead Wyverns

This rocky hilltop was clearly once an aerie, once the home to a family of wyverns. Once. A ring of stacked rocks surrounds a clutch of shattered eggs, and winged, reptilian corpses lie draped over and around the nest and the dry earth. This happened within the last day or two, you'd guess; the blood is dried, but the bodies have only begun to rot.

A number of small bits—fangs, stingers, wingtip claws—are missing, having been meticulously cut loose from the corpses.

If you'd like, you can add an encounter here—a few wyverns returning to find the rest of the family dead—but otherwise, this isn't a combat encounter. Rather, it's simply a sign of the reach and extent of the ongoing monster hunt.

It's also an opportunity for the characters to learn about one of the hunt's participants, if they haven't already. A DC 20 Wis (Survival) check allows the characters to track the hunters who killed these wyverns back to the town of Vath (see encounter **P**).

L. A Sacred Grief

The leaves of the thick woodland canopy drum and rattle overhead, plucked at by a slow drizzling rain that never reaches you or the soil and undergrowth over which you walk. The shadows of the forest around you, broken only by dappled patches of fading sun, grow suddenly darker without obvious cause or warning.

No... Not "darker," not quite. Heavier. As though the gloom has taken on additional meaning, additional weight.

Let the characters take whatever precautions they wish at this point. After a few moments of additional travel, continue.

The boles part like a curtain to reveal a clearing, marked only a smattering of smaller trees and a gentle, shallow-sloped hill. The raindrops, falling faintly before you or gathered on the leaves, seem to glow with silvery inner light. The air is heavy, weighing against your back and shoulders, like a burden you might never set down.

Atop the hill, somehow more solid, more real, than everything else around it, an equine figure kneels on four bent knees. The white of its coat, through brilliant, snowy, pales beside the gleam of its single horn and the silvery sheen in its eyes.

Sprawled atop the grass before the magnificent creature is a second unicorn, but this one lies oh so still. The brilliance of its coat is marred by dried blood; the sheen has left its eyes, never to return, and its horn... Is simply gone, leaving only a ragged, blade-bitten stump.

The grieving creature does not move, does not turn your way, but you hear a voice in your head all the same. It is the sound of the forest itself, the whispering of rustling branches, the song of life weighted down by grief. "Have you come to kill me, too?"

There's sadly little the characters can do here. The deceased unicorn cannot be brought back with a mere *raise dead*; even if the soul of a celestial being were free to do so, it will not return to a body that has lost its sacred horn. Its grieving mate, other than the initial question to the characters, doesn't say much. After a few moments it rises to slowly depart, fading away — perhaps *teleporting*, perhaps simply ceasing to be — as it goes. The dead unicorn vanishes along with it.

If the characters show any sign of suitable respect or shared grief, it speaks in their minds once more before it is gone.

"Avrandt. I haven't it in me to remain in this wretched place, not even to seek justice. If you care to do so, though, the murderers came from a place called Avrandt."

M. Manticore Massacre

Vultures, the occasional hyenas, and vast clouds of flies range through this high grassland, feasting on drying blood or cooling corpses. Several manticores, or sometimes just parts of manticores, lie scattered throughout the area like a child's broken toys.

Like encounter **K**, this is primarily a showcase that the hunt goes on. Again, this is not a combat encounter unless the GM chooses to add a few lingering survivors. With a DC 20 Wis (Survival) check, the characters can track the hunters back to the town of Corvul (see encounter **O**).

N. Perytons

This encounter occurs back within the borders of Aachen (unless you decide otherwise), but its exact position can vary. The mark on the map is just one possibility; all that matters is that there's a town or village present. The best use of this encounter is as evidence that the monster threat is indeed beginning to cross the Amrin; run it either if characters need a bit more incentive to take on the adventure in the first place, or if they return to civilization to resupply themselves with goods that cannot be readily acquired out in the Unclaimed Lands.

What first appeared to be a massive cloud passing before the sun suddenly splits apart, dissolving into well over a dozen furiously screeching horrors! Wings and antlers casting impossible shadows across the thatched roofs and screaming civilians, they plummet with talons outstretched.

Individually or even in small groups, these creatures pose no threat at all to characters of the characters' level. Unfortunately for them, there are no fewer than 17 **perytons** in this flock! Even worse, they're smart enough to spread out and dive from multiple angles, making it difficult to catch many of them in a single spell or area effect. While they focus on the party once the characters prove themselves dangerous, they're initially happy to attack whatever prey seems convenient, meaning the characters are again in a position where they need to protect civilians.

Peryton (17): **AC** 13; **HP** 33 (6d8+6); **Spd** 20ft, fly 60ft; **Melee** gore (+5, 1d8+3 piercing), talons (+5, 2d4+3 piercing); **SA** dive attack (extra 2d8 damage on melee, dives 30ft or more straight toward target before the attack), multiattack (gore, talons); **Resist** normal weapons; **Str** +3, **Dex** +1, **Con** +3, **Int** −1, **Wis** +1, **Cha** +0; **Skills** Perception +5; **Senses** keen sight and smell; **Traits** flyby (doesn't provoke opportunity attack when it flies out of enemy's reach); **AL** CE; **CR** 2; **XP** 450.

If their numbers are reduced to 5 or fewer, the perytons attempt to flee.

O. Corvul

A small but thriving community in the hills at the far west of the Unclaimed Lands, Corvul consists of one large central town, a smaller village a short ways south, and some sprawling hillside vineyards. It is, in terms of population, the smallest of the three fiefdoms involved in the monster hunt/competition, but also the wealthiest per capita. The terrain is gentle, more rolling than steep, and relatively green. For more, reference the "Unclaimed Lands Fiefdoms" sidebar.

As mentioned previously, Corvul is ruled by Baroness Ruvaka (female human college of valor **Brd10**).

Seeing Baroness Ruvaka

Anyone in town can direct the characters to the baroness's home at the center of town; not that this should be necessary, since it's visible from pretty much anywhere in Corvul. If and when the characters head that way, read the following.

The so-called "keep" of Baroness Ruvaka is little more than a single tower, surrounded by a few outbuildings and huddled within an outer wall that's not much more than a thick fence. Still, given the size of this "barony," it's actually a fairly decent effort at a defensive bastion. Certainly the hard-eyed and heavily armored soldiers standing at the main gate look as though they take their duties seriously enough.

The characters have enough of a reputation that, if they request to see the baroness, they'll eventually be granted an audience. That said, Ruvaka is busy and needs to keep up appearances, so they won't be allowed in immediately. Assume a delay of 1d4+1 days. A DC 20 Cha (Persuasion) check reduces the delay by 1, plus 1 additional day for every additional 5 points of success, to a minimum of 1 day. (So, 2 days with a roll of 25, 3 with a roll of 30, etc.)

If, however, the characters averted the oni and ogre attack (encounter **H**), or helped defend the village against them, Ruvaka sees them immediately upon request.

Several of the keep's soldiers escort you through the gate and then through the heavy outer doors of the tower itself. You pass through a few short stone halls, echoing with footsteps and the voices of minor functionaries, until you arrive in what appears to be as much sitting room as audience chamber. A number of cushioned sofas and divans circle an owlbear-skin rug and a small table, which itself offers a selection of wines and juices.

Sitting comfortably on one of those sofas on the opposite side of the table, and studying a list or report of some sort, is the woman you've come to see. Her features are sharp, striking; her hair and skin both quite dark, her gown — cut for comfort more than fashion — a creamy off-white. She offers you a friendly if not particularly sincere smile, and gestures for you to have a seat. A second wave of her hand sends your escorts to go stand at attention by the door.

If the characters did well by her people in encounter **H**, she begins by thanking them for their action. Otherwise, she politely but directly moves straight to the point, asking the characters what it is they wish of her.

Ruvaka is a reasonable woman, and when she learns the characters wish her to stop the monster hunt, she's willing to hear them out. She's sympathetic and more than a bit concerned if they explain the problems and possible political fallout of what's happening down along the Amrin River.

Once the characters have finished their request, and any conversation or questions that follow, read the following.

For long moments Baroness Ruvaka seems to study the wine glasses on the table, clearly lost in thought. Finally, without looking up, she speaks.

"I cannot back out of the competition alone. I simply cannot afford the loss of face or political prestige, and anyway, it would do no good in terms of solving your problems. You would have to convince Sir Habahn and Duke Fiodmar to cease their hunts as well.

"There is also..." She pauses a moment, finally meeting your eyes.

"Not many know this, but I have another reason for wanting the hunt to continue.

"Years ago, before my time, a dragon dwelt in the wilds not far from here. Many of my generation believe this to be mere legend, but I know it for fact. My father, who ruled here before me, lost several close companions to a halfbreed creature we later discovered to be the offspring of this repulsive wyrm. It was technically a fever that killed him, but he was greatly weighted down by grief; he might not have fallen ill, might not have succumbed to his illness, had his spirit not already been weakened.

"It's been, I confess, a bit of an obsession of mine since then. I don't pretend to know if I could, or would, ever truly seek vengeance on the dragon for adding to the monsters of my lands. I'm not even entirely sure I truly blame the creature for its spawn's actions. Nevertheless, I must know everything I can about it before I can make such decisions. I've hoped to flush it out with the hunt, if it still dwells nearby. Or, if not the dragon itself, then one of its offspring who can give me its name and tell me if it still lives.

"If you can do that for me, where my own hunters failed — and, yes, convince my competitors that they, too, must end their efforts — I will happily call off my part of the hunt."

It's possible, if you began the adventure with encounter **D**, that the characters *already* have this information. If so, and they share it, Ruvaka is initially a bit skeptical, but a DC 15 Persuasion check — or an offer to accept questioning under *zone of truth* or similar magic, if she can provide it — eventually convince her of their honesty.

If the characters don't already have that information (or cannot convince her that they do), they can acquire it from any of the various half-dragon creatures scattered throughout the region. The hydra at encounter **G**, the dragons or dracolisk random encounters, or even Fiodmar himself can provide them with Khythontorryx's name and the fact that he lives in the general vicinity, but no longer in this part of the Unclaimed Lands. You can add additional offspring as well, if need be.

How hard it is for the characters to find one of them is up to you. You can drag it out, leaving it to random chance as they continue the adventure, or you can plant rumors of half-dragons among some of the other monsters and NPC encounters, allowing the heroes to track them down with relative alacrity.

In either case, when the characters deliver the information, Ruvaka is both surprised and grateful, and — once they can also convince the other two lords to back down — keeps her word and calls her hunters off.

Encounter P: Vath

Vath stands amidst a stretch of overgrown plains, a small island amidst a sea of tall grasses. A single town and surrounding farms, Vath's inflated sense of its own importance is obvious from the first approach. The abatis (a defensive wall of branches and spiked logs) surrounding it is far larger than it really needs to be, and a handful of the buildings within are made of stone rather than wood. Vath really wants to be a small city, rather than a country town, and if it needs to wear a bit of makeup and play dress up to look the part, it's willing to do so.

Again, other than the above, see "Unclaimed Lands Fiefdoms" for more detail. The ruler of Vath is Sir Habahn the Gray (male half-elf battlemaster **Ftr9**).

Unclaimed Land Fiefdoms

Sooner or later, and on multiple occasions, the characters are going to find themselves entering the main towns of Unclaimed Lands "fiefdoms." These communities tend to be thriving relatively well for the area, and may have stronger militias and fortifications than might be expected, but are otherwise unremarkable. In civilized lands such as Aachen, these might not even appear on local maps. Here in the Unclaimed Lands, however, they form the heart of numerous independent "states." A large village—maybe two or three—and the surrounding farmlands, vineyards, and grazing fields are baronies, dukedoms, even kingdoms. Or so they call themselves, and nobody gainsays them, because anyone in a position to do so is actually making the same claims for themselves.

As previously mentioned, Corvul, Avrandt, and Vath aren't the only "village-states" in the immediate area. Until the characters begin gathering more information and receive some names from people, they have no reason to distinguish those three from the others.

Use the following description when the characters enter their first village-state, then simply refer back to it — with modifications for nearby crops and terrain, weather, number/prominence of soldiers on the streets, etc. — for the next ones. Most of these villages look very much like one another. (You'll want to come up with a few names for the "non-plot-specific" towns and their lords.)

Thick fences, abbattises, and other wooden palisades divide this community from the wilderness beyond, but once inside it resembles a hundred other small towns in a hundred other places. Buildings of lumber and thatch stand in rough blocks, with streets of dirt running between them. Farmers and workers wander those byways, accompanied by the clump of hooves and the creaking of old wagon wheels.

Yet there's something different about this place. Guards and militiamen stand at attention or walk beside the peasants, remarkably well armed for so small a community. And even the meanest citizen holds his or her head with a sense of pride not often found in similar looking towns.

They're something special, out here in the Unclaimed Lands. A state unto themselves that, however small and however poor, has thus far held its own.

For the record, characters can purchase very basic equipment — rations and supplies, tools, clothing, etc. — in any of these towns for more or less standard prices. They can purchase light armor and common simple weapons. For heavier armors, less common weapons, costly spell components, specific gems, alchemical items, spellcasting services, and the like, they'll have to return to Aachen (or some other civilized region).

Rumors

If the characters ask around any of these towns/mini-kingdoms for rumors and information about the monster hunt, they may attempt a DC 10 Charisma check. The people know that the hunt is ongoing, and that several local lords are involved, but they don't necessarily know *why* the hunt began. As to who's involved, well, that's where it gets tricky, and where the characters need to be careful which rumors they listen to.

In Vath, Corvul, and Avrandt, the citizens know well that their own lord is one of those engaged in monster hunting. They've seen too many expeditions come in and out, with trophies held high, to remain ignorant. If the characters are in one of these three towns when they ask around about which lords are involved, the citizens offer the names of 3 or 4 lords. Of those, 1 is their own lord; 1 is another lord who is genuinely involved; and the remaining 1 or 2 are false leads. (The people aren't lying to the characters; they've just believed rumors that aren't true.)

If the characters are in any of the other communities when they ask this question, the citizens there know that their own lords *aren't* heavily involved. They still give the characters 3 or 4 names; one is a lord who is genuinely involved, and the other 2 or 3 are false rumors.

(For example, if the characters are in Corvul when they gain this information, they will hear that Ruvalka is involved; they will hear that *either* Habahn or Fiodmar is involved; and they will hear the names of one or two other lords whom the peasant believe are involved, but aren't.)

Obviously, the characters don't know that a false rumor is false. Thus, if they intend to learn who the culprits are via rumor gathering, they'll have to go to multiple towns and see which names keep coming up, or see if the peasants name their own lord in the process.

Seeing Sir Habahn

Habahn is, like the community he formed, pretentious. He's also selfish, gluttonous, and greedy, but masks it all in a façade of chivalry and nobility. He uses a false honor to cloak his utter lack of it, and isn't honestly fooling much of anyone.

At the precise center of town stands a squat stone structure, more of a lordly manor than any sort of castle or keep. Just getting enough rock here to construct the thing, in the midst of the grassland, must have been a monumental endeavor.

An iron fence surrounds the property, revealing an estate of paths, trimmed grasses, and the occasional garden. Despite the house-like structure of the building, though, it doesn't feel much like a home. The ostentation is clearly deliberate, and the fencing, thick walls, and regular patrols give it a definite fortress-like air.

Atop the highest peak of the roof flaps a banner, showcasing a black silhouette of a lancer atop a rearing mount, against a field of gray.

Characters must make a DC 25 Cha (Persuasion) check when attempting to schedule a audience with Sir Habahn. On a success, the self-proclaimed knight will see them in 1d6+1 days. For every 5 points by which the characters beat the DC (30, 35, etc.) the delay decreases by 1 day (to a minimum of 1). If the characters fail the check, the delay *increases* by 1 day, plus one additional day for every 5 points by which the missed the check. (So, 2 days for a roll of 20, 3 days for a roll of 15, and so forth.)

However, offering the guard captain at the gate to Habahn's estate a bribe grants a bonus on this Cha check; +1 for every 200gp-worth of "gift."

Once their appointment finally comes around, the guards attempt to demand that the characters surrender their weapons before being admitted. They won't press, however, figuring it's not worth the effort or trouble.

The central chamber of the manor looks like a modern version of an old barbarian lord's drinking hall. The ceiling soars high overhead, crisscrossed with support beams. Trophies of every imaginable sort hang along the walls: from old weapons and shields to the heads of dire wolves and the claws and tail spines of manticores. A dozen of the lord's favored sycophants sit along the long table, feasting on roast meats and foamy ales.

At the head of the table sits a large man in gleaming plate; his hair is just growing out of neat trim, and his face is ruddy, flushed. He is clearly a lover of food and drink, but the way he moves and carries himself in his armor suggests real power and strength beneath the fleshy exterior.

"We have guests!" he calls out, gesturing with a turkey leg. "Come, sit! Dine with us!"

It is, of course, entirely up to the characters if they want to join the feast first, or get right to the point of their visit. Sir Habahn looks displeased with them if they interrupt, but otherwise it makes no real difference to him. Once the characters introduce the topic of their visit, Habahn orders the feasters out, leaving only himself and a handful of his guards in the room with the characters.

Once Habahn has heard the characters out, continue with the following.

The large knight slowly strokes his chin, takes an idle sip from his mug. "Were I speaking only for myself," he says, "I would of course end the hunt immediately. It disturbs me that we've had such an unfortunate impact on our neighbors to the south. But it is *not* only about me. This hunt has brought substantial commerce and other income to Vath, as well as increasing our influence among our fellow communities out here in the Unclaimed Lands. I couldn't possibly take that from my people now.

"Not without... alternate economic benefits."

A DC 12 Wis (Insight) check, or simply players who are paying attention, reveals this to be a steaming load. Nevertheless, the knight stands by his argument; it's going to take a bribe to get him to stop, even if it's phrased as "economic aid" for his town. (He also, like Ruvaka, requires the characters obtain a commitment from the other two lords to also back down.)

It's vaguely possible to threaten Habahn into backing off without cost, but this requires a DC 30 Cha (Intimidate) check, makes the characters a lifelong enemy, and may cause political repercussions in the future.

If the characters offer a bribe of at least 1000gp, they can convince him to end his hunt with a DC 25 Cha (Persuasion) check. For every additional 200gp beyond the first 1000, they gain a +1 bonus on the check.

Q. Avrandt

Located at the edge of the woodlands, Avrandt is the largest of the three competing provinces. The main town claims no fewer than three smaller satellite villages, and many acres of farmland. It's otherwise fairly similar to any other regional communities; as always, see "Unclaimed Lands Fiefdoms" for more.

What the characters likely don't realize at first — though they may have some suspicion, if they've encountered the unicorn at encounter **L** — is that Duke Fiodmar isn't just another petty lord engaged in prideful rivalry. There is power here in Avrandt, power and an almost bestial malevolence.

The being currently calling itself "Fiodmar" is a **half-green dragon doppelganger Pal15 (oath of vengeance)**. He is the offspring of Khythontorryx, and a seething cauldron of hatred for both his father and for civilization. Fiodmar dreams of setting the human nations at war, and leading a "monster" uprising to carve out a new kingdom of beasts and horrors, with himself as its king. He killed the original Duke Fiodmar and took his place some years ago, and has been slowly amassing wealth and knowledge. The competition of the monster hunt wasn't his idea, but it offered him an opportunity he could not pass up.

Seeing Duke Fiodmar

A large wooden fort and palisade on the north end of town seems to be the seat of authority for Avrandt, to judge by the stream of messengers and petitioners going in and out. Laborers and craftsmen work on the outer defenses and the inner walls, strengthening and enlarging the structure. Clearly, someone's concerned about defenses, perhaps even preparing for war. The laborers don't seem especially happy about it, either. Red-faced and exhausted, they look as though they've been at this for some time now.

Unlike the other two rulers, Fiodmar agrees to see the party within only an hour or two of their request. He instructs his messenger to play this up as respect for their reputations, but in fact Fiodmar's anxious to learn just what these interlopers want, and what threat they might pose to his plans.

Apparently, Duke Fiodmar thinks highly enough of himself to warrant something awfully close to a genuine throne room. His audience chamber has vaulted ceilings of twenty feet or higher. A broad walkway runs down the center from the door to... Not a throne, precisely, but a hefty, heavily cushioned chair that sits in the broad-armed embrace of an enormous stone statue. Rows of benches sit to each side, creating the look and feel of a royal court, even if only a few functionaries sit in those pews.

Leaning back in the throne is a lean, balding man whose rich robes of office cannot quite conceal the leather armor beneath; clearly, he wishes to both look the part and be ready for any trouble that might arise.

He doesn't look *exactly* like the statue, but there's enough similarity to suggest it may have been modified from its original design to more closely resemble him.

"I am honored by your visit," he tells you in deep, arrogant tones, "but my time is limited. What do you want?"

Fiodmar is clearly not taken with the idea of ending the hunt. He demands, first and foremost, that the characters convince the others to back off as well. Unlike Ruvaka and Habahn, it's not enough for him that the characters promise they will do so. If they don't already *have* a commitment from the others, Fiodmar won't even continue the negotiation, telling them to return if and when the others have agreed to cease the hunt.

If the characters have already gotten those commitments, or if they go get them and then come back, continue with the following.

Duke Fiodmar rises from his throne and begins to pace. He negligently waves a hand as he does so, ordering guards and functionaries out. The door shuts with a booming echo, so that only you and he remain in the audience chamber.

"You must understand," he tells you as he walks, back and forth, back and forth, "this hunt is very important to me. If this discussion is going to go anywhere, I need from you a favor that you may not be willing to provide.

"I need you *to die!*"

Fiodmar makes certain to make this pronouncement when he's some distance from the throne and the statue behind it. After all, he wouldn't want the characters to be able to catch him *and* his **stone golem** in a single attack or area effect! He and his golem attack immediately.

Note: While Fiodmar is not a new monster per se, and all of his abilities and traits come from the core rules, the sheer number of special abilities to which he has access makes him something of a complex combatant. As such, Fiodmar has a long-form stat block in the **Monster Appendix**, where his powers are given in substantially more detail.

Fiodmar , Male Half-Green Dragon Doppelganger Pal15 (oath of vengeance): AC 21; **HP** 253 (23d8+69); **Spd** 30ft; **Melee** *frost brand rapier* (+11, 1d8+8 piercing plus 1d6 cold plus 1d8 radiant), slam (+11, 1d6+6 bludgeoning plus 1d8 radiant); **SA** channel divinity (*abjure enemy* or *vow of enmity*), divine smite, multiattack (rapier x2 or slam x2), poison breath (recharge 5–6, poison gas in 15ft cone, 6d6 poison damage, DC 11 Constitution save for half); **Resist** poison; **Immune** charm, disease, fear; **Str** +0 (+3), **Dex** +6 (+9), **Con** +3 (+6), **Int** +0 (+3), **Wis** +1 (+9), **Cha** +3 (+11); **Skills** Deception +8, Insight +6, Intimidation +8, Persuasion +8; **Senses** blindsight 10ft, darkvision 60ft; **Traits** ambusher, aura of courage*, aura of protection*, cleansing touch (x3/long rest, divine sense, dueling fighting style*, improved divine smite*, lay on hands (pool of 75 hit points), read thoughts, relentless avenger, shapechanger, surprise attack; **AL** NE; **CR** 14; **XP** 11,500. (**Monster Appendix**)
*These are already incorporated into Fiodmar's stats.
　　Spells (slots): 1st (4); 2nd (3); 3rd (3); 4th (2). *Note:* Fiodmar does not prepare spells; he uses his spell slots *only* to empower Divine Smite.
　　Equipment: leather armor, shield, *frost brand rapier*.

Stone Golem: AC 17; **HP** 178 (17d10+85); **Spd** 30ft; **Melee** slam (+10, 3d8+6 bludgeoning); **SA** multiattack (slam x2), slow (recharge 5–6; one or more creatures within 10ft; can't use reactions, speed halved, can only make one attack, can take action or bonus action but not both, for 1 minute; DC 17 Wisdom save negates, can repeat at the end of its turn each round); **Immune** charm, exhaustion, fright, non-adamantine normal weapons, paralysis, petrify, poison, psychic; **Str** +6, **Dex** –1, **Con** +5, **Int** –4, **Wis** +0, **Cha** –5; **Senses** darkvision 120ft; **Traits** immutable form (immune to any spell or effect that would alter its form), magic resistance, magic weapons; **AL** U; **CR** 10; **XP** 5900

*Note: Remember to add Fiodmar's Charisma bonus to the golem's saves when they are within 10ft.

Fiodmar is far too angry and far too prideful to acknowledge that these adventurers can defeat him, and the golem mindlessly obeys orders. Both fight to the death.

The doppelganger is more than willing to talk or argue with the characters during combat, and feels no need to hide anything at this point. As such, they might be able to get some information out of him even as they fight, including the name of his draconic parent and the fact that he seeks to lead a veritable nation of monsters to wipe out the humans of the Borderlands.

Fortunately, Fiodmar reverts to his natural form when he dies, so when the chaos finally dies down and the guards work up the nerve to burst

---

A Hidden Evil

It's possible that the characters might discover earlier than intended that Fiodmar isn't what he appears to be, perhaps through the use of various detection spells. If so, he and his golem attack immediately, working to eliminate any witnesses among the guards or courtroom aids, as well as the characters.

On the other hand, if the players don't discover Fiodmar's true nature on their own, you might decide not to have him reveal himself here. The doppelganger could make for a good recurring hidden villain in your campaign. If you don't feel the need to have this adventure wrap itself up, consider having him pretend to acquiesce to the characters' requests. (Maybe he gives them a side quest like Ruvaka did, just to make it all seem on the up and up.) Then, when the heat's off, he can resume his efforts at driving monsters south into Aachen through some other means.

---

through the door and find out just what the hell's going on, the characters have plenty of evidence for their claims.

R. Sour Grapes

Defeating Fiodmar, and getting Ruvaka and Habahn to agree to stop their hunt, doesn't mean things are quite over for the characters. There are now several bands of monster hunters who are out of a very lucrative job, and while most aren't willing to challenge the characters over it, our old friend Dovrath isn't quite so timid.

He and his team attack the characters at a time and location of your choosing; they hope to catch the party unawares, but if the characters don't drop their guard and are about to reach civilization, Dovrath throws caution to the wind and attacks anyway.

Dovrath, Male Human Archmage: AC 12 (15 with *mage armor*); **HP** 99 (18d8+18); **Spd** 30ft; **Melee** dagger (+6, 1d4+2 piercing); **Ranged** dagger (+6, 20ft/60ft, 1d4+2 piercing); **SA** spells (Int +9, DC 17); **Immune** charm, divination spells, mind-reading, psychic damage; **Resist** normal weapons due to *stoneskin*; **Str** +0, **Dex** +2, **Con** +1, **Int** +5 (+9), **Wis** +2 (+6), **Cha** +3; **Skills** Arcana +13, History +13; **Traits** magic resistance; **AL** CN; **CR** 12; **XP** 8400.
　　Innate Spells: at will—*disguise self, invisibility*
　　Spells (slots): 0 (at will)—*fire bolt, light, mage hand, prestidigitation, shocking grasp*; 1st (4)—*detect magic, identify, mage armor*, magic missile*; 2nd (3)—*detect thought, mirror image, misty step*; 3rd (3)—*counterspell, fly ,lightning bolt*; 4th (3)—*banishment, fire shield, stoneskin**; 5th (3)—*cone of cold, scrying, wall of force*; 6th (1)—*globe of invulnerability*; 7th (1)—*teleport*; 8th (1)—*mind blank**; 9th (1)—*time stop*
　　*already cast
　　Equipment: dagger, spellbook

Imriss, Female Human Assassin: AC 15; **HP** 78 (12d8+24); **Spd** 30ft; **Melee** shortsword (+7, x2, 1d6+3 piercing plus 7d6 poison [DC 15 Constitution saving throw for half]); **Ranged** light crossbow (+7, 80ft/320ft, 1d8+3 piercing plus 7d6 poison [DC 15 Constitution saving throw for half]); **SA** sneak attack (1/turn, 4d6 damage); **Str** +0, **Dex** +3 (+7), **Con** +2, **Int** +1 (+5), **Wis** +0, **Cha** +0; **Skills** Acrobatics +7, Deception +4, Perception +4, Stealth +11; **Traits** assassinate (on first turn, tactical advantage on attack against creature that hasn't taken a turn, and any hit against a surprised creature is a critical hit), evasion (effect that allows a Dex save half, take no damage on success and only half on fail); **AL** CN; **CR** 8; **XP** 3900.
　　Equipment: leather armor, poison (x10), shortsword, light crossbow, 20 bolts

Torval and Yndra, Male and Female Human Monster Hunters (Gladiator variant): AC 16; **HP** 112 (15d8+45); **Spd** 30ft; **Melee** spear (+10, 2d6+4 piercing, or 2d8+4 piercing if used two-handed), shield bash (+10, 2d4+4 bludgeoning plus the target is knocked prone if Medium or smaller, DC 15 Str negates); **Ranged** spear (+10, 20ft/60ft, 2d6+4 piercing); **SA** multiattack (melee x3 or ranged x2); **Str** +7 (+10), **Dex** +2 (+5), **Con** +3 (+6), **Int** +0, **Wis** +1, **Cha** +2; **Skills** Athletics +10, Perception +4, Survival +4; **Traits** brave, brute, parry (reaction, +3 AC against one melee that would hit); **AL** N; **CR** 5; **XP** 1800.
　　Equipment: studded leather, shield, 3 spears.

These guys are pissed, but they're not suicidal. Torval and Yndra surrender or attempt to flee if reduced to fewer than 30 hit points; Imriss does the same if below 20. Dovrath himself *teleports* away — with one or more of his companions if possible, but by himself if necessary — if he's reduced to 20 hit points, or if all his companions have surrendered, fled, or dropped.

While the characters are defending themselves, they're better off not killing these particular opponents. Yes, leaving them alive means the characters have some new enemies, but it'll only be these four. If the characters actually kill them, not only does this draw some questions from the authorities back home, but the characters have now earned the enmity of many of the region's other adventurers. Thus, whether or not they live, Dovrath's team are likely to be a source of trouble for the characters for some time to come.

Lingering Issues

The fact that the hunt has ended doesn't mean the monsters instantly cease what they're doing and return home. Many won't realize the threat has passed. Others might prefer their new hunting grounds. It's still going to require multiple expeditions to drive them back from the Amrin, and not everyone in Aachen is yet convinced that doing so is necessary. The characters may have further adventures, or at least further argument and negotiation, ahead of them.

If the party was promised a reward by representatives of either Aachen or Bard's Gate, their employers honor the agreement. Whether Khythontorryx does or not, however, depends on how much of an effort the characters actually made to avoid killing his offspring (other than Fiodmar), and whether Fiodmar himself was killed. Assuming the dragon is satisfied with their performance, he appears some days later to keep his end of the bargain — and keeps a very close eye on the characters for the foreseeable future, watching to see if they can continue to be useful tools, or if they're becoming a threat he should eliminate. If the latter, he's very likely to make a deal with some of the region's disgruntled adventurers to strike at the characters, rather than doing so directly. This most peculiar hunt may be ended, but its repercussions might still be felt for months or years to come.

Ectarlin's Last Ride

Strange happenings along the northern shore of Amrin Estuary are threatening Eastreach Province's lucrative coastal trade. Merchant vessels are found adrift at sea or grounded out along the shoals and marshlands of the coast — their cargo holds partially looted and their crews vanished without a trace. It's up the adventurers to get to the bottom of the mystery — but that mystery runs far deeper than anyone suspects.

Ectarlin's Last Ride involves careful investigation, challenging combat, and roleplaying as the characters attempt to discover what force was behind the attacks on the derelict ships. In the end, the heroes end up battling very different foes than the ones they set out to fight — and might find themselves defending those they first set out to vanquish.

This adventure is designed for a party of 4–6 characters of 14th level.

Adventure Background

All merchants know to avoid the Lowwater Road that runs up the eastern coast of Eastreach Province — a wild and dangerous track. Virtually all trade between Eastgate, at the end of Amrin Estuary, and Eastwych, on the coast of Eastreach Province, sails on board the small merchant craft that ply the coastal waters. However, starting four weeks ago, a sudden disruption to the previously safe coastal trade routes has set a rising panic among the traders of two lands.

When a slow coaster named the *Blue Boar* was three days late for arrival on a cargo run to Eastwych, small boats were quickly dispatched to see if the vessel had run aground. *Blue Boar* was found

three days later, drifting far beyond the mouth of the Amrin Estuary with no crew and her holds ransacked. Over the following four weeks, four additional vessels have met the same fate — two running north from Eastgate to Eastwych, and two running the southerly return route. In the last three instances, the ships were fast caravels, carrying additional guards hired by the merchant houses — and it made no difference. Two of the ships were found grounded in the marshland south of the Lowwater road. The others were found adrift, heading out past Telar Brindel toward the open sea.

In all five instances, the holds of the missing ships had been ransacked. Merchant clerks charged with tallying the cargo consistently reported that the lightest, most valuable commodities had been taken, even as larger, bulky trade goods were left behind. Though some reported seeing clear signs of combat on board the derelicts, no bodies have yet been found.

The ransacking of the holds speaks to pirates as the power behind the attacks on the drifting ships, while the killing and dumping whole crews suggests a particularly bloodthirsty band of cutthroats newly operating along the coast. However, the merchant guilds whose ships have been targeted have had poor luck convincing the authorities to investigate. The League of Estuary Lords (all of whom owe fealty to Bard's Gate) argue that the attacks are obviously the responsibility of Eastreach Province, since the pirates are clearly based along and striking from the marshes along the Lowwater Road. The local lords of Eastreach are just as adamant that since the attacks are happening in the Estuary, the problem belongs to the cities of Eastgate and Bard's Gate. Having had enough of political squabbling, the merchants whose ships are being targeted are taking matters into their own hands.

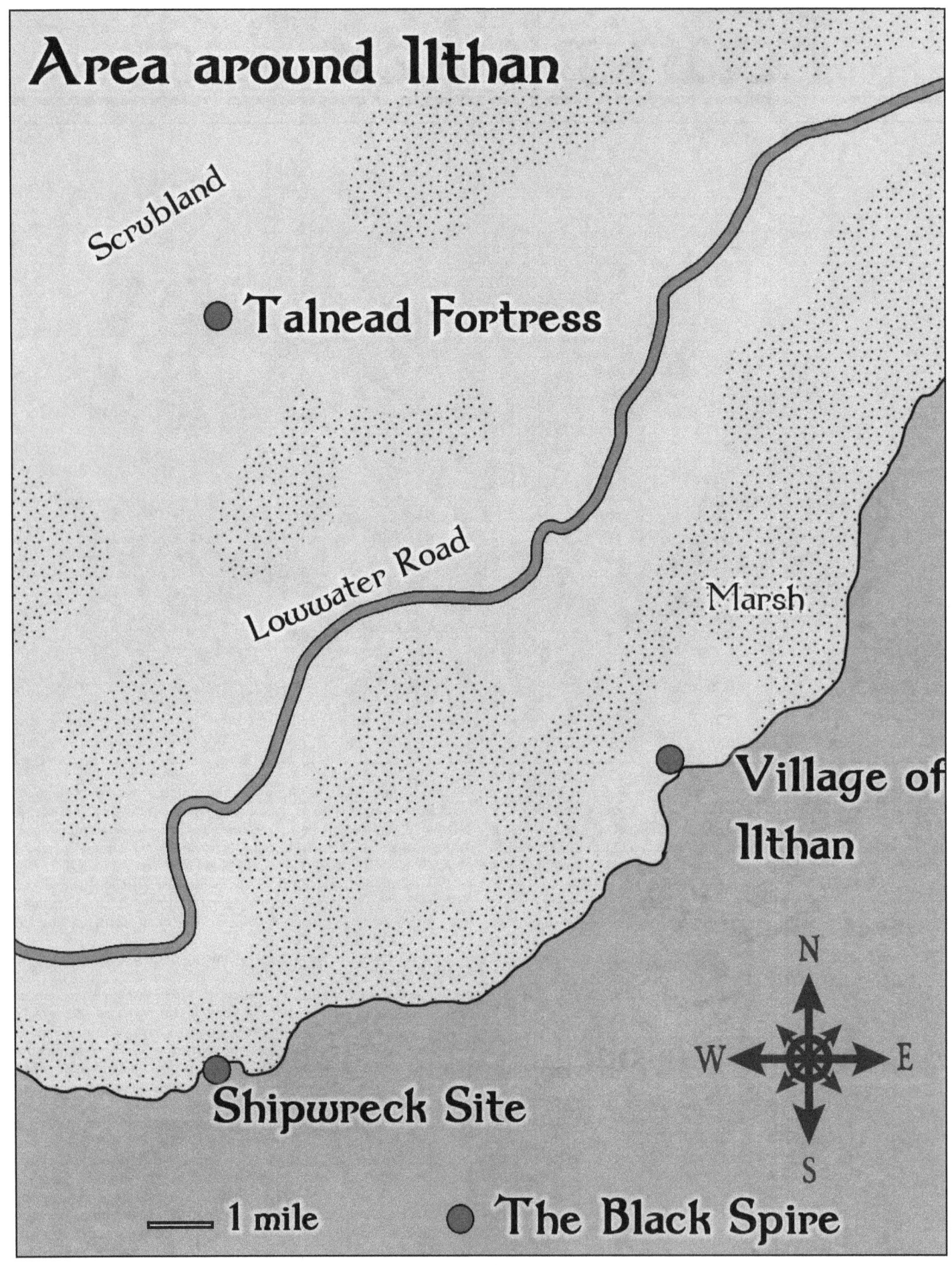

Area around Ilthan

Scrubland

● Talnead Fortress

Lowwater Road

Marsh

● Village of Ilthan

N
W E
S

● Shipwreck Site

— 1 mile ● The Black Spire

The Real Story

Although pirates operating along the seacoast are a part of the fate of the derelict ships, they are not the cause of it. Rather, the reappearance of an ancient undead power on a small island called the Black Spire has unleashed a pack of ravenous undead called soulstealers, which hunt by night for bodies and souls. The undead attack the ships of the coast because they are constrained to a fixed area around their undead lord — a once-powerful lich they call the Dread Master, now imprisoned in his dark island tomb. But as the Dread Master's power grows, so does the range of his servants, and all the coast and the lands beyond will soon be potential targets for his dark hunger.

The Dread Master and his spectral servants are not the only undead haunting the Amrin–Eastreach coastal borderlands, however. A century ago, a legendary knight named Ectarlin was the local freelord who fought against — and was slain by — the lich. With the Dread Master's return to power, Ectarlin has returned as a mad ghost driven to fulfill his mission to protect the folk of the Lowwater lands. With him is the ghost ride: the spectral shades of the warriors who once followed Ectarlin into battle, and who promise to turn the Amrin coast into a battleground once again.

Heroes for Hire

Based on their individual or group reputation as adventurers who can get things done, the characters are sought out by representatives of merchant guilds in Eastgate or Eastwych (depending on where they happen to be). A merchant clerk named Bando Larna is the envoy to the adventurers. Meeting in private, he gives the characters the backstory presented above and presents the merchant guilds' offer — 250gp per character up front, plus another 250gp each for the destruction of the pirate operation responsible for attacking the lost merchant ships.

While rumors of the attacks have spread, a true understanding of their full scope has not, and the merchant lords would like to keep it that way. As such, they hope the characters can uncover the truth of what's happening along the estuary — and quickly. The characters are not being hired to guard any particular ship; rather, the merchant guilds want them to patrol the Lowwater Road along the estuary, looking for signs of pirate activity and taking the fight to the bloodthirsty buccaneers.

Alternate Hooks

If the heroes-for-hire setup doesn't appeal to you or the players, feel free to make use of the following options, or create your own.

Right Place, Right Time: Though few locals and fewer merchants travel the Lowwater Road, the dangers of the road and the surrounding marsh- and scrubland might simply seem a pleasant walk to a 14th-level party. If the characters have business that takes them north or south along the road, they might simply happen across the encounter that kicks off **Ghosts on the Water**, the first part of the adventure.

Lost Friends: One or more NPCs the characters know were among the crew members lost on the derelict ships (either sailors or mercenaries hired for protection after the initial disappearances). The adventurers can use this personal connection to strike out along the Lowwater Road, seeking retribution for fallen friends, or hoping perhaps that the missing NPCs might still be alive.

Ghosts on the Water

Whatever hook you use to inspire the characters' involvement in the mystery of the derelict ships, the action kicks off along the Lowwater Road, close to the mouth of Amrin Estuary where it meets the Sinnar Ocean. In the dark of night, a pirate raid in progress draws the characters into the adventure.

Lights in the Night

This initial encounter takes place late at night, when the soulstealers are active and the local pirate band known as the Black Ghosts are taking unwitting advantage of the undead creatures' dark deeds. Whether the characters are traveling by dark, camped out for the night along the Lowwater Road, or have set a watch for possible pirate activity, mysterious lights are the clue that draws them in.

The wind is blowing off the estuary, with the night-chilled tang of salt air thankfully overpowering the fetid scent of marsh that's followed you through the day's ride along the Lowwater Road. The moon is veiled by the clouds that have threatened rain all day, setting a wan, gray light across the landscape.

At the top of an escarpment where the Lowwater Road defies its name to temporarily twist above the surrounding marshland, you have a good view of the land around you, all the way to the sea. Against the dimness of the night, a sudden flare of light shines out to the west, then is just as suddenly gone. After a moment, it appears again — the light of a lamp or lantern being swung in a wide arc, up and down, in some kind of signal.

A successful DC 12 Wis (Survival) check judges that the signal came from close offshore and no more than a half-mile ahead. The light was a scout from the Black Ghost pirate band having spotted and reached the scuttled merchant coaster *Gull's Egg*, and signaling that the ships crew has vanished, as the pirates expect. In the time it takes the characters to make their way toward where they saw the light, the *Gull's Egg* has been grounded and the pirates are quickly relieving the ship of its remaining cargo.

Salvage Operation

As the characters draw close, they see the Black Ghosts at a distance — a band of humans all dressed in dark leather and black masks. An equal mix of men and women, the pirates hail from a village along the southern flank of the Forest of Hope. But though they are actively looting the scuttled ship, they are not the agents behind its fate, as the characters will learn.

Following a haphazard path through the marsh, you take shelter behind a stand of gnarled and rotting willow trees. Along the shore a hundred paces ahead, you see a small merchant coaster run aground, its deck heaved over at a steep angle. Its sails are still fully set and filled out by wind blowing in off the darkened coast. Even in the faint haze of cloudy moonlight, you can see figures in small boats plying the choppy water between the foundering ship and the shore. The sailors move with quick purpose and are in black from head to foot — including the masks that cover their faces.

Two figures are in each of two pinnaces moving to and from the ship. One figure rows while the other holds a crossbow at the ready — the same weapon seen in the hands of sentries standing watch along the shoreline, where even more pirates sort through barrels and boxes spread across the beach, quickly packing select goods onto a dozen pack horses.

The Black Ghosts are 3 pirate captains (**bandit captain**) leading 12 pirates (**bandit**). The characters can take any number of approaches to dealing with the pirates.

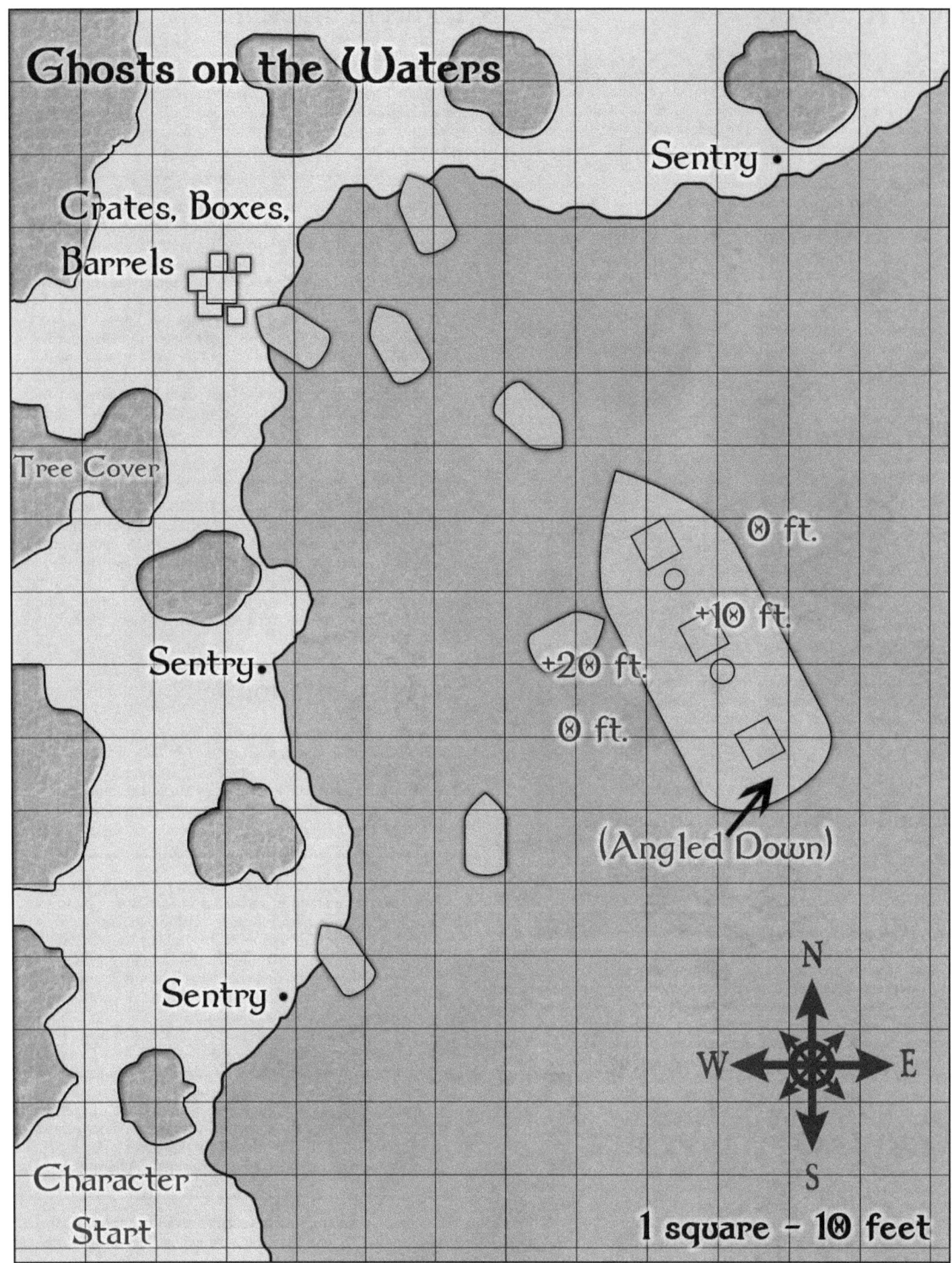

Ghosts on the Waters

Sentry •

Crates, Boxes,
Barrels

Tree Cover

⊗ ft.

+10 ft.

+20 ft.

⊗ ft.

Sentry•

(Angled Down)

Sentry •

N

W ⟷ E

S

Character
Start

1 square – 10 feet

Moving in Quietly

The characters can use stealth to approach through the marsh, either to try to take out a sentry with surprise or to gain access to the water. Each character must make successful DC 15 Dex (Stealth) check to escape the notice of any of the alert sentries, who call out an alarm if any character is spotted (see "Shore Fight," below). Because none of the pirates have darkvision, the dark night makes the shore area lightly obscured, granting tactical disadvantage on Wis (Perception) checks to spot intruders.

Characters who get past the nearest sentry can reach a pinnace dragged up on shore, and have the option of slipping out to the *Gull's Egg* before deciding how to deal with the pirates. Each boat can hold up to six characters while empty of cargo. Each round of rowing the boat at a full speed of 30ft per round across the choppy water requires a successful DC 12 Str (Athletics) check. On a failed check, a character moves the boat only 15ft. Hardy characters can take to the water and swim up to the ship with successful DC 15 Str (Athletics) check.

Once at the ship, characters can easily board it by climbing up any of the numerous ropes hanging down from the deck. It takes a successful DC 12 Str (Athletics) check to climb up one of the wet ropes. Characters climbing out of view of the shore can slip onto the ship unseen. Any character climbing within view of the shore must make a successful DC 15 Dex (Stealth) check to avoid notice. On a failed check, the character is spotted and a shouted alarm goes up along the shore. See "Pirate Escape," below.

See "The Gull's Egg," below, if the characters explore or fight on the grounded ship.

Shore Fight

Given the party's level, both a direct assault and an attempt to order the pirates to stand down are reasonable options — and lead to the same result. The wary pirates respond aggressively to the appearance of any characters. The first pirate to spot a character shouts out a warning that is quickly repeated from pirate to pirate, alerting the entire company in short order (including the pirates rowing out to and currently on the ship).

Pirates on the shore attack at once, firing crossbows as they take cover behind their boats and the stacks of crates and barrels brought in from the ship. Pirates in boats immediately head back to shore at 30ft per round (and making one crossbow attack per round), then beach their boats and join the fight. The two pirates presently on the ship take 2 rounds to get to their boat, then row back behind the others. The pirate captains meet any characters who close to melee, but the pirates hold back with ranged attacks for as long as possible. For characters in melee, the rocky shore is covered with intermittent patches of difficult terrain.

Pirate Captain (3): AC 15; HP 65 (10d8 + 20); **Spd** 30ft; **Melee** scimitar (+5, 1d6 + 3 slashing); **Ranged** light crossbow (+5, 80ft/320ft, 1d8 + 3 piercing); **Str** +2, **Dex** +3, **Con** +2, **Int** +2, **Wis** +0, **Cha** +2; **AL** NG/N; **CR** 2; **XP** 450.
   Equipment: leather armor, scimitar, dagger, light crossbow, 10 bolts.

Pirate (12): AC 12; HP 11 (2d8 + 2); **Spd** 30ft; **Melee** scimitar (+3, 1d6 + 1 slashing); **Ranged** light crossbow (+3, 80ft/320ft, 1d8 + 1 piercing); **Str** +0, **Dex** +1, **Con** +1, **Int** +0, **Wis** +0, **Cha** +0; **AL** NG/N; **CR** 1/8; **XP** 25.
   Equipment: leather armor, scimitar, dagger, light crossbow, 10 bolts.

Pirate Escape

All members of the pirate company assume that the characters are an official patrol out of Eastgate, and they have no interest in surrendering just to be executed by the crown. The Black Ghosts are savvy fighters, though, and will fall back if they see that the battle is turning against them. If four members of the group are killed, a call goes up from a surviving pirate captain or pirate to "Break for the bog!" After a final salvo of crossbow fire, the pirates split up to run separate courses for the Lowwater Road, abandoning the treasure and the horses. They then make their way individually into the dark marsh beyond the road, eventually returning to the village of Ilthan (see the next section).

You can play out a chase between the characters and a fleeing pirate, but the pirates know the marsh well and have tactical advantage on all Wis (Survival) checks they make to navigate it. The speed of the pirates' flight makes them relatively easy to track, (see "Developments," below), though doing so is easier by daylight.

The Gull's Egg

The *Gull's Egg* is a small merchant coaster of simple construction — little more than a single open deck, a cargo hold beneath that doubles as crew's quarters, and a bilge beneath. The ship is listing badly but solidly grounded, and is in no danger of shifting further.

The angle of the decks makes all areas of the listing ship difficult terrain, and allows characters to move along most of the main deck without being seen from the shore. A character moving along the upper edge of the deck becomes visible from the shore, and must make a successful DC 12 Dex (Stealth) check to avoid being spotted.

Though most of the cargo the *Gull's Egg* was carrying was lashed down, beaching the ship has sent many crates and barrels tumbling toward the lower edge of the deck, both on the main deck and in the cargo hold below. Access from the main deck to the cargo hold is through one of three wide ladderways. The pirates are using the middle ladderway to carry goods from the cargo hold up to the deck.

Main Deck

The main deck of the *Gull's Egg* is piled high with crates holding raw wool and rough cloth. The pirates are ignoring these bulky goods in favor of more valuable booty in the cargo hold.

The main deck is where the unfortunate crew of the ship made their futile stand against the soulstealers that have been hunting the waters of Amrin Estuary. A character who searches the debris along the lower edge of the deck (mostly loose rope, gaffs, shattered crates, and spilled bales) can make a successful DC 13 Int (Investigation) or Wis (Perception) check to find three scimitars, two of which are streaked with blood. (This was the result of the ship's crew turning against each other when stricken by the domination effect of the soulstealer's Mind Wrack.)

Cargo Hold

Unlike on the main deck and the shore, the pirates have lanterns lit to help their work in this area, filling the hold with bright light. This smaller space is filled with barrels, boxes, and crates holding wine and brandy, aged cheeses, smoked meats, fine cloth, finished clothing, pottery, and furs. The pirates are quickly and methodically ransacking this deck to cull the most valuable and portable goods.

As with the main deck above, many of the crates and barrels here have pitched to the lower edge of the deck and are piled high along the wall. A rich smell of wine and brandy fills the air from a number of shattered casks. (Though the brandy is normally flammable, it has been diluted with enough wine that there is no risk of fire in this area.)

Any character who wants to do so can spend 10 minutes searching the cargo hold to claim goods weighing a total of 50 pounds and worth 100gp, to a maximum of 1000gp worth of goods for the party.

Pirates at Work

If the characters arrive on the ship while the pirates are unloading, they find two pirates in the cargo hold sorting the most valuable casks and boxes. Their boat is lashed to a rope on the shoreward side. If the characters do not cause an alarm to be raised while they are on the ship, another boat carrying two more pirates arrives at the ship after 1 minute, tying up on the shoreward side. It not interrupted, the four pirates move back and forth between the deck and the hold for 5 minutes, transferring crates, barrels, and boxes to the boat. Two pirates then row back to the shore, and another boat arrives 1 minute later to repeat the process.

The pirates are focused on their work but wary. To hide from pirates moving on the ship where they can see a character requires a successful DC 15 Dex (Stealth) check. If the pirates on the ship become aware of the characters, they immediately shout an alarm toward the shore and race for their boats. If attacked, the pirates use the Disengage action in an attempt to escape. If prevented from reaching their boats, they dive overboard and swim back to shore.

Questions and Answers

A character who searches the bodies of any dead pirates finds only their weapons and clothing, but any quick assessment shows that all the pirates' gear (including their boats) is second rate and well worn. Any horses left behind are in average-to-poor health and show no brands or other markings.

Any pirates knocked unconscious and captured can be questioned once the fight is done. As long as they believe the adventurers are officials of either Eastreach Province or Amrin Estuary, captured pirates are stoically silent. They know that giving up any information will bring the law down on their families and their village (see the next section, **Darkness in Ilthan**), and all are willing to die in order to protect those they leave behind. It takes a successful DC 13 Cha (Persuasion) check to convince surviving pirates that the characters are independent of the law.

Anell Thale is the ranking surviving member of the Black Ghosts, and the pirate who talks to the adventurers if they earn her trust. A veteran sailor, Anell is a human female, thirty-five years old, and uses **pirate captain** statistics. (Use these statistics for her even if all the pirate captains in the encounter were killed.)

Anell will answer the characters' questions as long the adventurers leave all surviving pirates untied and agree to let them go when the talk is done. If the characters insist on binding the pirates, Anell refuses to trust them.

Successfully talking with Anell reveals the following information.

• The Black Ghosts are normally fisherfolk and scavengers, eking out a living collecting salvage along the shoreline of Amrin Estuary. Their small oared boats are moored near their village, from which the Black Ghosts patrol the marshy shore on the lookout for crates and barrels lost from or washed off the many merchant vessels that sail the coast.

• The pirates are opportunists, not brigands, though they know that makes no difference as far as the law is concerned. Living as scavengers leaves them open to accusations of theft and piracy, so all their salvaged goods are shipped to and sold through back channels in Carterscroft.

• Four weeks ago, members of the Black Ghosts spotted a derelict coaster (the *Blue Boar*) drifting toward shore at sunset. With no crew seen, the sailors of the Black Ghosts made a risky open-water crossing to investigate. Finding the ship deserted but fully stocked with cargo, they helped themselves to the most valuable goods, then turned the tiller and sent the ship out to sea.

• Four times since then, the sailors of the watch have scouted for and found deserted ships, looting them by dark of night. On each occasion, the ships' crews had already vanished without a trace.

"I'll tell you true," the pirate says, "we might not work the right side of the law, but we do no one any harm. What's lost is gone to the merchant lords in Eastgate, but what's found will feed my family. There's no shame in what we do — but I swear on my family, there's no blood crime neither. Those ships were empty before we got to them, each and every time. I don't know what's taking their crews, but it's not us."

A successful DC 12 Wis (Insight) check confirms the truth of Anell's tale. However, a check result of 15 or higher gives a character the sense that the pirate is hiding something as well — and is fearful. It takes a DC 15 Cha (Persuasion) check to convince Anell to open up.

"I spoke truth when I said I don't know what happened to the merchant crews. No one's seen nothing, and I promise

---

you, we've been watching. But I heard something. The second time out, finding a merchant cog out of Eastwych sailing circles past the estuary mouth. Foggy it was that night, and I heard a scream coming from out of the mist behind us. A voice high and dark. I've never heard its like before, and won't again if I'm lucky."

Screams in the Night

On their previous salvage operations, the pirates have worked to get on and off the derelict ships quickly. Their instincts to not linger on the deserted ships were apt, as the characters learn shortly after they take control of the situation around the *Gull's Egg*.

This encounter most likely occurs while the characters are exploring the ship or the shoreline (including at the end of any interrogation of surviving pirates). If the characters leave the shoreline area quickly (most likely because they are attempting to track the fleeing pirates by night), set this encounter in rough swampy terrain interrupted by patches of difficult terrain.

Over the hiss of wind, a sudden shriek rises from the nighttime gloom. A creature of nightmare surges forward out of the darkness — a serpentine mass of shattered bone that glides above the ground. Its wide maw opens as it screams again, revealing a vortex of churning bone fragments that gleam like sharpened teeth.

If Anell Thale has spoken with the characters, she recognizes the scream. Any surviving pirates flee if they are able, vanishing into the darkness of the marsh as the soulstealers close in around the adventurers. The soulstealers have been driven back to this area by the presence of the

---

Lost Moments

The most pernicious power of the soulstealers found throughout this adventure are those undead creatures' Mind Wrack feature, which can steal away the recollection of their victims. Encourage roleplaying from the players of characters who suddenly forget the events of previous minutes, reminding them that from their characters' perspective, they're suddenly in the middle of a fight they don't remember starting, with foes they might never have seen before. In most cases, afflicted characters will need to rely on other characters to tell them what's going on.

If the players are extremely unlucky, it's possible that everyone in the party might lose the memory of an entire encounter and the events leading up to it. If this happens, it's up to you to decide how to play out the absence of the characters' knowledge. If your players are up to a roleplaying challenge, the characters might revisit the scene of a forgotten encounter with no idea what happened, forced to investigate their own adventuring handiwork and reclaim the clues that have been taken from them.

A particularly ambitious GM with a roleplay-heavy group might consider actually starting the adventure this way, rather than via any of the options given above. You can throw the characters into the deep end, having them missing several days of memory and only slowly realizing that the battles they are investigating actually involved them! They would have to piece together what happened, meeting people for the first time who already know them and fighting unknown enemies who recognize them.

This, of course, requires that the characters have already failed a number of saves "off screen," so do this *only* if your group of players are of the sort to appreciate the drama, and won't be frustrated by the "GM fiat" necessary to get them there.

spectral lord Ectarlin and the ghost ride, which follows just a half-minute behind them. Having been interrupted in their hunting, 5 **soulstealers** embrace the opportunity to take the adventurers as new sacrifices to their Dread Master.

Soulstealer (5): AC 16; **HP** 105 (14d8 + 42); **Spd** 20ft, fly 40ft; **Melee** claws (+6, 1d8 + 5 slashing); **SA** mind wrack (*dominate person*, DC 15 Wis; *modify memory*, DC 15 Int), multiattack (claw x 4); **Immune** exhaustion, fright, necrotic, poison, restrain, stun, unconscious; **Resist** normal weapons; **Str** +4, **Dex** +2, **Con** +3 (+5), **Int** +2, **Wis** +2, **Cha** +0; **Skills** Perception +8; **Senses** darkvision 60ft; **Traits** incorporeal shift, mind wrack, unearthly destruction; **AL** NE; **CR** 6; **XP** 2300. (**Monster Appendix**)

Mind and Memory

The soulstealers feed on the body and essence of their prey, consuming flesh and spirit with their attacks. They focus on heavily armed warriors first, setting them against their allies with Mind Wrack if they can. They then turn their attention to spellcasters to minimize the chances of magic being used against them.

Though the soulstealers are rapacious, they are highly intelligent and driven by a strong sense of self-preservation. They flee when the ghost ride appears in pursuit of them (see below).

The Ghost Ride

In the 6th round of combat, or the round following the destruction of a second soulstealer (whichever comes first), a ghastly shrieking is heard from the marsh, in the direction from which the soulstealers appeared.

Over the horrid screaming of the phantasmal undead as they twist between you, the distant marsh comes alive with a guttural shrieking. A flare of pale light heralds the appearance of a dozen spectral riders, all racing toward you on translucent steeds, tabards flowing on the wind. The tall warrior who leads them is an imposingly regal figure, his long hair held back by a gleaming circlet. Two spectral hounds glow bright white where they race silently alongside his ghostly steed. Streamers of glowing grey mist shred off all the warriors' weapons, raised for attack as they charge in.

The 12 **spectral wardens** (see the sidebar) all sit astride ghostly steeds whose hooves beat the air without touching the ground. The warriors wear a uniform style of chain mail, and ride with a precision that suggests a military company. The tabards they wear all show the same sigil — a trident encircled by grape vines — that the characters might recognize (see "Developments," below).

Though the presence of the ghost ride might alarm the characters (especially those having a tough time in the fight against the soulstealers), the spectral wardens are not a threat. In pursuit of the soulstealers, the newly arrived ghosts take little notice of the adventurers unless the characters attack them. They otherwise remain focused on the greater threat, driving the soulstealers away from the characters and into the marsh 1 round after they appear.

The characters' last sight of all the spectral creatures is the glowing haze of the ghost ride vanishing into darkness. If the characters attempt to pursue, they see the warriors of the ghost ride destroy the remaining soulstealers in 3 rounds, then slowly fade away, their work done.

Developments

A character who inspects the body of a slain soulstealer notes fading runes embossed into its countless bones. With a successful DC 18 Int (Arcana) check or a *detect magic* spell, the character senses that the runes

---

Ectarlin and the Spectral Wardens

A spectral warden is a variant good-aligned **ghost** whose actions are driven by its failure to fulfill some oath of bond or protection, and whose spirit cannot pass on until it has completed its task or atoned. The spectral wardens in this adventure use the standard ghost stat block but have the following additional features.

• A spectral warrior has Str 14 (+2) and Con 13 (+1).

• Its increased Con gives a spectral warrior 55 hit points (10d8 + 10).

• *Radiant Rage.* As a bonus action, the spectral warden can alter its withering touch attack to deal radiant damage instead of necrotic damage.

• *Ghost Steed.* The spectral warden sits astride a ghostly steed that grants it a speed of 60ft. The steed cannot attack, be attacked, or interact with other creatures.

• *Resilient Faith.* Until its unfulfilled mission is completed, a spectral warden cannot be destroyed. If it is reduced to 0 hit points, the ghost manifests again at full strength after 24 hours.

• A spectral warden loses the ghost's Possession feature.

Ectarlin is a powerful spectral warden with the following statistics.

• Ectarlin has maximum hit points (90 hp).

• He has a +3 bonus to saving throws.

• *Regeneration.* Ectarlin regains 10 hit points at the start of his turn. If he takes radiant damage, this trait doesn't function at the start of Ectarlin's next turn.

• *Multiattack.* Ectarlin makes two withering touch attacks using his spectral mace. If he hits with both attacks (either targeting the same creature or two creatures), all enemies within 10ft of Ectarlin take 9 (3d6) radiant damage.

• Ectarlin's challenge rating is 8.

---

bind the undead horror to the creature that created it, and that the binding allows the soulstealer to move only a limited distance from its creator. (See the **Monster Appendix** for more information.)

In the aftermath of the pirate raid, the characters have two ways to proceed. Where the pirates' packhorses have been tethered and left behind, a mere DC 8 Wis (Perception) check finds a rough path leading into the marsh. With successful DC 15 Wis (Survival) checks, the characters can follow the trail back to the pirates' home settlement of Ilthan and continue the adventure in **Darkness in Ilthan**. Following any of the fleeing pirates leads to the village as well, but keeping along those erratic trails requires successful DC 20 Wis (Survival) checks.

A character who succeeds on a DC 12 Int (History) check recognizes the trident-and-vine sigil seen on the spectral riders' tabards, and recalls it as belonging to a loyalist knight of Foere named Lord Arnast Ectarlin. See "What Anell Knows" in the next section, and provide the characters with the information in the first and last bullet points. A successful DC 17 Int (History) check recalls the rough location of Ectarlin's former fortress of Talnead in relation to a recognizable landmark on the Lowwater Road, allowing the characters to set a course through the wilderness to find it. The adventure then continues in **Fallen Talnead**.

Darkness in Ilthan

The characters pursue the pirates known as the Black Ghosts from the site of the scuttled *Gull's Egg* to their home village. The isolated village of Ilthan is set on a marshland promontory south of the Lowwater Road, and is one of only a handful of permanent settlements along the southeast flanks of the Forest of Hope. Built on the bones of a long-abandoned estate, the village is home to some one hundred and fifty souls, all of whom — adults and children alike — work the water. A small, sheltered

Forking Paths

The players can take on the adventure in two slightly different ways, depending on where they choose to go at the end of **Ghosts on the Water**. If they next take on **Darkness in Ilthan**, that section becomes part 2 of the adventure, and is followed by **Fallen Talnead** as part 3. If the characters instead decide to go to Ectarlin's fortress first, **Fallen Talnead** becomes part 2 of the adventure and **Darkness in Ilthan** becomes part 3.

Whichever section of the adventure becomes part 3, it ends with the special encounter detailed in **The Ghost Lord's Sorrow**. The adventure then concludes with **The Black Spire**.

Illo 1 - Flowchart

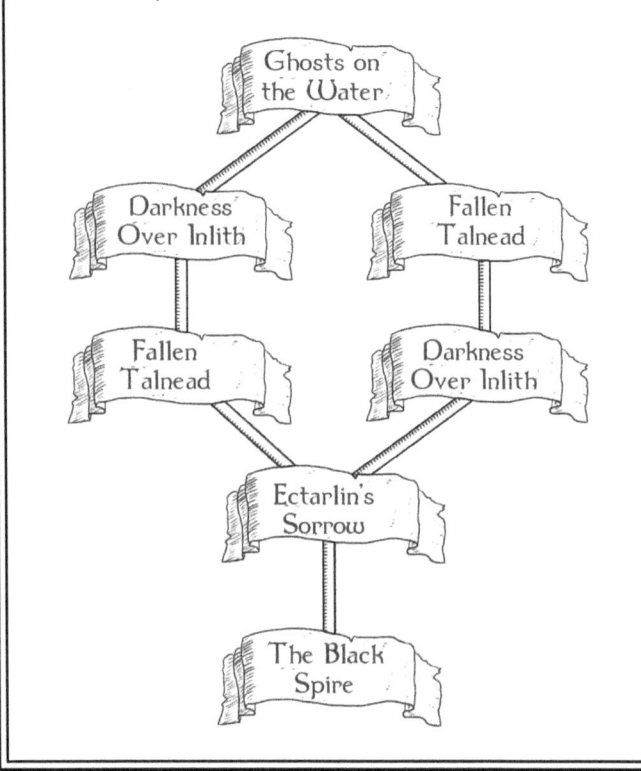

inlet below the village features rough docks where the villagers moor the boats they use for fishing and their more lucrative salvaging activities.

The pirate villagers are not the real threat in the adventure, but the characters might enter Ilthan expecting trouble and ready to fight depending on the outcome of **Ghosts on the Water**. However, even if the adventurers take a "kill first, ask questions later" approach, any mayhem they start in the village changes with the arrival of the ghost ride and an undead horde intent on destruction.

Finding Ilthan

The day is dark when the characters set out for Ilthan, with gray skies threatening rain. The length of the journey depends on whether the characters are setting out from the wreck site of the *Gull's Egg* or from Talnead Fortress.

From the wreck site, the horse track leads from the water's edge through the marsh, sticking to high points of relatively dry land that make it easy to follow. The characters can make their way to the outskirts of the village in 2 hours with no risk of becoming lost. If the characters instead follow the tracks of one or more of the escaping pirates, holding the trail requires two successful DC 15 Wis (Survival) checks to avoid becoming lost. Characters moving at night make these checks with tactical disadvantage. Each failed check adds 1 hour to the journey.

If the characters went to Talnead Fortress before traveling to Ilthan, they must return to the wreck site of the *Gull's Egg*, then follow the pirates' horse track to the village. See **Fallen Talnead** for information on the journey from the wreck site to the fortress. For the return journey, characters have tactical advantage on checks made to avoid becoming lost. Additionally, when the characters return to the wreck site, they find that the horses and the most valuable of the abandoned cargo on the beach have been reclaimed.

Wandering Monsters

For each hour of the characters' journey to Ilthan, roll 1d10. On a result of 10, roll 1d6 and consult the table below to see what occurs. (Note that encounters 1–3 can only occur once each.)

Ilthan Random Encounters

1d6	Encounter
1	1 **adult black dragon**
2	2 **ghasts** + 8 **ghouls**
3	3 **green hags** (coven)
4	1 **hobgoblin captain** + 2d12 **hobgoblins**
5	2d4 **ogres**
6	1d4 **shambling mounds**

Dragon, Adult Black: AC 19; **HP** 195 (17d12+85); **Spd** 40ft, fly 80ft, swim 40ft; **Melee** bite (+11, 10ft, 2d10+6 piercing plus 1d8 acid), claw (+11, 2d6+6 slashing); **SA** acid breath (recharge 5–6, 60ft line 5ft wide, 12d8 acid, DC 18 Dex half), frightful presence (120ft, frightened for 1 min, DC 16 Wis repeat), multiattack (frightful presence, bite, claw x2); **LA** detect, tail (+11, 15ft, 2d8+6 bludgeoning), wing (2 actions, 10ft, 2d6+6 bludgeoning, knock prone, DC 19 Dex, flies up to half speed); **Immune** acid; **Str** +6, **Dex** +2 (+7), **Con** +5 (+10), **Int** +2, **Wis** +1 (+6), **Cha** +3 (+8); **Skills** Perception +11, Stealth +7; **Senses** blindsight 60ft, darkvision 120ft; **Traits** amphibious, legendary resistance (3/day); **AL** CE; **CR** 14; **XP** 11,500.

Ghoul: AC 12; **HP** 22 (5d8); **Spd** 30ft; **Melee** claws (+4, 2d4+2 slashing plus paralysis for 1 min, DC 10 Con) or bite (+2, 2d6+2 piercing); **Immune** charm, exhaustion, poison; **Str** +1, **Dex** +2, **Con** +0, **Int** –2, **Wis** +0, **Cha** –2; **Senses** darkvision 60ft; **AL** CE; **CR** 1; **XP** 200.

Ghast: AC 13; **HP** 36 (8d8); **Spd** 30ft; **Melee** claws (+5, 2d6+3 slashing plus paralysis for 1 min, DC 10 Con repeat) or bite (+3, 2d8+3 piercing); **Immune** charm, exhaustion, poison; **Resist** necrotic; **Str** +3, **Dex** +3, **Con** +0, **Int** +0, **Wis** +0, **Cha** –1; **Senses** darkvision 60ft; **Traits** stench (5ft, poisoned until start of next turn, DC 10 Con), turning defiance (30ft, tactical advantage on saves against turn effects); **AL** CE; **CR** 2; **XP** 400.

Hag, Green: AC 17; **HP** 82 (11d8+33); **Spd** 30ft; **Melee** claws (+6, 2d8+4 slashing); **SA** illusory appearance, innate spells (Cha, DC 12), invisible passage; **Str** +4, **Dex** +1, **Con** +3, **Int** +1, **Wis** +2, **Cha** +2; **Skills** Arcana +3, Deception +4, Perception +4, Stealth +3; **Senses** darkvision 60ft; **Traits** amphibious, mimicry—imitation detect on DC 14 Wis (Insight); **AL** NE; **CR** 3; **XP** 700.

    Innate Spells: at will—*dancing lights, minor illusion, vicious mockery*

Hag Coven: When all three members are within 30ft of each, they have additional spellcasting abilities but must share the spell slots among themselves. The caster level is at 12th with Int +5, DC 13.

Spells (slots): 1st (4)—*identify, ray of sickness;* 2nd (3)—*hold person, locate object;* 3rd (3)—*bestow curse, counterspell, lightning bolt;* 4th(2)—*phantasmal killer, polymorph;* 5th (2)—*contact other plane, scrying;* 6th (1)—*eyebite*

Hobgoblin: AC 16; **HP** 11 (2d8+2); **Spd** 30ft; **Melee** longsword (+3, 1d10+1 slashing); **Ranged** longbow (+3, 150ft/600ft, 1d8+1 piercing); **SA** martial advantage (1/turn, extra 2d6 with weapon if target is within 5ft of ally); **Str** +1, **Dex** +1, **Con** +1, **Int** +0, **Wis** +0, **Cha** −1; **Senses** darkvision 60ft; **AL** LE; **CR** 1/2; **XP** 100.

Hobgoblin Captain: AC 17; **HP** 39 (6d8+12); **Spd** 30ft; **Melee** greatsword (+4, 2d6+2 slashing); **Ranged** javelin (+4, 30ft/120ft, 1d6+2 piercing); **SA** martial advantage (1/turn, extra 3d6 with weapon if target is within 5ft of ally); **Str** +2, **Dex** +2, **Con** +2, **Int** +1, **Wis** +0, **Cha** +1; **AL** LE; **CR** 3; **XP** 700.

Ogre: AC 11; **HP** 59 (7d10+21); **Spd** 40ft; **Melee** greatclub (+6, 2d8+4 bludgeoning); **Ranged** (+6, 30ft/120ft, 2d6+4 piercing); **Str** +4, **Dex** −1, **Con** +3, **Int** −3, **Wis** −2, **Cha** −2; **Senses** darkvision 60ft; **AL** CE; **CR** 2; **XP** 450.

Shambling Mound: AC 15; **HP** 136 (16d10+48); **Spd** 20ft, swim 20ft; **Melee** slam (+7, 2d8+4 bludgeoning); **SA** engulf (grappled target is blinded, restrained, and unable to breathe, DC 14 Con or 2d8+4 bludgeoning), multiattack (slam x2, if both hit, then grappled then engulf, escape DC 14); **Immune** blind, deaf, exhaustion, lightning; **Resist** cold, fire; **Str** +4, **Dex** −1, **Con** +3, **Int** −3, **Wis** +0, **Cha** −3; **Skills** Stealth +2; **Senses** blindsight 60ft (blind beyond); **Traits** lightning absorption; **AL** U; **CR** 5; **XP** 1800

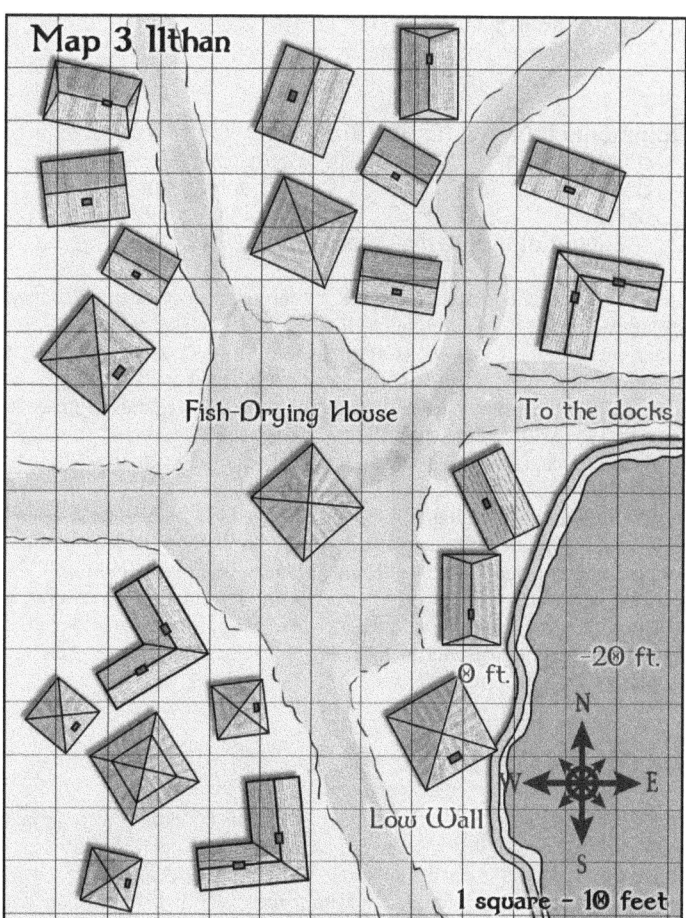

Map 3 Ilthan

Fish-Drying House

To the docks

Low Wall

1 square – 10 feet

Random encounters are with creatures hunting in the marshes and scrubland for food or protecting their nesting areas. Some creatures might be noticed at a distance, giving the characters a chance to avoid combat or set an ambush, at your discretion.

Approaching the Village

Signs of chimney smoke mark the site of the village well before the characters reach it. In the aftermath of the adventurer's appearance at the shipwreck site, the villagers have gone to great lengths to hide all evidence of their salvaging activities, and have set a rough watch along the four main paths leading to the village. Villagers pretending to be out collecting firewood keep a wary eye out for intruders, and will hustle back to warn the others at the first sign of the adventurers.

A character can spot a villager on inconspicuous watch before the party is spotted with a successful DC 13 Wis (Perception) check. Approaching along a main path means the party is spotted automatically. By moving onto side trails and succeeding on a DC 13 group Dex (Stealth) check, the characters can make it past the sentries and approach the village unseen.

Making an Entrance

Whether the adventurers approach openly or by stealth, Ilthan and its people show no sign of threat or trouble.

The village seems no different than any other poor borderlands settlement, though the stone foundations of its larger buildings show where those structures were built on the bones of older ruins. From the placement of those ruins and the remains of a low wall skirting a drop-off along the edge of the promontory on which the village is set, the site has the look of some long-gone estate that once overlooked the sea below.

The rough houses of the settlement and the poor clothing of its inhabitants show their hardscrabble existence. When they are first spotted, the adventurers are greeted by the nearest villagers, who are surprised to see any folk traveling so far off the road, and who immediately attempt to sell the characters a selection of fish. "The best on this coast. Peamouth chub, starry flounder, tomcod, and dogfish, fresh or salted."

Any character who makes a successful DC 13 Wis (Perception) check to scan the village from within notes a lack of children on the street — the result of the adults hiding them within the houses in case of violence. If the check result is 18 or higher, a character notes multiple faces watching from behind shuttered windows.

First Line of Offense

As was seen at the wreck site of the *Gull's Egg*, the folk of Ilthan can look after themselves. They are cautious and will not be goaded into combat, treating abusive characters lightly and suggesting that the party move on if they have no business in the village. However, if the characters attack any villagers or attempt to take hostages, the folk of Ilthan react.

The assembled adults of Ilthan comprise **5 pirate captains**, **15 pirates**, and **40 commoners**, all of whom are willing and able to fight. The remaining villagers (children and those too old or infirm for battle) quickly flee their houses and head for shelter in the cellars beneath the fish-drying house (see "What Anell Knows," below).

Pirate Captain (5): AC 15; **HP** 65 (10d8 + 20); **Spd** 30ft; **Melee** scimitar (+5, 1d6 + 3 slashing); **Ranged** light crossbow (+5, 80ft/320ft, 1d8 + 3 piercing); **Str** +2, **Dex** +3, **Con** +2, **Int** +2, **Wis** +0, **Cha** +2; **AL** NG/N; **CR** 2; **XP** 450.
    Equipment: Leather armor, scimitar, dagger, light crossbow, 10 bolts.

Pirate (15): AC 12; **HP** 11 (2d8 + 2); **Spd** 30ft; **Melee** scimitar (+3, 1d6 + 1 slashing); **Ranged** light crossbow (+3, 80ft/320ft, 1d8 + 1 piercing); **Str** +0, **Dex** +1, **Con** +1, **Int** +0,

Wis +0, **Cha** +0; **AL** NG/N; **CR** 1/8; **XP** 25.

> **Equipment**: Leather armor, scimitar, dagger, light crossbow, 10 bolts.

Commoner (40): AC 10; HP 4 (1d8); **Spd** 30ft; **Melee** club (+2, 1d4 bludgeoning); **Ranged** light crossbow (+2, 80ft/320ft, 1d8 piercing); **Str** +0, **Dex** +0, **Con** +0, **Int** +0, **Wis** +0, **Cha** +0; **AL** NG/N; **CR** 0; **XP** 10.

> **Equipment**: Club, light crossbow, 10 bolts.

In the first round after hostilities begin, each adventurer takes two crossbow attacks from commoner villagers hidden in nearby houses, who attack through the windows. (Commoners in this encounter have a light crossbow attack, as indicated in the short stat block above.)

Characters who remain in the open during subsequent rounds continue to draw crossbow fire, while characters who seek cover are quickly engaged by the pirate captains and pirates. These accomplished warriors focus on lightly armored characters, wanting to neutralize spellcasters quickly and hoping to gain an advantage by taking hostages. Any character dropped to 0 hit points by the villagers is knocked unconscious, at which point the villagers shout out for parley and Anell Thale appears (see below).

If the characters quickly gain the upper hand against the pirates (as is likely, given their level), look to the arrival of the ghost ride to prevent the fight from becoming a rout of the villagers. See "Ilthan Under Attack," below, for more information.

Low Profile

The villagers wear none of the gear or weapons the pirates were armed with during the raid, and no outward connection between the pirates and Ilthan can be seen. Pirates from the raid who might be recognized are well out of sight, though any character who inspects the half-dozen boats at dock recognizes the same style of pinnace as those seen and abandoned at the wreck site. However, any discussion of the pirates is met by blank looks and concern. The villagers claim to be aware of intermittent piracy along the coast, but say that they stay close to the marshy shore with their fishing boats, neither looking for nor finding trouble.

If the characters make any threats or trouble, the villagers are ready for them in "First Line of Offense," above. If the characters make any overtures of simply wanting to talk about what happened at the *Gull's Egg* wreck site, Anell Thale steps out from a nearby house to treat with them. (If the characters spoke to Anell after the pirate raid and she was subsequently killed, her sister Eryn Thale is the new leader of the village, and takes Anell's place below.)

What Anell Knows

The adventurers' interaction with Anell varies depending on how they dealt with the pirates in **Ghosts on the Water**, and whether they've come to Ilthan before or after visiting **Fallen Talnead**. The proud pirate captain deals evenly with the adventurers, and responds to insults and bravado in kind.

The Pirate Raid: If the characters got no information out of the pirates the previous night, Anell can first reveal the information detailed in the "Questions and Answers" section, previously. Once the characters are aware of Anell's story, she uses the visual evidence of the village to underline its truth. Even with their recent run of wealth gained by salvaging the mysterious derelicts, the Black Ghosts and the people of Ilthan remain only one step above destitute.

Under Ilthan: If Anell is pressed about the goods taken from the derelict ships, she takes the characters to a fish-drying house with a secret trapdoor concealed under several hundred-pound sacks of salt. (If the characters need to search for this access, the door cannot be found unless the sacks are moved. Even then, it takes a successful DC 22 Int (Investigation) check to find the trapdoor seams along the flagstones of the floor.)

A stone-lined tunnel runs down beneath the ground, part of a cellar under the former estate on which the village was built. The villagers hold their captured booty in the niches and side passages of these cellars, which are close to bursting with the Black Ghosts' recent spoils. These goods include bolts of fine cloth, candlesticks, sheepskins, supple leather, ingots of copper and brass, pottery, spices, cheeses, wine, brandy, and salt. Though a few shelves hold jewelry, art objects, and other goods of real value, any inspection by the adventurers shows that the wealth here is far from excessive. (If a value is needed, the Black Ghosts' loot is worth a total of 500gp, but would take considerable effort to move.)

Legends of Talnead: If the characters have been to Talnead and fought the ghostly Lord Ectarlin, Anell can add to their knowledge about Ectarlin's legacy. If the characters have not yet visited Talnead but ask Anell what she knows about the trident-and-vine sigil borne by the ghost ride, she shares what she knows as well.

Successfully talking with Anell reveals the following information.

• The frontiers of Eastreach are filled with fallen freeholds, all established by lords who tried to tame those lands. One of the most legendary of those lords was Arnast Ectarlin, a loyalist knight of Foere. A hundred years ago, Ectarlin dreamed of seeing the north shore of Amrin Estuary settled and the Forest of Hope tamed. His heroic efforts to clear monsters and bandits from his doomed freehold have become a local legend.

• Lord Ectarlin was a legendary naval commander and knight, equally at home aboard ship or riding the field. His power as freelord resided in the skill and dedication of his cavalry, whose patrols kept the freehold safe from the edge of the forest to the marshlands. Ectarlin's plan was to see the Lowwater Road made safe for travel, anchoring a broad expanse of settlements along the coast.

• Ectarlin's fight to keep his claimed lands safe was successful for a time, with estates and protected villages built over a period of twenty years. (The ruins on which Ilthan is built are the site of one such estate.) In the end, though, the evil that prowls the Sinnar coast was too much to fight against. In response to word of undead attacking fishing villages along the coast, Ectarlin and his best riders rode forth to deal with the threat. They were never seen again.

• The seat of Ectarlin's power was the fortress of Talnead — a small keep set on a narrow bluff overlooking the freelord's lands. In the aftermath of Ectarlin's fall, several of his knights claimed Talnead Fortress and his legacy, attempting to continue the work he started. However, monstrous incursions from the Forest of Hope and the Lowwater marshes soon overwhelmed them. The last of Ectarlin's riders scattered, with the villages they had protected abandoned soon thereafter.

The Legend of the Ghost Ride

The recent appearance of the ghost ride within the Lowwater Marshes is not something the villagers have any previous experience with. Having avoided the attention of the soulstealers attacking merchant ships along the coast, they have not yet witnessed any of the deadly battles the adventurers and the pirate salvage band saw at the end of **Ghosts on the Water**. If the characters bring up the ghost ride, several villagers admit to having seen a strange trail of luminescence out along the water in the dark of night in recent weeks, but they have no additional knowledge or information.

Ilthan Under Attack

At some point during the characters' interaction with the villagers, Ilthan comes under "attack" by Ectarlin and the ghost ride. The spectral wardens are not the true threat, however. Rather, they are following their ancient orders to protect the settlements of the Lowwater, and are responding to the Dread Master's return to power.

The Ghost Ride Appears

Time the appearance of the ghost ride to any opportune moment. If the characters strike a detente with Anell Thale and the villagers, the howling can arise when the adventurers are inspecting Ilthan's stores of stolen goods or sitting down to talk with the village leader. If the characters take a more confrontational approach or engage the villagers in combat, have the ghost ride appear to interrupt the fight before too much damage is done.

> The steady wind pushing gray storm clouds in off the sea is suddenly filled by a familiar shriek. A guttural cry rises from the marsh to the south of the village, then is joined

by other voices, growing louder now. Against the darkness of the cloud-shrouded day, a pulse of light appears through the trees, heralding the appearance of some twenty ghostly riders. The same regal figure you saw leading them along the shore rides at the head of the column once more, his ghostly hounds close behind.

The ghost ride pours into the village as **20 spectral wardens** divided into two groups, all mounted on their ghostly steeds and with one group led by Ectarlin. The two groups fork around the village, one circling clockwise while the other circles anticlockwise. The incorporeal creatures pass through the walls of houses on the edge of the village, sending the inhabitants of those houses screaming into the streets in response to the ghosts' Horrifying Visage.

Ectarlin, Spectral Warden: AC 11; **HP** 90 (10d8 + 10, max); **Spd** 0ft, fly 60ft; **Melee** withering touch (+5, 4d6 + 3 necrotic or radiant); **SA** horrifying visage (60ft, DC 13 Wis, 1 min.), multiattack (withering touch x2; two hits, 10ft, 3d6 radiant); **Immune** cold, charmed, exhaustion, frightened, grappled, necrotic, paralyzed, petrified, poisoned, prone, restrained; **Str** +2 (+5), **Dex** +1 (+4), **Con** +1 (+4), **Int** +0 (+3), **Wis** +1 (+4), **Cha** +3 (+6); **Senses** darkvision 60ft; **Traits** ethereal sight, etherealness, ghost steed, incorporeal movement, radiant rage, regeneration 10, resilient faith; **AL** NG; **CR** 8; **XP** 1100.

Spectral Warden (20): AC 11; **HP** 55 (10d8 + 10); **Spd** 0ft, fly 60ft; **Melee** withering touch (+5, 4d6 + 3 necrotic or radiant); **SA** horrifying visage (60ft, DC 13 Wis, 1 min.); **Immune** cold, charmed, exhaustion, frightened, grappled, necrotic, paralyzed, petrified, poisoned, prone, restrained; **Str** +2, **Dex** +1, **Con** +1, **Int** +0, **Wis** +1, **Cha** +3; **Senses** darkvision 60ft; **Traits** ethereal sight, etherealness, ghost steed, incorporeal movement, radiant rage, resilient faith; **AL** NG; **CR** 4; **XP** 1100.

Describe the appearance of the ghost ride as sealing the villagers in, trying to ensure that the players perceive them as a threat. However, the spectral wardens attack only under the following circumstances.

• If any adventurer or villager attacks a spectral warden, the warrior breaks formation to make one withering touch attack in response, dealing minimum damage if it hits. It then returns to its place in the ranks and continues to race around the village.

•.If any spectral warden comes within 50ft of an evil or neutral player character, or a character who possesses a magic item of neutral or evil alignment, that warrior breaks out of formation to race toward the character and attack. (The ghosts respond to the relative power of the characters compared to the pirates and commoners, but you can have neutral or evil villagers singled out as well if you choose.) Spectral wardens attacking characters of an ambiguous moral bent believe they are attacking the servants of the Dread Master, and deal full damage with their attacks. However, these attacks against the characters break off as soon as greater threat of the soulstealers and their undead followers appear.

When the spectral wardens first appear, assume that a half-dozen villagers attack with their crossbows, incurring retaliatory attacks that the adventurers will witness. The ghost ride's subsequent actions depend on whether these initial attacks inspire the characters to come to the villagers' defense or to urge a cessation of hostilities (if one or more characters rightfully intuits that the ghost ride is not the real threat).

Undead Assault

The spectral wardens of the ghost ride have been drawn to Ilthan by the imminent appearance of the soulstealers and a force of local undead that have been drawn to the Dread Master's power. After 3 rounds of initial combat with Ectarlin and the ghost ride (or 3 rounds of the characters recognizing that the ghost ride is not a threat and directing the villagers to fall back and wait), the undead surge into the village. The spectral wardens

of the ghost ride immediately break off any hostilities with the characters and the villagers, turning their attention to the real threat.

The shrieking cries of the spectral riders grow more intense, and you suddenly see the reason why. More spectral shapes advance down all four of the main paths into the village — the serpentine bone creatures you saw along the water, with a pack of spectral undead flying among them.

Battle in Ilthan

The attack force consists of **3 soulstealers**, along with **9 specters** that have risen in response to the Dread Lord's servants moving farther afield. If you use a battle grid for combat, use whatever portion of the village map is appropriate to the size of your table, with other parts of the fight (see "Handling the Battle") happening "off screen."

Soulstealer (3): AC 16; **HP** 105 (14d8 + 42); **Spd** 20ft, fly 40ft; **Melee** claws (+6, 1d8 + 5 slashing); **SA** mind wrack (*dominate person*, DC 15 Wis; *modify memory*, DC 15 Int), multiattack (claw x 4); **Immune** exhaustion, fright, necrotic, poison, restrain, stun, unconscious; **Resist** normal weapons; **Str** +4, **Dex** +2, **Con** +3 (+5), **Int** +2, **Wis** +2, **Cha** +0; **Skills** Perception +8; **Senses** darkvision 60ft; **Traits** incorporeal shift, mind wrack, unearthly destruction; **AL** NE; **CR** 6; **XP** 2300. (**Monster Appendix**)

Specter (9): AC 12; **HP** 22 (5d8); **Spd** 0ft, fly 50ft (hover); **Melee** life drain (+4, 3d6 necrotic); **Immune** charmed, exhaustion, grappled, necrotic, poison, paralyzed, petrified, restrained, unconscious; **Resist** acid, cold, fire, lightning, normal weapons, thunder; **Str** −5, **Dex** +2, **Con** +0, **Int** +0, **Wis** +0, **Cha** +0; **Senses** darkvision 60ft; **Traits** incorporeal movement, sunlight sensitivity; **AL** CE; **CR** 1; **XP** 200.

Houses in the village block line of sight and provide three-quarters cover to characters hiding around a corner or going inside to look out the windows. (Add doors and windows to houses as you see fit.) Ranged combatants and spellcasters can take good advantage of this cover when attacking from a distance, but such characters quickly become targets for the wrath of the undead.

The low wall that edges the promontory is a potential threat to creatures fighting near it. Any creature pushed over the wall — or that flees in that direction under the effect of a soulstealer's Mind Wrack — goes over the edge and must make a successful DC 13 Dex saving throw to grab the edge. On a failed save, the creature falls 20ft to the 5ft deep water along the shore, taking 2d6 bludgeoning damage. It takes 2 rounds and a successful DC 12 Str (Athletics) check to climb back up the promontory, though a character might need to spend additional time to claim weapons or other gear dropped in the water.

Handling the Battle

Rather than roll dice for the attacks of the villagers, the spectral wardens, and the monsters alike, simply consider the effect those third-party combatants have on each other and on the adventurers in combat. At the end of each round, any soulstealer or specter engaged by villagers (whether fighting by themselves or alongside the adventurers) takes 1 slashing or piercing damage per villager, as appropriate to the villagers' weapons. Additionally, any adventurer fighting alongside three or more villagers against the same monster has tactical advantage on attack rolls against that monster. (If two adventurers are fighting together, each must have three different villager allies to gain tactical advantage in this way.)

As long as the villagers are fighting alongside the characters, the undead focus their attacks on the characters, recognizing them as the greater threat. Among all the villagers fighting the undead on their own, 1d4–1 villagers of your choice drop to 0 hit points each round.

The spectral wardens of the ghost ride focus all their attacks on the undead. For each spectral rider in the fight, the combined undead take

1 damage each round, divided as you see fit. You can have a number of spectral riders converge on one creature to maximize the damage dealt, or have them spread out to apply minimal damage to all the undead.

In addition to any spectral riders that might have been destroyed by the adventurers in the opening stages of combat, one more spectral rider is destroyed each round by the attacks of the undead.

Victory and Aftermath

Driven to a frenzy by the presence of Ectarlin and the ghost ride, all the undead in this encounter will fight until destroyed. However, the final actions of the ghost ride depend on whether the characters have already visited Talnead Fortress or not. See "Developments," below, for more information.

In the aftermath of the battle, the villagers must tend to their dead and wounded. Assume that half the villagers dropped to 0 hit points during the fight have died by the battle's end, but the other half are unconscious and can be stabilized.

Assuming the party didn't simply stand back to let the villagers fight the undead on their own, any lingering animosity among the villagers toward the adventurers is set aside. If the characters still haven't gotten the full story of the Black Ghosts and their experiences with the derelict ships (as might be the case for a party more interested in fighting than talking), Anell Thale fills in any missing details (see "Questions and Answers" in the first section of the adventure). Having recognized the sigil on the tabards of the ghostly warriors, she can also tell the characters about Lord Ectarlin's legend and legacy (see "What Anell Knows," above).

Developments

When the undead are defeated, Ectarlin and the ghost ride depart *if the characters have not yet undertaken the* **Fallen Talnead** *section of the adventure*. (Ectarlin and the ghost ride both reappear in that section.) The spectral riders circle the village once more after the last undead is destroyed. As he rides past, Ectarlin singles out any evil or neutral characters, shrieking out: "None touched by evil will claim these lands!" Ectarlin then leads the ghost ride at a run out of the village, where the quickly fade from sight.

In the aftermath of the attack, the characters have seen the protective role taken on by the ghost ride, even as they might have felt the brunt of attacks by the spectral wardens. However, if they have not visited Talnead before coming to the village, the connection between the ghost ride, the soulstealers, and the derelict ships remains undetermined. However, the ghost ride's connection to Talnead makes that fallen fortress the next stop in their investigation. All the people of Ilthan know Talnead Fortress and how to reach it, but the pirate folk will not accompany the characters there. Anell Thale describes the ruins as monster haunted and best avoided. Continue with the **Fallen Talnead** section.

If the characters have already played **Fallen Talnead**, the destruction of the last undead instead becomes the starting point for the characters to treat with him. Go to **The Ghost Lord's Sorrow** to play out the end of this section of the adventure.

Any character who inspects a slain soulstealer notes the same fading runes seen in **Ghosts on the Water**. A successful DC 18 Int (Arcana) check or a *detect magic* spell reveals the binding magic that connects the soulstealers to the Dread Master. If the same check was successfully made previously, a character senses that the range of control over the creatures has expanded since the earlier fight, allowing the soulstealers to reach the village. Savvy characters will surmise that the threat of the soulstealers has the potential to grow if their range increases again.

Fallen Talnead

The former fortress of Lord Arnast Ectarlin is a ruined tangle of fallen stones half-swallowed by scrub pine, set on the northern flank of Amrin Estuary. Built atop a narrow sandstone bluff that overlooked Ectarlin's

former domain, the estate was abandoned shortly after the freelord's fall. Wild beasts and bandits have claimed the ruins at points in the past, and local folk give the site a wide berth. As such, no one knows that Lord Ectarlin's shade has been drawn back here by his failed mission to protect his lands.

Finding Talnead

The ruins of Talnead Fortress are 5 hours from the wreck site of the *Gull's Egg* and 4 hours from Ilthan, with both routes requiring the characters to make their way along unmarked trails. Following either route requires two successful DC 13 Wis (Survival) checks to avoid becoming lost. Each failed check adds 1 hour to the journey.

A lightning-struck tree spotted from the Lowwater Road marks the point where a rough track winds from the marsh and into the scrubland. Following the trail through rough stands of pine and tangles of wild grass proves nearly as difficult as navigating the marshes south of the road. But in time, you see the land begin to rise toward the sandstone bluffs where you have been told Ectarlin's fortress will be found.

Wandering Monsters

For each hour of the characters' journey to Talnead, roll 1d10. On a result of 10, roll 1d6 and consult the table below to see what occurs. Note that encounters 1, 3, and 5 can each occur only once.

Talnead Random Encounters

1d6	Encounter
1	1 adult green dragon
2	2d10 dire wolves
3	2 ghasts + 8 ghouls
4	1 hobgoblin captain + 2d12 hobgoblins
5	1d10 manticores
6	2d4 ogres

Random encounters are with creatures hunting in the marshes and scrubland for food or protecting their nesting areas. Some creatures might be noticed at a distance, giving the characters a chance to avoid combat or set an ambush, at your discretion.

Dragon, Adult Green: AC 19; **HP** 207 (18d12+90); **Spd** 40ft, fly 80ft, swim 40ft; **Melee** bite (+11, 10ft, 2d10+6 piercing plus 2d6 poison), claw (+11, 2d6+6 slashing); **SA** frightful presence (120ft, frightened for 1 min, DC 16 Wis repeat), multiattack (frightful presence, bite, claw x2), poison breath (recharge 5–6, 60ft cone, 16d6 poison, DC 18 Con half); **LA** detect, tail (+11, 15ft, 2d8+6 bludgeoning), wing (2 actions, 10ft, 2d6+6 bludgeoning, knock prone, DC 19 Dex, flies up to half speed); **Immune** poison; **Str** +6, **Dex** +1 (+6), **Con** +5 (+10), **Int** +4, **Wis** +2 (+7), **Cha** +3 (+8); **Skills** Deception +8, Insight +7, Perception +12, Persuasion +8, Stealth +7; **Senses** blindsight 60ft, darkvision 120ft; **Traits** amphibious, legendary resistance (3/day); **AL** LE; **CR** 15; **XP** 13,000.

Ghoul: AC 12; **HP** 22 (5d8); **Spd** 30ft; **Melee** claws (+4, 2d4+2 slashing plus paralysis for 1 min, DC 10 Con) or bite (+2, 2d6+2 piercing); **Immune** charm, exhaustion, poison; **Str** +1, **Dex** +2, **Con** +0, **Int** −2, **Wis** +0, **Cha** −2; **Senses** darkvision 60ft; **AL** CE; **CR** 1; **XP** 200.

Ghast: AC 13; **HP** 36 (8d8); **Spd** 30ft; **Melee** claws (+5, 2d6+3 slashing plus paralysis for 1 min, DC 10 Con repeat) or bite

(+3, 2d8+3 piercing); **Immune** charm, exhaustion, poison; **Resist** necrotic; **Str** +3, **Dex** +3, **Con** +0, **Int** +0, **Wis** +0, **Cha** −1; **Senses** darkvision 60ft; **Traits** stench (5ft, poisoned until start of next turn, DC 10 Con), turning defiance (30ft, tactical advantage on saves against turn effects); **AL** CE; **CR** 2; **XP** 400.

Hobgoblin: AC 16; HP 11 (2d8+2); **Spd** 30ft; **Melee** longsword (+3, 1d10+1 slashing); **Ranged** longbow (+3, 150ft/600ft, 1d8+1 piercing); **SA** martial advantage (1/turn, extra 2d6 with weapon if target is within 5ft of ally); **Str** +1, **Dex** +1, **Con** +1, **Int** +0, **Wis** +0, **Cha** −1; **Senses** darkvision 60ft; **AL** LE; **CR** 1/2; **XP** 100.

Hobgoblin Captain: AC 17; HP 39 (6d8+12); **Spd** 30ft; **Melee** greatsword (+4, 2d6+2 slashing); **Ranged** javelin (+4, 30ft/120ft, 1d6+2 piercing); **SA** martial advantage (1/turn, extra 3d6 with weapon if target is within 5ft of ally); **Str** +2, **Dex** +2, **Con** +2, **Int** +1, **Wis** +0, **Cha** +1; **AL** LE; **CR** 3; **XP** 700.

Manticore: AC 14; HP 68 (8d10+24); **Spd** 30ft, fly 50ft; **Melee** bite (+5, 1d8+3 piercing), claw (+5, 1d6+3 slashing); **Ranged** tail spike (+5, 100ft/200ft, 1d8+3 piercing); **SA** multiattack (bite, claw x2 or tail spike x3); **Str** +3, **Dex** +3, **Con** +3, **Int** −2, **Wis** +1, **Cha** −1; **Senses** darkvision 60ft; **Traits** tail spike regrowth (up to 24); **AL** LE; **CR** 3; **XP** 700.

Ogre: AC 11; HP 59 (7d10+21); **Spd** 40ft; **Melee** greatclub (+6, 2d8+4 bludgeoning); **Ranged** (+6, 30ft/120ft, 2d6+4 piercing); **Str** +4, **Dex** −1, **Con** +3, **Int** −3, **Wis** −2, **Cha** −2; **Senses** darkvision 60ft; **AL** CE; **CR** 2; **XP** 450.

Wolf, Dire: AC 14; HP 37 (5d10+10); **Spd** 50ft; **Melee** bite (+5, 2d6+3 piercing plus knock prone, DC 13 Str); **Str** +3, **Dex** +2, **Con** +2, **Int** −4, **Wis** +1, **Cha** −2; **Skills** Perception +3, Stealth +4; **Skills** Perception +3, Stealth +4; **Senses** keen hearing and smell; **Traits** pack tactics; **AL** U; **CR** 1; **XP** 200

Approaching the Ruins

Once the characters are within sight of the bluff, they can survey the area to get the lay of the land.

The trees become sparser as you advance, giving way to dry grass thrust up in intermittent patches from the sandy soil. The open vista gives you a clear glimpse of your destination — a dominant bluff thrust up from the surrounding scrubland. There's no sign of ruins to be seen within the tangle of trees marking the crest of the bluff, but even from a distance, you can see the dark line of a cart track winding its way up and around to its height.

Features of the Ruins

The sandstone bluff on which the ruins stand has crumbled away over time. Any character moving along the track must make a successful DC 13 Str (Athletics) check at three points along the way to scramble up and around broad clefts where the ground has fallen away to a depth of 10ft. On a failed check, the character slips and drops to the bottom of the cleft, taking 1d6 bludgeoning damage. Characters who rope themselves together when bypassing the clefts have tactical advantage on these checks.

Characters can avoid the path in favor of scaling the sheer bluff. Doing so requires DC 15 Str (Athletics) checks, made with tactical advantage by characters who rope themselves together. Characters who scale the bluff can enter the ruins anywhere on the map, avoiding or delaying the encounter at the fallen gates.

A thick stone wall once surrounded the fortress atop the bluff, but it has crumbled away in many places. Where the wall still stands, it is 15–20ft

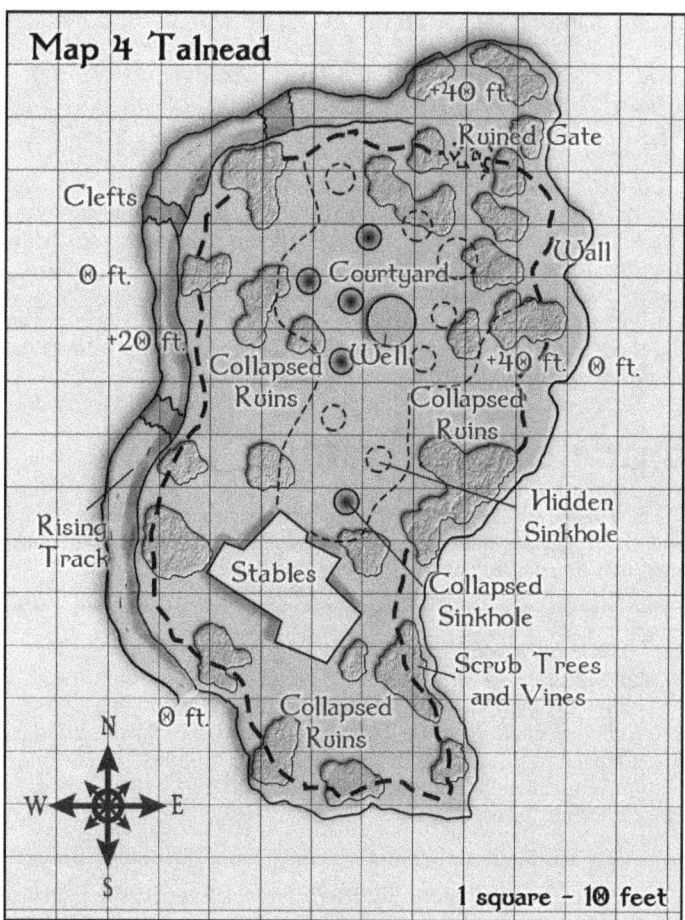

tall and requires a DC 10 Str (Athletics) check to climb.

Thick patches of ivy and stands of scrub pine grow across the top of the bluff. These areas provide half cover and are difficult terrain.

Ambush at the Gate

The track along the side of the bluff leads up to the remains of the keep's wall and its main gate.

A tangle of rusted iron and shattered stone marks where a great arched gate once stood as the entrance to Talnead's central courtyard. Thick clumps of ivy growing tenaciously from the crumbling sandstone of the bluff hedge it in from either side, but the open area around the gate is strewn with the skeletal remains of hundreds of birds.

The gate is now the domain of a pack of hunting spiders — currently comprising **5 giant spiders** and **10 swarms of insects (spiders)** — that feed on the birds that once flocked to the bluff. Those birds have fled with the arrival of Ectarlin and the ghost ride, however, and the ravenous spiders are desperate for new prey. With a clear view of the track, they have set themselves up in ambush as the characters approach.

Inspection of the dead birds from a distance shows, without any required check, that their remains are well dried, their bones bleached white by the sun. If a character succeeds at a DC 15 Wis (Perception) check, he or she also spots 1d4 spiders or swarms hidden in the greenery.

Giant Spider (5): AC 14; HP 26 4d10 + 4); **Spd** 30ft, climb 30ft; **Melee** bite (+5, 1d8 + 3 piercing plus poison 2d8, DC 11 Con); **SA** web (recharge 5–6, 30–60ft, +5, restrained); **Str** +2, **Dex** +3, **Con** +1, **Int** −4, **Wis** +0, **Cha** −3; **Skills** Stealth +7; **Senses** blindsight 10ft, darkvision 60ft; **Traits** spider climb, web sense, web walker; **AL** U; **CR** 1; **XP** 200.

Swarm of Insects (Spiders) (10): AC 12; HP 22 (5d8); **Spd** 20ft, climb 20ft; **Melee** bite (+3, in space, 4d4/2d4 piercing); **Str** −4, **Dex** +1, **Con** +0, **Int** −5, **Wis** −2, **Cha** −5; **Senses** blindsight 10ft; **Traits** spider climb, swarm, web sense, web walker; **AL** U; **CR** 1/2; **XP** 100.

Characters can attempt to flee from the spiders by leaving the area, but they run the risk of being caught in a sinkhole collapse in the courtyard (see below). That in turn might trigger the appearance of water elementals from the fortress's well. If the water elementals attack, any surviving spiders circle the fray to pick off wounded characters.

If the characters avoid the spiders by avoiding the gate, feel free to add them to the water elemental encounter or have them appear as the characters are exploring the ruins.

Shattered Courtyard

The erosion of the courtyard's sandstone foundations has created a number of open sinkholes — and a more dangerous array of weakened areas that are ready to collapse.

> The central court of the fortress is set with irregular slabs of cracked and weathered slate, many of which have collapsed down into sinkholes where the sandstone bluff has eroded away. Beyond the courtyard, most of the fortress has collapsed to rough piles of stone shrouded by vines and scrub pine. Only a single building remains standing, on the far side of the courtyard.

The presence of the water elementals in the well (see below) has eroded and weakened the sandstone of the bluff over long years. A DC 10 Int (Nature) check reveals that the erosion of the exposed sinkholes has been caused by water, but at levels far in excess of what the bluff should have received as rain, even over decades.

Hidden Sinkholes: With a successful DC 17 Wis (Perception) check made while moving across the courtyard, a character spots the nearest hidden sinkhole. A character who taps the ground ahead with a pole or other long implement can hear a telltale echo that grants tactical advantage on the check.

A character who walks across a sinkhole without noticing it triggers a collapse, and must succeed on a DC 13 Dex saving throw to grab the edge. (Treat scrambling up from the edge of a sinkhole as standing up from being prone.) On a failed save, the character plunges 10ft down into the sinkhole, taking 1d6 bludgeoning damage from the fall and 1d6 bludgeoning damage as the sandstone walls crumble in. A character must succeed on a DC 20 Str (Athletics) check to escape the collapse and climb out of the pit. It costs 30ft of movement to escape the bottom of a sinkhole.

While caught at the bottom of a sinkhole, a character has tactical disadvantage on attack rolls, and on Dex checks and saving throws.

Moving Across the Ruins: Characters wishing to avoid walking across the courtyard without using magic can do so by moving across the precarious ruins with a successful DC 13 Dex (Acrobatics) check each turn. On a failed check, a character triggers a partial collapse of the ruins, which crumble around the character to deal 1d4 bludgeoning damage.

Elemental Well

> At the center of the courtyard, a broad well is marked out by a stone ledge rising above the flagstones. Even at a distance, water within the well sets up rippling waves of light along its inside edges.

The fact that water is moving within the well might tip the characters to the presence of the 2 **water elementals** that dwell there. The elementals were magically summoned and permanently bound to the well when

Talnead was built, providing clean water for the fortress and the residents of nearby villages. The elementals have long raged against their binding, creating storms of water that have weakened the bluff and caused its buildings to crumble as their foundations shifted.

Water Elemental (2): AC 14; HP 114 (12d10 + 48); **Spd** 30ft, swim 90ft; **Melee** slam (+7, 2d8 +4 bludgeoning); **SA** whelm (recharge 4–6, DC 15 Str, 2d8 + 4 bludgeoning, grappled, restrained, and can't breathe), multiattack (slam x2); **Immune** exhaustion, grapple, paralysis, petrify, poison, prone, restraint, unconscious; **Resist** acid, normal weapons; **Str** +4, **Dex** +2, **Con** +4, **Int** −3, **Wis** +0, **Cha** −1; **Senses** darkvision 60ft; **Traits** freeze, water form; **AL** N; **CR** 5; **XP** 1800.

The enraged elementals rise from the well to attack when they sense the movement of creatures above them. The first time any character triggers a sinkhole, one elemental rises with a gurgling moan 1 round later, then moves to attack. The second elemental rises the following round. If no sinkholes are triggered, both elementals rise at the same time if any character comes within 10ft of the well.

Each elemental fights until reduced to 20 hit points or fewer, then retreats back to hide at the bottom of the well, 40ft below the courtyard. The well is filled with 30ft of water, effectively giving the elementals three-quarters cover against ranged attacks made from above, and blocking line of effect for spells.

Detect magic notes the binding magic suffused into the stones of the well. A *dispel magic* spell can be cast on the well at any point to break the binding magic (the equivalent of a 12th-level spell). If the binding is broken, the elementals vanish.

Spectral Stables

The only extant part of the fortress is the great stone stables that once housed the horses of Lord Ectarlin's cavalry. With the reappearance of the ghostly lord, his long-dead knights have been summoned back to ride once more.

> The open doorway of the fortress's only surviving structure is set with the sigil of a trident wrapped in grape vines, but its empty stone shell gives no hint of its former function. As you approach, a faint glimmer is seen in the darkness beyond the door — flaring to reveal thirty spectral horses standing motionless in ranks of ten, each ridden by a ghostly warrior in chain mail. These spirits slowly turn their heads toward you, horses and riders alike staring you down with unblinking white eyes.

The spectral wardens that follow Ectarlin stand in stasis in their former stables, waiting for their lord's call to ride when he next senses the power of the Dread Master. Ectarlin himself — possessed by a dark madness that drives his vengeance — is the only threat here.

The Ghost Lord

As soon as any creature advances beyond the threshold of the stables, Ectarlin takes form within the darkness. Depending on whether the characters have seen Ectarlin only at the wreck site of the *Gull's Egg* or at the ship and in Ilthan, adjust the description accordingly.

> Stepping beyond the doorway produces no new response in the motionless ranks of riders as they watch you. But from the far side of the empty building, a brighter pulse of light flares. A howl of pain and rage rises as the leader of the ghostly riders appears, his spectral horse clawing its way out of the darkness and his glowing hounds close behind. The

tall warrior's eyes blaze with light, his spectral riders shifting back as he spurs forward. Swinging a heavy mace around his head, he shouts out a single word — "Vengeance..."

Ectarlin targets evil or neutral characters first while his **2 ghost hounds** tear into other combatants. If all of the characters are of good alignment, Ectarlin focuses on heavily armored warriors first, driven to a state of rage by the party's intrusion into his sanctum.

Ectarlin, Spectral Warden: AC 11; **HP** 90 (max 10d8 + 10); **Spd** 0ft, fly 60ft; **Melee** withering touch (+5, 4d6 + 3 necrotic or radiant); **SA** horrifying visage (60ft, DC 13 Wis, 1 min.), multiattack (withering touch x2; two hits, 10ft, 3d6 radiant); **Immune** cold, charmed, exhaustion, frightened, grappled, necrotic, paralyzed, petrified, poisoned, prone, restrained; **Str** +2 (+5), **Dex** +1 (+4), **Con** +1 (+4), **Int** +0 (+3), **Wis** +1 (+4), **Cha** +3 (+6); **Senses** darkvision 60ft; **Traits** ethereal sight, etherealness, ghost steed, incorporeal movement, radiant rage, regeneration 10, resilient faith; **AL** NG; **CR** 8; **XP** 1100.

Ghost Hound (2): AC 14 ; **HP** 57 (6d10 + 24); **Spd** 0ft, fly 40ft; **Melee** bite (+6, 1d8 + 3 piercing); **SA** howl (60ft fear, DC 12 Wis, 1d4 min), multiattack (bite x2); **Immune** cold, exhaustion, fright, necrotic, poison, unconscious; **Resist** normal weapons; **Str** +3, **Dex** +2, **Con** +4, **Int** −2, **Wis** +1, **Cha** +0 ; **Senses** darkvision 60ft; **Traits** magic resistance; **AL** N; **CR** 4; **XP** 3900. (**Monster Appendix**)

Ectarlin's shattered mind sees this fight as a battle of honor, and the ghost ride does not join him in attacking the adventurers. However, their ghostly presence makes combat more difficult. As the fight progresses, the riders begin to circle faster and faster around the characters, hemming them in within a field of spectral white light. The area of the fight is lightly obscured for all living creatures, including those with darkvision. Additionally, any creature making a saving throw against becoming frightened while in the area does so with tactical disadvantage.

Ectarlin and his hounds pursue foes out of the stables and onto the courtyard, but they will not pursue past the gate of Talnead.

Developments

If Ectarlin is reduced to 20 hit points or fewer, he falls back and fades away *if the characters have not yet undertaken the **Darkness in Ilthan** section of the adventure.* (The ghostly lord reforms at full strength to reappear in that section.) As he fades away, the spectral lord swears dark oaths against the characters before he goes, shrieking that, "No forces of evil will stand against Ectarlin's ride!"

*If the characters have already played **Darkness in Ilthan**,* reducing Ectarlin to 20 hit points or fewer instead becomes the starting point for the characters to treat with him. Go to **The Ghost Lord's Sorrow** to play out the end of this section of the adventure.

If the characters elect to destroy Ectarlin completely, they are unable to engage with the ghost lord at this stage of the adventure. You'll need to improvise how to handle the party's next move. Then at an opportune moment, have Ectarlin and the ghost ride reappear after 24 hours wherever the characters are, seeking revenge. Try to work some of the details revealed in **The Ghost Lord's Sorrow** (below) into that subsequent fight, helping the characters realize that Ectarlin has information they need.

The Ghost Lord's Sorrow

Lord Ectarlin has been drawn back to the mortal realm in response to the evil of the Dread Master risen again. However, the half-mad ghost

does not recognize the truth of his existence — and cannot do so without the adventurers' help.

The characters must first come to understand the state of Ectarlin's fractured mind, then try to help the ghost come to terms with his fate. As they do, Ectarlin shares his own story, explaining the sudden appearance of the soulstealers that have been attacking ships along the coast — and hinting at the greater evil that controls them.

Treating with Ectarlin

This part of the adventure is not a separate scenario. Rather, it is a single social interaction encounter that plays out at the end of the third part of the adventure — either **Darkness in Ilthan** or **Fallen Talnead**, depending on the order the players chose when tackling those two sections.

If this encounter comes at the end of the fight in Ilthan, Ectarlin and the ghost ride surround the characters in the aftermath of the last undead foe falling. If it comes at the end of the exploration of Talnead Fortress, Ectarlin and the ghost ride surround the characters (if Ectarlin carried the fight), or the ghostly lord falls back into a defensive posture with his riders behind him (if the characters reduced him to 20 hit points or fewer).

This part of the adventure can be played out entirely as a roleplaying scenario, with you judging the players' success or failure strictly on their ability to make use of what they know of Ectarlin, to appeal to his heroic nature, and to engage the broken ghost. Alternatively, you can use rules for social interaction encounters to allow the characters to influence Ectarlin with Cha (Deception or Persuasion) checks, or to augment their roleplaying with such checks. (The ghostly lord does not respond to attempts at intimidation.) If you run this encounter as entirely check-based, Ectarlin's starting attitude is hostile and affecting the ghostly lord's attitude requires a successful DC 20 check.

The Mind of the Ghost Lord

Though Ectarlin's heart remains pure, a hundred years of undeath have thoroughly corrupted the former freelord's thoughts. He dwells now in a place between worlds, aware only of his failed mission to create a safe haven along the Amrin–Eastwatch borderlands, and drawn to the power of the risen Dread Master who destroyed him a century ago.

The spectral lord draws himself up in the saddle, his mace gripped tight in a mailed hand. "I am Ectarlin!" the figure shrieks, its voice hanging momentarily on the air as a shimmer of light. "You will tell me who you serve. I protect these lands from evil. I will ride to the Black Spire, and on my return, the bards will sing..."

Then suddenly, the knight falters, his form seeming to break apart, then coalesce once more. A ripple passes through the assembled spectral riders and their mounts, as if they sense a disturbance in the ghost lord's power. He gazes past you now, his voice cracking with unexplained fear. "The dreams tell me I have been gone, but the dreams lie. The darkness lies. I have not gone. I have only slept..."

As a sudden wind begins to rise, the ethereal figures of the ghost ride begin to shred. The spectral horses snort their fear as their riders silently clash weapons on shields. "I am Ectarlin!" their leader shouts again as he faces his troops. "I protect these lands from evil! Gather my banners! To the Black Spire we ride!"

Then a sudden convulsion twists through the knight again. His body shimmers and shifts, threatening to tear away to mist as he shouts a cry of fear and rage. He turns toward you once more. "I am Ectarlin. You will tell me who you serve..."

Ectarlin's Story

As the adventurers interact with Ectarlin, use the success of the players' roleplaying or the characters' social interaction ability checks to reveal some or all of the following information. Ideally, try to frame

Ectarlin's statements and story as responses to information raised by the characters. However, this encounter is not an interrogation. If the characters simply ply Ectarlin with questions, he reverts back to mad ranting in the manner above.

(This information builds on what the characters learned from Anell Thale in Ilthan. If, for some reason, the characters have not yet gained all that information, incorporate it into this encounter.)

• **Return of the Ghost Ride:** After reappearing in the material realm, Ectarlin called the ghost ride to him through sheer force of will. *"The dreams said I slept, but it cannot be that so many years have passed. My riders come to my command, as always. My sigil still stands over my lands and holdings. The free folk know that I will protect them."*

• **Ectarlin's Quest:** The ghostly lord has been drawn back to the mortal realm by a resurgence of the power of the Dread Master — the lich who slew the freelord a century ago and doomed his soul to endless sorrow. *"In the dreams, I am called. I hear his name, I see his face, I sense his presence. The Dread Master, he is called. But he must be dead. I set out to kill him so long ago..."*

• **The Last Ride:** The final threat that Ectarlin and his mounted warriors rode out against long ago was the same undead the characters have fought. *"We heard the news from the villages, of serpents of bone swimming through wave and air alike. Driving folk mad with their touch, turning friend on friend. Consuming the dead, flesh and bone and marrow. Nothing left even to burn in the dark aftermath."*

• **The Black Spire:** The undead that attacked the coastal villages under Ectarlin's protection a hundred years before were eventually traced to a small, rocky isle known as the Black Spire. *"We knew the Black Spire to avoid it. Shallow shoals there would tear the hulls from ships at low tide. But there were legends as well, which we ignored to our own peril."*

• **The Dread Master's Power:** The lich known as the Dread Master was a figure of ancient legend entombed in the black spire, and who created the soulstealers as his servants. *"The lich was bound, the legends said. Helpless and starved in his Black Spire tomb. But even helpless, he shaped bone and spirit from the dead of the sea to do his bidding. And so did his evil rise again."*

• **The Dread Master's Fall:** In the final battle, Ectarlin and his soldiers took to the sea, and were nearly victorious. *"We set forth in ships, my riders and I, and threw ourselves against the Black Spire. The Dread Master laid death among us, but I fought to him and cleaved him to destruction. I felt him fall ere I died. Ere I... died...?"*

Ectarlin's Fall

The critical component in restoring Ectarlin's mind is getting the beleaguered ghost to understand that he and his company have all been dead for a hundred years. If the characters don't bring him to this realization (or if they fear to do so and try to avoid the subject), have Ectarlin come to that conclusion himself as the characters coax more of his story out. When Ectarlin understands the truth, the ghostly lord's madness fades away, replaced by sorrow and rage.

Ectarlin's expression grows dark, an unseen wind whipping his form to spectral tatters. "I am dead, then. I have failed and left these lands to fester and fall. To be defended by new heroes." Spinning around on his spectral steed, the ghost lord screams to the riders assembled around him. "Our journey is done! Our hope has failed and our mission ends. Ride with me, friends! Ride with me to our end!"

A storm wind erupts from the ground and sky at once, driving dust that scours and blinds you. But through the haze, you see the spectral figures of the ghost ride torn away by that wind, vanishing one by one. As the wind dies as suddenly as it came, Ectarlin, his head hung in sorrow, is the last to go.

Developments

When Ectarlin vanishes, he leaves a trace of his essence and goodness behind. Each character is imbued with the *boon of Ectarlin*, gaining

tactical advantage on saving throws against the spells and special abilities of evil creatures for 24 hours.

Though the characters might assume that Ectarlin and the ghost ride are gone, the spectral wardens reappear in the last section of the adventure to fight alongside the adventurers. When they do, the characters' overall success in treating with Ectarlin determines the effectiveness of the spectral fighting force.

When this encounter is done, consider the characters' roleplaying, or assess the result of their attempts to use ability checks to improve Ectarlin's attitude. Assign the characters' efforts to engage the spectral lord a value from 1 (minimal success) to 4 (full success). This number becomes important during the opening battle of **The Black Spire**.

The Black Spire

From Ectarlin, the characters have gained knowledge of a heretofore unknown island called the Black Spire — and heard hints of a dark power that lurks there.

The Black Spire is a local landmark long gone from history and legend, making Ilthan the best place to seek information on it. Anell Thale and the other villagers know of the Black Spire, but only as a shipping hazard to be avoided, and as a place where folk of the coast sometimes collect eggs from the seabirds that nest along the spire's rocky shores. One villager — a fisher name Dolman — knows the island best, but for all the wrong reasons.

"My brother Shamus died on the Black Spire a month back," Dolman says. "His leg goes lame sometimes, makes it so pulling nets is hard on him. He used to sail to the spire to go egging at the gull rookery. One day he went out and never came back by dusk. Next day, we found his boat still tied up along the shore. He must have fallen to the water and never come back up."

Dolman can provide the characters with a description of the island (see below) and notes the presence of a narrow cave carved out along one side of its rocky spire. He says that he and his brother investigated the cave once but found nothing of interest inside. (In truth, the cave hides the secret entrance to the Dread Master's tomb.)

The lore recounted by Ectarlin should be enough to convince the characters to investigate the Black Spire. If they need additional persuasion, Anell Thale wants to investigate and requests the party's assistance.

The Dread Master Reborn

The legends of the lich known as the Dread Master were lost to memory centuries ago, when he was hunted down and overthrown by his enemies. Not content with simply destroying the lich, however, those enemies sought to impose an eternity of torture on him, imprisoning him — with his phylactery — beneath the Black Spire, to decay forever with no supply of souls to sustain him.

But though the Dread Master was physically prevented from escaping the tomb, long years of imprisonment reduced the lich to a mental essence that was able to slip beyond the wards that bound him. On two occasions, the Dread Master was able to seek out and claim the life force of sentient creatures visiting the island, restoring him to minimal power. With that power, he used his mental essence to create the foul undead soulstealers from the bones and spirits of sailors drowned on the shoals around the Black Spire. Sending his servants out to claim new souls for him, the Dread Master's power grew.

The first time the Dread Master returned to power, Ectarlin's forces came to the island to confront him. In a devastating battle, Ectarlin's knights were slain to the last by soulstealers, and the freelord himself fell in the act of destroying the Dread Master's physical form — and before the lich's phylactery could be destroyed. For a hundred years, the Dread Master slumbered again as nothing more than mental essence, until claiming the soul of the fisher-pirate Shamus a month ago set him once again on the path to recover his power.

Reaching the Black Spire

Any of the folk of Ilthan can show the characters how to find the Black Spire or provide suitable directions. Anell Thale offers to sail the characters there with an escort, or the characters can borrow a pinnace from the Ilthan docks. (Characters who prefer to strike out on their own can also claim any boat left at the wreck site of the *Gull's Egg*, assuming too much time has not passed.)

> The coast has only just disappeared behind you when you see a dark shape rising from the water. The Black Spire is a fang-shaped pinnacle of rock rising 50 feet or more above the water, with a broad, rocky island at its base. The near vertical slope of the spire thrusts straight up from the water along the island's south side, but the north is a broad, rocky plateau marked with seabird nests and stained white with guano.

If the characters journey to the island with folk from Ilthan, they are accompanied by Anell (a **pirate captain**) and 5 **pirates**, taking two boats. The characters can divide themselves between the boats and allow the pirates to sail, or one boat can carry just the party if enough adventurers have proficiency with water vehicles.

The waters around the island are calm enough to allow the characters to easily reach it by boat. Using flying or teleportation magic is also an option — and gives the characters a potential edge against the ambush that awaits them.

Death from the Deep

The soulstealers that serve the Dread Master are on patrol in the waters around the Black Spire, and attack as soon as any threat comes within 200ft of the island, whether by boat or by air. If the characters teleport directly to the shore, the soulstealers instead rise up from around the island to attack. Go to "The Isle of the Spire," below, then rework the following read-aloud text and the appearance of the ghost ride accordingly.

> As you draw closer, you see no signs of movement or activity on the island — not even birds along the rocky shore of the nesting ground. But suddenly, a surge of motion from beneath you sends a lurch through the boat, as a pack of soulstealers shoot forth, shrieking, from under the dark water.

Soulstealer (5): AC 16; HP 105 (14d8 + 42); **Spd** 20ft, fly 40ft; **Melee** claws (+6, 1d8 + 5 slashing); **SA** mind wrack (*dominate person*, DC 15 Wis; *modify memory*, DC 15 Int), multiattack (claw x 4); **Immune** exhaustion, fright, necrotic, poison, restrain, stun, unconscious; **Resist** normal weapons; **Str** +4, **Dex** +2, **Con** +3 (+5), **Int** +2, **Wis** +2, **Cha** +0; **Skills** Perception +8; **Senses** darkvision 60ft; **Traits** incorporeal shift, mind wrack, unearthly destruction; **AL** NE; **CR** 6; **XP** 2300. (**Monster Appendix**)

The soulstealers attack characters in boats or in the air, attempting to drive them down into the water. A soulstealer can forego its attack to attempt a DC 20 Str check to swamp a boat. If it succeeds, any character in the boat must succeed on a DC 15 Dex saving throw or end up in the water. Swimming in the open water requires a successful DC 15 Str (Athletics) check. (All the pirates of Ilthan are expert swimmers, and make it to the Black Spire safely even if their boats are capsized.)

Spectral Allies

A fight on the open water with the soulstealers would normally be a deadly affair, but the adventurers quickly gain an unexpected advantage. Their efforts to restore Ectarlin's mind and learn his story have focused the spectral lord. Feeling the power of the Dread Master surge again, Ectarlin manifests with his warriors for one last ride.

The timeliness of the appearance of the ghost ride is determined by how well the characters engaged Ectarlin in **The Ghost Lord's Sorrow**. The ghost ride appears, at the end of the round, 4 rounds after the soulstealers appear, minus the number you assigned to the characters' efforts (from 1 to 4). Characters who achieved only minimal success engaging Ectarlin must engage the soulstealers for 3 rounds on their own. Characters who managed to fully engage the spectral lord see the ghost ride appear in the first round of combat.

> From far behind you, a guttural shrieking rises even above the sound of battle. A pulse of white light flares above the dark water, which comes alive with movement as two score ghostly knights surge toward you. Their spectral steeds lash the sea to foam as they race across it, their streaming banners showing the trident wrapped with vines. In the vanguard of the ghostly force, Ectarlin rides with mace in hand, a light of vengeance burning in his eyes.

The ghost ride reaches the site of combat in 1 round, whereupon the spectral riders fall upon the soulstealers in a fury. The characters are free to continue on to the Black Spire, watching as Ectarlin and his knights lay waste to the foul undead. (If the characters try to engage in the battle, Ectarlin cries out, "This fight is ours! Get to the safety of the shore!")

The Isle of the Spire

When the characters reach the island, they find no sign of further danger but make a grisly discovery.

> Patches of white that you initially took for guano-crusted rocks are actually the skeletal remains of dozens of humanoids, their flesh stripped clean to leave shattered skulls and bones behind. The state of the remains and the presence of blood flies swarming around dripping pools of marrow suggests that these unfortunates have been only recently killed — a few weeks ago at most.

The seabirds that once dwelled here fled a month before, when the Dread Master reformed once more. The skeletal remains are the unfortunate crews of the ships the soulstealers have assaulted in recent weeks, their skeletal bodies returned here so their souls could be consumed by the Dread Master.

The cave entrance that Dolman spoke of is easily seen from the shore. A character that searches the cave with a successful DC 18 Int (Investigation) check finds a secret trapdoor concealed beneath a covering of packed earth and rock. A *detect magic* spell also locates the trapdoor, which is protected by powerful abjuration magic. A successful DC 15 Int (Arcana) check or an *identify* spell reveals that an area beneath the island is permanently warded to prevent the passage of undead creatures (similar to the effect of a *scroll of protection from undead*).

Opening the trapdoor requires a successful DC 18 Str (Athletics) check. The undead ward (placed here when the Dread Master was entombed centuries ago) is too powerful to be dispelled.

Tomb Entrance

While the characters explore the cave, they see and hear the ghost ride engage the soulstealers behind them. Whether the characters wait for that fight to finish or descend into the tomb quickly, Ectarlin and his hounds appear at their side as soon as the trapdoor is opened.

> "The tomb of the Dread Master," Ectarlin says. "The evil that does not sleep. We will finish this fight now, my friends." But even as the ghostly lord pushes forward, you

see his spectral form suddenly shot through with sharp lines resembling black iron bands. His steed and his hounds all shriek with fear as they stumble back.

"My power wanes," Ectarlin whispers. "The wards that hold the dread lich in this tomb bar me now from passing within. I cannot complete this fight. The living must be the architects of the Dread Master's fate. Go. I will ensure, at least, that none of his vile minions enter to strike at you from behind."

The Tomb of the Dread Master

Beneath the trapdoor, the characters find a spiral stone staircase cut into the rock. This descends 30ft to a landing that opens up to a broad chamber, 50ft across.

Steps lead down from the landing to a rough-walled chamber of black stone. Seawater drips from the ceiling and pools along the floor, the air before you shimmering with shadow. Across from the landing, a chaotic mass of rusted armor, corroded and shattered weapons, and splintered bones have been piled up in the vague shape of a throne, upon which sits a skeletal figure clad in tattered crimson robes.

The lich's empty eye sockets glow a baleful red as it rises and suddenly shimmers into four distinct figures. "Heroes, are you, seeking the glory of those who tried and failed to kill the Dread Master before? Or mere rabble come to feed me? Either way, your souls are mine."

Thankfully for the characters, the Dread Master has not yet had enough time to restore himself to the level of power that routed Ectarlin and his forces. (In fact, the lich's threat to steal the characters' souls is a hollow one, as he is unable to cast *imprisonment* and must rely on the soulstealers to claim souls for him until he can.) However, the diminished lich is still a potent threat.

The Dread Master uses the lich stat block, but with the following adjustments:

• The Dread Master takes a –2 penalty to saving throws (already included in the short stat block, below), and can use legendary resistance only once per encounter, rather than the standard three times.

• He is not immune to the exhaustion or paralysis.

• He has access only to spells of 7th level and lower, but has full slots for those spells. He cannot cast *plane shift* while within the tomb, and cannot cast *dimension door* to leave the tomb.

• The Dread Master can use any of the lich's legendary actions, but he has no lair actions in his prison.

• The Dread Master's challenge rating is 17.

Dread Master: AC 17; HP 135 (18d8 + 54); Spd 30ft; **Melee** paralyzing touch (+12, 3d6 cold plus DC 18 Con, paralyzed, 1 min); **SA** spells (Int+10, DC 18); **LA** cantrip, disrupt life, frightening gaze, paralyzing touch; **Immune** charm, fright, normal weapons, poison; **Resist** cold, lightning, necrotic; **Str** +0 (–2), **Dex** +3 (+1), **Con** +3 (+8), **Int** +5 (+10), **Wis** +2 (+7), **Cha** +3 (+1); **Skills** Arcana +18, History +12, Insight +9, Perception +9; **Senses** truesight 120ft; **Traits** legendary resistance (x1 only), rejuvenation; **AL** CE; **CR** 17; **XP** 18,000.

> **Spells (slots):** 0 (at will)—*mage hand, prestidigitation, ray of frost;* 1st (4)—*detect magic, magic missile, shield, thunderwave;* 2nd (3)—*detect thoughts, invisibility, Melf's acid arrow, mirror image;* 3rd (3)—*animate dead, counterspell, dispel magic, fireball;* 4th (3)—*blight, dimension door;* 5th (3)—*cloudkill, scrying;* 6th (1)—*disintegrate, globe of invulnerability;* 7th (1)—*finger of death, plane shift*

When the battle begins, the Dread Master has already cast *mirror image* to protect himself (it lasts for 9 rounds once combat starts). He then prepares his most effective offensive spells in subsequent rounds, targeting a spellcaster with *disintegrate* and a martial character with *finger of death,* then falling back on *fireball* and *cloudkill* against the maximum number of characters.

If hard pressed in melee, the Dread Master uses his Frightening Gaze legendary action to attempt to drive a foe back. Otherwise, he uses Disrupt Life each round in the hope of destroying the heroes quickly.

The Tomb: Black shadow fills the Dread Master's tomb, making all areas lightly obscured, even to creatures with darkvision. Any area spell that deals fire damage temporarily clears away the shadow in its area for 1 round after the spell is cast. Magical light from a spell of 2nd level or lower has no effect on the shadow.

The water pooling along the floor makes much of the area difficult terrain.

Allied Forces: Anell and her pirates accompany the party into the tomb if the characters have been consistently above board in their dealings with the villagers since **Ghosts on the Water**. The pirates cannot damage the lich with their normal weapons. However, their presence in the fight can lend aid to the adventurers. In each round of combat during which any pirates fight alongside the characters, one character can gain tactical advantage on attack rolls made against the lich. Alternatively, one character can impose tactical disadvantage on saving throws made by the lich against the character's spells or special abilities.

The players must decide which character gains this benefit at the start of each round. It cannot be granted in response to a failed attack roll or a successful save by the lich.

Developments

The Dread Master wears his phylactery, and if the lich is slain, it can be easily destroyed to prevent his reappearance.

Characters who investigate the Dread Master's tomb find that the lich has a left a record of sorts scratched in Common into the stone of the walls. Much of it is insane rambling, but an hour's study allows the characters to learn the broad details touched on in the "The Tomb of the Dread Master," above, though the details of who originally imprisoned him have been lost.

Treasure

Any character who pokes around the lich's makeshift throne can easily deduce that this macabre fixture is all that remains of those members of Ectarlin's company who died here a hundred years before. With a DC 15 Wis (Perception) check, a character spots a gleam of steel deep within the pile, and a *detect magic* spell reveals magic at the same location. By carefully disassembling the throne, the characters reveal three magic items that have survived the decades — a pair of *boots of striding and springing,* a set of *adamantine chain mail,* and Ectarlin's *mace of disruption* — identical to the spectral mace his ghost now wields.

Ectarlin's Farewell

When the characters emerge from the tomb, they find the soulstealers defeated. The surface of the Black Spire is covered with a grisly array of bones where the undead fell. The members of the ghost ride are on their spectral steeds once more, lined up to both sides of Ectarlin where he waits.

When he hears news of the lich's destruction, Ectarlin nods gravely. If he sees his mace and the other items in the possession of good characters, he tells them he is proud to have them carry on his legacy. If a neutral or evil character wields Ectarlin's mace, his mood turns dark, but he accepts this outcome of the characters' successful fight against the Dread Master. "By your bravery, you have earned the right to wield the power I once wielded. I pray you find a course for your life that will let you prove worthy of that power."

Ectarlin then turns away as he calls to his riders. "Follow me, friends. We ride home." Then surging out across the water, heading away from the coast, the spectral wardens and their horses fade away.

Spoils and Rewards

In addition to the magic items found in the Dread Master's tomb, if the characters were hired to identity and defeat whatever was behind the derelict ships, they are spectacularly successful. Returning to Bando Larna with the full story of what was behind the disappearing crews earns them their agreed-upon fee, plus a bonus of 500gp each. (If the characters took up the adventure for some other reason, or even by happenstance, word of their exploits gets back to the merchant guilds, and an award of 1000gp each is granted to them by the grateful merchant guilds.) In addition, the characters gain the notice of many of the more powerful lords and merchants of Eastgate and Eastwych.

Assuming that a party of self-centered characters don't turn the pirate-scavengers of Ilthan over to the authorities, the adventurers gain the lifelong allegiance of Anell Thale and her people, and a reputation for heroic deeds that spreads throughout the isolated settlements of the estuary coast and the Forest of Hope.

In addition to the monetary reward, the characters are also granted title to the lands that were once Ectarlin's. Though the damage done by the elementals means that his fortress of Talnead cannot be repaired, the characters have it in their power to try to establish a new order in the wild borderlands between Amrin Estuary and Eastwatch — and perhaps to make good on the legacy of peace and prosperity that Ectarlin was denied.

Appendix: New Monsters

Balban (Brute Demon)

XP 1800 (CR 5)
CE Large fiend (demon)
Init +2

DEFENSE

AC 15 (natural armor)
HP 143 (15d10 + 60)
Save Int +1, Wis +5
Immune lightning, poison
Resist acid, cold, fire
Vulnerable radiant

OFFENSE

Speed 40ft
Charge. If the balban moves at least 15ft straight toward a target and then hits it with a gore attack on the same turn, the target takes an extra 11 (2d10) piercing damage. If the target is a creature, it must succeed on a DC 16 Str saving throw or be pushed up to 10ft away and knocked prone.
Multiattack The balban makes two slam attacks.
Melee slam (+8, 10ft, 2d6+5 bludgeoning), gore (+8, 1d10+5 piercing)

STATISTICS

Str 20 (+5), **Dex** 14 (+2), **Con** 22 (+6),
Int 6 (−2), **Wis** 14 (+2), **Cha** 10 (+0)
Languages Abyssal, telepathy 120 ft (demons only)
Skills Athletics +8, Survival +5
Senses blindsight 30ft, darkvision 120ft

TRAITS

Double Damage Against Objects. A balban's powerful fists are particularly effective against objects. A balban deals double damage against an object.
Magic Resistance. The balban has tactical advantage on saving throws against spells and other magic effects.

ECOLOGY

Environment Abyss
Organization solitary, pack (1d4), or mixed squad (1d4 balban and 2d6 manes)

Roughly humanoid in shape, a balban stands 10–12ft in height and weighs about 5000 pounds. It sports a muscular chest over a squat, pot-bellied abdomen, massive arms, and columnar legs. Its slate gray skin hangs loose and leathery, paler on its face and belly, darker on its back and legs. Red and black horns used with their gore attack curve back from the head, these spiral and twist upward, like an antelope.

In the armies of the Abyss, balbans provide the important service of siege-breaker. Their ability to break objects is unrivaled. If a demonic general needs a gate smashed, a wall toppled, or a siege-engine dismantled, it sends a balban to do it.

Balbans have limited intelligence, but a very dedicated focus and delight in their destructive missions. Of the lesser demons, a balban is most likely to be accompanied by manes. They dislike dretches because of the smaller creatures' smell (even though immune to the effects of their stench).

Source: Demon, Balban (Brute Demon) from *The Tome of Horrors Complete*, Copyright 2011, **Necromancer Games, Inc.**, published and distributed by **Frog God Games**; Author Scott Greene.

Fiodmar, Duke of Avrandt

XP 11,500 (CR 14)
NE Medium monstrosity (shapechanger)
Init +6

DEFENSE

AC 21
HP 253 (23d8+69)
Save Str +5, Dex +11, Con +8, Int +5, Wis +6, Cha +8
Immune charm, disease, fear
Resist poison

OFFENSE

Speed 30ft
Multiattack Fiodmar makes two melee attacks in any combination.
Melee *frost brand rapier* (+11, 1d8+8 piercing plus 1d6 cold plus 1d8 radiant)
Melee slam (+11, 1d6+6 bludgeoning plus 1d8 radiant)

STATISTICS

Str 11 (+0), **Dex** 22 (+6), **Con** 16 (+3),
Int 11 (+0), **Wis** 12 (+1), **Cha** 16 (+3)
Languages Common, Draconic
Skills Deception +8, Insight +6, Intimidation +8, Persuasion +8
Senses blindsight 10ft, darkvision 60ft

TRAITS

Ambusher Fiodmar has advantage on attack rolls against any creature he has surprised.
Aura of Courage Fiodmar and friendly creatures within 10ft can't be frightened while he is conscious.*
Aura of Protection Whenever Fiodmar or a friendly creature within 10ft of him must make a saving throw, the creature gains a +3 bonus to the saving throw. He must be conscious to grant this bonus.*
Channel Divinity Fiodmar chooses which of the following two options to use. He must then finish a short or long rest to use his Channel Divinity again.
• **Abjure Enemy** As an action, Fiodmar chooses one creature within 60ft that he can see. That creature must make a DC 16 Wisdom saving throw, unless it is immune to being frightened. Fiends and undead have disadvantage on this saving throw.
On a failed save, the creature is frightened for 1 minute or until it takes any damage. While frightened, the creature's speed is 0, and it can't benefit from any bonus to its speed.
On a successful save, the creature's speed is halved for 1 minute or until the creature takes any damage.
• **Vow of Enmity** As a bonus action, Fiodmar can utter a vow of enmity against a creature he can see within 10ft, using his Channel Divinity. He gains advantage on attack rolls against the creature for 1 minute or until it drops to 0 hit points or falls unconscious.
Cleansing Touch Fiodmar can use his action to end one spell on himself or on one willing creature that he touches. He can use this feature 3 times. He regains expended uses when he finishes a long rest.
Divine Sense As an action, Fiodmar can open his awareness. Until the end of his next turn, he knows the

location of any celestial, fiend, or undead within 60ft of him that is not behind total cover. He knows the type (celestial, fiend, or undead) of any being whose presence he senses, but not its identity. Within the same radius, he also detects the presence of any place or object that has been consecrated or desecrated, as with the *hallow* spell.

He can use this feature 4 times. When he finishes a long rest, he regains all expended uses.

Divine Smite When Fiodmar hits a creature with a melee weapon attack, he can expend one paladin spell slot to deal radiant damage to the target, in addition to the weapon's damage. The extra damage is 2d8 for a 1st-level spell slot, plus 1d8 for each spell level higher than 1st, to a maximum of 5d8. The damage increases by 1d8 if the target is an undead or a fiend.

Dueling Fighting Style When Fiodmar is wielding a melee weapon in one hand and no other weapons, he gains a +2 bonus to damage rolls with that weapon.*

Improved Divine Smite Whenever Fiodmar hits a creature with a melee weapon, the creature takes an extra 1d8 radiant damage.*

Lay on Hands Fiodmar has a pool of healing power that replenishes when he takes a long rest. With that pool, he can restore a total of 75 hit points.

As an action, he can touch a creature and draw power from the pool to restore a number of hit points to that creature, up to the maximum amount remaining in his pool.

Alternatively, he can expend 5 hit points from his pool of healing to cure the target of one disease or neutralize one poison affecting it. He can cure multiple diseases and neutralize multiple poisons with a single use of Lay on Hands, expending hit points separately for each one.

Poison Breath Fiodmar exhales poisonous gas in a 15-foot cone. Each creature in that area must make a DC 11 Constitution saving throw, taking 21 (6d6) poison damage on a failed save, or half as much damage on a successful one.

Read Thoughts Fidomar magically reads the surface thoughts of one creature within 60ft. The effect can penetrate barriers, but 3 feet of wood or dirt, 2 feet of stone, 2 inches of metal, or a thin sheet of lead blocks it. While the target is in range, Fiodmar can continue reading its thoughts, as long as his concentration isn't broken (as if concentrating on a spell). While reading the target's mind, Fiodmar has advantage on Wisdom (Insight) and Charisma (Deception, Intimidation, and Persuasion) checks against the target.

Relentless Avenger When Fiodmar hits a creature with an opportunity attack, he can move up to half his speed immediately after the attack and as part of the same reaction. This movement doesn't provoke opportunity attacks.

Shapechanger Fiodmar can use his action to polymorph into a Small or Medium humanoid he has seen, or back into his true form. His statistics, other than its size, are the same in each form. Any equipment he is wearing or carrying isn't transformed. He reverts to his true form if it dies.

Spells Fiodmar is a 15th-level paladin, and would normally use Charisma as his spellcasting ability. However, Fiodmar does not prepare spells for casting. He uses his spell slots *only* to empower his Divine Smite ability.

1st Level (x4)
2nd Level (x3)
3rd Level (x3)
4th Level (x2)

Surprise Attack If Fiodmar surprises a creature and hits it with an attack during the first round of combat, the target takes an extra 3d6 damage from the attack

*(Modifiers for this trait are already accounted for in Fiodmar's stats, above.)

GEAR
leather armor, shield, *frost brand rapier*

The being currently calling itself "Fiodmar" is a half-green dragon doppelganger, the offspring of Khythontorryx, and a seething cauldron of hatred for both his father and for civilization. Fiodmar dreams of setting the human nations at war, and leading a "monster" uprising to carve out a new kingdom of beasts and horrors, with himself as its king. He killed the original Duke Fiodmar and took his place some years ago, and has been slowly amassing wealth and knowledge. The competition of the monster hunt wasn't his idea, but it offered him an opportunity he could not pass up.

Ghost Hound

XP 1100 (CR 4)
N Medium undead
Init +2

DEFENSE
AC 14 (natural armor)
HP 57 (6d10 + 24)
Save Con +6
Immune cold, necrotic, and poison damage; fright, poison, exhaustion, unconscious
Resist bludgeoning, piercing, and slashing damage from normal weapons

OFFENSE
Speed: 0ft, fly 40ft
Multiattack: A ghost hound attacks twice with its bite.
Melee bite (+6, 1d8 + 3 piercing)

STATISTICS
Str 17 (+3), **Dex** 15 (+2), **Con** 18 (+4),
Int 6 (−2), **Wis** 12 (+1), **Cha** 10 (+0)
Languages understands the commands of undead creatures but does not speak.
Skills Stealth +4
Senses darkvision 60ft

TRAITS
Howl: A ghost hound can unleash a frightening howl as an action. Any creature within 60 feet of the ghost hound must make a successful DC 12 Wis saving throw or become frightened for 1d4 minutes. A successful saving throw renders a character immune to the howling of ghost hounds until after the character's next long rest.

ECOLOGY
Environment: Temperate and tropical forest
Organization: Pair or pack (3–6)

Ghost hounds are the spectral shades of hunting dogs or guard dogs that have accompanied their masters to undeath. Typically found in the service of ghosts, wights, specters, and other purpose-driven undead, these spectral hounds use their frightening howl to hem in foes and drive them toward their masters.

Though dogs are the most common manifestation of these undead, the ghost hound stat block can be used to represent a spectral undead version of any similarly sized trained guard creature or hunting creature.

Jaundool (Pallid One)

XP 50 (CR 1/4)
CE Small humanoid
Init +5

DEFENSE
AC 13
HP 27 (6d6 + 6)
Vulnerable radiant damage

OFFENSE
Speed 20ft, burrow 10ft
Multiattack A jaundool bites once and makes one attack with its claws or dagger.
Melee bite (+5, 1d4+3 piercing), claw (+5, 1d6+3 slashing), bone dagger (+5, 1d4+3 piercing plus poison)
Ranged bone dagger (+5, 20ft/60ft, 1d4+3 plus poison)

STATISTICS
Str 8 (–1), **Dex** 16 (+3), **Con** 13 (+1),
Int 8 (–1), **Wis** 15 (+2), **Cha** 8 (–1)
Languages Pallid One, broken Common
Skills Perception +4, Stealth +5, Survival +4
Senses darkvision 60ft

TRAITS
Burrowing Attack Jaundools can burrow under opponents and make a claw attack with tactical advantage from below. The target makes a DC 13 Dex save. If the save fails, the pallid one attacks with advantage, and if the attack is successful the opponent is grappled. If the check succeeds the pallid one attacks normally and the victim is not grappled.
Daylight Vulnerability A jaundool must make a DC 13 Con save every hour that it is exposed to daylight, and takes one level of exhaustion with each failed save.
Poison Jaundool bone daggers are treated with verdice, a poison extracted from underground fungi. Anyone struck by a pallid one's dagger attack must make a DC 14 Con save or be poisoned for 1d4 hours, and a second DC 11 Con save or be blinded for 3d6 minutes. After a successful attack the pallid one must take an action to reapply another dose of poison for it to be used again. A jaundool normally carries 5 doses of poison.
Stealthy Jaundools always have tactical advantage on Stealth checks that take place in darkness or underground.

ECOLOGY
Environment any underground
Organization solitary, band (2–7) or horde (6–24)

Jaundools are the degenerate remnants of a race that ruled this part of the world countless millennia ago and worshipped the demon-god known as the Pallid King. Though they once built vast underground cities and networks of tunnels, today they dwell in squalid burrows amidst the crumbling ruins of their old settlements. Their communities rarely number more than two or three dozen, and their lives are miserable shadows of their race's ancient greatness.

Physically pallid ones resemble gnarled, hairless ratlike humanoids with tiny black eyes and weak, malformed limbs. Despite their feeble appearance they are strong burrowers, and still retain enough of their old knowledge to craft bone and stone tools or weapons and extract the verdice poison from underground fungal growths.

The Pallid King

XP 1800 (CR 5)
CE Large Fiend
Init +6

DEFENSE
AC 15 (natural armor)
HP 97 (13d10 + 39)
Save Str +7, Con +6, Wis +6
Immune cold
Resist bludgeoning, piercing and slashing from normal weapons
Vulnerable radiant

OFFENSE
Speed 40ft, fly 20ft, burrow 10ft
Multiattack The pallid king attacks with one bite and two claws
Melee bite (+7, 1d8+4 piercing), claw (+7, 1d6+4 slashing)

STATISTICS
Str 18 (+4), **Dex** 12 (+1), **Con** 16 (+3),
Int 12 (+1), **Wis** 16 (+3), **Cha** 11 (+0)
Languages Common, telepathy 60ft
Skills Perception +6
Senses darkvision 120ft

ECOLOGY
Environment subterranean
Organization solitary or clan (pallid king and 3d6 pallid ones)

The demonic creature known as the Pallid King once ruled the powerful civilization that occupied Keston Province long before even the founding of the Lost City of Barakus. In time, as its subjects dwindled and fell into decadence, it was also worshipped by the corrupt humans who also inhabited the region, until they were wiped out and the Pallid King slain by Hyperborean adventurers. The Pallid King's bloodline persisted however, lingering as a tiny black speck on the soul of some of its human descendants, and with the right rituals and sacrifice, it might yet be reborn.

This represents the Pallid King at its rebirth — relatively weak and underpowered. With time, worship and more sacrifice, it will grow to a truly terrifying demon hybrid, its evil spirit corrupting the innocent and drawing more under its domination. Any future statistics are entirely up to the GM.

Soulstealer

XP 2300 (CR 6)
NE Large undead
Initiative +2

DEFENSE
AC 16 (natural armor)
HP 105 (14d8 + 42)
Save Con +5
Immune exhaustion, fright, poison, necrotic, restrain, stun, unconscious
Resist bludgeoning, piercing, and slashing from normal weapons

OFFENSE
Speed: 20ft, fly 40ft
Multiattack The soulstealer attacks four times with its claws.
Melee claw (+6, 10ft, 1d8 + 5 slashing)

STATISTICS
Str 19 (+4), **Dex** 14 (+2), **Con** 17 (+3),

Int 14 (+2), **Wis** 14 (+2), **Cha** 10 (+0)
Languages: Understands all the languages of its creator but does not speak
Skills Perception +8
Senses darkvision 60ft

TRAITS

Incorporeal Shift As a bonus action, a soulstealer can make itself incorporeal until the start of its next turn. While incorporeal, it can move through solid objects and living creatures as though they were difficult terrain. If it becomes corporeal inside an object, the soulstealer takes 1d10 force damage. If the soulstealer becomes corporeal inside any other creatures, each creature takes 1d10 force damage.

A soulstealer that has engulfed one or more bodies using its Unearthly Destruction action option cannot use its Incorporeal Shift.

Lifesense A soulstealer can automatically pinpoint the location of any living creature within 120ft, and it knows how close to death the creature is.

Mind Wrack A living creature struck twice by a soulstealer's claw attack must make a DC 15 Wis saving throw. On a failed save, the creature falls under the soulstealer's control for 1d6 rounds, as if affected by *dominate person*. When this effect ends, the creature must make a DC 15 Int saving throw or lose all memory of the previous 10 minutes, as if the memory was eliminated by a *modify memory* spell.

If a creature is subject to this effect multiple times, its memory losses do not overlap, but are cumulative. For example, a creature affected twice by Mind Wrack loses all memory of the previous 20 minutes. The *dominate person* effect can be removed with *dispel magic*, but the loss of memory can be undone only with a *greater restoration* spell.

Unearthly Destruction As an action, a soulstealer can engulf a Large or smaller creature that has died within 1 round, consuming its body and soul. A creature that is engulfed by the soulstealer has its flesh stripped from it, leaving only skeletal remains that become part of the soulstealer's form. The creature's gear is discarded by the soulstealer.

While a creature is engulfed by a soulstealer, its soul is not free for the purpose of *resurrection* and similar effects. A soulstealer can invoke its unearthly destruction on up to one Large or four Medium or smaller dead creatures before it is sated. It then typically returns to its creator, who can make use of the trapped souls.

If a soulstealer is destroyed, creatures it has engulfed are left tangled up in the creature's mass of bones, but any souls it has engulfed are freed.

ECOLOGY

Environment: Any
Organization: Pack (3–12)

The soulstealer appears as a serpentine mass of bones that continually grind and shift as the creature moves. It has no limbs, but shoots forth spiked bone claws with which it attacks.

These foul undead are created by dark and secret rituals, and remain forever under the control of their creator. The process of creating a soulstealer requires the skeletal remains of a minimum of ten Medium or five Large sentient creatures, and destroys the souls of those creatures to fuel the soulstealer's dark purpose. The bones of a soulstealer are marked with glowing runes that bind it to its creator.

A soulstealer can move only a limited distance from its creator — 10 miles for each point of the creator's challenge rating or character level. If the creator's challenge rating increases, or if the creator goes up in level, the effective range of the soulstealer increases.

While within 100 feet of a soulstealer, its creator can draw a soul from it with a successful DC 20 Int (Arcana) check. On a failed check, the soul is freed. On a successful check, the soul can be used by the creator (consumed, channeled into a dark ritual, used to create an undead creature, and so on). Soulstealers are often created by necromancers, liches, night hags, and other creatures that traffic in souls.

If a soulstealer's creator is killed or destroyed, it goes berserk, attacking all creatures it meets until it is destroyed.

Wildshadow

XP 1800 (CR 5)
NE Small Fey
Init +5

DEFENSE

AC 15
HP 67 (15d6 + 15)
Save Dex +8, Wis +6

OFFENSE

Speed 40ft, fly 50ft
Multiattack The wildshadow attacks once with its rapier and once with its dagger in melee, or with two darts at range.
Melee rapier (+9, 1d8 + 9 piercing plus *wild thrall*), dagger (+9, 1d4 + 9 piercing plus *wild thrall*)
Ranged dart (+9, 20ft/60ft, 1d4 + 9 piercing plus *wild thrall*)

STATISTICS

Str 13 (+1), **Dex** 20 (+5), **Con** 13 (+1),
Int 12 (+1), **Wis** 16 (+3), **Cha** 18 (+4)
Languages Common, Elvish, Sylvan
Skills Deception +7 Perception +6, Stealth +8, Survival +6
Senses darkvision 120ft

TRAITS

Charm As an action, the wildshadow targets one humanoid it can see within 30 feet of it. If the target can see the wildshadow, the target must succeed on a DC 17 Wisdom saving throw against this magic or be charmed by the wildshadow. The charmed target regards the wildshadow as a trusted friend to be heeded and protected. Although the target isn't under the wildshadow's control, it interprets the wildshadow's requests or actions in the most favorable way it can.

Each time the wildshadow or the wildshadow's thralls or companions do anything harmful to the target, it can repeat the saving throw, ending the effect on itself on a success. Otherwise, the effect lasts 24 hours or until the wildshadow is killed, is on a different plane of existence than the target, or takes a bonus action to end the effect.

If a creature's saving throw is successful or the effect ends for it (for any reason other than the 24 hours duration), the creature is immune to the wildshadow's Charm for the next 24 hours.

Innate Spellcasting The wildshadow's spellcasting ability is Charisma (spell save DC 17). The wildshadow can innately cast the following spells, requiring no material components:

At will: *dancing lights, mage hand, minor illusion, prestidigitation, vicious mockery*
3/day each: *disguise self, entangle, fog cloud, hypnotic pattern, major image, phantasmal force, silent image, suggestion*
1/day: *confusion*

Magic Resistance The wildshadow has advantage on saving throws against spells and other magical effects.

Superior Invisibility As an action, the wildshadow magically turns invisible until its concentration ends (as if concentrating on a spell). Any equipment the wildshadow wears or carries is invisible with it.

Wild Enchantment Any normal weapon that has been in the wildshadow's immediate possession for 3 or more days becomes a darker color, almost black and slightly greenish, and behaves in all ways like a +1 enchanted weapon. If the weapon is piercing or slashing, it also gains the ability to inflict the *wild thrall* disease. Once such a weapon has been out of contact with the wildshadow for 3 or more days, it loses all magical properties and returns to normal.

Wild Thrall Any time a piercing or slashing weapon affected by the *wild enchantment* trait does damage to a target, that target must succeed on a DC 17 Constitution saving throw or be infected by the *wild thrall* disease. While infected, the target has disadvantage on all Wisdom checks (but not attacks or saving throws), due to hallucinations and extreme mood swings. The target may make a new save every round to shake off the effects, but all such saves after the initial one are at disadvantage. Additional exposures to the disease (through subsequent damage) may re-infect the target normally. This initial stage of the magical disease may also be cured by *lesser restoration, remove curse,* or *dispel magic.* Undead, constructs, elementals, and oozes are immune to the *wild thrall* disease, as are creatures ordinarily immune to magical diseases and creatures of a CR that exceeds the wildshadow's own by 4 or more.

If a target is reduced to 0 hit points while infected with the disease, the target does not fall unconscious or die, even if instant death would ordinarily apply. Instead the target recovers 4d8+2 hit points (or its maximum hit points, whichever is lower) but falls under the telepathic control of the wildshadow who caused the disease. The target retains all stats and abilities, but its personality becomes subdued, almost blank. If a PC, the character becomes an NPC under the wildshadow's control until the thrall is broken. The thrall stage of the disease may be cured by a successful *dispel magic* (DC 17), or by *greater restoration.* When the *wild thrall* is cured, the target immediately makes a DC 17 Constitution save, taking 4d8+2 points of necrotic damage on a failed save, or half as much damage on a successful one, as the departing magical disease takes back the health that it gave. Curing the disease with a *heal* or *wish* spell avoids this damage.

The wildshadow can control up to four thralls (enthralled targets) at a time. If the wildshadow gains a fifth thrall, the thrall with the highest CR is immediately freed of the wildshadow's control, but takes damage as described above. The disease must still be cured normally.

If the wildshadow dies, any thralls are freed of the *wild thrall* but immediately suffer damage as above. Again, the disease must still be cured normally.

ECOLOGY
Environment any forest
Organization with 1d4 thralls (any monsters or NPCs under the wildshadow's Wild Thrall power)

A wildshadow is an evil fey creature, born, some say, of the darkest desires that whisper between trees at the hearts of the deepest forests. Others claim they are some vile crossbreed between a pixie and a fiend. Wildshadows enjoy the pain of other intelligent beings and seek it out as a pleasant hobby, but they can be protective or even benevolent toward simple animals, vermin, and plants.

To maximize the effectiveness of their *wild thrall,* wildshadows sometimes kill less powerful thralls in their control, in order to make room for control of a more powerful enthralled target. They also favor thralls with healing abilities.

A wildshadow tends to be beautiful in an eerie way, extremely thin, deathly greyish or pale of skin, with inky black hair and blood red eyes.

They have black moth wings with dark red markings like terrible eldritch symbols inked in blood. Though often charming and personable when you can see them, some of the most evil wildshadows exude a subtle, chilling aura while invisible, especially at night, often only discernible to those with mystical ability.

Zemicek, Greater Ogre Mage (Oni)

XP 7200 (CR 11)
LE Large giant
Init +0

DEFENSE
AC 17 (skin armor and natural armor)
HP 178 (17d10+85)
Save Dex +4, Con +9, Wis +5, Cha +9
Resist fire
Immune poison

OFFENSE
Speed 30ft, fly 30ft
Multiattack Zemicek attacks four times, with either his claws or his glaive
Melee glaive (+10, reach 10 ft., 2d10+6 slashing or 1d10+6 slashing in Small or Medium form), claw (+10, reach 5 ft., 1d8+6, true form only)

STATISTICS
Str 22 (+6), **Dex** 11 (+0), **Con** 20 (+5),
Int 15 (+2), **Wis** 13 (+1), **Cha** 20 (+5)
Languages Common, Giant, Infernal
Skills Arcana +6, Deception +9, Perception +5
Senses darkvision 120ft, poor depth perception

TRAITS
Innate spells Zemicek can cast the following innate spells, using Charisma as his spellcasting ability (attack +9, DC 17). Zemicek doesn't need material components to cast these spells.
at will—*darkness, fire bolt, invisibility*
1/day—*charm person, cone of cold, gaseous form, misty step, sleep*
Magic attacks Zemicek's natural and weapon attacks are considered magical.
Regeneration Zemicek regains 10 hit points at the start of his turn if he has any hit points remaining.
Change shape Zemicek can magically polymorph into a humanoid of up to Medium size, into a Large giant, or back into its true form. (Other than size, statistics are the same regardless.) His glaive transforms with him, and both revert to true form and size upon his death.
Fiendish adaptation (recharge 5–6) When Zemicek is hit by an attack that would do cold, lightning, or psychic damage, he can gain resistance to that attack type (and thus suffer half damage from the attack). This resistance lasts the rest of the combat, and he can't change the damage type during that time until and unless this power recharges (5 or 6).
Poor Depth Perception Zemicek has tactical disadvantage on any attack roll against a target more than 30ft

---

GEAR
skin armor (armor constructed from humanoid and giant "leather"), glaive, *fetish necklace.*

After the Wilderlands Clan War, the house of Zemicek was all but in ruins. Although the wizened oni survived the hostilities, it was for that

The Fetish Necklace of Zemicek

Unique Wondrous Item

The *fetish necklace of Zemicek* is a grisly little thing: a necklace made of bound twine with over a dozen severed tongues dangling from it. The *fetish necklace* is a unique, non-artifact wondrous item that occupies the neck/amulet slot, though it can be worn or carried anywhere on one's person and still bestow the same effects. It has three chief properties:

• While worn or carried, it provides a +1 natural armor bonus to the bearer's AC.

• If the bearer adds a tongue to the *fetish necklace*, the former owner of that tongue is rendered permanently silent, even beyond death, until and unless the tongue is removed or the *fetish necklace* is destroyed. In the meantime, attempts to speak with or otherwise commune with the accursed soul are doomed to fail.

• Carrying the necklace is not inherently evil, but it is insidiously corruptive. Every time the bearer lays the killing blow (or spell, etc.) on a sentient enemy with a tongue (e.g., a human), the bearer must make a DC 14 Wis save. Failure creates a compulsion to cut out the fallen enemy's tongue and add it to the *fetish necklace*. (Assume room for about 3 dozen tongues, but if it runs out of room, the power of the item is such that the bearer feels compelled to shed old or useless tongues to make room for new ones.) This compulsion isn't so strong that it can't be overcome by intervention from others, but absent that, the bearer will do everything possible to add to the item's grim collection.

very reason that his star fell from the firmament of fortune, as he had actively counseled both his people and the various ogre tribes of the mountains *against* the margoyle-led scheme; and when the others came to him, seeking the support and the arms of his tribe, he refused them. When the lands of men went on to repel his cousins' invasion, as he foresaw they would, those who survived retreated to the mountains and castigated the house of Zemicek for failing to assist, for allowing this shameful defeat when it could and rightfully should have stood with its kin, as so many other ogre and ogrillon tribes had. Collectively, the others cast him and his people out, taking over his lands and homes as punishment for betraying shared blood, and sending the house of Zemicek into Forlorn exile.

Directionless, Zemicek wandered the mountains for months, seeking answers to a purpose fulfilled but punished nonetheless, until at last he came to the northern marches of the Forlorn, a beautiful but stark land riven by deep canyons and honeycombed with dark, twisting caverns. It was in this place that Zemicek found both renewed purpose and a means to his own tragic end.

On a lonely Road, Map 1

1 square – 5 ft.

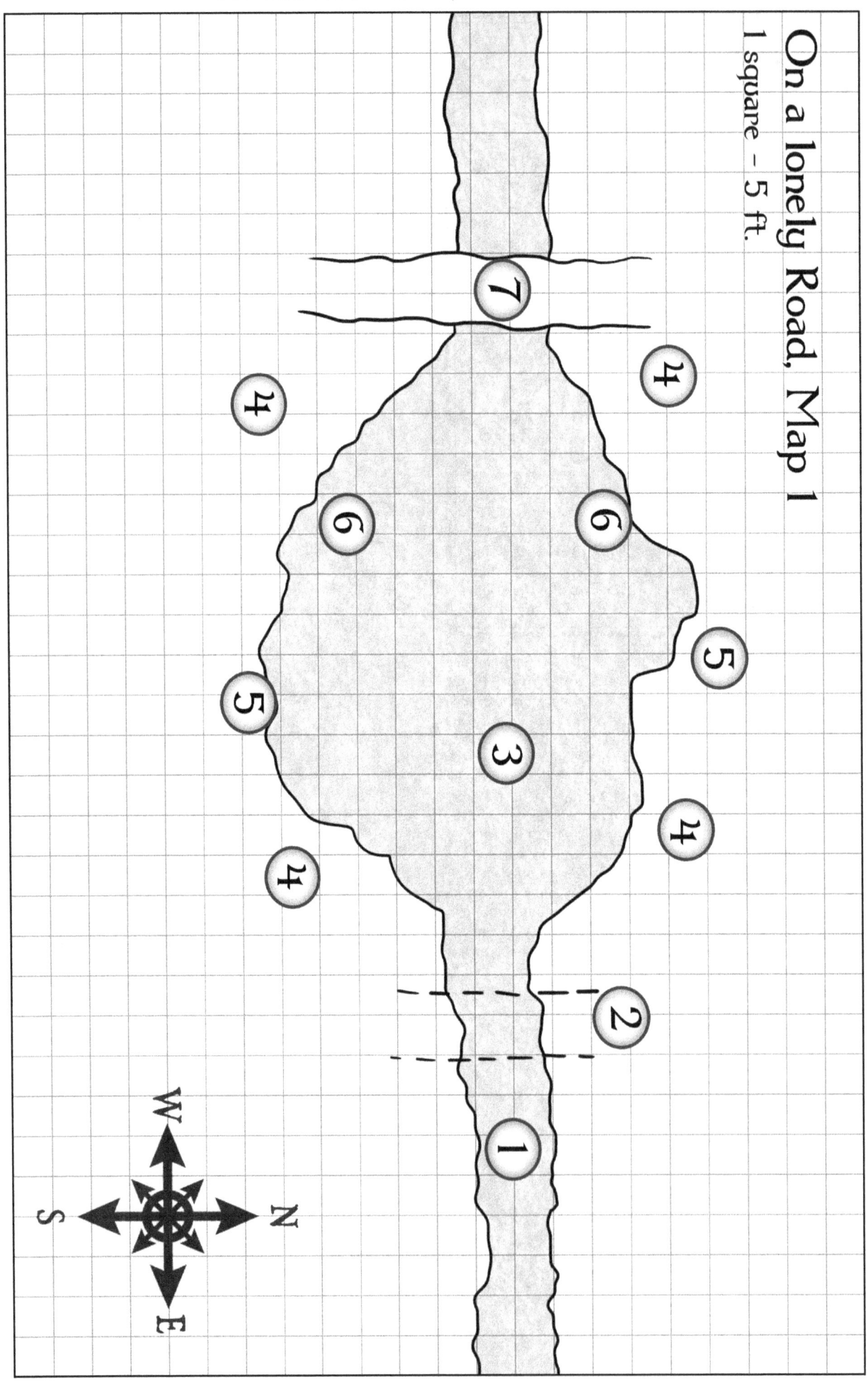

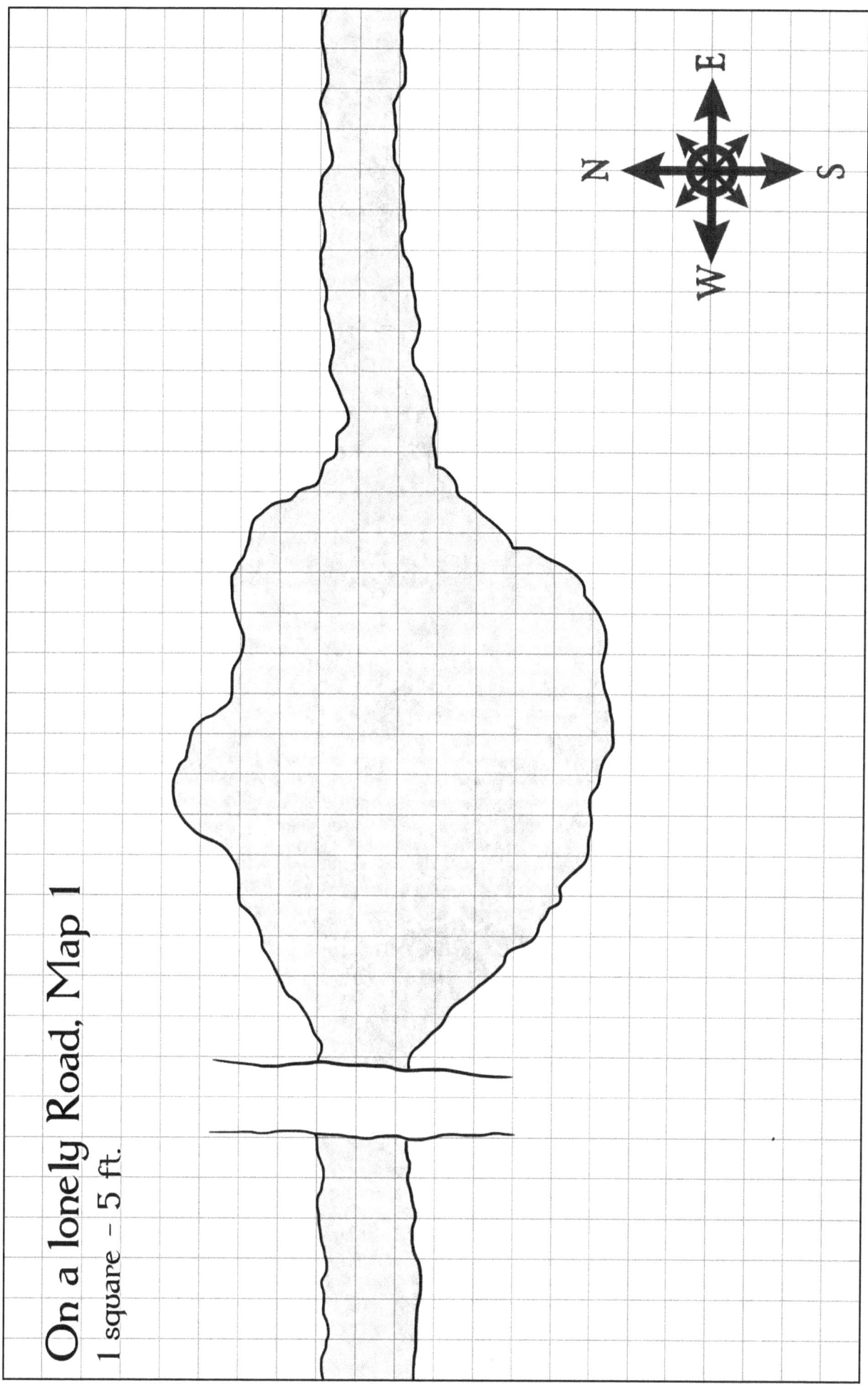

On a lonely Road, Map 1
1 square – 5 ft.

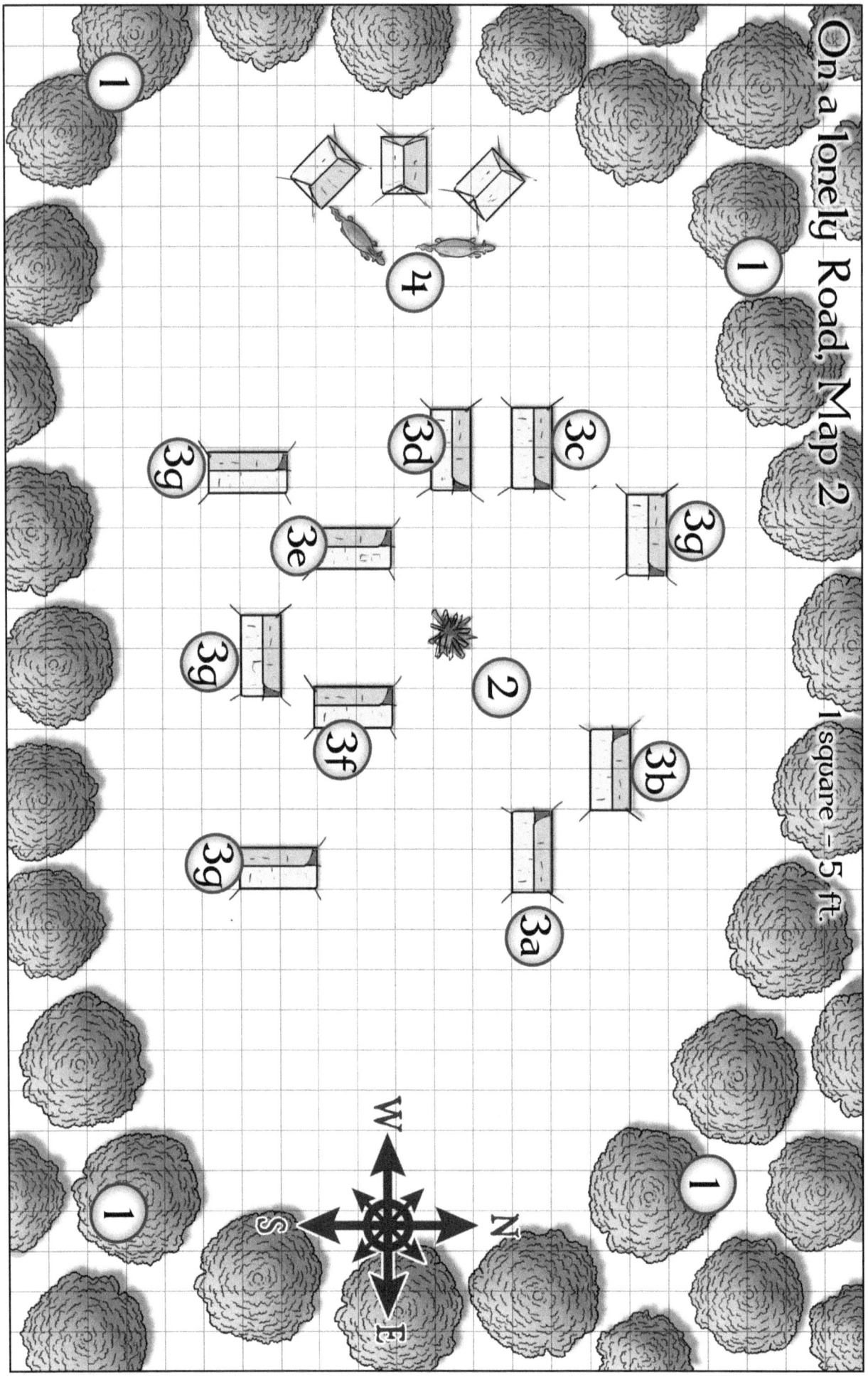

On a lonely Road, Map 2

1 square = 5 ft.

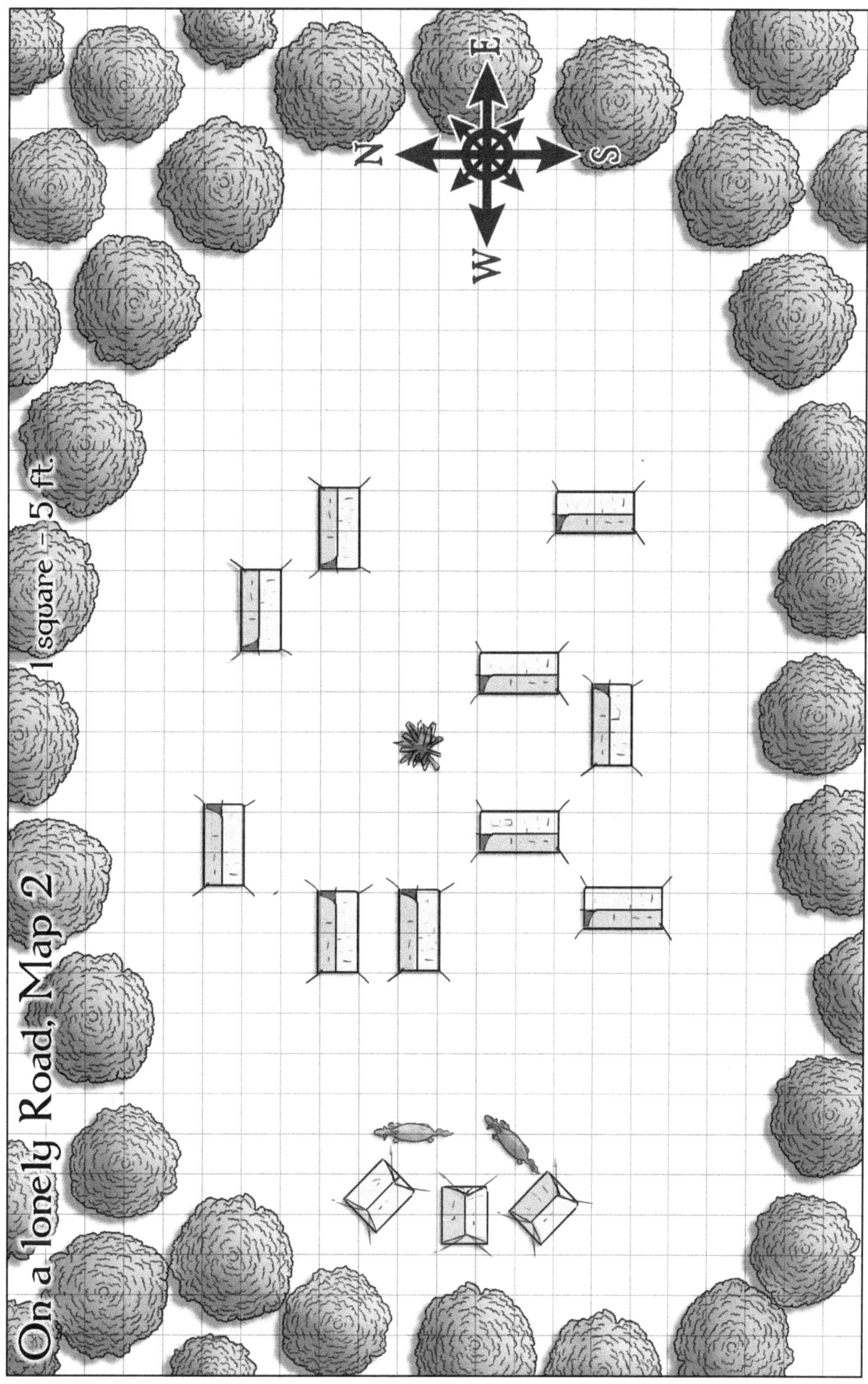

On a lonely Road, Map 2

1 square = 5 ft.

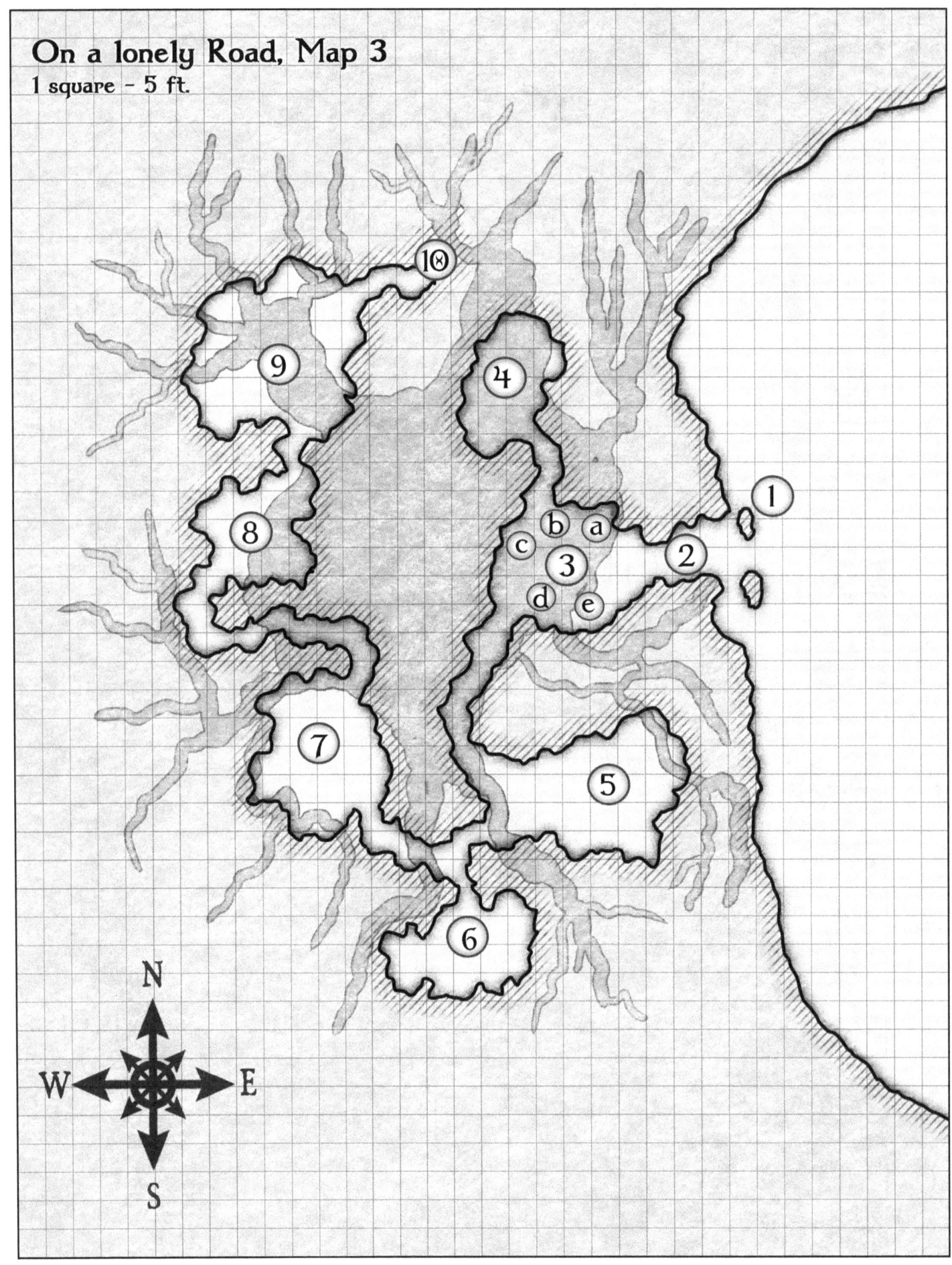

On a lonely Road, Map 3

1 square - 5 ft.

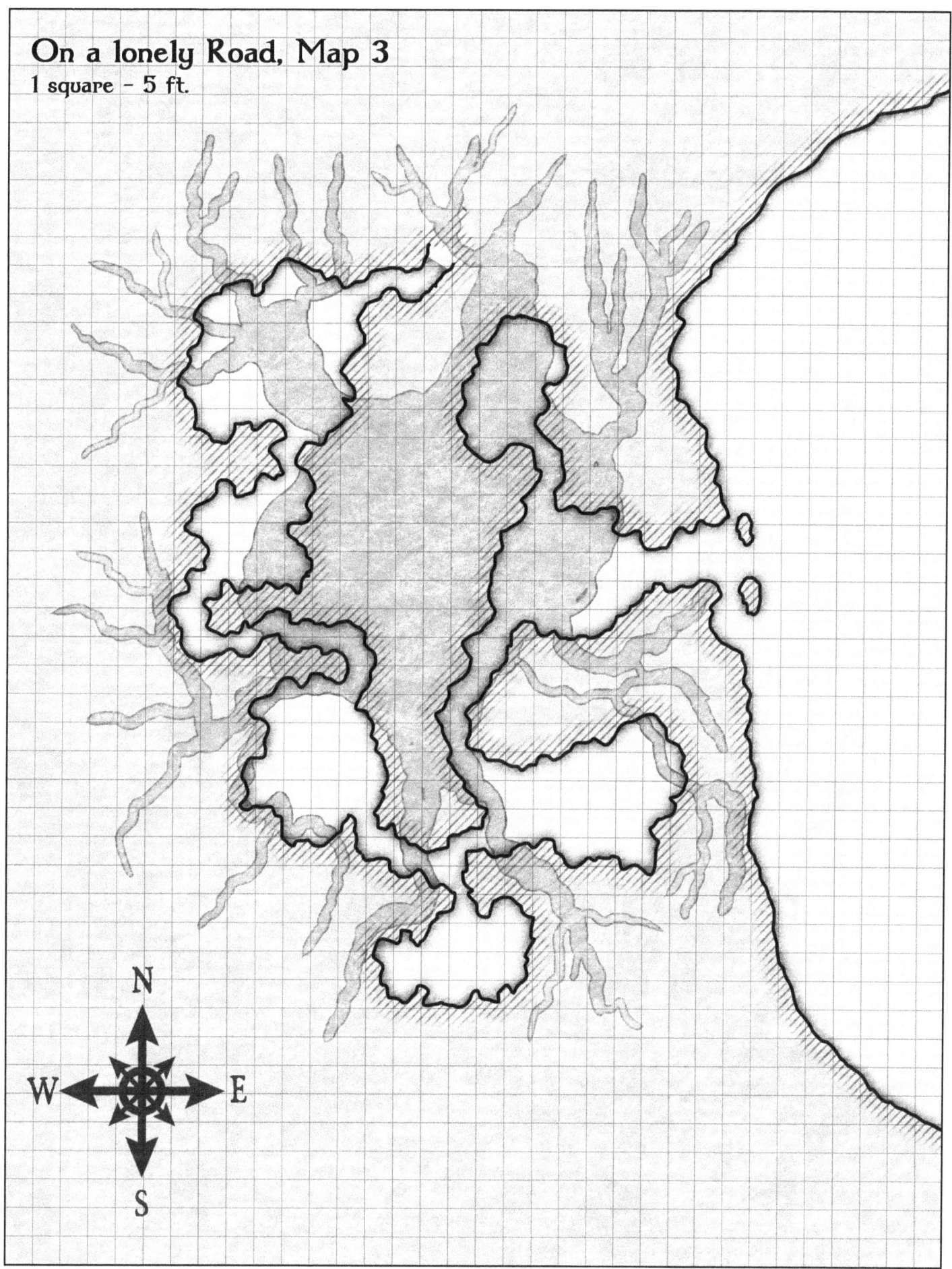

On a lonely Road, Map 3
1 square - 5 ft.

N
W E
S

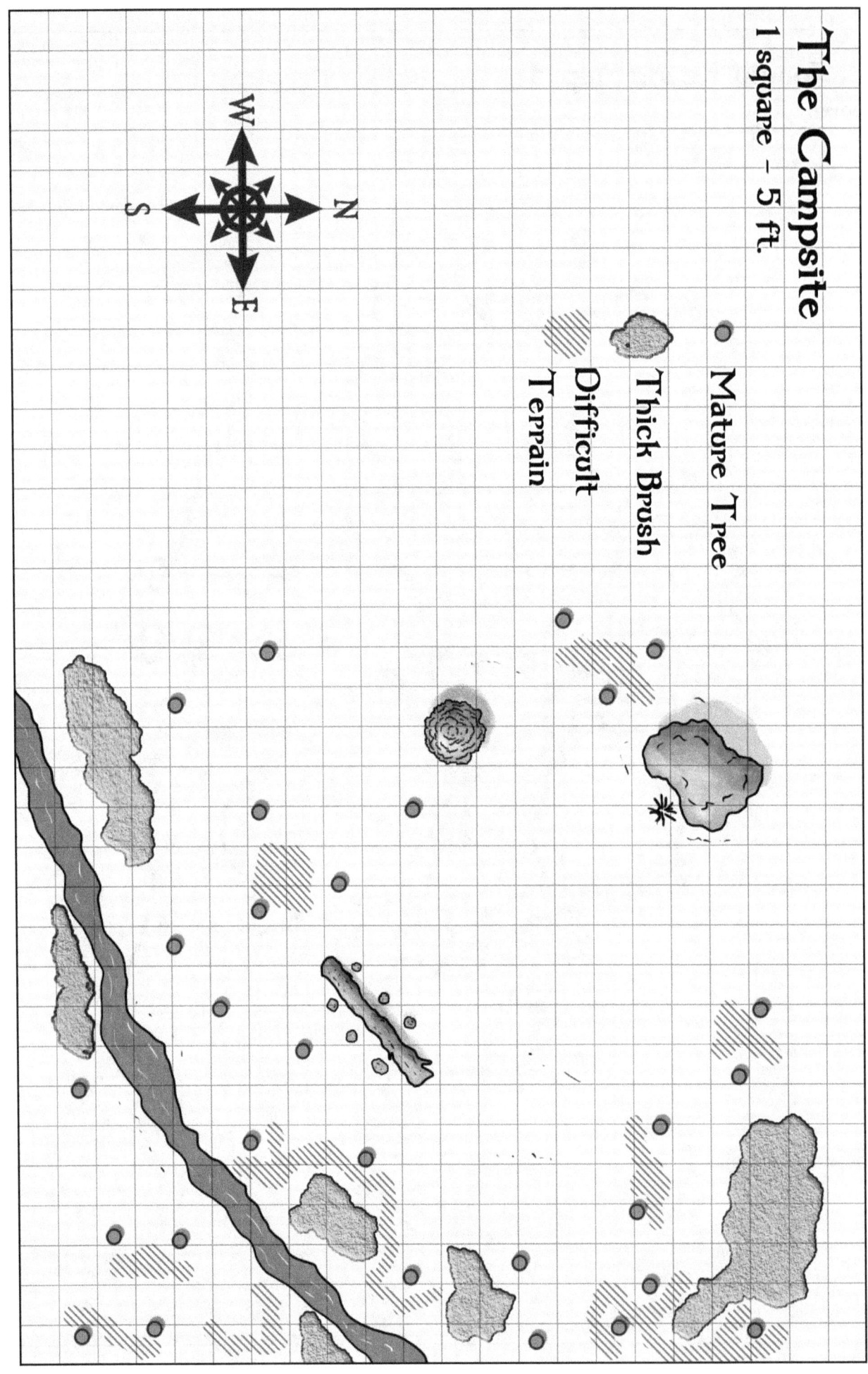

The Campsite
1 square – 5 ft.

- Mature Tree
- Thick Brush
- **Difficult Terrain**

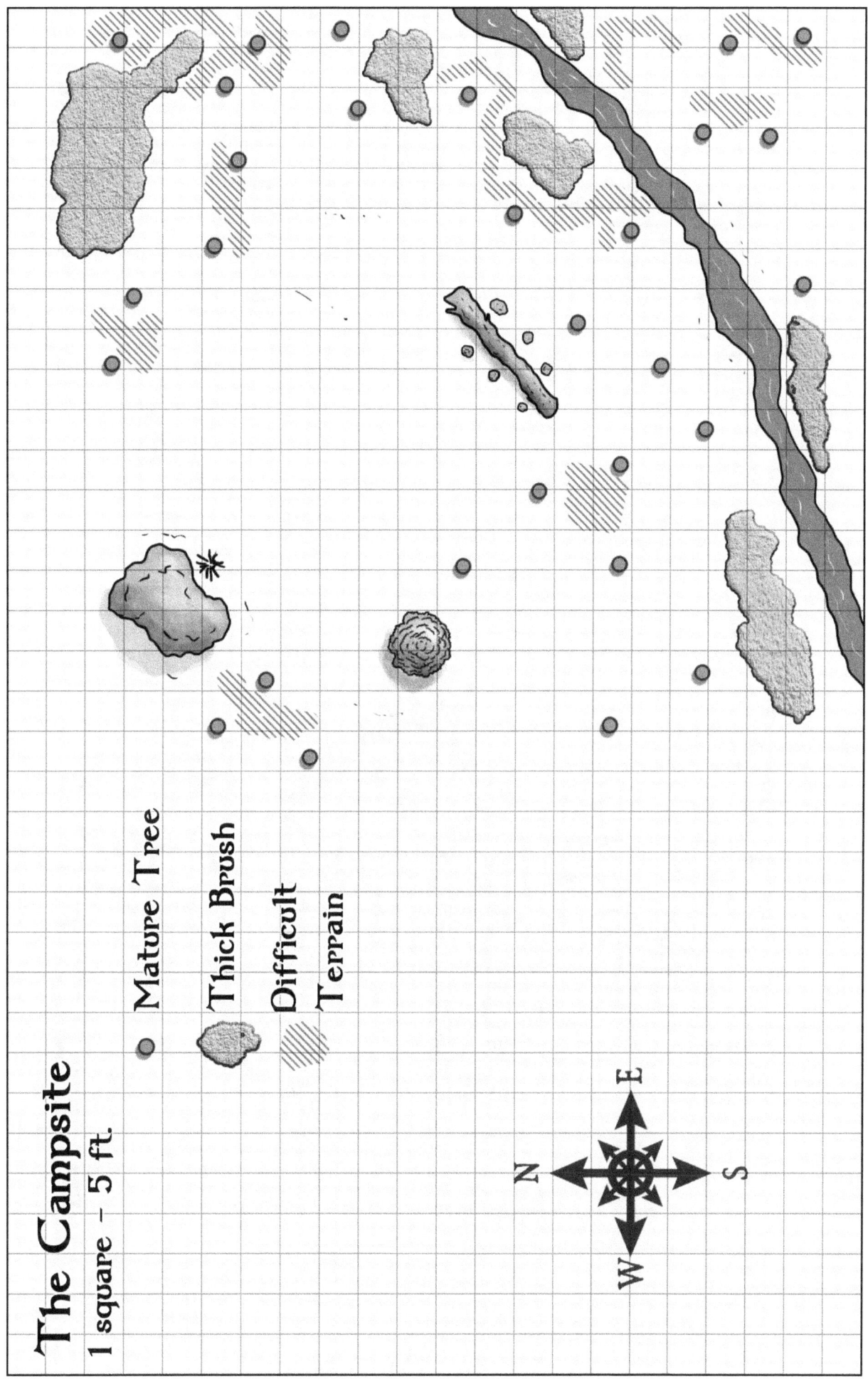

The Campsite
1 square – 5 ft.

● Mature Tree

Thick Brush

Difficult Terrain

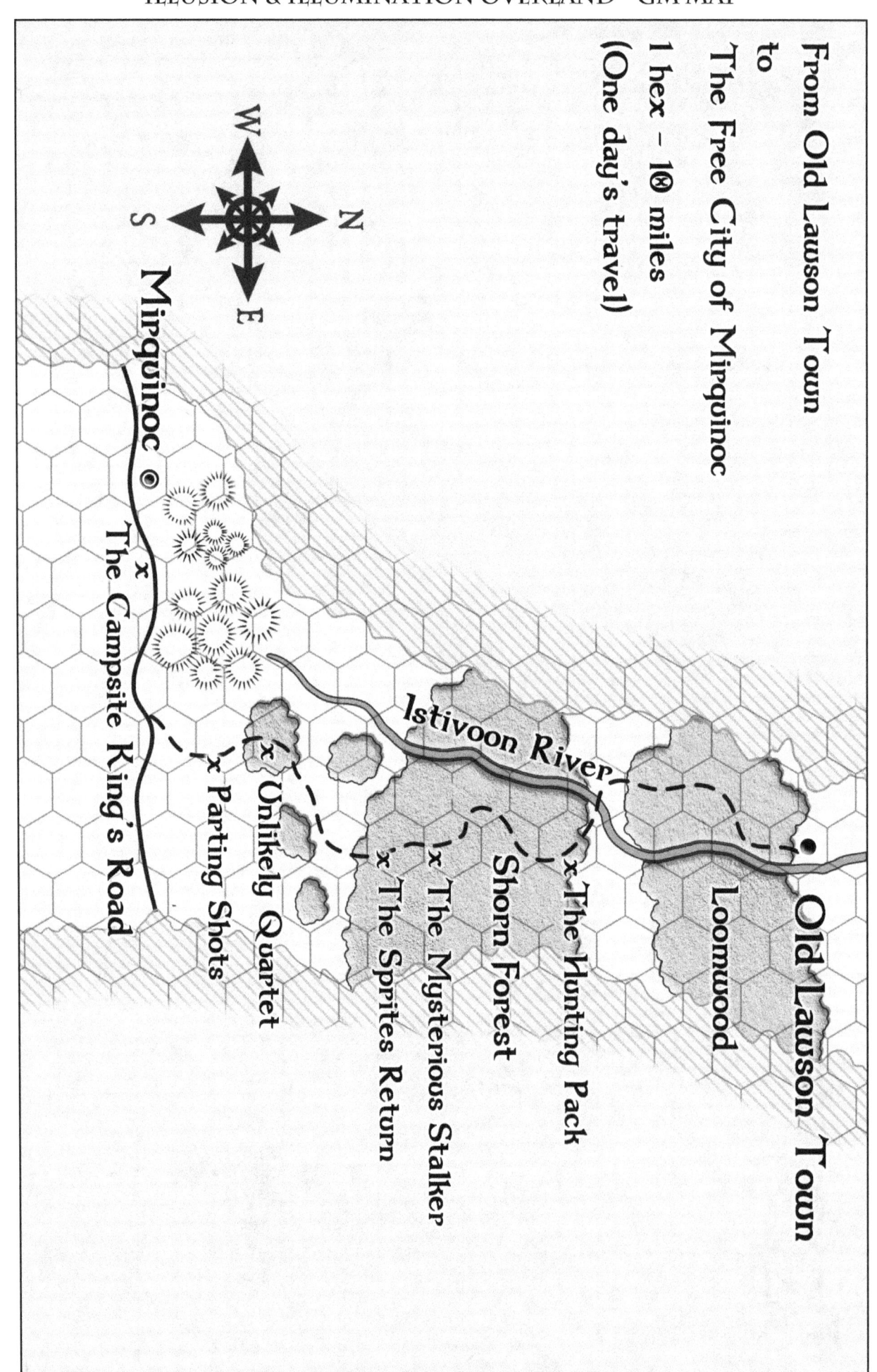

From Old Lawson Town
to
The Free City of Mirquinoc
1 hex – 10 miles
(One day's travel)

Mirquinoc

The Campsite King's Road

x Parting Shots

x Unlikely Quartet

x The Sprites Return

x The Mysterious Stalker

Shorn Forest

x The Hunting Pack

Istivoon River

Loomwood

Old Lawson Town

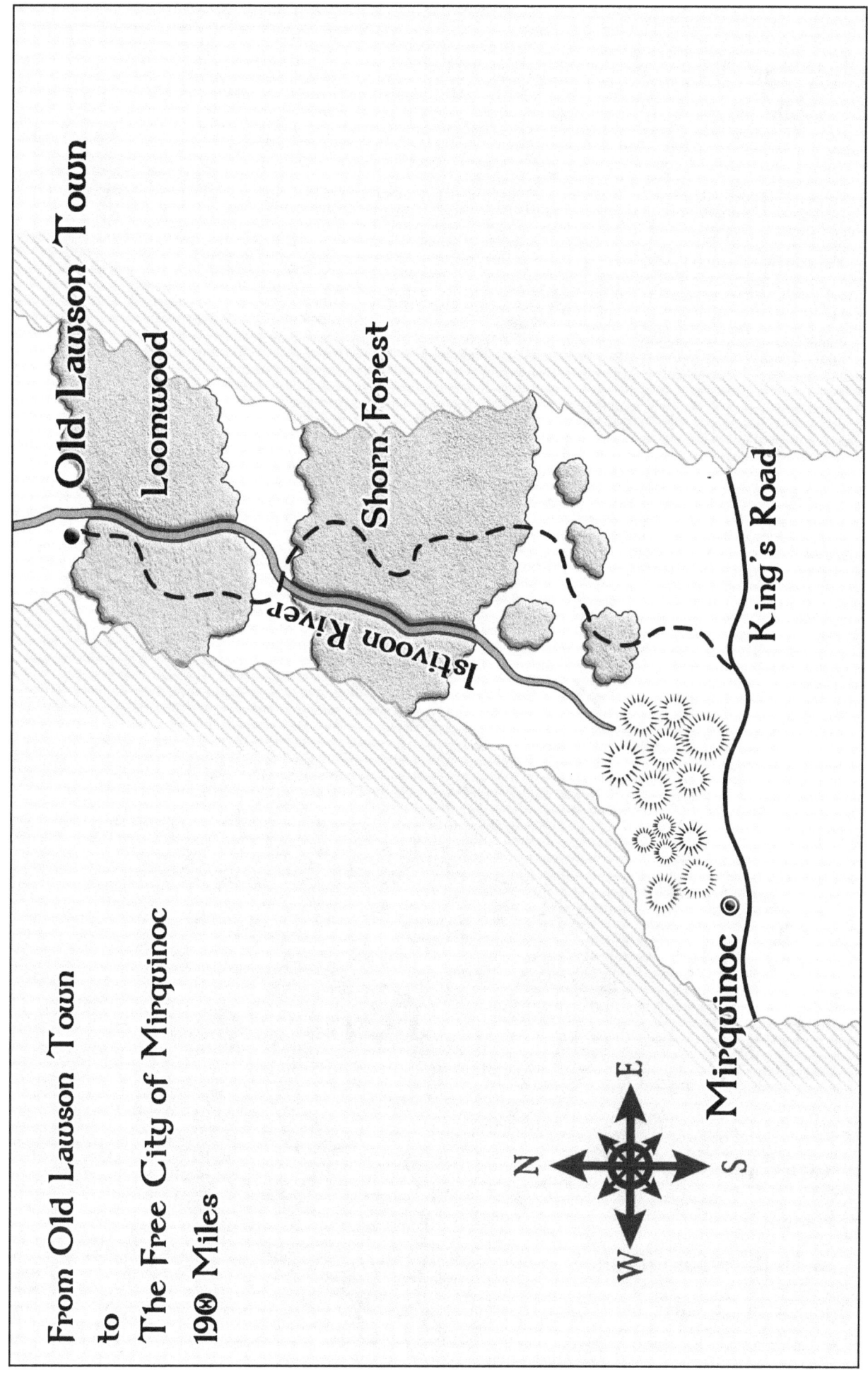

Old Lawson Town

Loomwood

Shorn Forest

King's Road

Istivoon River

From Old Lawson Town
to
The Free City of Mirquinoc
190 Miles

Mirquinoc

N
E
S
W

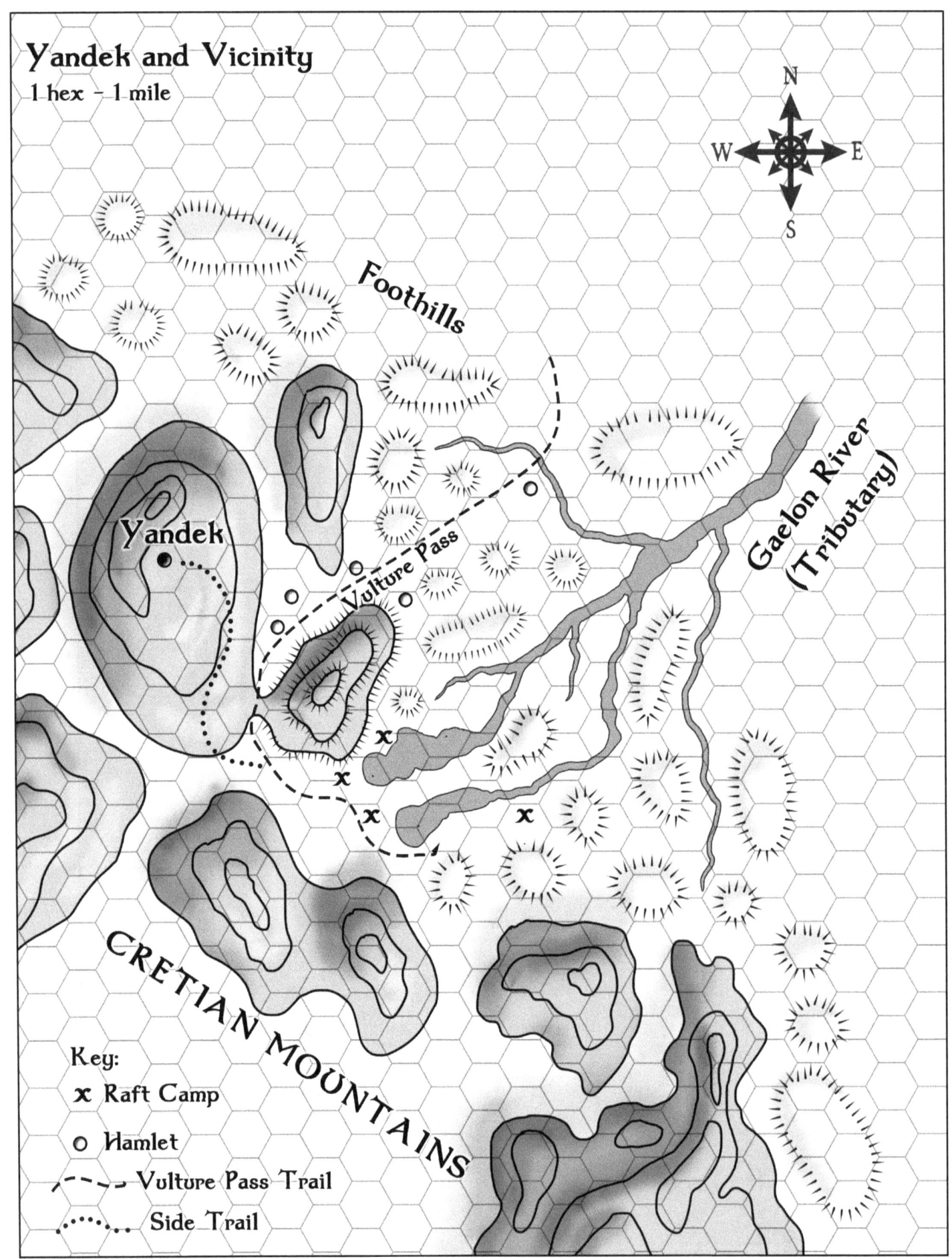

Yandek and Vicinity
1 hex ~ 1 mile

Foothills

Yandek

Vulture Pass

Gaelon River (Tributary)

CRETIAN MOUNTAINS

Key:
x Raft Camp
o Hamlet
- - - - Vulture Pass Trail
.... Side Trail

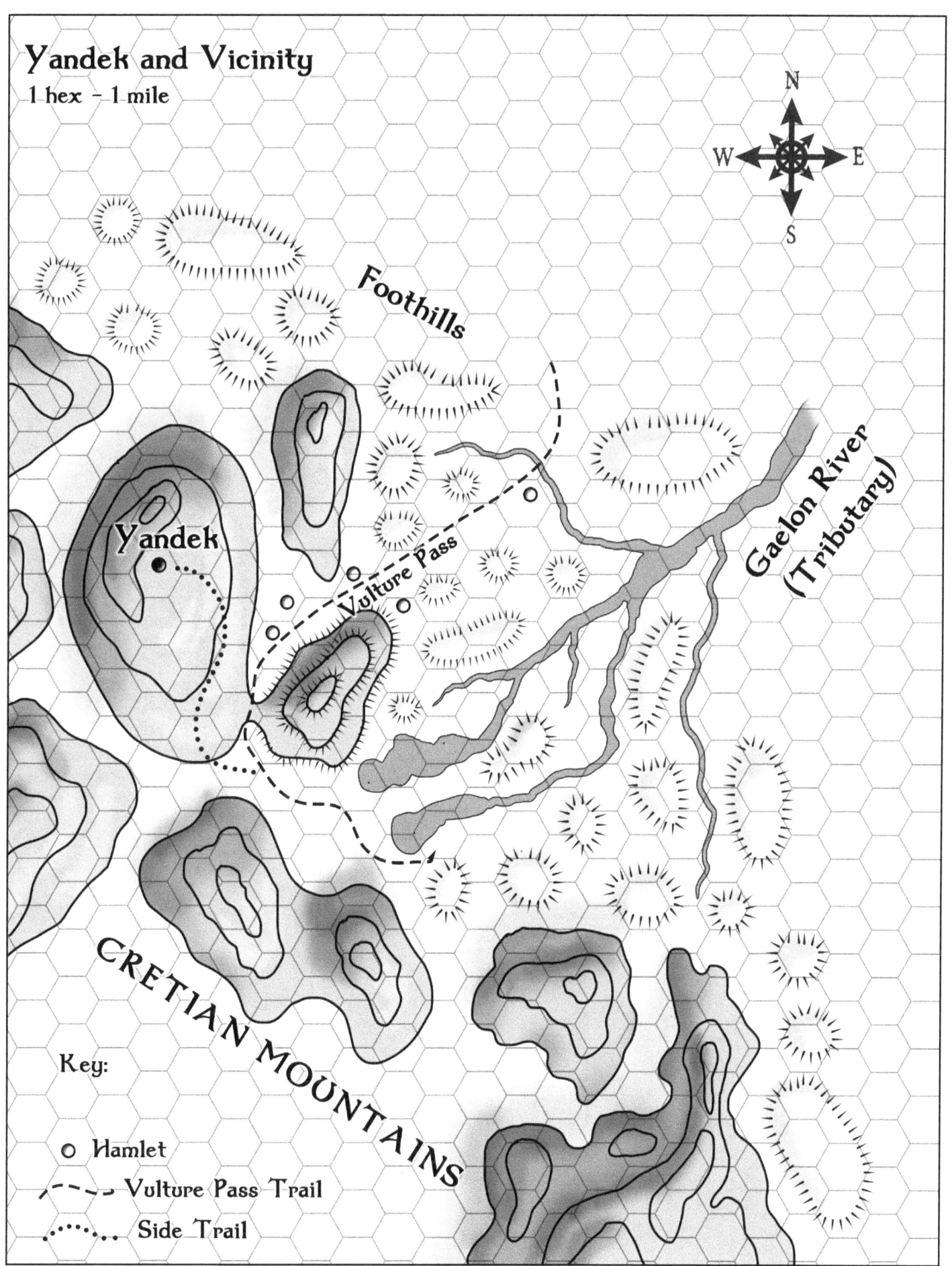

Yandek and Vicinity

1 hex – 1 mile

Foothills

Yandek

Vulture Pass

Gaelon River
(Tributary)

CRETIAN MOUNTAINS

Key:

o Hamlet

– – – Vulture Pass Trail

...... Side Trail

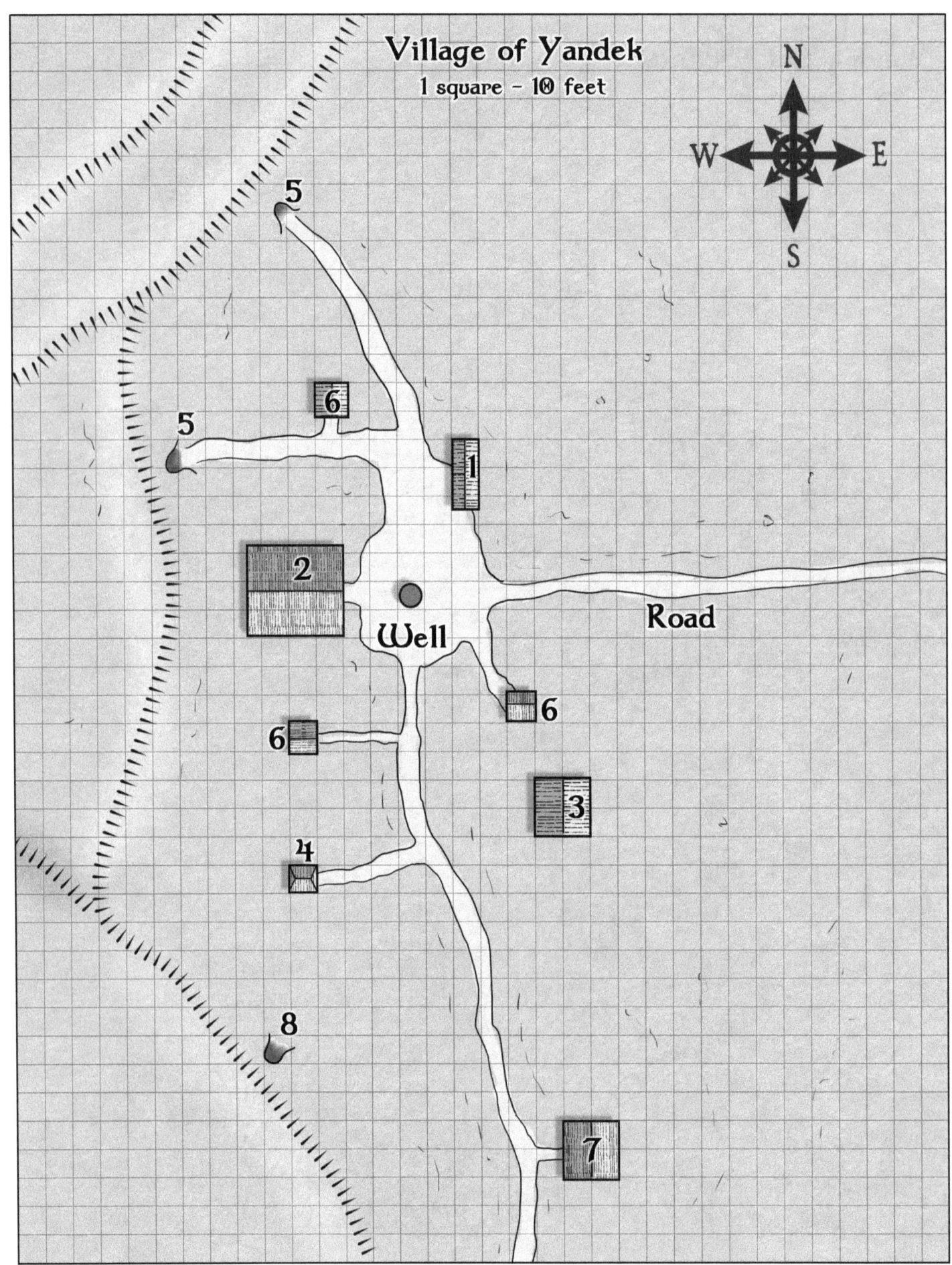

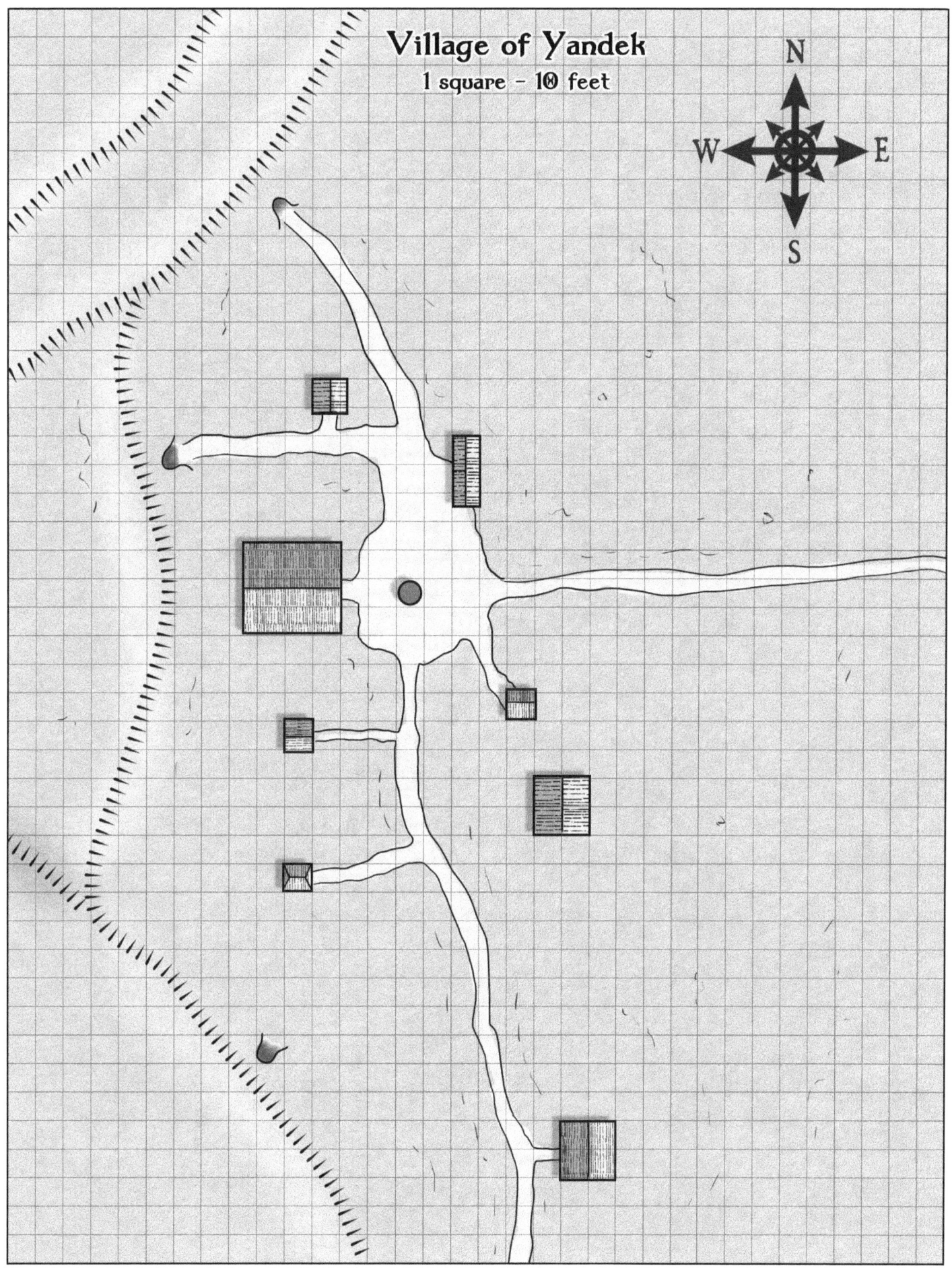

Village of Yandek
1 square - 10 feet

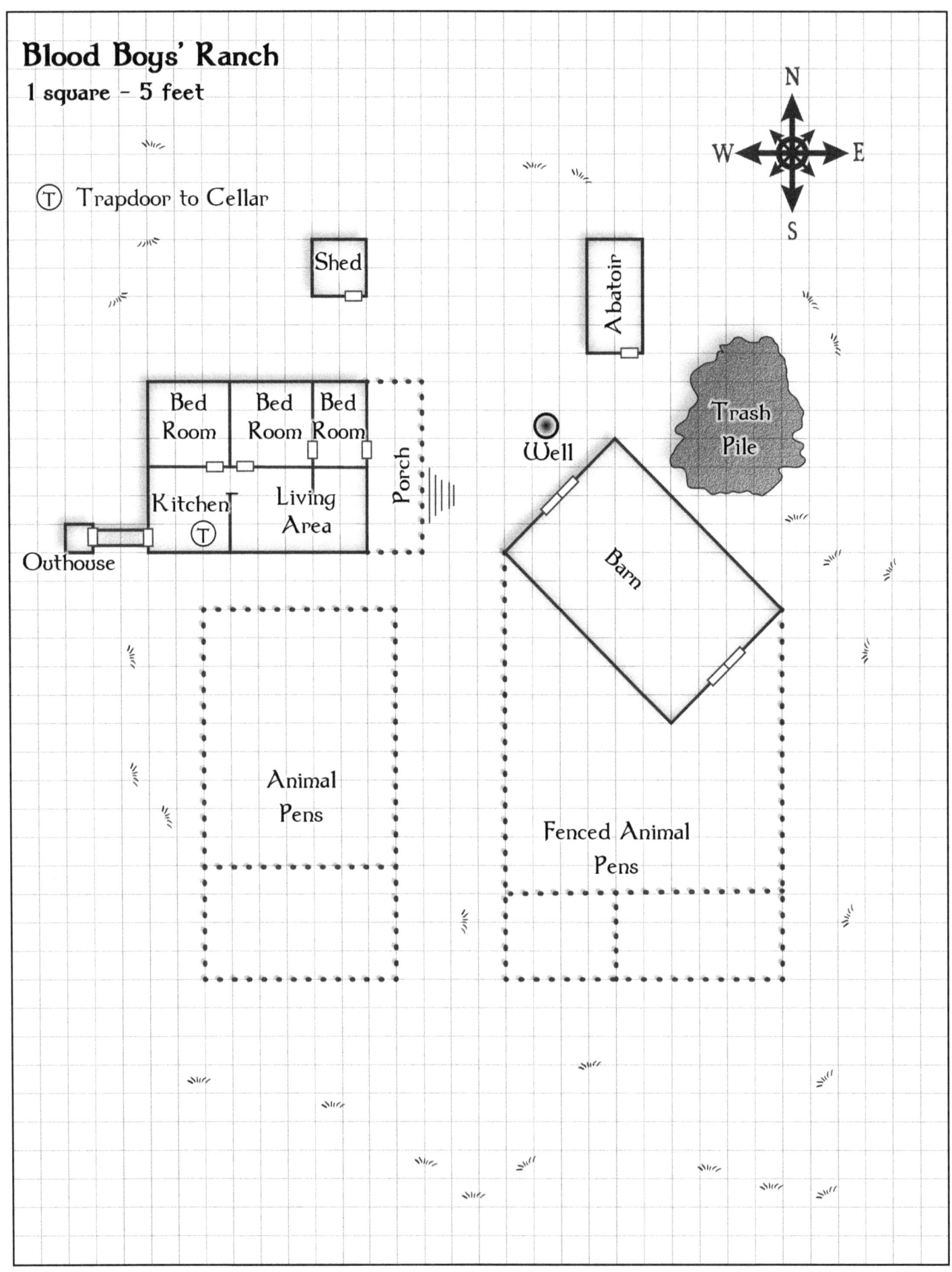

Blood Boys' Ranch

1 square – 5 feet

T Trapdoor to Cellar

Shed

Abatoir

Trash Pile

Bed Room

Bed Room

Bed Room

Porch

Well

Kitchen

Living Area

Outhouse

Barn

Animal Pens

Fenced Animal Pens

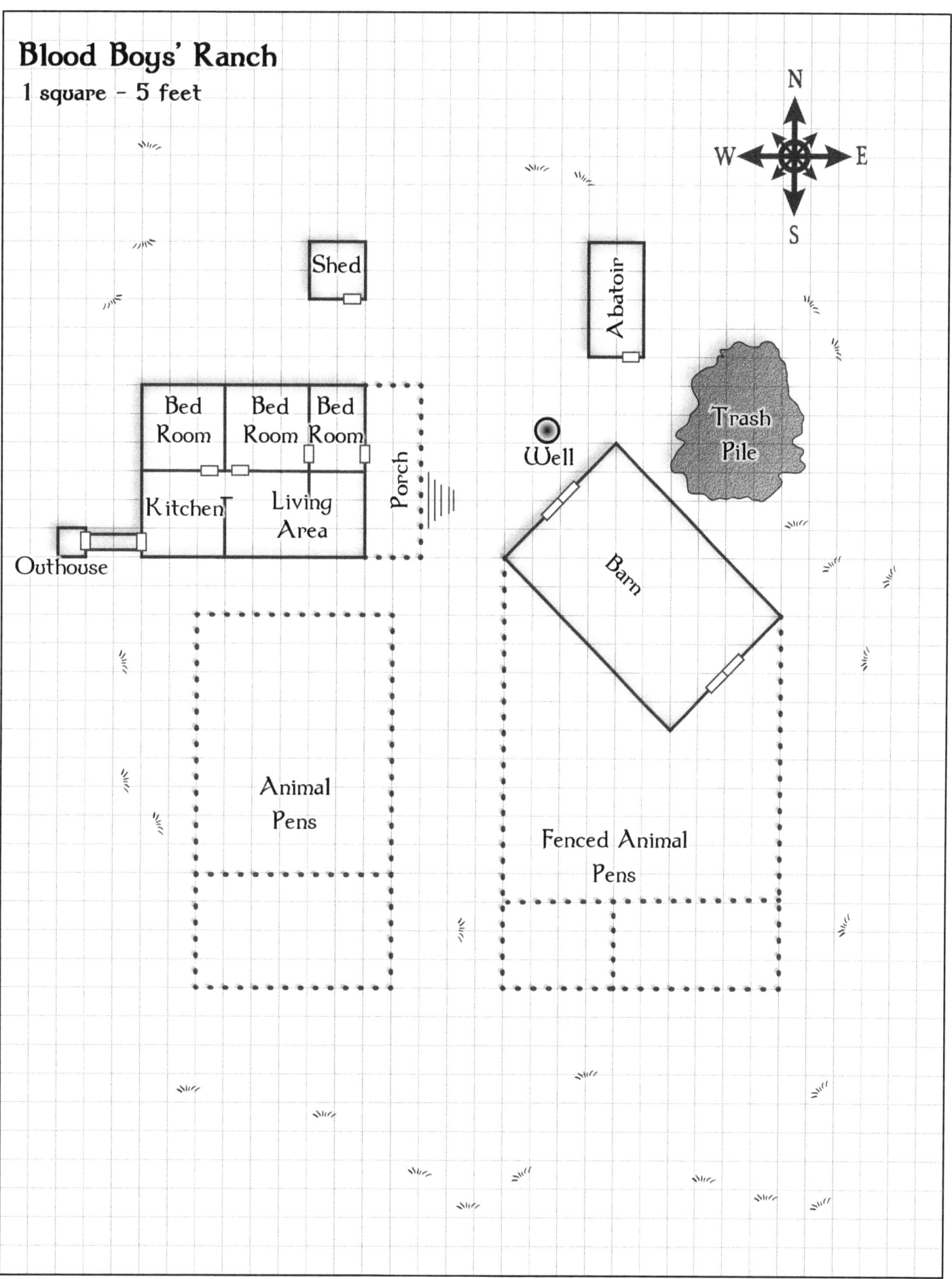

Blood Boys' Ranch
1 square - 5 feet

The Mines

1 square – 10 feet

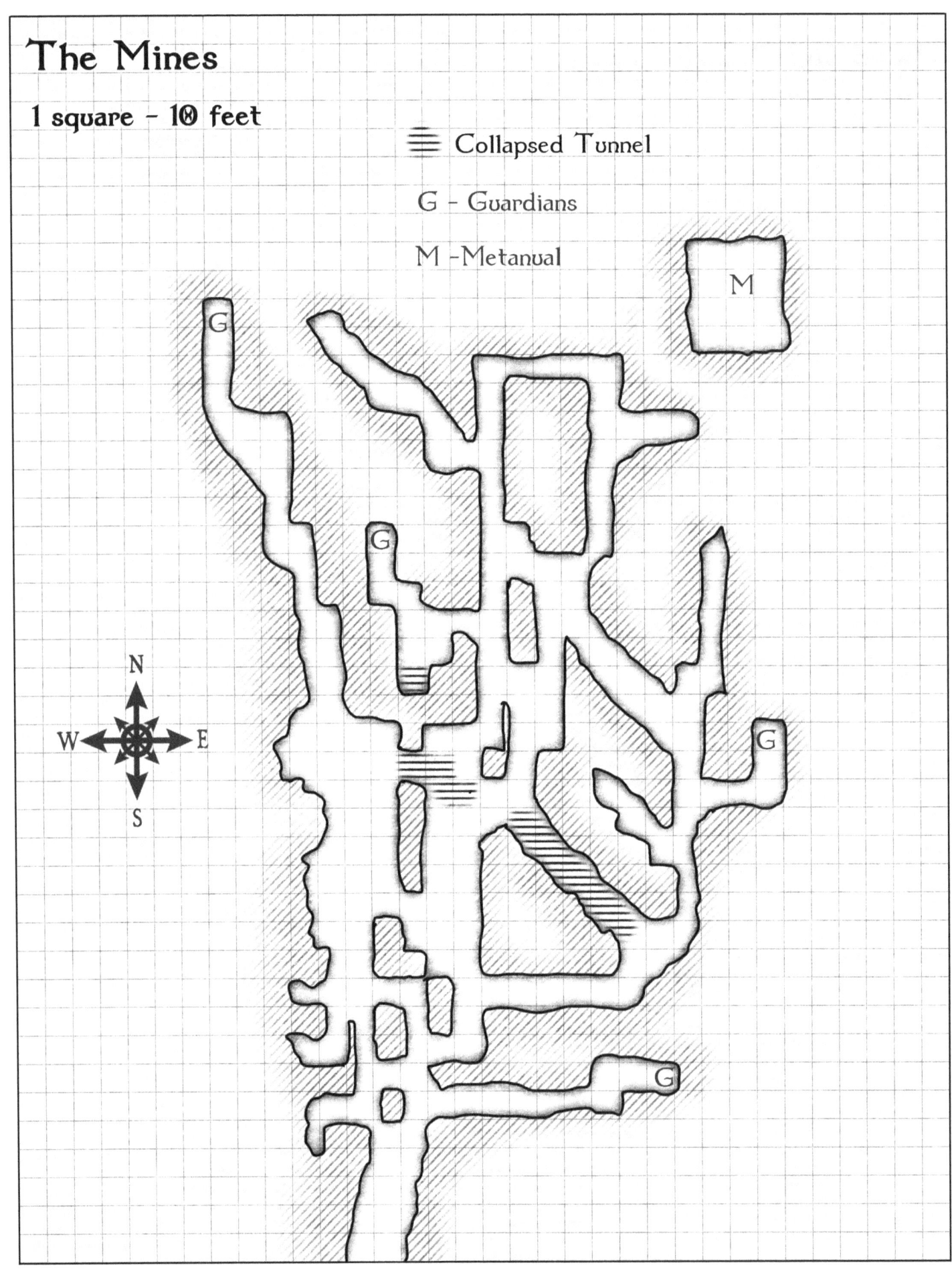

≡ Collapsed Tunnel

G – Guardians

M – Metanual

The Mines

1 square - 10 feet

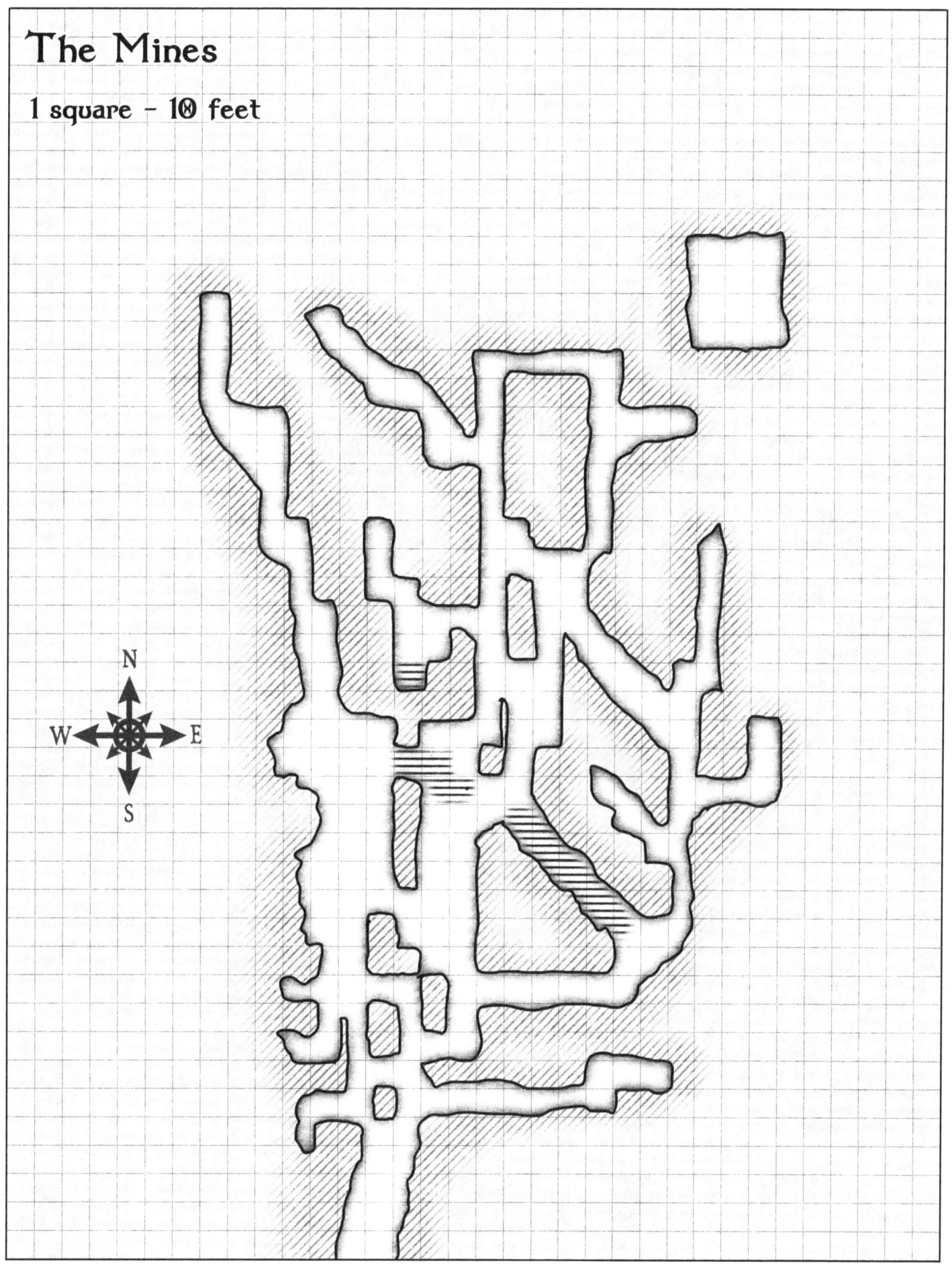

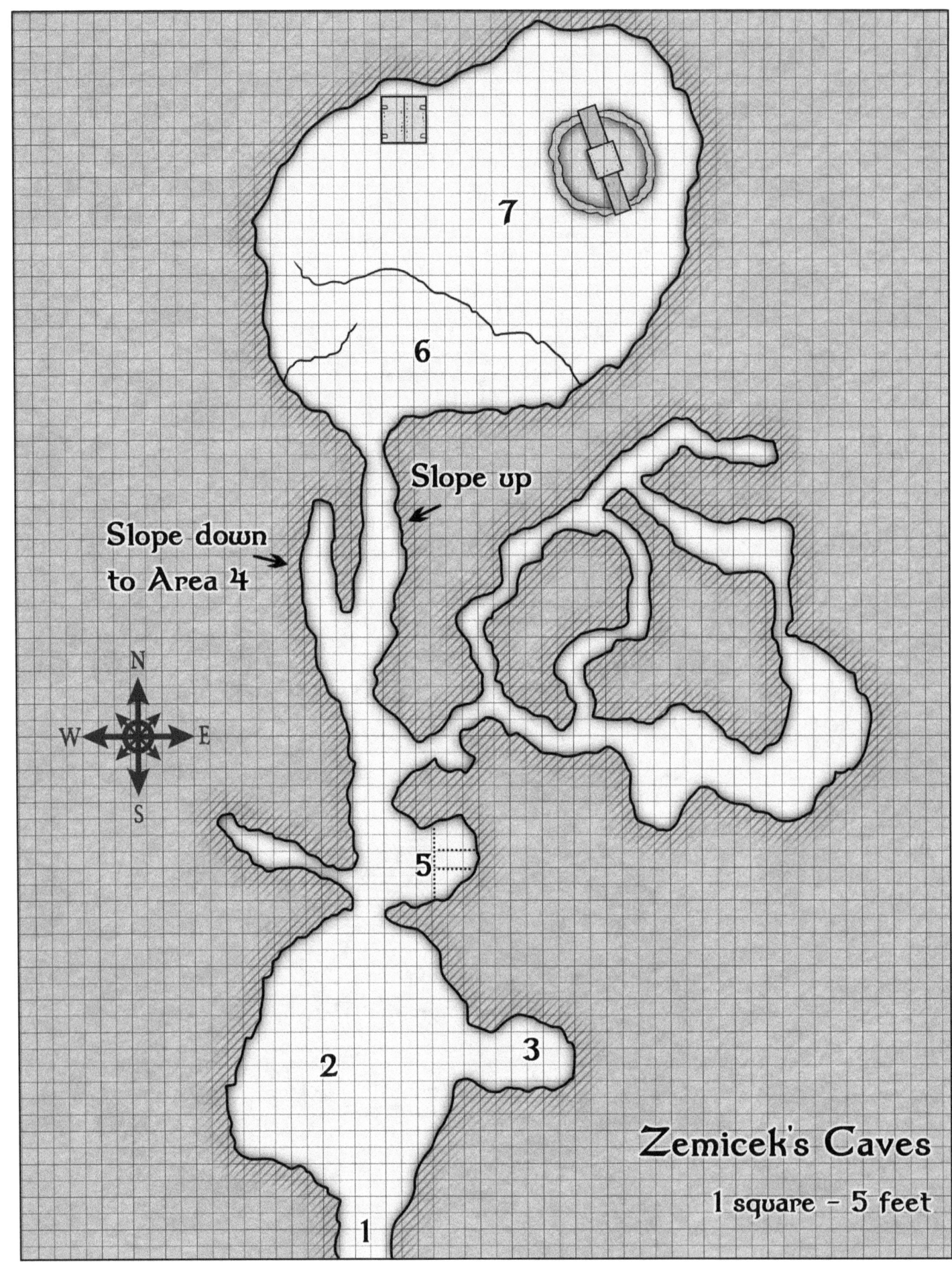

Slope up

Slope down
to Area 4

7

6

5

2

3

1

Zemicek's Caves

1 square – 5 feet

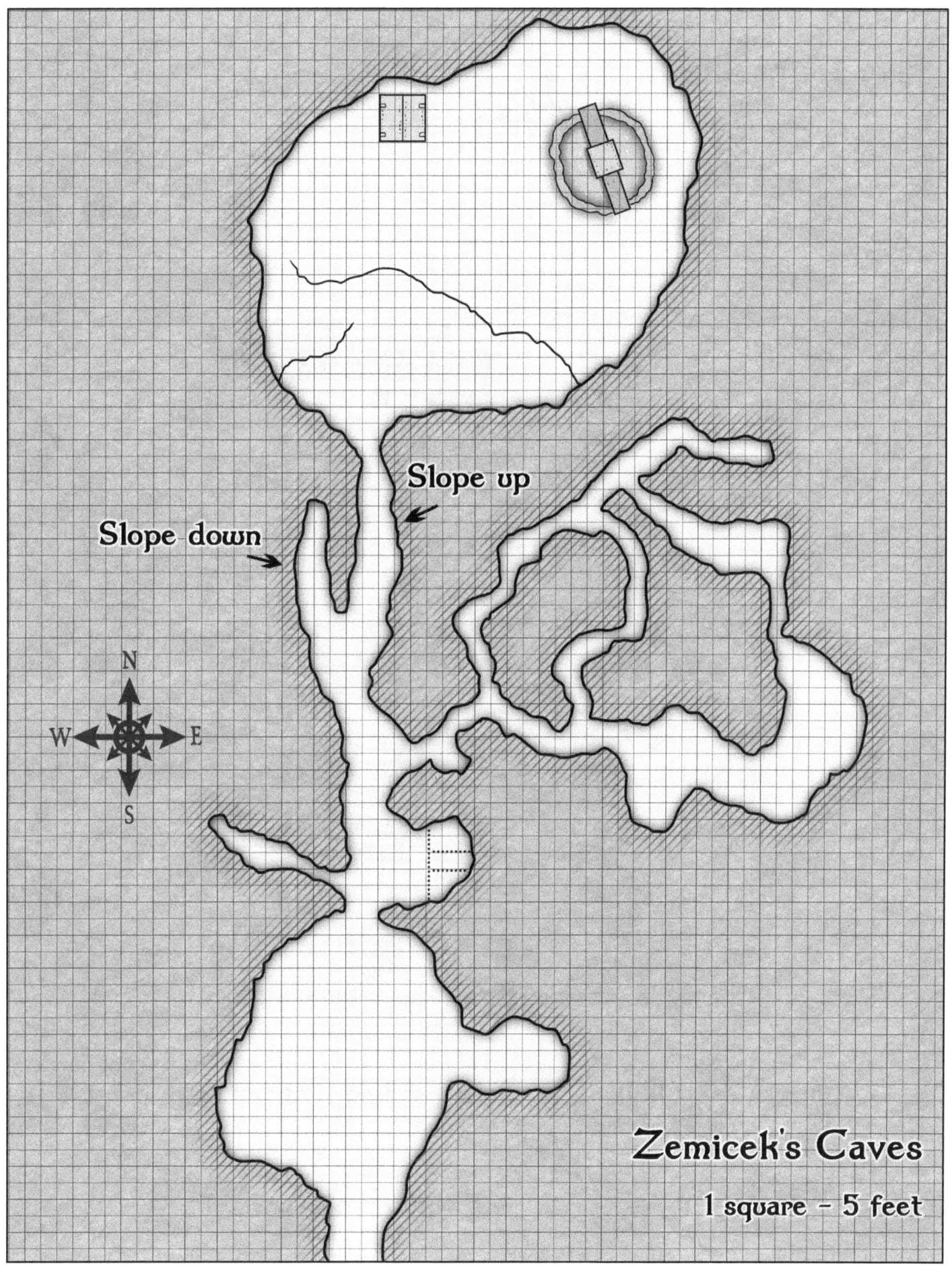

Slope up

Slope down

N
W E
S

Zemicek's Caves

1 square - 5 feet

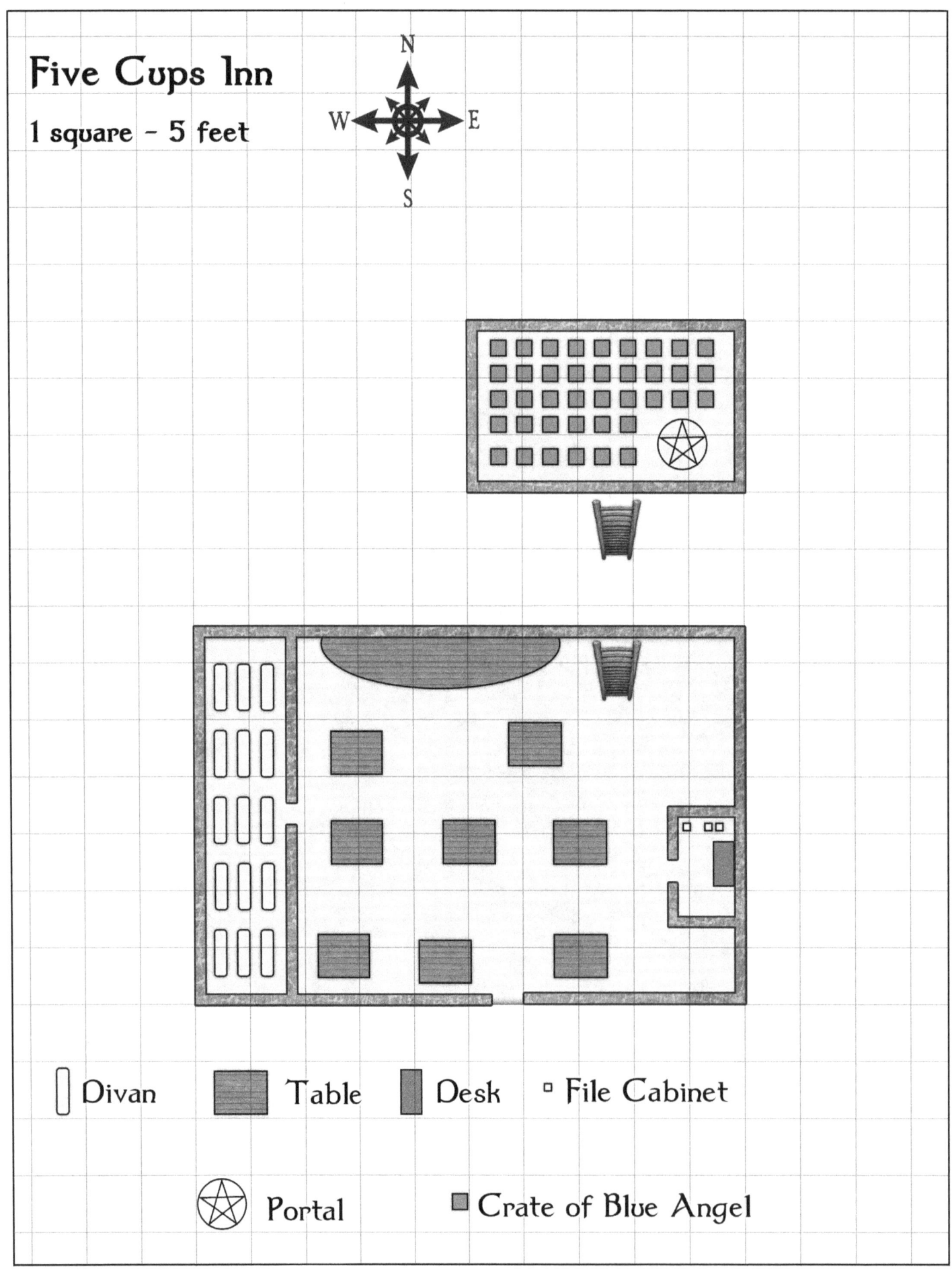

Five Cups Inn

1 square - 5 feet

| Divan | Table | Desk | □ File Cabinet |

Portal | Crate of Blue Angel

Five Cups Inn

1 square - 5 feet

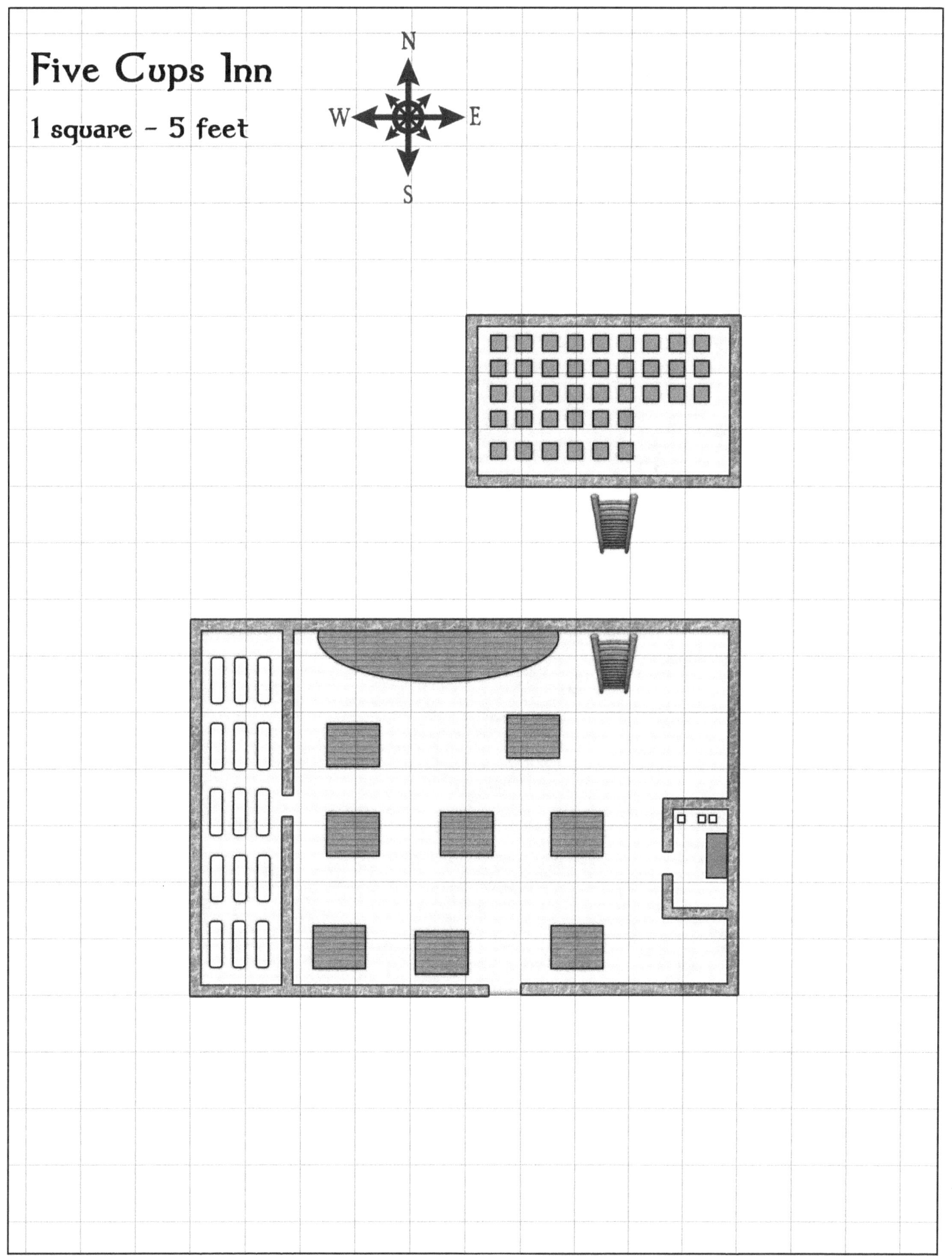

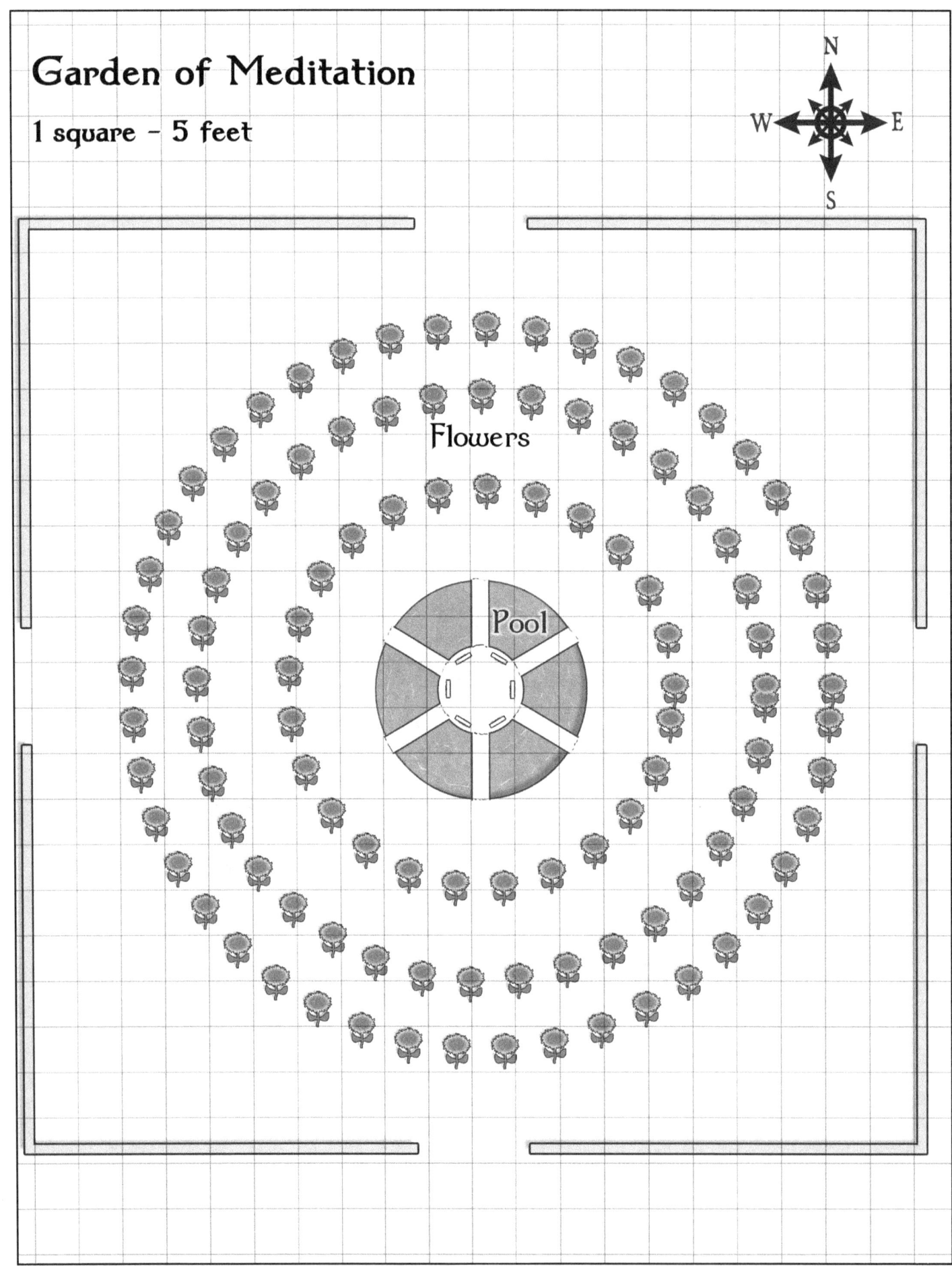

Garden of Meditation

1 square - 5 feet

Flowers

Pool

Garden of Meditation

1 square – 5 feet

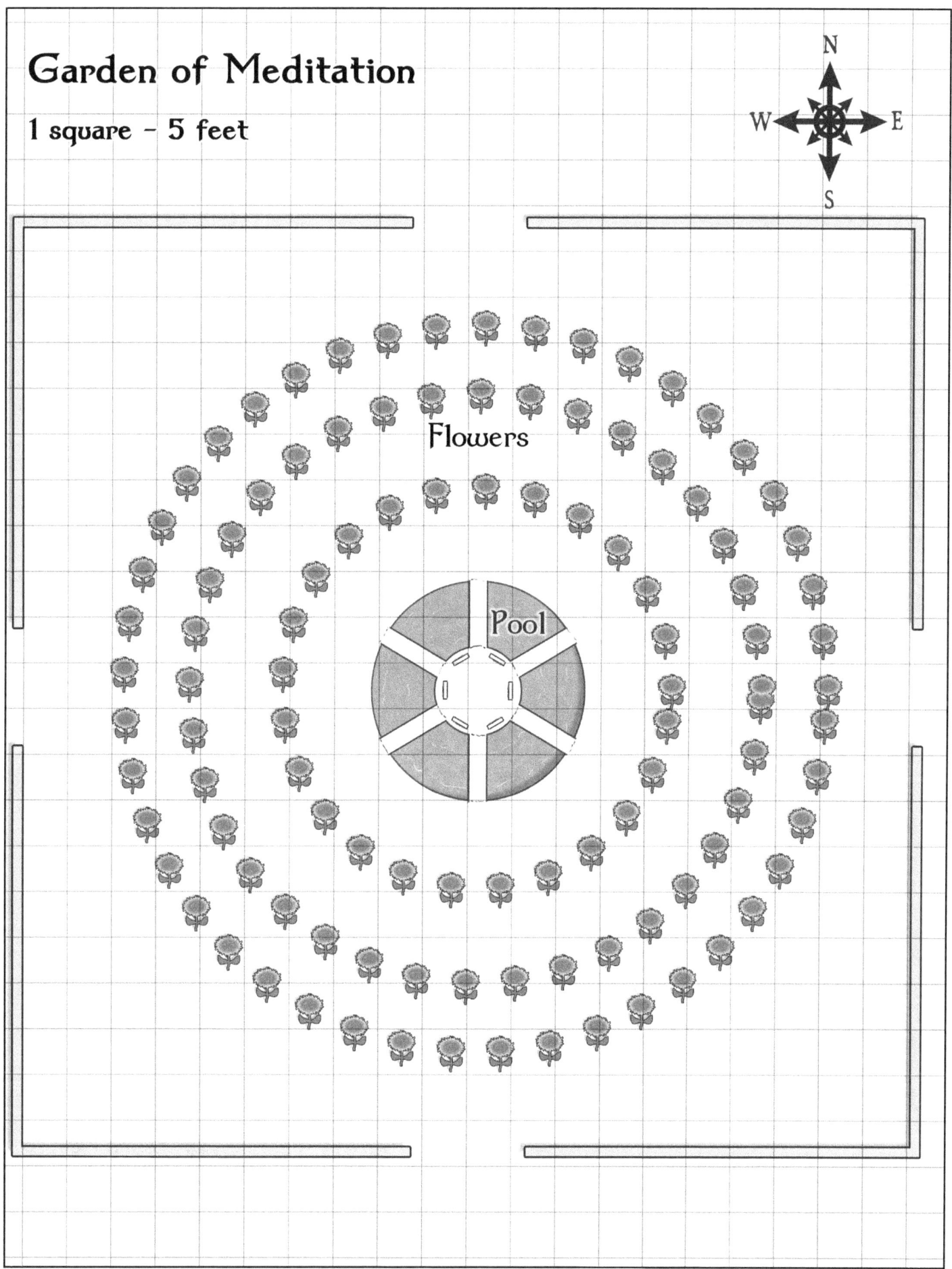

Flowers

Pool

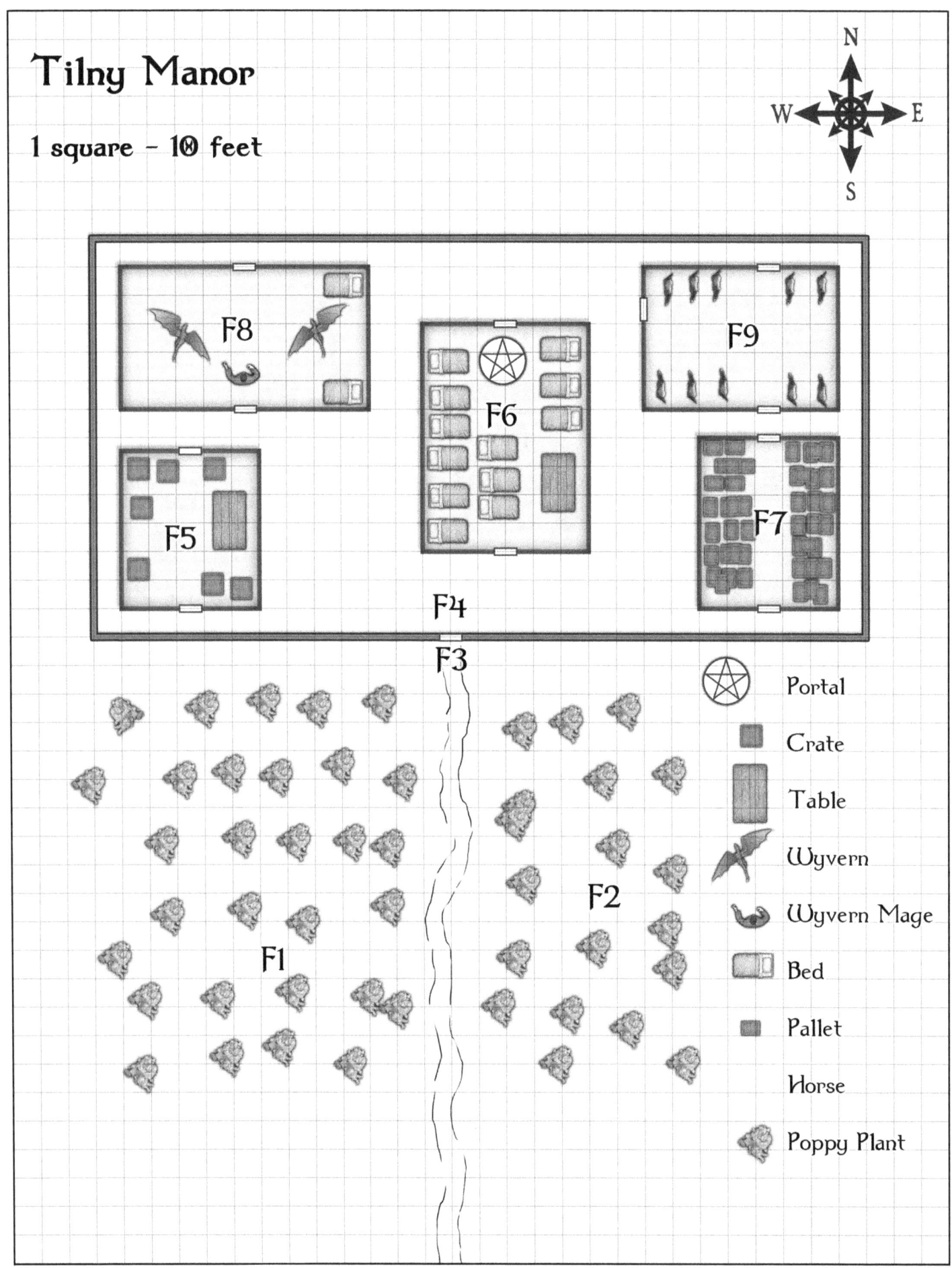

Tilny Manor

1 square – 10 feet

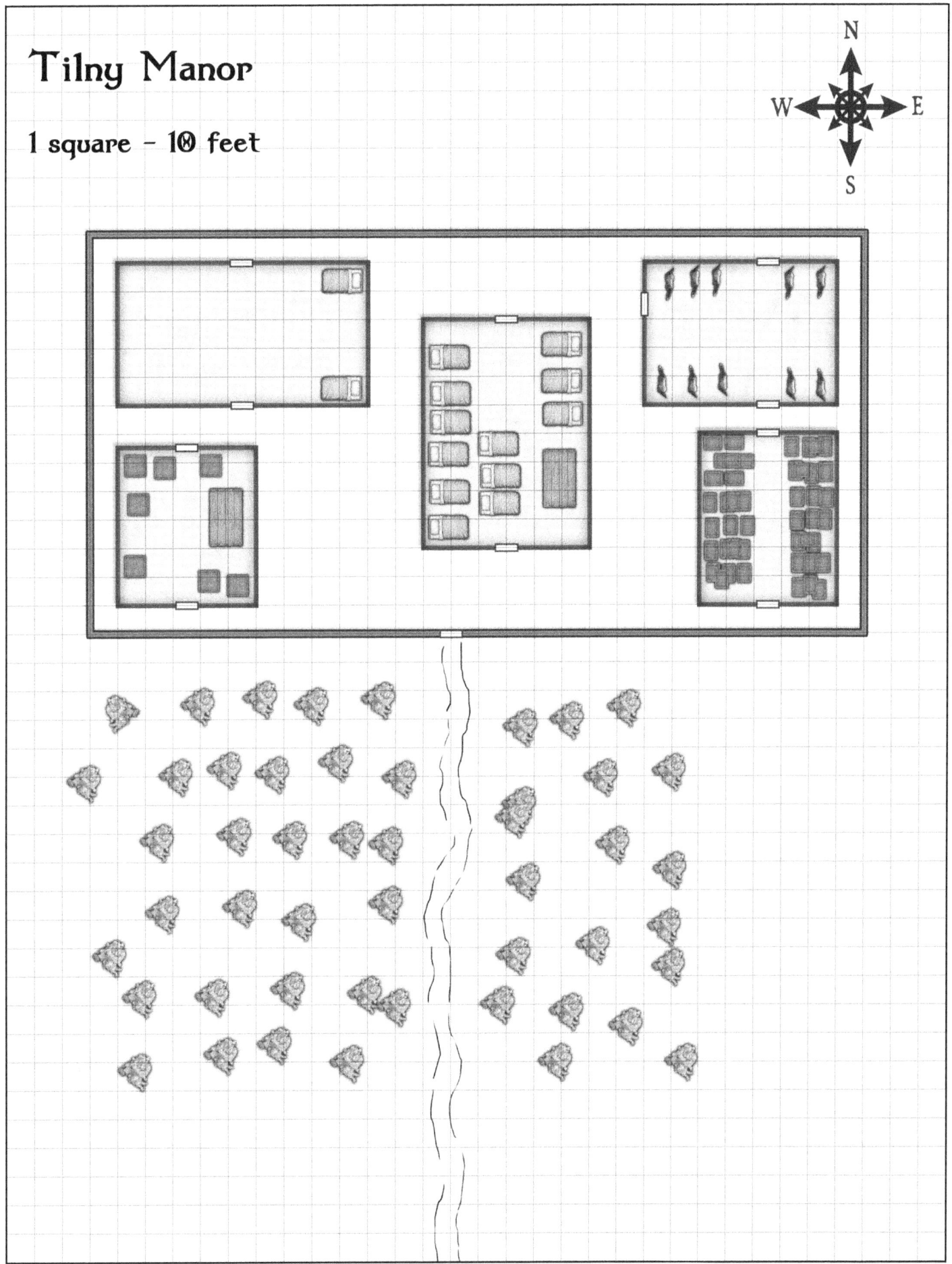

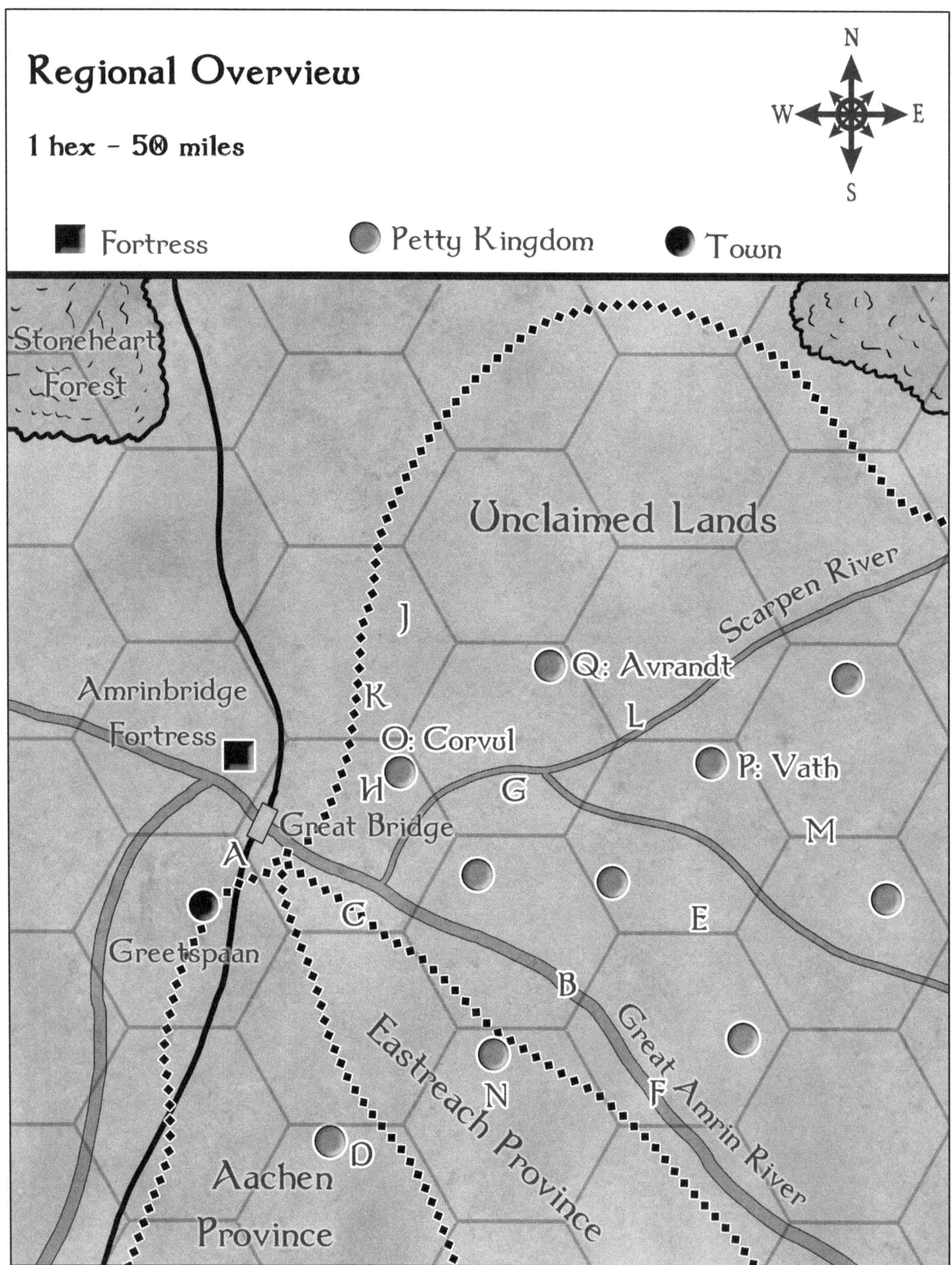

Regional Overview

1 hex – 50 miles

■ Fortress   ● Petty Kingdom   ● Town

Stoneheart Forest

Unclaimed Lands

Scarpen River

J

K

Amrinbridge
Fortress

O: Corvul

H

Q: Avrandt

L

P: Vath

M

G

A

Great Bridge

C

E

Greetspaan

B

N

Eastreach Province

Great Amrin River

F

D

Aachen
Province

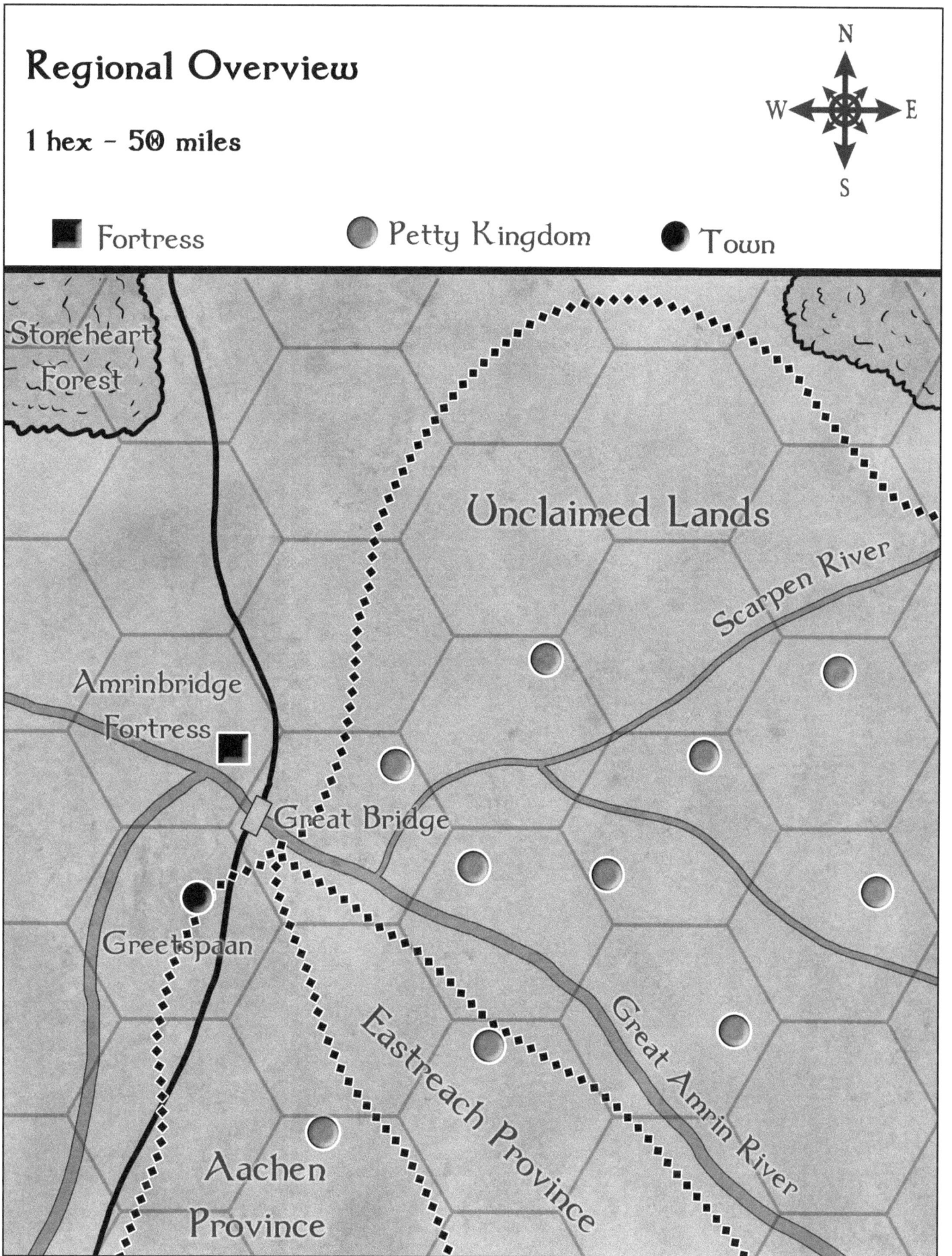

Regional Overview

1 hex - 50 miles

■ Fortress   ◐ Petty Kingdom   ● Town

N
W E
S

Stoneheart Forest

Unclaimed Lands

Scarpen River

Amrinbridge Fortress

Great Bridge

Greetspaan

Eastreach Province

Great Amrin River

Aachen Province

Ghosts on the Waters

Crates, Boxes, Barrels

Tree Cover

Sentry •

Sentry •

Sentry •

Character Start

Sentry •

⊗ ft.

+10 ft.

+20 ft.

⊗ ft.

(Angled Down)

N

W   E

S

1 square - 10 feet

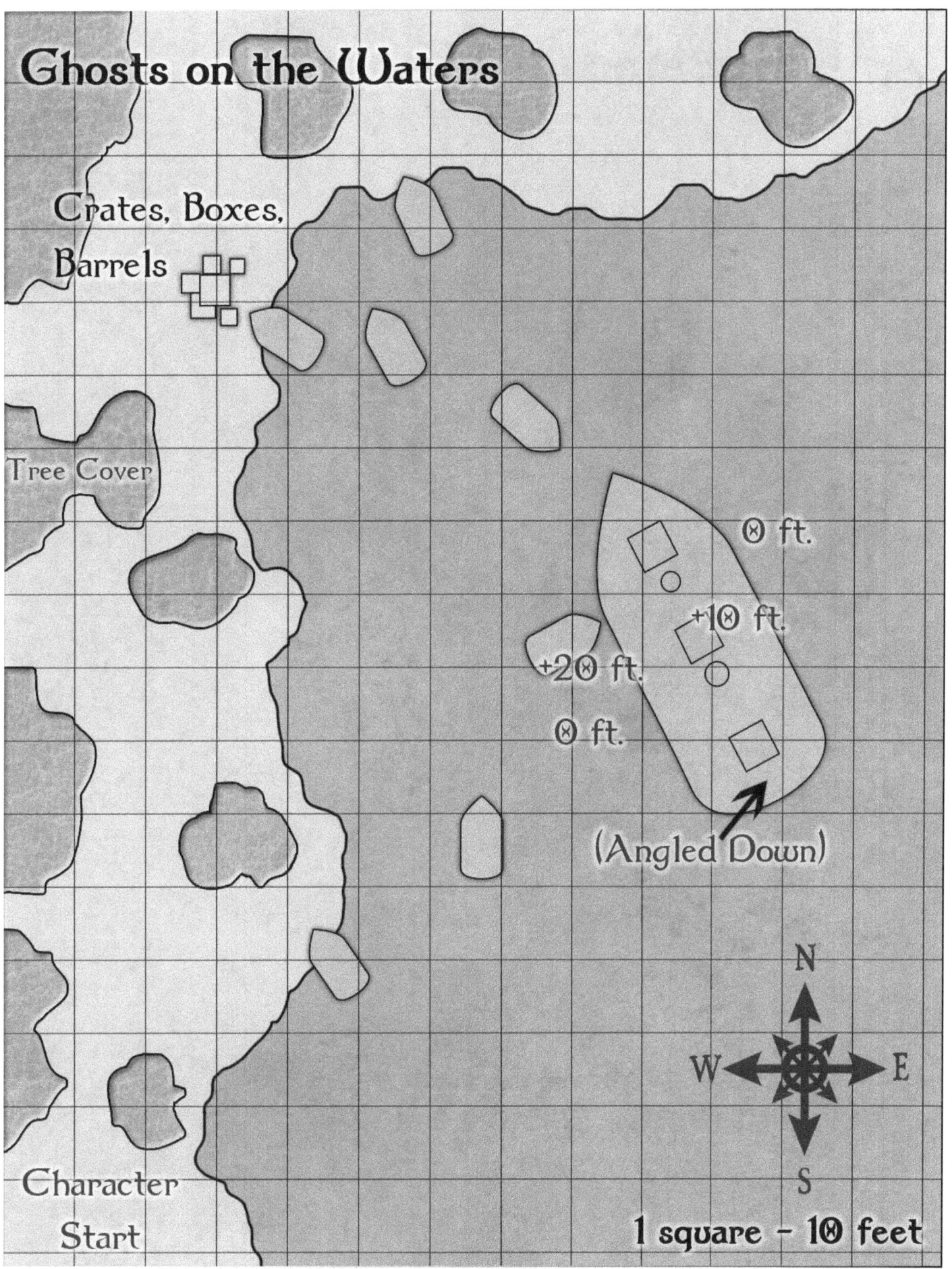

Ghosts on the Waters

Crates, Boxes, Barrels

Tree Cover

⊗ ft.

+10 ft.

+20 ft.

⊗ ft.

(Angled Down)

N

W   E

S

Character Start

1 square - 10 feet

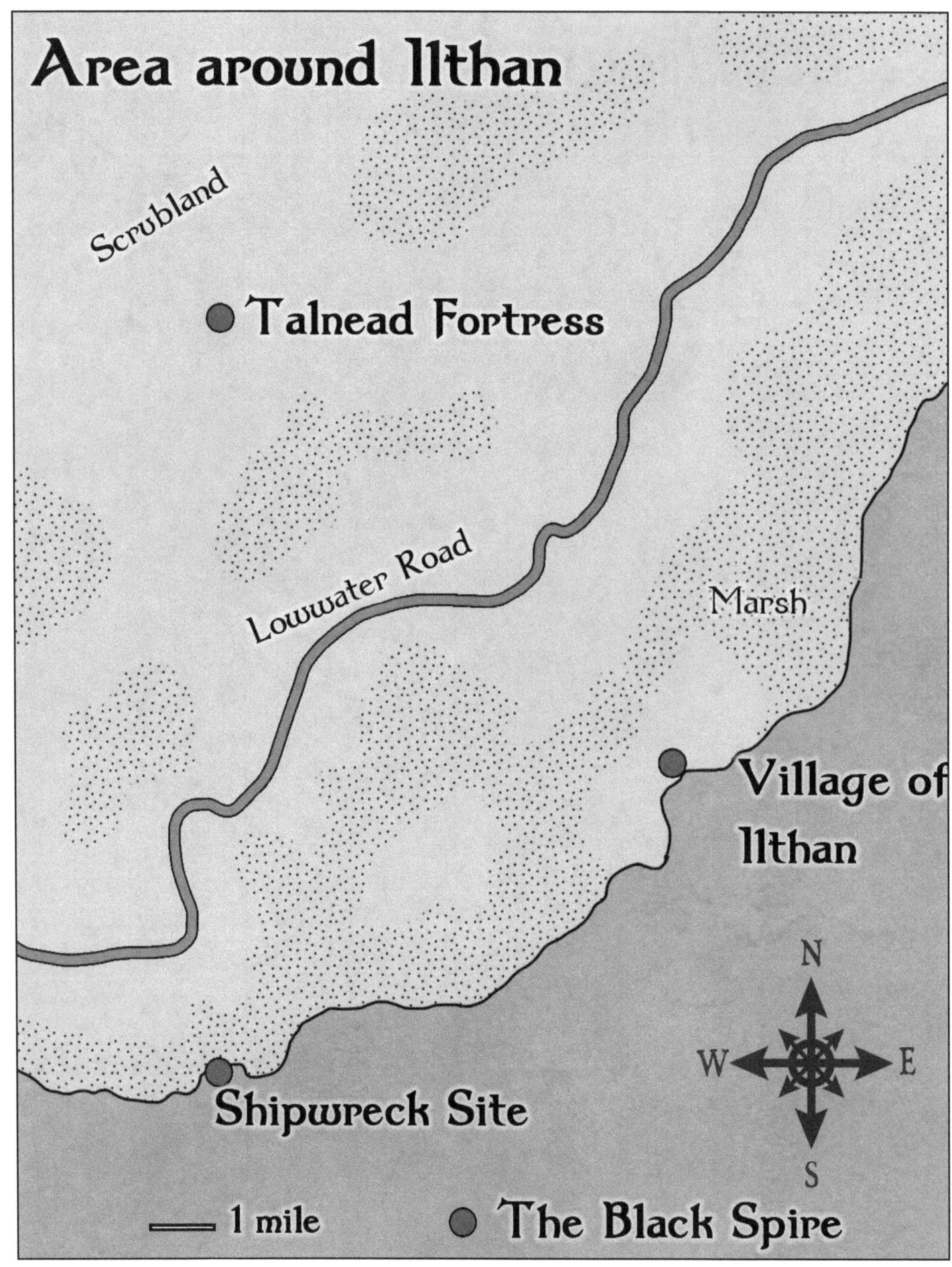

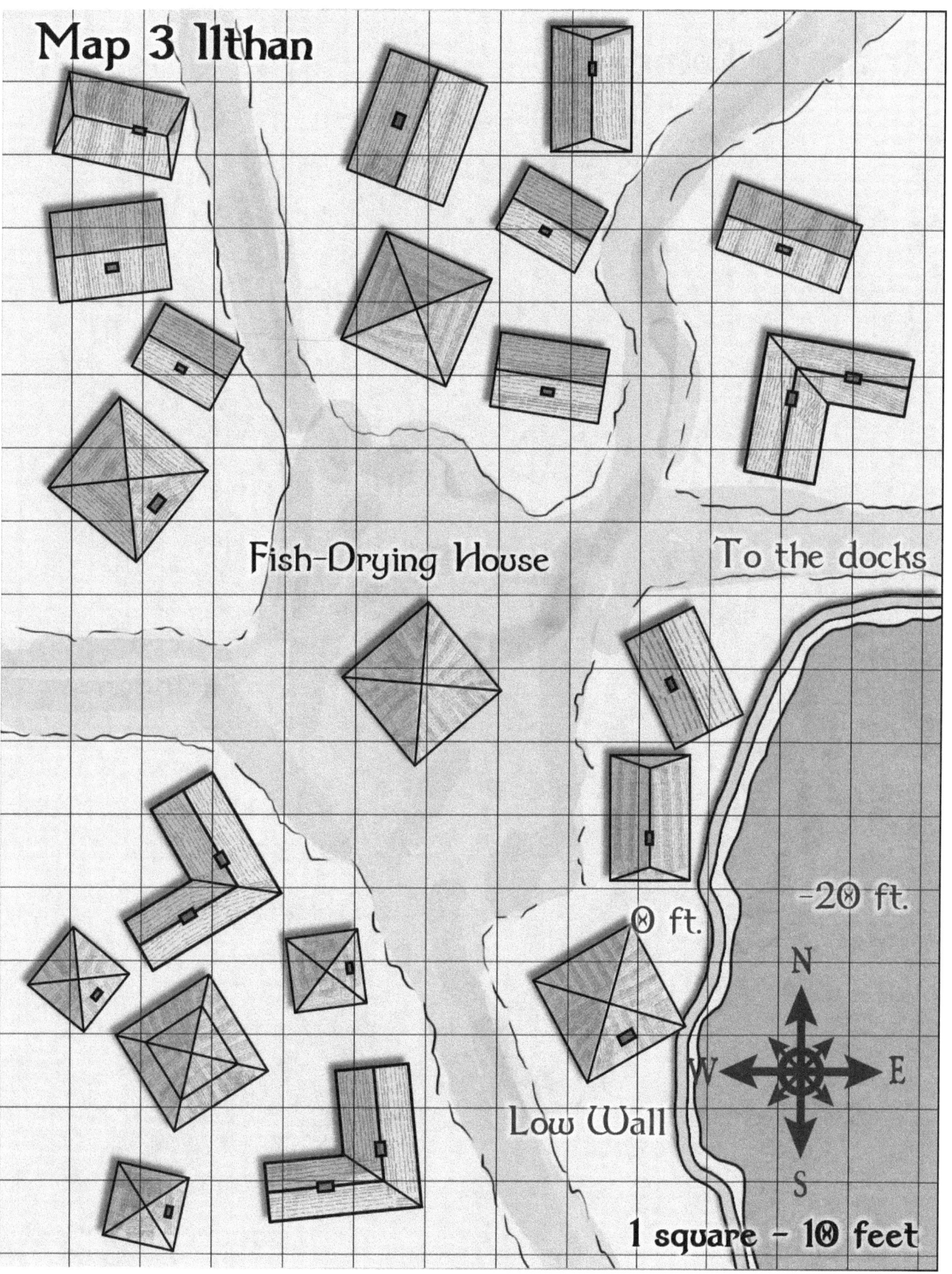

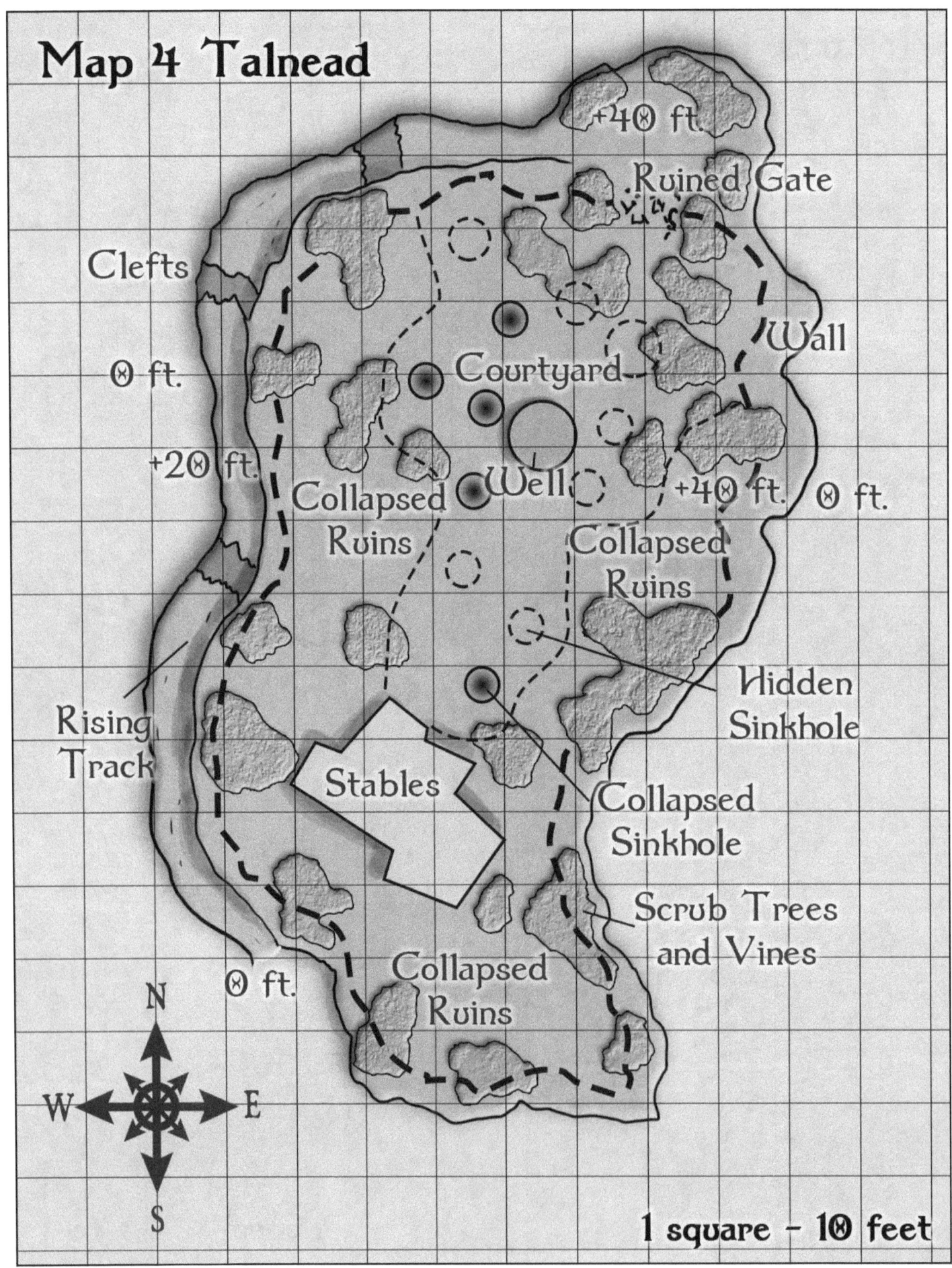

Map 4 Talnead

+40 ft.

Ruined Gate

Clefts

0 ft.

Wall

Courtyard

+20 ft.

Well

+40 ft.   0 ft.

Collapsed
Ruins

Collapsed
Ruins

Hidden
Sinkhole

Rising
Track

Stables

Collapsed
Sinkhole

Scrub Trees
and Vines

0 ft.

Collapsed
Ruins

N

W   E

S

1 square – 10 feet

LEGAL APPENDIX